DIANA'S INCREDIBLE JOURNEY

BOOK ONE

FALL OF MENDACIUM

BY

EVA ROBLINS

Cover Design by EbookLaunch

ISBN 978-0-9861861-6-5 - EBOOK
ISBN 978-0-9861861-8-9 - PAPERBACK

www.evaroblins.com

IN MEMORIAM

Ariana Binave (2004 - 2018)

Ariana was a lovely child who departed our world far too young. She was outgoing, always friendly with a perpetual smile of friendship on her face. Her Dad said, "She was like sunshine even when it was dark." According to one of her dear friends, Ariana was an angel on earth, and she always said, "Live life beautifully." Yes, Ariana, we will live life beautifully, as we fondly recall your wonderful spirit and your infectious smile. Your loving family and friends and the faculty, and classmates at William Henry Oliver Middle School, Nashville, Tennessee truly miss you. We will think of you often as you smile upon us from Heaven. Rest in Peace our lovely, sweet, precious Angel.

Sydney Renee Manley (2010 - 2018)

Sydney was a true warrior, a heroine in the eyes of thousands. She knew how to make others laugh. She always put others' feelings before her own. She never gave up. She visited other children who were suffering from cancer so that she could help to bring smiles to their faces. Sydney organized a toy drive that brought in thousands of toys for cancer patients and their families. During her battle with cancer, Sydney's beautiful smile never left her face. Her gorgeous eyes, happy attitude, infectious smile and generous heart were an inspiration to others around the world. Finally, when she had decided in her courageous way that she had enough, enough of the surgery, treatments, chemotherapy, being poked with needles, she decided it on her terms. She would decide when she would fly into the arms of Jesus. So, for those of us who might be jealous that Sydney got to meet Jesus before we did, we shall always remember her touching words. "I know you're jelly I get to see Jesus first, but if you're gonna be jelly be strawberry jelly. It's the best!" We miss you, "Super Sydney." And we love you. Thank you for blessing all our lives with your amazing presence. Rest in Peace our lovely, sweet, precious Angel.

Other Works by Eva Roblins

Eva Roblins and the Enchanted Gate, Book One: Return of the Princess

Eva Roblins and the Enchanted Gate, Book Two: Conquest of the Hidden Valley

Freddy Meets Carmen the Talking Mouse

*Gloves for José -
A Brief Tale of Love and Compassion*

DEDICATION

With Love and Respect to Diana Jane Fowler
with an awesome and coolio yepity yep yep

~ ~ ~

"If there is something I frown on more than anything, it must be lying. Lying is worse than stealing. Stealing is tangible. It can be seen and touched. And one can always replace stolen items. On the other hand, lying is invisible and can remain hidden for the longest time. Once discovered, a lie can never reverse its trickery, renew trust in another or heal a broken heart." ~ Diana

"It's better to ignore ignorance than to travel the path of foolishness." ~ Diana

"Well, as Dorothy had said in the Wizard of Oz, 'Toto, I have a feeling we're not in Kansas anymore,' I am fairly certain we are not in a place or era of my time.'" ~ Diana

"They remind me of overripened, nasty peas in a bully pod." ~ Diana

"Right now, only four percent of nearly five billion dollars of research funds go to research for childhood cancer. Children with cancer deserve as much as a chance to live as adults." ~ Charles

"I know you're jelly I get to see Jesus first, but if you're gonna be jelly be strawberry jelly. It's the best!" ~ Sydney

"A bully was bullying others while being bullied by bullies. How ironic is that? When will it stop? Will it ever stop?" ~ Diana

"Like the nightmarish scenes you've witnessed and the battles you fought here in the World Beyond, your scars are yours and yours alone. Your scars and the suffering in your heart are yours to bear and nobody else's." ~ Charles

~ ~ ~

PREFACE

Diana and my novel began with a simple question, as I asked her something along these lines. "How would you like to be in a book?" I had already published a book that included Diana's fictional character, Dianise. Fortunately, Diana did not think I was going crazy. She replied, "Sure!"

I asked Diana for input to our story, assorted little-known things I mention in the acknowledgments page. As I worked through the plot of our story, I knew it would, by hook or by crook, focus somewhat on softball. Diana is the catcher on a ladies travel softball team. She is very talented, and her superb athleticism is apparent.

But a fictional novel about softball? Too constrained, too narrow and, although I love softball, too uninteresting for my liking. I mean, why read about softball when you can watch it on television or watch Diana at Play? I needed something more.

Diana told me about her lifelong ghost, Charles. He plays tricks on her and her friends. I also have a ghost, Jessica. So, I can relate to her having a ghost. Everybody should have a ghost with whom they can talk to - (when no one else is around!). Therefore, Charles became a primary character in our story. I also created three other primary characters. One is "I Dunno," Diana's protector pixie. Another is Jayvyn (Life Spirit), Diana's noble steed. I will talk about the third character in a moment.

I understood that our protagonist, Diana, needed to be a heroine. I thought, why not make Diana a softball heroine? But, how to connect softball with Diana's fictional character in an interesting way? Then an epiphany struck me like a hammer knocking me on my noggin.

Like the theme in my other published novels, I touched on the scourge of bullying. But, this time with a different topic. Adult bullying. Then, I added a bit more drama. I tied bullying to deceit, fabrications, and lies, all matters of falsehoods, resulting from a ladies' championship softball tournament. I added corruption, threats and illegal, criminal innuendoes for good measure.

Then another epiphany hit me. I would split Diana into two separate beings. Her personae would be in two places at once! I understood at the onset that having two separate timelines, with two of Diana's beings in two different worlds, would be difficult to pen. However, once I pursue a dream, I never quit. I kept writing.

In our story, Diana in the Real-world would navigate the tumultuous road of bullying, lies, deceit, corruption, scams, and threats as she sought the truth. Meanwhile, her double would battle the same falsehoods in the World Beyond. Diana in the Real-world would be a normal teenager doing what teenagers do. Diana in the World Beyond would use her intelligence, longbow, and sword to battle evil creatures. Naturally, as she battled evil creatures, she also met friendly, peace-loving creatures along the way.

Finally, I needed a villain. Certainly, the bully(s) in our story were villains. Diana in the Real-world would have to contend with those. Meanwhile, Diana in the World Beyond would need a villain as well. I thought, "Wait a minute here! Why not have a villain common to both worlds!"

The words *lie, lying, falsehood, fraud, etcetera*, translate in Latin to *Mendacium*. So, I thought, why not make Mendacium our common villain! I went a few steps further by giving Mendacium two other names to which I refer to him in our story. *The King of Deceit and He who is Unmerciful.*

There you have it. Diana, the heroine softball player in the Real-world battles, in an emotional sense, bullying, deceit, corruption, and lies after lies brought about by Mendacium's wickedness. While at the same time, her primary warrior persona in the World Beyond battles Mendacium and his evil cohorts in a more physical sense, as the Heroine Youngster of the World Beyond, Empress Artemis-Diana.

In closing, I offer this. Our story is about a fictional fourteen-year-old female who overcomes insurmountable odds to make our world a better place. As such, teenagers can relate to our story. However, it is important to mention. Our story also deals with the scourge of bullying, an issue common to all ages. Also, since our story has no bad language, it is suitable for pre-teens, as well as for adults.

I hope you enjoy our story; God-willing, the first of many in the series, *Diana's Incredible Journey.*

ACKNOWLEDGMENTS

I must recognize my friend, the Real-world teenager, Diana, to whom I proudly dedicate our book of fiction. Diana's likeness is the central character of this novel. As the storyline evolved from a thought and a prayer to writing it, up until its completion, Diana furnished essential input. She provided me with countless ideas concerning the idiosyncrasies, habits, and likes and dislikes of her fictional character likeness. Quips in our story such as *yepity, yep, yep; coolio* and *Nnnnnoooooooooooo,* I owe to Diana. Other similarities presented in a fictional manner in our story also originated with Diana. These include our fictional character's taste in music, her love of Chinese orange chicken and, yes, unquestionably, her fondness for French fries with a dab of ketchup on the side. These are but a few of the many examples of Diana's invaluable input to the storyline. I cannot take an iota of credit, and I am deeply indebted to her.

Diana is an intelligent, inquisitive, and talented young lady. Her grasp of the fine arts and her reading of great books, along with her accomplished acting ability, are the basis for many scenes in our story. Her active involvement in athletics such as softball and roller skating attests to her athleticism and team spirit. Her physical prowess made it much easier to project her character likeness as a powerful, determined and resolute young lady, a warrior of uncharacteristic tenacity who has to persevere against all the odds.

Unlike many of her peers, Diana would rather play sports, write, draw, or read a great novel than gawp at a video screen. Stating this is not to say video games are prejudicial and that she doesn't play Xbox games. On the contrary. She does play video games. They are a fantastic respite from the humdrum of modern life. Just the same, it is encouraging to recognize a teenager who patterns her daily routine around flexibility rather than technology. It goes without saying. Diana lives her life to its fullest.

More importantly, Diana is respectful, mannerly, humble, and a positive role model for others. She goes out of her way to make people happy. Everyone she sees, whether old or young, she says hello to without hesitation. I have yet to meet a more outgoing, bubbly teen with a positive outlook on life like Diana. Her attributes attest to her inner strength and yes, undoubtedly, to the love, respect, and attention given to her by her parents. To her parents, I say thank you. You have done a marvelous job of teaching Diana everything there is to know about righteousness and respect for others.

Until I penned our novel, I have never asked another person for input when writing my novels. Therefore, I am indebted to Diana for helping to enrich our novel's storyline. Her invaluable assistance is one of the many reasons why, when I refer to this novel, I describe it as *our* novel. For it belongs to Diana as much as it belongs to me. After all, it is for, about, and lovingly dedicated to Diana as her courageous character likeness, Empress Artemis-Diana, battles evil as the Youngster Heroine of the World Beyond!

Thank you, Diana. You are brilliantly coolio!
Stay awesome.
~ Ed

~ ~ ~

INTRODUCTION

SETTING THE STAGE

"You're out!" the umpire screams.

Cheers of jubilation erupt on the field and in the bleachers of the home team. Slightly less audible are the loud moans and groans of the visiting team and its adoring fans. Suddenly, raucous boos and boisterous chants, "Fire the ump! He's a cheat!" immediately follow from the visiting team's bleachers. These dissenting calls and chants nearly drown out the home team's jubilant cheers.

"But sir," the girl cries as she dusts dirt from her uniform. "I was safe. The catcher never tagged me! You must believe me. I was safe, sir! Honestly!" She points to the home team's catcher, Diana and adds, "Ask the catcher, sir. She will tell you the truth. I was safe by a mile."

The girl had just hammered a stinging line drive over the center fielder's head. She ran the bases, but when she slid into the home plate, she was called out.

The girl is Sally Turndle, a tall, athletic brunette who excels in softball, volleyball, and basketball. Her softball teammates and admiring fans affectionately call her Home Run Sally. Her nickname comes as no surprise. She is the team's fastest baserunner and top hitter with 22 homers and 41 RBI's this season alone.

The stern-faced umpire, Mister Reynolds, is well known by the local schools' female softball teams as a strict, no-nonsense umpire. His daughter, Regina, is the star pitcher on the home team. It comes as no surprise that a perception exists throughout the league that Mister Reynolds' sometimes questionable calls continually favor his daughter's softball team.

Mister Reynolds glares at Sally, his piercing dark gray eyes conveying more anger than his words will utter in a few seconds.

Sally begins to plead her case once more, that she had slid beneath Diana's tag. Her animated actions as she throws her hands high in the air and yells at the umpire are difficult to watch. Then she points to something that Mister Reynolds has clutched in his hand.

In reply to her rebellious actions, Mister Reynolds says in a loud voice, "I said you are out!" At that point, to the surprise of everyone who is watching the spectacle behind home plate, he points his thumb to the visiting team's stands. "Out of the game! Ejected! Please leave the field now!"

He turns his back to Sally who looks understandably shocked and is now in tears due to Mister Reynolds' ejecting her from the game. As Mister Reynolds tucks a folded piece of paper into his pocket, he yells more loudly than necessary to the visiting team's dugout.

"Batter up! We still have this and one more inning to go. So, please hurry up!"

Mister Reynolds bends over to sweep dirt from the home plate. Diana gently tugs on his shirtsleeve to get his attention. She begins to say something, but before she opens her mouth, she notices the desperate gestures of her coach.

Her coach is Mister Downey. He is outside the dugout waving his hands high in the air and vigorously shaking his head back and forth. Diana immediately understands what he is trying to tell her. Coach does not want her to talk to the umpire and risk him ejecting her from the softball championship game as he did to Sally. She nods her head in recognition with what Coach just told her via his non-verbal actions. She picks up her catcher's face mask from the ground and crouches behind the home plate.

The next batter is Sarah Cousins, the clean-up batter. Sarah is the second-best hitter on the visiting team's roster. The first pitch to Sarah is a strike, in Diana's opinion just outside the corner, but probably too close for the umpire to call.

After the second pitch, the umpire yells, "Strike two! The count is oh and two." His call elicits a chorus of boos and robust shouts from the visiting team's fans.

"The ump is blind! The ump's a cheat!"

Diana frowns as she ponders, "I'm pretty sure that was a ball, in the dirt. Sure, it was a drop ball, but I had to scoop it up. I'm lucky it didn't go past me." Then she thinks the unthinkable. "Is the ump trying to throw the game? Is he trying to throw the game in our favor?"

To avoid being hit in the shin by the next thrown ball, Sarah must jump to her left.

The umpire yells, "Ball! The count is one and two."

The visiting team in the dugout and the fans in the bleachers cheer loudly. Chants of, "Go Sarah go, go Sarah go!" reverberate from the visiting team's fans.

Diana smiles. "Good. It looks like the ump is back on board with fair calls."

The next pitch is another ball. It is low in the dirt, nearly uncatchable, but Diana manages to scoop it up. The umpire calls the following pitch a ball as well.

"Full count!" the umpire yells as he moves to brush dirt from the plate. "Three and two."

Sarah fouls the next pitch along the left field line. She fouls the following pitch over the backstop.

The final pitch forces Sarah to once again move out of the batter's box to her left. The umpire yells, "Strike three! You're out!"

Sarah does not walk back to the dugout. She stands to the left of the home plate for a moment as if she wants to protest the call. However, she thinks better of it. She does not want the umpire to have grounds to eject her from the game. She quickly walks to the dugout.

Diana cringes as she thinks, "That was a ball if I have ever seen one. Certainly, I moved my mitt to the center of the plate after I caught it to make it look like a strike. That is what us catchers are supposed to do. But it was a darned ball, not a strike."

In Diana's mind, the umpire had now misjudged two calls, purposely calling two players of the visiting team out when they weren't. He also had ejected their star hitter from the game. She wonders if Mister Reynolds is purposely missing the calls or if he needs new glasses. As she squats and readies herself for the next batter, she ponders everything that is happening in this, the most exciting game of her young life.

"If there is something I frown on more than anything, it must be lying. Lying is worse than stealing. Stealing is tangible. It can be seen and touched. And one can always replace stolen items. On the other hand, lying is invisible and can remain hidden for the longest time. Once discovered, a lie can never reverse its trickery, renew trust in another and heal a broken heart."

CHAPTER ONE

ASTONISHING EYE OPENERS

Part I: Charles

Diana has trouble falling asleep despite the time, 2:30 in the morning on a school day. She had a super-fun birthday the day before, Thursday, June 18. The thrilling excitement of the softball championship game made her birthday even more special. She received loads of cool presents, to include a new catcher's mitt and her very own catcher's face mask. She also received new roller skates.

Another birthday gift, a tiny package the size of a jewelry box, remains unopened. Diana had discovered the beautifully wrapped gift in her softball bag. The giver of the mysterious gift did not reveal who he or she is. The gift is sitting on her bedside table, some inches from her reach. She has been tempted on more than one occasion to open it since she discovered it. But she figures she will wait until daybreak to open it.

She is lying in her bed propped up on her pillows. Her head is cradled in the palms of her hands as she stares at the ceiling. Her eyelids are heavy, but she cannot seem to do anything but toss and turn. She is overly excited, still jumpy due to yesterday's excitement. Not only had her team won the ladies' championship softball game; her teammates had voted her most valuable player, the team's softball heroine for the game. That everything super cool happened on her birthday has made her happy beyond words.

Notwithstanding her euphoria, she has no clue what is in store for her. In fact, the thrill of winning the ladies' championship softball game for her team on her birthday is going to be nothing compared to what the future will bring. More of this later.

She smiles as she rethinks the last few minutes of the game, a game she knows she will never forget. It was the bottom of the ninth inning, overtime for the two teams since the league normally plays only seven innings. It was a tie ballgame with the score nothing to nothing. There were two outs. Diana was at bat with her team's bases loaded.

The final count against her was 3 and 2, a full count with three balls and two strikes. One more strike and the championship softball game would end in a tie. Then again, if she could only get a hit, her team would win! She was understandably nervous.

She calls to mind her time at bat. She had swung awkwardly at the first pitch connecting with nothing but thin air. That was strike one. The next throw by the pitcher was a ball, way outside to the right of the plate. The count was then 1 and 1, one ball and one strike. Diana slammed the third pitch foul along the third base line. The count displayed on the center field scoreboard inched up to 1 and 2, one ball and two strikes.

The next pitch was low in the dirt. It nearly got away from the visiting team's catcher. The count was now 2 and 2, two balls and two strikes.

Diana recalls that her spirits were sinking at that point. One more strike and the game would be over, a tie. Her heart was beating wildly with both fear and excitement. Then, the unthinkable happened. The fifth pitch was a strike, catching the left corner of the plate. She was out, or so she thought. Her team had lost.

Diana vividly recalls she had shrugged her shoulders in defeat. She was visibly dejected. Shaking her head, and with her shoulders hunched over, she slowly turned to walk away from the plate. As if in a distant dream, she imagined she could hear the moans and groans of her teammates and from the home team bleachers. She had failed them!

Then, to her amazement, the umpire yelled at that very moment, "Ball three, just outside the corner!" The home team fans began screaming over and over, "Yes, Dynamite, yes! You can do it! Go, Diana, go!"

Diana had been incorrect. She had thought it was a strike. But no, the umpire said it was a ball!

She returned to the plate and swung practice swings a few times. She bent her knees and stared intently into the pitcher's eyes. The count was full, 3 and 2. The game was not over. She still had a chance! Her team might win.

Diana twirls a lock of her long brown hair with her fingers. She frowns as she continues to stare dreamily at the ceiling. As a catcher who has probably seen a thousand or more pitches in her short softball career, she recognizes a strike when she sees one. She remembers thinking to herself at the time, "That was a strike. I should have been called out. But I'll take a ball for sure!"

Despite her relief at not being called out, she remembers being upset at the time nonetheless. She felt the umpire had once again purposely messed up a call, probably to help his daughter's team, her team, to win the championship tournament. Then again, perhaps what she saw as a strike was a ball. There is no way of knowing without a photograph or a video taken at the precise time the ball sailed over the plate. Notwithstanding the gnawing doubt she still feels in her heart, and yes, a tinge of guilt for the umpire's presumed missed call in her favor, she smiles. She resumes recalling the final moments of the ladies' championship softball game.

As she nervously stood at the plate, the umpire had ceremoniously walked between the pitcher's mound and the home plate. He turned to face the crowd. He stated loudly, "Two outs! The score is tied nothing to nothing. We have a full count." He pointed to his left in the direction of the ominous thunderstorm clouds slowly approaching from the west.

"The visiting and home team coaches and I agree. It is a matter of safety for the two teams as well as for the fans. If there is no score at the end of this, the ninth inning, I will call the game despite the lack of a winner. Then the league's commissioners must decide whether to reschedule the game or to declare the ladies' softball championship game a tie." As he walked to the plate, he looked directly at Diana and yelled, "Batter up!"

With the umpire's pronouncement and the ballpark's attention once again focused on her, Diana became even more nervous. She felt that her knees were shaking and that her heart was racing a mile a minute. Her lips, mouth, and throat felt parched. Her breaths were coming and going in brief, shallow gasps. She could barely catch her breath.

Her predicament was crystal clear. If they won the game, if she somehow were able to drive the third base runner home, she would be a heroine. On the other hand, if she struck out, she would always be remembered as the catcher who denied her team the ladies' softball championship trophy.

For what seemed like an eternity, but was probably less than thirty seconds, the visiting team's pitcher and Diana looked each other square in the eye. The pitcher placed her mitt beneath her armpit, and then she proceeded to rub the ball between her hands more slowly than necessary. She sneered nastily at Diana, and then she popped her chewing gum loudly. She shook her head back and forth with a noticeable air of defiance. She was trying to intimidate Diana. The pitcher's message to Diana was obvious.

"You're toast."

In return, Diana purposely swung her bat with two slower than usual practice swings. She sneered at the pitcher in return. She set her lips in a straight line, squinted her nose, and narrowed her eyes. Lightning bolts of defiance flashed in the pupils of her eyes. She bent over to pick up a fistful of dirt, all the while never taking her eyes off of the pitcher. She rubbed the dirt between her hands, and then she nonchalantly tossed the dirt to the ground in front of the home plate. The wind caught some of the dirt. It sailed right at the feet of the pitcher. She took a final practice swing and readied for the pitch.

The home and visiting teams' dugouts were deathly silent. You could hear a pin drop in the ballpark, that is how quiet it was. An eerie hush had also fallen over both teams' bleachers. The only noticeable sounds, other than the far-off thundering within the gathering storm clouds, was Diana's rapidly beating heart and her slow, purposeful breathing. She took one final practice swing and readied for the pitch.

She watched with dreaded trepidation as the pitcher wound up for the pitch. Diana's bold composure had immediately changed. She was certain the pitcher was going to throw a curve! She hated curves. She could never hit curves! She would strike out! She would lose the ladies' softball championship game for her team!

Her eyes widened to the size of saucers the split second the ball left the pitcher's hand. Then she felt the unmistakable *twang* reverberate to her hands as the bat connected squarely with the ball. Her instinct told her the ball she had just hit was traveling in the direction of the third baseman. Maybe she even hit the ball to the shortstop! She did not bother to watch the ball's trajectory as it rocketed from her bat. She lowered her head and ran to first base as quickly as her long legs could carry her.

As a reflective, highly gifted and astute teenager, Diana immediately recognized at that very moment that everything to follow her hit was out-and-out karma. It was what it was. There would be no changing destiny. If her hit was a foul ball, that was okay. She would get another chance at bat. However, she seriously doubted if she could step up to the plate again without passing out with sheer nervousness.

If the ball were hit directly to the third baseman, the second base runner would be forced out. If it were a hit to the shortstop, an easy toss to the second baseman would get the first base runner out. Then the game would end in a tie. And she knew she would be devastated for not winning the game for her team, for her school. Of course, one of the infielders could bobble the ball, make an error. Then everything would be up for grabs.

As soon as Diana stomped on first base, she turned around and watched with uncertainty as her teammates spilled out of the dugout. They were cheering, their hands waving excitedly in the air. They were running in her direction! It was then that she had looked toward the left part of the ballfield where she had hit the ball.

The third baseman was standing stock still, dejected, seemingly in shock. Tears were streaming down her face. The shortstop was prostrate on the infield, facing toward third base with the arm of her glove hand outstretched as if she had dived for something out of reach. She was furiously slapping the ground with her mitt. She was screaming over and over, "No, no, no!"

Then Diana saw it, in left field, about ten feet in front of the left fielder. The ball that she had just hit had rolled to a stop midway between the infield and the outfield. It suddenly dawned on her why her teammates were celebrating. She had hit a soft line drive just beyond the infield, dab smack in the middle of the third baseman and the shortstop. She had driven in the winning run! The ladies' softball championship trophy was theirs!

Within seconds, her teammates lifted her high on their shoulders. Then twenty girls gleefully walked the bases, first base to second, and then to third, and finally to home. All the while they were screaming and laughing and yes, crying tears of extreme happiness. They had won the ladies' softball championship tournament in nine innings with a hard-fought score of one to nothing!

Shortly after the game, Coach treated the entire team to McDonald's. There, with family cameras and smartphones happily snapping pics, the league's commissioner presented Coach with the league's ladies' softball championship trophy. Then, to the surprise of everyone present, Coach pulled two huge cardboard boxes from beneath a table. With boisterous shouts of congratulations filling the restaurant, Coach proceeded to present each of the team's players with a shiny softball trophy. The inscription on the trophies read *Ladies' Softball Championship Winner!* Then, much to Diana's slight embarrassment but absolute delight, Coach presented her with a second trophy. It read, *Ladies' Softball Championship MVP (Most Valuable Player).*

Diana stretches and sighs deeply. Yesterday was one of the best days of her teenage life. Suddenly, she hears a soft noise, a scratching noise like someone is writing on a whiteboard. She turns on her bedside lamp. She glances around the room. Seeing nothing out of the ordinary, she snaps off the lamp. Then, just as the scratching noise resumes, she looks up at the ceiling. She covers her mouth with her hand and manages to stifle a scream as three words slowly appear on the ashen ceiling of the darkened room.

Lies! Lies! Lies!

"Charles?" Diana whispers. "Is that you? If so, please speak to me. Tell me what those words imply that I just saw on the ceiling."

She is calling out to her lifelong ghost, Charles, an unseen being that haunts her. Charles seems harmless enough, friendly in fact. He likes to pull tomfooleries, as she refers to them, on Diana and her friends. Whenever Charles pulls a tomfoolery when her friends visit, her friends gleefully yell in unison, "It's Charles!"

Charles' tomfooleries or pranks consist of strange stuff like opening doors, switching lights on and off, making things fall, changing the volume of Diana's radio, little things like that. His pranks are relatively innocent but super fun to witness. Diana's friends look forward to Charles *haunting* them whenever they visit her. But, if the words on the ceiling are truly Charles' doing, this is the first time he has tried to communicate with her. Then again, this is the first time he has tried to frighten her.

She glances at her smartphone to read the time. It is now 3:19 in the morning. Just as she is about to set her phone on the bedside stand, a notification appears on its screen. She squints her eyes to read the faint words.

"Too many lies against me, Diana. Too many devious entities are calling me a liar. In the closet. Come to me, Diana!"

She whispers with obvious foreboding in her soft voice, "Oh my God! This is getting too creepy. First, there are words on the ceiling, and now I'm getting scary notifications on my phone that aren't even texts! I'm outta here."

She throws back the covers and leaps out of bed. She hastily pulls on her robe and slides her feet into her slippers. As she does, she cannot help but look at the closet. She thinks that it may be her imagination since she is tired. But, she swears that the closet door is slowly opening by itself! As if to confirm her worries, she hears the telltale squeak of the door's hinges.

She ponders, "I'm glad I didn't oil those noisy hinges!"

She turns to dash out of her bedroom. She figures that perhaps it is better if she sleeps on the couch. Granted, she knows she will not sleep well. The couch is too lumpy. But, she is too restless, and she cannot fall asleep anyway, so it does not matter where she lays her head. In any event, she needs to get out of her bedroom. Now!

She scrambles to her bed to retrieve her comforter. As she hastily tears the comforter off her bed, she looks at the closet. It is then that she sees it. A bony, skeleton-like hand. From inside the closet.

Clutching at the opening door! She shrieks in terror. She wants to run but for some reason, she cannot. She screams a second time.

Suddenly, an intense light blinds her. She slowly opens her eyes, shielding them from the intense light with her hands. She sees her mother standing in the middle of her bedroom. Her mother whispers, "I'm sorry to have turned on the light. But you were screaming. What is it, Diana? Are you okay?"

Diana is surprised to see she is not standing. She is lying in bed with her blanket pulled close to her chin. She looks past her mother to stare at the closet door. She breathes in deeply, and then she sharply exhales with an accompanying sigh of relief. The closet door is just as she left it before going to bed. It remains closed.

She whispers, "It's nothing Mom, just a bad nightmare I guess. I'm okay, thanks. I love you. Goodnight."

She turns onto her side and closes her eyes. She is bone-tired and desperately needs to sleep. She has no idea if what she imagined was real or if it was a nightmare. But one thing she knows for certain. She will not sleep well tonight if at all despite her tiredness.

The unusual scraping noises begin once again. Diana tries to ignore them thinking that she undoubtedly is imagining the noises as before. Or, just maybe, she is already asleep and dreaming. If she is dreaming she hopes this latest dream does not turn into a nightmare.

She whispers, "But that scraping noise! It is quickly getting to be a pain in the butt! It reminds me of someone writing on a whiteboard with a greasy Sharpie!"

She slowly opens one eye and then the other. Her head is still beneath the covers, well, not entirely beneath the covers. Her eyes, nose, and lips are peeking out but only slightly. Why at her age she covers the back of her head when she sleeps is beyond her reckoning. When her mom asks her why she sleeps that way, Diana shrugs it off saying her room is a bit chilly. But she even sleeps that way when it is too hot in her room.

She cautiously glances at the closet door. The ambiance of the room is shadowy, but she is certain that the closet door remains closed. Thank goodness! And, one thing is for certain. Given all that she witnessed in her nightmarish dream, she fully intends to never, never,

never oil the door's squeaky hinges no matter how loudly they squeak. If something or other is going to leap out at her from the closet at night, she wants to hear it coming. So, squeaky hinges it is going to be for now on and always!

She turns on her phone's flashlight app. She slowly twists the phone in her hand so that the light illuminates each corner of the room. Everything seems normal, except.

"Wait! What is that? On the mirror on top of my bureau? Tiny writing!" She scrambles out of her bed. She stands motionless for a split second. Then she pinches her forearm firmly to make certain she is awake and not in another stupid nightmare. "Ouch! That hurts! I guess I'm not dreaming."

As she rubs her forearm where she pinched it all too firmly, she crouches low as if she does not want anyone to see her. Then she drops on her hands and knees. She slowly crawls on all fours to her bureau. Placing her hands on top of the bureau, she slowly pulls herself up to peer guardedly at the round handheld mirror.

"Yes, there is writing on the mirror. It is pretty sloppy and very faint, but I can read it easily enough. Let's see what it says." Her heart seemingly leaps into her throat as she reads the scrawled note.

"Diana. We need to talk. Charles."

She cannot believe what she is seeing. She grabs the mirror off the bureau and crawls back to her bed. Once her blanket is enveloping her body and surrounding the back of her head, she whispers into the mirror, "Talk, but how?" Then, logically assuming that Charles probably is not inside the mirror but somehow writing on it, she glances around the room with anticipation.

"Where are you? How are you doing this, writing on the mirror? And how do I know that you're Charles and not the owner of that creepy hand opening the closet door that I imagined in my nightmare?" Just as she says this, dread seizes her heart. She holds her breath.

"Those are the closet door hinges squeaking. The door is opening!" She is ready to dash out of her bedroom. But, for some reason, she hesitates. Suddenly, scraping noises on the mirror resume again just as the closet door slams shut.

Her heart is now racing like crazy. She is scared out of her wits. She looks away from the closet door to stare at the mirror. Charles, or at least she hopes it is Charles, had hastily scrawled one word on the mirror in capital letters just as the closet door was opening.

"CEASE!"

She reckons that Charles had ordered whatever it was in the closet to cease, to stop. She watches in awe as words miraculously begin to appear on the mirror yet again.

"Diana, we need to talk. But not out loud. As of yet, he cannot see. But his hearing is astute. He also has limited magical powers. Charles."

Diana whispers, "Okay, Charles. Gosh, I hope you are who you say you are. If not, I'm going to scream as loudly as I can, and then I will run out of here, clear across town if I have to!" Words rapidly appear on the mirror.

"Do not scream. Do not run. Trust me."

"But how can we talk, Charles, if not out loud? I don't know sign language or anything." She places her index finger to her temple in thought. "And I don't have anything to write with on the mirror."

Her phone suddenly lights up. The note app appears on its screen. She notices the time. It is 3:25 am.

She whispers, "Oh, you want me to talk to you by using notes?"

Words on the note app read, "Yes! We can talk by using your cell phone. But first, you should charge it. The battery is almost dead. Charles."

She notices that the cell phone's battery needs charging. It is at one percent. Given all that has happened in the wee hours of this morning, she is understandably bewildered. She is also very sleepy. All she can manage to do is drowsily gawp at the phone's screen as she speedily connects her phone to the charger.

She types on her phone, "Okay, Charles." She stops typing momentarily to cover her mouth as she yawns deeply. Realizing that she is overly courteous to an unseen ghost on the other end of her phone, she renews her typing as her yawning persists. "What happens now? And what is that scary thing in my closet that I dreamed? It is freaking me out!"

"Not in your closet," Charles replies. "All around. Everywhere."

Diana is suddenly wide-eyed. She sits up on her bed and reaches over to turn on her bedside lamp. Trembling yet again, she glances around her bedroom nervously. She quickly types, "Everywhere? All around? What in the world does that mean? You're scaring me, Charles!"

Charles' reply appears on her phone. "Sorry. You asked."

"Well, explain what you mean by the word everywhere! Dang, Charles! I've never experienced such a creepy thing in my whole life except, of course when you first started haunting me. Now that was creepy! But I am used to you now. So are my friends. Besides, you're not scary. But that eerie thing in the closet is!"

"What I meant by 'everywhere,' 'all around' is complicated,'" Charles replies. "Lies, deceit, dishonesty, treachery, call them what you want, they are everywhere."

"Well, that makes perfect sense, Charles. But what in the world does this have to do with me?"

Charles types, "Your unopened birthday gift. Open it, if you please."

"I was going to wait until morning. It is a small gift which means it's jewelry. Besides, I like the wrapping. Why should I open it now?"

"Because I asked you to. Besides, it IS morning." Charles includes a smiling face emoji at the end of his typewritten words.

Diana hesitates slightly. She quickly types on her screen. "Wait a minute, Charles. Two questions. First, that creepy thing sent a notification to my phone. Is he, or it, reading what we type on notes? Second, do you know what the gift is?"

Charles types, "I shall answer the second question first. Yes, I know what the gift is. First question. I blocked him."

Diana is somewhat offended and a slight bit angry at Charles' response. She murmurs in a singsong sarcastic tone, "I blocked him. I blocked him. Harrumph! Well, it's nice to know *I* have control over *my* phone." With a purposeful, agitated groan, she roughly grabs the gift off of her bedside stand. As she does, another missive from Charles appears on her notes app.

"I heard that!" Charles follows his typewritten words with a wide-eyed face emoji.

In spite of her weariness, Diana cannot help but laugh at Charles' typewritten reply. She types, "Sorry. I didn't mean to offend you. I'm tired, that's all. I love you, Charles."

Charles replies with a heart emoji.

Diana removes the outer wrapping of the gift. She is amazed to see that a beautifully engraved leather box encloses the gift. There is an inscription on the box. She reads the inscription out loud in a hushed whisper.

"Honesty is the First Chapter in the Book of Honor ~ James Hall 521 BC."

The light on her bedside lamp abruptly dims. Then a chilly breeze rushes into the bedroom. Amazingly, the closed window's curtains sway slightly with the breeze. Diana begins to shiver a little. Pulling the blanket up to her neck, she takes a deep breath. Her heart is racing as she unhurriedly opens the box.

*****

Part II: More Ghosts!

Diana is thrilled beyond words when she sees what the jewelry box contains. A small, lovely lightning bolt charm of a dark blue color rests on a downy pillow of white. The lightning bolt charm is attached to an adjustable black leather string necklace. A small circular medallion with the letter *D* in calligraphy is attached to the charm's clasp. Diana is not certain if she imagines it, but the charm seems to glow ever so slightly in the room's dim light. She stares lovingly at the jewelry and considers the implication of this birthday present and the reason why she wanted to delay to open it. Her heart tells her that the lightning bolt charm is a symbol of good luck. She cannot wait to place the necklace around her neck. Nevertheless, something tells her now is not the time. Her thoughts return to Charles.

She types on her phone, "Goodness, Charles, I love the charm. It is very pretty. But what does it have to do with me?" She closes the jewelry box to look at the inscription on the outside. "Who is James Hall? Also, is 521 BC a date? I assume it is a date, but I want to make certain."

Charles types, "James is my brother. And yes, 521 BC is a date, five hundred twenty-one years before the birth of Christ."

Diana's stares at her phone for the longest time. She is both surprised and excited to discover that Charles has a brother. Her stormy blue-grey eyes open wide, their pupils blazing with the customary little lightning bolts, in this case, of eagerness. She types, "Your brother? Goodness, Charles, I think that is very coolio because I never knew you had a brother. Why didn't you tell me?"

Typewritten words unhurriedly appear on her phone's screen. They read, "You never asked, Diana."

Diana types, "Well, I guess I didn't." She scratches her head absentmindedly, and then she quickly types, "Quite frankly, it never occurred to me to ask. Let's be honest here. A teenager having her very own gentle ghost is pretty cool in and of itself, wouldn't you agree? So, why would I ask if you had a brother? Besides, you never communicated with me until this morning." Just as she finishes typing, she notices the time as it updates on her phone. It is 3:47 am, Friday, June 19. She stretches her arms out wide and yawns.

Despite yesterday's birthday celebrations, winning the girl's softball championship and, naturally, the weirdness and excitement of this morning, she feels crummy. She glances at her phone to look at the time yet again. It is 3:52 am. A whole five minutes have passed since the last time she looked! She reckons she fell fast asleep while sitting up as she waited for Charles to respond.

"Darn! I need to get some sleep. I can barely keep my eyes open." She stretches her legs before her and wiggles her toes. "And my muscles are aching from squatting so long on the softball field. The game seemed much longer than nine innings. Talking to Charles is pretty cool, but I'm bushed!"

Her cell phone lights up. Typewritten words slowly appear on the screen. As Charles types the words, he occasionally backspaces what he has written. It appears to Diana that he is purposely careful with his choice of words. As she waits for him to finish typing, she closes her eyes. Her head rolls to the left causing her to awaken suddenly. Then, a few seconds later, she is nodding off yet again. Just as her chin rests on her chest, her phone vibrates. Charles is trying to get her attention.

Charles' typewritten words say, "You should have asked me, Diana. I think it is important for you to know that you should have asked. All these years I waited for you to ask via your thoughts."

Diana quickly types, "My thoughts? Charles, if you do not mind me asking, can you read my mind, my thoughts?"

"Yes, Diana, I can comprehend your thoughts every time you mention my name out loud or in a thought process. I can even grasp your thoughts when you are in school or on the softball diamond. Like when you said in your mind a few seconds ago, 'Talking to Charles is pretty cool, but I'm bushed!'" Diana unconsciously moves her hand to cover her mouth. She feels ashamed.

"Oh, I am very sorry, Charles. All these years, I've been focusing on how cool it is to have a ghost, bragging to my friends. And throughout, I've never questioned you either aloud or in my thoughts about you and your family. All I thought about was how cool it was to have my very own ghost. I'm truly sorry for being self-centered, Charles. Please forgive me for my rudeness."

Charles types, "It's all good, Diana. If you please, place the necklace around your neck. Right now is the moment in time that you should learn the truth. And trust me, do not be alarmed at what happens after you place the necklace around your neck."

Diana sets her phone on the bedside table. She opens the box and removes the necklace. She carefully places the necklace around her neck. As she does, she immediately notices she does not feel the least bit tired! Miraculously, the achiness in her muscles has also disappeared. Somewhat startled, but surprisingly unafraid, she stares straight ahead awe-struck as a ghostly vision unhurriedly appears at the far end of her bedroom. The ghost's image is not entirely like that of a Real-world person. That is because a translucent grayish-white aura surrounds its form from head to toe. Otherwise, the ghost's form takes shape as something resembling a human.

She can hardly control her emotions as her heart races with excitement. She wants to run out of her bedroom, but Charles had told her not to be alarmed, to trust him. The ghost, definitely a male, is handsomely beautiful. Since he is an apparition, there is no actual coloring of his skin, hair, and eyes or even his clothes. Be that as it may, his almond-shaped eyes flicker with a flush of triumph and joy.

He has bristly eyebrows and defined cheekbones. His Roman nose and defined cheekbones surround a full mouth. While it is barely noticeable, Diana can make out a sand-rough stubble on his chin. He appears to be in his middle to the late twenties, perhaps even in his thirties. He stands about six-feet tall, slender but with well-developed, striking muscles. He is wearing what appears to be old-fashioned clothes, perhaps from the Unenlightened Period or even during ancient times. The ghost seemingly glides above the floor to stand near Diana's bed. He bows deeply.

Nearly out of breath with anticipation, Diana whispers, "Charles?"

The ghost replies, "No, Diana. I am not Charles. I am James, James Hall, Charles' older brother." He extends his hand saying, "It is a pleasure to make your acquaintance finally, Diana."

Diana reaches to take James' hand in hers. Her hand goes right through his. Having her hand pass right through his causes delicate wisps of grayish-white smoke to curl around both of their hands. Flabbergasted and sort of embarrassed thinking she could shake a ghost's hand, she quickly jerks her hand back.

She whispers, "Oh, I am very sorry, James. Please excuse me if I have offended you in any way. I logically figured that you were Charles. I also thought I could somehow shake your hand, that I could touch it." She giggles. "I hope you understand. You are the first ghost I have seen. And my goodness! Where are my manners?" She places her right hand on her heart as a display of warmth. "It is a pleasure to meet you as well." She glances around the bedroom expectantly. "But where is Charles? I cannot see him."

Charles thoughts immediately enter Diana's mind.

"I am here beside you as well, Diana, obviously not in a physical form like my brother, but always near, but a whisper and a heartbeat away." He adds with a chuckle, "Unlike James who is merely here to escort you to our world."

"Oh my goodness," Diana whispers with an understandable tone of surprise in her voice, "to your world? But Charles." She looks at James who is now kneeling on the floor beside her bed. "But Charles, James, I do not want to go anywhere." She stretches and rubs her legs beneath her blanket. "Although my legs no longer hurt and I'm not sleepy, which is pretty amazing, I'm quite content right here at home in my happy place." She shakes her head back and forth with disagreement with what Charles had said.

"No. I do not need to go anywhere. Besides, today is a school day, even if it'll be a pretty easy day since we won the ladies' softball championship. Also, I do not want to leave my parents, my brothers, Billy and Dan, my home and my friends. They will worry about me."

She stares at her phone. Then she exclaims, "Goodness, Charles, it just occurred to me! You no longer have to type on my phone app or write on a mirror to talk to me. I can read your thoughts. This latest revelation is coolio, Charles!" She looks up at James once more.

"James, I do not need to go anywhere. I am quite content right here."

"Diana, you shall be perfectly safe with me," James says. "I shall endeavor to ensure no harm comes to you while you are in our world." He frowns. "Although I must tell you, I am afraid you may confront some danger."

Charles' thoughts enter Diana's mind. "Diana, your family is asleep right now. There is no need to worry."

"But when they wake up," Diana cries, "they will not find me here, and they will worry themselves sick."

James says, "Diana, you will journey to our faraway world of unbelievable beautiful scenes, strange creatures, and, as I said, you may encounter a bit of danger. At the same time, while you are journeying in our world, another part of you, your double, will remain behind. The other part that remains behind will function as normal. She will attend school, eat, sleep, and even hang out with her, or perhaps I should say, your friends.

"And you, the part journeying to our world, you will have the capability to occasionally glimpse into the comings and goings of your other half as she goes about her normal daily routine. However, you cannot influence her actions in any way. While she will be you, you will also be you, if that makes sense. So, as it relates to your parents, Diana, they will never even know you are gone."

Diana whispers, "That is very coolio. I will be in two places at once. I can hardly believe it. But how do I know I can trust you? After all, I am a female teenager, and I do not want to go to a faraway world with two ghosts, two male ghosts at that. It simply is not proper." She tilts her head and smiles sheepishly just as her face blushes. "I hope you understand what I am saying."

Charles' thoughts enter Diana's mind yet again.

"True, Diana, and your concern is reasonable. That is one of the many reasons why I am your lifelong friend. You truly are a respectable young lady. Your values are proper. You are very intelligent and amazingly talented. I would never be a lifelong friend, a ghost, of someone of lesser qualities."

James turns his head to the left. He whispers, "That is why my good friend April will accompany us." He smiles. "It is only proper and fitting that a kind woman escorts you, a woman with unparalleled character and graciousness such as yours."

Charles' thoughts enter Diana's mind yet again. As his words form in her mind, she is certain she detects a hint of jealousy in his words.

"James is your masculine escort, your protection in case of trouble. One does not move from your world to ours without a suggestion of misfortune and, as James said, the potential for peril. Besides, you and I will meet in my world soon enough."

James laughs at his brother's words. As Diana stares at him, she is certain that if he had any color to his form, his alluring eyes would most certainly be hazel.

He says, "Indeed. Given that Charles is younger than me by many years, he is unable to escort you, notwithstanding that he is your lifelong compassionate ghost. Or, as those of us in our world like to refer to ourselves, your lifelong *protective soul*."

Diana says, "Well, okay then, I guess that is only appropriate, to have a female escort me. So, when will I get to meet April?"

Just as she asks her question, a second apparition or, more correctly, Diana reasons, a protective soul, appears at the far end of her bedroom.

Like James' vision a few moments earlier, April's image forms slowly. The same grayish-white aura surrounds her figure. April is noticeably older than James, perhaps in her mid-thirties or maybe even early forties. She stands just about five-foot three-inches. She is gorgeous! Her inspiring .beauty is evident in the crease of her lovely brows and the up-curve of her full lips. But her eyes, her eyes show the true beauty and compassion of her soul. Diana instantly knows April is a person who she can trust, in whom she can confide if the need ever arises.

As her image continues to emerge, an unmistakable breeze in Diana's bedroom causes April's full-length gown to billow. Her gown appears satiny, long and loose. The high semicircular collar is at its head. Like James, there is no true color to April's form. Just the same, Diana envisions that April is a redhead. Her full-length hair that cascades in curls past her shoulders is unmistakably lava-red even though there is no actual color to it. A puff of the soft breeze in the bedroom sweeps through her supposed reddish hair.

April has a shapely, slender figure. Her eyes are a pale-white. Once again, Diana thinks that if she could see April's true eye color, they would be a dazzling rapture-blue. A pair of arched eyebrows looks down on her sweeping eyelashes. Her barely noticeable ears tucked beneath her long hair frame a cute button nose. It is also very apparent that April has freckles, on her face, her nose, her neck, and even on her lips. She is undoubtedly the most beautiful woman that Diana has ever seen. In fact, she thinks the lovely woman standing in the center of her bedroom is so elegant she looks like she is the head of a royal family. She looks like a princess, maybe even a queen.

April curtsies elegantly. She walks to Diana's bed, and then she places her hands on her heart. Diana recognizes the gesture as one of friendship. She copies April's gesture.

April whispers, "Diana, I am ready to escort you to our world. We call it the World Beyond." She smiles the most tender smile imaginable. "Are you ready?"

Diana looks around her bedroom. Tears well up in her eyes once more. She consciously pulls her blanket up tight to cover her head. In a muffled voice that belies her fear, she nervously replies under her blanket, "Not really, April. To tell you the truth, I'm really afraid. How do I know I can trust you, that I will be okay, that I won't be gone long? More importantly, I'm concerned about my parents. They will worry themselves sick if they somehow discover the real me is not here."

In what Diana assumes is a whisper, Charles' thoughts enter her mind.

"As I said, Diana, I will also be nearby, but a whisper away. I have never disappointed you, have I? After a few seconds, he adds, "Do you trust *me*, Diana?"

Diana has to admit she trusts Charles, probably just as much as she trusts anyone else in the world. Her muffled response as she hides from view beneath the blanket reflects that trust.

"Yes, Charles, I trust you. You know that. I always have. You've been very kind to me. You've brightened many otherwise gloomy days with your innocent pranks. In fact, you've helped me to make friends. I know that may sound superficial, but it's true. As my friends came to know you, they also came to know me as someone in whom they can confide, someone they can trust. Like you, Charles, I will never abandon a true friend. So, yes, I trust you. If you say everything is going to be okay, I trust your words, unequivocally. But I am still very scared."

She peeks from beneath her blanket. She stares at April in disbelief. April's form is no longer grayish-white! She looks just like your everyday kaleidoscopic human from head to toe!

All of a sudden, she throws back her blanket. She leaps out of her bed. She rushes to hug April exclaiming excitedly, "Oh my God, April. You look exactly like the character, well, the description actually, of Queen April in the Enchanted Gate series of novels! My likeness is a character in the novels too. I'm an elf called Dianise! Dianise has amazing magical powers, levitation, and apportation!"

She backs away from April to get a better look at the beautiful woman. As she stares into April's rapture-blue eyes, she exclaims, "Your similarity to Queen April on the ancient Isle of Spardom beneath the sea is amazing, strikingly amazing! You even have the exact red hair and freckles as I imagined them from the books!" She embraces April yet again. "In fact, you look just like your daughter Eva, the Princess, well, as I imagine her from her portrayal in the books."

April moves closer so she can whisper into Diana's ear.

"Why, Diana, otherwise known as the multi-talented Professor Dianise of the Academy of Spells and Enchantments, it would appear that you have discovered my secret without me even telling you. Yes, indeed, my dear, I am the same Queen April of Spardom. Princess Eva is my daughter, as is the present queen of the Isle, my lovely child Lindsial." She gently pushes away from Diana and looks into Diana's eyes.

She says, "Nevertheless, the journey on which you are about to venture has nothing to do with Spardom or any of its current, turbulent events. Or, I am sad to say, any of its elves or bizarre Spardom creatures, to include the evil wizard, Zarof. But, I guarantee you will not be disappointed as you journey. You will meet many bizarre creatures and yes, as James alluded to, you will encounter danger." She places her hands on Diana's shoulders.

"Diana, your journey is all about you and your quest for right-eousness." She smiles deviously. "Yes, Diana, I know what you have been thinking. You seek the truth about yesterday's championship softball game. You are elated and disheartened at the same time. As you venture on your soon-to-be incredible journey, you will hopefully find actual honor in your quest for the truth." She smiles. "So, what do you say, my dear? Are you ready?"

Diana hugs April tightly one more time. The nervousness in her unsteady words is apparent as she replies.

"Well, I guess so, April." After a few seconds, she pushes away from April. She stares into April's eyes, eyes that seem to cry out, *you can put your faith in me!* With a renewed expression of determination on her face and the telltale little lightning bolts dancing in her stormy, blue-grey eyes, Diana exclaims in a whisper, "Yes, April. You are correct. I have been thinking about the championship game since yesterday. That is why I couldn't sleep, not because we won because I think I struck out. That probably explains why I had that terrible nightmare, the one about that creepy thing, a ghost I guess, opening the closet. It freaked me out, I dare say! I am thankful that Charles came to my aid." She looks at the ceiling and whispers, "Thank you very much, Charles."

Charles replies in her mind, "It was no biggie, Diana, honestly. You would have done the same for me."

Diana reflects privately in her thoughts, "Yes, Charles, yes indeed. I would certainly do the same for you. I love you."

Her cell phone sitting on her bedside table suddenly vibrates. She reaches for it and cannot help to laugh as emoji after emoji scroll across the screen. The seemingly endless strings of emoji's are broadly smiling faces with huge hearts for eyes. Finally, after a few more lines of loving emoji's, Charles types on her phone's notes app, "I love you too!"

Diana breathes in deeply. In a confident whisper, she says to April, "Okay, I'm ready." Moving her hands alongside her body, she adds, "But, first I should change my clothes, don't you think? Journeying in pajamas isn't my thing if you know what I mean." She laughs.

April smiles. "I am afraid you do not have anything in your closet that is appropriate for our world, Diana. So."

Before April can finish her sentence, Diana sarcastically exclaims as she stares at the closet door, "Yeah, nothing but a creepy, totally scary apparition, that's what is in my closet!" Her eyes are glowing with loathing, the tiny lightning bolts dancing in her pupils like crazy. With a serious scowl, she looks at April expectantly. "But it was only a dream, you know, that thing in my closet, am I correct?"

April takes both of Diana's hands in hers. She squeezes them firmly.

"No, Diana, it was not a dream. Or even a nightmare. What you think you envisioned, what you, in fact, saw with your own eyes, is *Mendacium*. Mendacium is a Latin word. Translation of the word in English is pure and simple. It means lies, deceit, untruths, and other words. Yes, Diana, I am afraid that Mendacium is real. He is a horrible, evil manifestation that, unfortunately, dwells in both of our worlds." She smiles as her hands squeeze Diana's yet again. "However, you must face up to Mendacium. If you do not, you will never attain actual peace in your heart and certainly, in your mind."

April gently squeezes Diana's hands three times. At first, Diana is not certain what the three squeezes of her hands imply. Then she remembers. On Spardom, the make-believe Isle beneath the sea, three squeezes of one's hands by an elf indicates, "I love you."

With a broad smile, Diana squeezes April's hands firmly four times in reply. Four squeezes of one's hands on Spardom means, "I love you too!" Then, with a worried look on her face, she looks squarely into April's eyes and says, "You will protect me, yes?" April nods her head.

Diana turns to address James. Unlike April, his form is still indistinct. She whispers, "And you, James. Will you also protect me?" James nods his head. Diana says, "Promise?" April and James both reply, "Promise."

Charles thoughts are immediately in Diana's mind. Unsurprisingly, his thoughts echo April and James' pledge. He says, "Promise."

Diana says, "Okay, I'm ready. How does it work? Will I be awake or asleep? It won't hurt, will it?"

April warmly smiles as she says, "No, Diana it will not hurt. All you have to do is to rub the lightning bolt on your charm necklace three times between your thumb and forefinger. It is that simple."

Diana smiles despite the worry that is gripping her emotions. She is rightfully worried and yes, very afraid. However, she ponders that she somehow knew it all along, in fact, from the very moment she opened the gift. She indeed has a quest. A quest for the truth, for the honor of something lurking in the back of her mind. All the same, she never dreamed that her longing for the truth would entail a journey to a different world.

"How had April put it? Ah, yes, she said it would be an incredible journey. I like the sound of that. *Diana's Incredible Journey.*"

She is rather certain that ambiguity looms in her future. All the same, she is eager to experience whatever the future holds. She loves adventure, and she is a proven risk taker. She also hopes that the journey on which she is about to embark is as unbelievable, far-fetched, and mind-blowing as everything that has happened to her in the past two days. If it is, she will have one awesome story to tell her friends when she returns!

She takes one last look around her bedroom. As she fiddles with the charm, she suddenly feels at ease. She slowly rubs the charm's lightning bolt three times between her thumb and forefinger. As she does, hateful words out of nowhere scream.

"It's nobody's business! Nobody, I tell you. Nobody at all!"

Diana begins to freak out. She wants to run, run away as quickly as she can and as far away as possible. But she does not. She stands up tall. Ignoring the torturing screams of Mendacium, she sets her lips in a straight line. The pupils of her wide-open eyes light up the room with dancing lightning bolts of irrefutable courage and defiance.

And then she is gone.

*****

Part III: Tranquility Beam

Utterly opaque darkness. These are the only words to describe Diana's visual sensation immediately after she rubs the charm's lightning bolt three times. She opens her eyes wide and stares. But she can see nothing but absolute darkness. At the same time, she imagines in her mind's eye that she is falling weightlessly in tight spirals through a narrow corridor. The weightless sensation is like floating, the stomach-lurching feeling you get when a roller coaster suddenly drops down its tracks. The only difference now is Diana feels as if her body is also spiraling or corkscrewing within the corridor.

The corridor, if, as Diana reasons, that is what it truly is, seems to zigzag this way and that from time to time. As her body weightlessly zigzags within the corridor, her hands, arms, legs, and occasionally her face, scrape the corridor's sides. As they do, prickly objects that feel like spears seem to scratch her skin a little. The spears are like static electricity shocks one feels when touching a doorknob after walking on a wool carpet during the dead of winter. Happily, the staticky shocks do not cause much pain. Despite this, they certainly are very annoying.

Diana's shallow breaths, perhaps better described as fleeting gasps, are racing in step with her rapidly beating heart. To further add to her unease, she abruptly senses a chill. The chill progressively turns to outright cold making her very uncomfortable. The cold triggers the hairs on her arms to stand on end and an army of shivers to run up and down her spine. She starts to shiver uncontrollably. Then, as quickly as the chilliness had arrived, it begins to dissipate slowly. A lukewarm sensation gradually replaces the chilling sensation, causing her to feel more comfortable as her body warms. But, before long, the warming sensation gradually intensifies. Then it becomes very hot causing her to feel ill at ease. The increase in temperature causes her to sweat profusely. Just as she thinks she cannot stand the hotness any longer, the chilling sensation begins to appear, and her comfortableness gradually returns.

After suffering a few of the chilling and warming episodes, she notices something interesting. The sensations seem to come and go and to rise and fall in a set pattern. On a hunch, she begins to count her heartbeats at the beginning of a warming session. After 100 heartbeats, the chill slowly returns just as the intense heat gradually leaves. One hundred heartbeats later, the warmth slowly arrives once more. Diana is somewhat relieved that she can now prepare herself mentally for the recurring changes in temperature. Be that as it may, the recurring temperature variations are now as annoying as the prickly shocks to her skin.

She also notices something else. Her heartbeats and breathing seem to slow progressively after each temperature variation cycle. It is almost as if her body is gradually acclimating to another environment as it continues to spiral weightlessly through the corridor. She also notices one additional phenomenon. As her heartbeat and breathing progressively slow, so does the spiral, or so she supposes. Be that as it may, the chilling and warming sensations still come and go every 100 heartbeats, give or take a heartbeat.

She has not spoken a single word this entire time. She has been too afraid to do anything but think as she glares into the opaque blackness and tries to endure the shocks and strange temperature fluctuations. Also, she has no inkling of the length of time she has been in this corridor if that is what it is. At long last, she gets up enough courage to see if she still can speak.

"Ahem, hello?" she whispers uncertainly. "Yepity, yep, yep! Whew, that's good. Not only can I talk, but I can also hear. Well, at least I think I can hear. Let's see if what I think I'm hearing is my voice and not an echoing in my mind."

Out of the blue, she starts to laugh as she recalls the time as a child she was in a plastic tunnel at a McDonald's play area. She had been surprised how her shouts had seemed to echo in a nearly inaudible way. They also sounded peculiar when they echoed. She yells at the top of her voice, "Hello, hello?" Her voice instantly echoes a gradually fading, "Hello, hello, hello, hello." She smiles to herself. "Well, my intuition was correct. I am in a corridor of some sort."

She says aloud, "Can anybody hear me?"

There is no response. The fact that there is no response causes Diana to worry.

"What if what I think I saw in my bedroom wasn't real? What if Charles is playing a prank on me, or worse yet, that nasty critter Mendacium is playing a nasty hoax on me? Did I see April and James? Or did I imagine them? Heck, maybe I'm still asleep, and all this weirdness is nothing but a bad dream. Also, where in the world are April and James? They promised they would accompany me. And Charles? Where is my loving ghost, my protective soul?"

She tries to reach out with her right hand to pinch her left arm to ensure that she is awake. She cannot. The centrifugal force of her spiral prevents her two appendages from touching. Suddenly, she feels something touching the tip of the forefinger of her left hand. She recoils and closes her hand into a tight fist.

She shouts, "Who or what is that! Don't you dare touch me! If you touch me again, I will strike you with my fist!"

A soft voice from somewhere nearby in the corridor replies, "It is okay, Diana. It is only me, April. I have been racing to catch up with you, but your ascension is really fast. It seems you have adapted to the tranquility beam much better than we had expected. I am very proud of you. You're a natural I dare say!"

"Whew!" Diana exclaims. "I was beginning to worry that." She stops midsentence and says, "Wait a minute! You said ascension. Have I been traveling skyward all this time? I thought I was traveling downward! It feels like I am tumbling downward out of control."

April laughs. "No, all this time you have been traveling upward. Each of the sensations you are feeling serves an important purpose. The sensation of falling through the tranquility beam helps to maintain your equilibrium. So, when you arrive in the World Beyond, you will adapt rather quickly and not undergo too much lightheadedness. The variations in temperature you are experiencing also serve a purpose. They are designed to acclimatize your body to the unique, airy atmosphere of the World Beyond."

Diana asks, "There is oxygen in the World Beyond, yes? I won't have to wear a helmet or anything, will I?"

April giggles, and then she inquires, "Since when do you not like wearing a helmet, Diana? You wear a helmet each time you are at bat during your softball games."

"Oh, not that kind of helmet. I am talking about a helmet that is hooked up to a canister of oxygen. It is the same as astronauts use in outer space."

"Oh, now I understand what kind of helmet to which you refer," April says with a chuckle. "No, Diana, the air is breathable, and the atmosphere is suitable for your body. It is different than what you are used to, that is all. Please allow me to portray the ecosystem of the World Beyond, so you will better understand the purpose of the tranquility beam.

"There are no oceans or seas or rivers or streams in the World Beyond. Then again, there is one very large lake. Those that dwell in the World Beyond refer to it as Lake Vita. There is no rainfall like in your world. Certainly, there is moisture to nourish life, but it arises from the bottom up, from the ground. We suspect the ground-seeping moisture originates from Lake Vita.

"Also, the World Beyond, unlike your world where pollution is rampant, is unspoiled. That's because there is no modern industry, such as factories and manufacturing plants. Likewise, there are no harmful chemicals to speak of, apart from those that occur naturally in nature. Because of the World Beyond's purity, the air is much cleaner than anything you have ever experienced. So, when you exit the tranquility beam, you will have adjusted to the World Beyond's environment."

"So, why is it that this corridor, I mean the tranquility beam, twists, and then it turns, and why do I feel like I am zigzagging through it?"

April replies, "Your perception of zigzagging through the beam is real. With every zig or zag, you pass an intersection of sorts within the beam. As an example, one intersection takes the traveler to an uninteresting land called Someplace in Time. Someplace in Time resembles a vast desert one would expect to see in your world. It is void of vegetation and any noticeable lifeforms. There is no water, no food, no entertainment, no sound, and sadly, no one with whom its residents can communicate.

"All the same, there are living beings in Someplace in Time, lots of beings. It is just that they cannot see, hear, touch, or talk to each other. The entire scene in Someplace in Time is unchanging, for lack of a better word. As the land's name implies, time stands still, and life is static. The land is for those who lack the ability, or desire to allow for a change in their lives. I visited Someplace in Time many years ago. It is a very uninteresting land. I was quite bored during my visit and very lonely. Perhaps loneliness is the land's worst feature."

Diana suddenly whispers, "Goodness, April, what is that noise? It sounds like thousands of insects. I can hear the distinctive sounds of the buzzing of bees, droning of wings, stridulating of crickets, and the hissing of, oh my goodness! I can hear the hissing of what sounds like bunches of spiders!"

"There is nothing to fear, Diana," April says. We just zigged near the Land of Insectum. Reference to the land as the Land of Insectum is inaccurate. But that is what everyone calls it, the Land of Insectum. Even though it is a land bursting with every imaginable insect, it is also crawling with arachnids, scorpions, mites, ticks, and spiders. As you know, the last creatures I mentioned technically are not insects."

Diana exclaims, "Spiders? I hate spiders! I do not have arachnophobia, at least I do not think that I do. All the same, spiders freak me out."

April inquires, "Why is that? Why do, as you say, spiders freak you out?"

"Well, one time during Halloween, after my little brother, Billy and I had finished trick-or-treating, we were counting, sorting, and trading our candy. Out of nowhere, this huge spider, probably bigger than a quarter started running from under the sofa. It was making this weird noise, kind of like a wind-up toy. It had super-creepy red eyes that glowed.

"When I first saw it, I thought it was a prank. After all, it was Halloween night. Then, as it came straight toward our piles of candy, I realized it was a real spider. I screamed as did my brother. My scream was a normal scream, at least I think that it was. But Billy's scream was a high-pitched, ear-piercing, blood-curdling, once-in-a-lifetime, incredible shriek.

"The two of us scrambled onto separate couches. Then I got enough courage to run upstairs to my dad. I was panting, completely out of breath on the stairway. I said - no, I think I stuttered, 'There's - there's a sp-sp-ider!' All my dad said in reply, in a calm tone of voice, 'Sounded like one.' Then he went downstairs to eliminate the nasty thing. Now you know why I hate spiders.'"

April's loud laughter seemingly echoes nonstop within the beam. She says, "I am sorry about your encounter with that spider. If it makes you feel better, there are few spiders in the World Beyond. Even so, those that live are enormous in comparison to spiders in your world."

A tremor races up Diana's spine and jolts her shoulders with a cold shiver. She is about to shout what she is thinking. "Enormous in comparison to spiders in my world?" But then, before she can voice her apprehension about enormous spiders in the World Beyond, April resumes talking.

"Okay, if you have noticed, Diana, we just zagged. To our right was the corridor humans know as Purgatory. In some religions, Purgatory is a place of punishment for souls who die in God's grace so that they may make amends for past sins. It supposedly prepares them for Heaven."

"I have heard of Purgatory," Diana whispers. "I would not like to go there, even for a short visit."

"No, Diana, surely you would not. And I seriously doubt a young lady of your honorable conduct will ever need to worry about even the briefest stopover there."

"That is nice to know, and I thank you," Diana replies softly with a long sigh of relief. "I try to live my life each day as a good person, helping others, being respectful. I try to make people laugh, and I am always ready to provide emotional comfort for those in need. Sure, I may listen to Hard Rock and Indie Rock, which some people find offensive, but I thoroughly enjoy those kinds of music. They make me happy.

"You know, April, people sometimes do not understand that teenagers have unique tastes in music, movies, and books. Just because our tastes are different does not mean we are not agreeable people. I mean, I respect others' choices, so why can't they respect mine?

"A while back, I participated in a play production with some of my classmates in drama class. Most of my classmates liked the play. A few others in my school thought they were kind of stupid. Every so often they would say, not to me personally, but to no one in particular, not so pleasant things." She sighs. "Sometimes I do not understand why people cannot be nice to everyone. Just because you do not like something does not mean you have to be nasty to others."

Diana stops talking briefly, and then she says with utmost sincerity in her voice, "It is comforting to know someone cares and accepts me for who I am. My mom and dad do as do my brothers. I also have an elderly friend who thinks highly of me as well. He always refers to me as intelligent, artistic, and he compliments me on, what he calls, my exceptional athleticism.

"Anyway, once again, I thank you, April. So, tell me, if you please. Does Mendacium's kingdom have an intersection of its own? If so, hopefully, we have already passed it. I do not want to go anywhere near that awful creature. Is his domain far away from the World Beyond?"

"Yes, and no," April replies. "Yes, there is an intersection for Mendacium. And no, his domain is not far from the World Beyond. In fact, his domain *IS* the World Beyond. He possesses it, Diana. He owns it as the kingdom's ruler."

Diana shouts, "What! You're telling me that Mendacium possesses, is the owner of the World Beyond? Goodness, April, if that is the case, I certainly do not want to go there! Please take me home."

"Diana, your concern is understandable. Yes, Mendacium is the Ruler of the World Beyond." She hesitates, and then she tenderly takes hold of Diana's hand. "I am sorry to tell you this, Diana, but I cannot return you to your home, to the Real-world, at least not until you find the truth that you seek."

"The truth!" Diana exclaims with a shout. "I could care less about the truth at this point if it means I have to square off with Mendacium in his land! I do not want to know the truth! Take me home!"

Diana's shouted words seem to echo within the confines of the tranquility beam much longer and much louder than usual. Strangely, her words hauntingly echo over and over in her mind as well.

"Take me home, take me home, take me home." Finally, her disparaging words fade away into the blackness.

Her awareness of what she just shouted to April causes her heart to sink. She winces as tears of outrage well up in her eyes. She is angry with herself by the way she appeared to give in easily to her doubts.

As she regains her composure, she mutters to herself, "I am not a quitter. I've never been a quitter, and I will never be afraid." She frees her hand from April's clutch. With an expression of renewed resolve on her face, she clenches both of her hands into tight fists.

"I am sorry, April, for shouting. Please forgive me. You are correct, one hundred percent correct. I honestly want to. No, that is the wrong word. I *must* know the truth. After all, my reputation is at stake here, as the supposed heroine of the softball championship game. And, while I have no desire to square off with Mendacium, I know I must do it for honor's sake. I apologize for being, well, for lack of a better word, a worrywart. But at least I voiced my fears." She laughs at the top of her voice. "And definitely, I got that out of my system as well."

April says with a laugh, "There is no need to apologize. Your reaction is logical. I would have voiced my doubts as well had I been in your shoes." Changing the subject, she says, "We will arrive soon, in fact, in less than a few moments. It is important for your mind to be clear when we arrive. Do you have any questions?"

"Yes, I have one question. What in the world are those prickly things that keep giving me shocks, like tingles from static electricity? They do not hurt much, but they sure are irritating!"

"I know the prickly sensations tingle a bit," April replies. "But they are harmless. Some are bursts of air that inject anodyne elements into your body. We call them *elemental attributes*. They are designed to increase your strong points. A few of the elemental attributes are courage, tenacity, and stamina.

"Other bursts of air do the exact opposite. They remove things from your body and your mind. We call these removals *opposing diminutions*. Some examples of opposing diminutions are indecision, fear, doubt, anxiety, dishonesty, and nervousness, things like that.

"Elemental attributes will help to make you a formidable foe when you, as you refer to it, square off with Mendacium. Conversely, removing some of your fears, doubts, etcetera, from your body, thanks to opposing diminutions, will make you less susceptible to failure."

Diana does not answer for a few moments as she considers April's words. When she finally replies, she counters with a chuckle and, as is her custom, straightforward words mixed with a bit of humor.

"Well, by now I should probably be comparable to a daring, awe-inspiring superwoman. Because those elemental and opposing things jabbed me at least a couple of thousand times!"

*****

Part IV: Mendacium

April unexpectedly yells just as a penetratingly bright light illuminates the interior of the tranquility beam.

"I know you are having trouble seeing well with the intense light. All the same, reach out to grasp my hand with yours, quickly! I am on your left. I will slow our ascent just a tad to enable you to move your arm without too much difficulty. Hurry, Diana, hurry! There is not much time!"

The unexpected intense light is very penetrating, extremely painful to Diana's eyes. It feels like it is boring behind her eyes deep into her brain. Because of the sudden pain, her eyes instinctively narrow as she seeks out April's hand. To make matters worse, she desperately wants to cover her eyes with her hands, to stop the agony her eyes are experiencing. Even so, she continues to fight with all her strength to counter the centrifugal force that is gripping her arms in its clutch. She grunts and groans as she uses every muscle in her shoulders, triceps, forearms, and wrists to try and reach out for April's fingertips. After much effort, she manages to touch April's fingertips. She gradually works her fingers up April's fingers until she is clasping April's hand.

She shouts, "April, what is it? Is everything okay? What is that overpowering light? It is hurting my eyes even though my eyes are tightly closed! And I cannot shield my eyes with my left hand because, if I do, I will slip from your clutch. Plus, my right hand is useless. I cannot move it. The spinning and turning are making it impossible to shield my eyes!"

"Diana, shush, if you please," April whispers. "Something is out there, something sinister. I can feel it."

Diana cries out, "What is out there? What do you feel? Please tell me what it is. You are frightening me!"

"Diana, not now. Trust me. Shush, my dear."

Abruptly, a frightening voice echoes throughout the beam. Diana wants to cover her ears against the tormenting cries of terror. But she cannot. Her right arm is whirling uselessly in front of her, and she does not want to let go of April's hand with her left.

"Don't be a fool, Diana! Why go with this old woman when you can join me, be my friend, be like me! Let go of the old woman's hands. Be strong. Be brave. Be the heroine you know in your heart that you are, that you deserve! Do not allow the old woman to deceive you! Come to me, Diana."

Diana screams, "Oh, my God! It's Mendacium! I can feel his presence, hear his voice. His presence is the same that I experienced in my bedroom! April, help me, please! Do not allow him to touch me!"

April does not reply. She is trying with all her inner strength to drive the deceitful demon from their presence.

To Diana's horror, an unseen, powerful force steadily works to pry open the fingers on her left hand. She struggles against the unseen force with all her strength. Despite her best efforts, the aching in the joints of her fingers is too much to bear. Her fingers are forced open one by one until only April and her forefingers are linked.

April says in a firm voice, "Diana! Stay with me. Do not allow him to defeat you. What you are facing at this very moment is only the beginning of your journey. If he triumphs here and now, you lose everything, everything you pursue. Do not break our bond. Focus, Diana, focus. You are stronger than he is. You can beat him!"

Diana continues to resist with all her strength. The unbearable agony in her forefinger is enormous. She cries out in anguish, "My God, April. My finger feels like it is going to break! I cannot hold on to your finger much longer."

"Then free yourself," the fearsome voice says. "All you have to do is release yourself from the old woman's finger. Then you will be liberated. And you can return home, to your comfortable bed and all of the wonderful things that you know you honestly desire."

Then the voice laughs hideous mocking tones that echo repeatedly. "Ha-ha-ha-ha-ha! Then you and I can be in your world together forever!"

Diana cries out, "I cannot stand this pain!" Just as she says this, her finger slips from April's grasp. She screams, "I am sorry, April. I think he has broken my finger as he pried my finger from yours! Gosh, it hurts badly!"

The terrifying voice's sickening laugh mockingly echoes within the tranquility beam's walls yet again.

"Ha-ha-ha-ha-ha! I have won. I knew it. You are nothing, Diana, nothing. You are weak, a loser. And all this time you thought you were a heroine. You should be ashamed of yourself. To think you thought you could defeat me, the powerful Mendacium. Ha-ha-ha-ha-ha!"

Diana shrieks in terror. She is staring into the opaque, black eyes of the evilest living thing imaginable. Mendacium! She watches horrified as the creature unhurriedly draws near, his disgusting barebones hands menacingly reaching out to grab her by her shoulders.

He whispers, "See, Diana. It is me, Mendacium. I have come for you, to receive you into my worldwide realm."

Diana cries out, "No, no, no! I despise you, Mendacium. You will not defeat me. And you will never win. I will win! I do not care how long it takes. You will go down. You can count on it!"

She opens her eyes even wider despite the pain of the blinding light. She stretches out her hand until her aching forefinger is once again touching April's hand. With a loud cry of agony caused by the intense pain that is shooting up her arm and across her shoulders, she lunges with all her strength to seize April's forefinger.

Tears of triumph are streaming from her eyes. She feels stronger, free from fear, invincible. In some way, she manages with brute strength to free her right hand from the powerful clutches of the spinning and twisting gyroscopic phenomenon. She points her finger menacingly at Mendacium as she glares a look of victory.

"Yes, Mendacium, I won this round. I now have one strike against you, with a count of oh and one. So, prepare to strike out, you loathsome, detestable devil, when I see you on the other side when we meet face to face! Yes, prepare yourself, Mendacium, 'cause you're going down!"

CHAPTER TWO

THE WORLD BEYOND

Part I: Empress

Diana unceremoniously enters the World Beyond. Due to no fault of her own, she arrives much too swiftly, her arms and legs thrashing senselessly in thin air as she tries to maintain her balance. The abrupt change in atmospheric pressure from inside the beam to the World Beyond causes her gaucherie.

To say her arrival seems comical goes without saying. She looks like someone clumsily soaring down the length of a curving playground slide who cannot do anything to slow the wild skid except crash to the ground bum first. The clumsy, wild, arms flailing, sidesplitting skid and its ending crash are what happens to Diana as the tranquility beam rudely ejects her.

When her rear end hits the ground, she exclaims forcefully, "Well, this is embarrassing, not to mention it hurts!" She rubs her bottom and hurriedly looks around to check if anyone is watching. There is no one in sight. She awkwardly tries to get to her feet and nearly falls backward. When she looks to see what she tripped over, she is astonished to see she is no longer wearing her pajamas. She is wearing strange clothes that hang around her ankles.

She cries out, saying, "Well, this explains why I almost fell on my butt yet again." She carefully flexes the forefinger on her left hand. It is a bit painful, but thankfully not broken. In fact, as the seconds slowly tick by, the throbbing in her finger gradually subsides. She gently shakes her hand. After a few moments, her finger heals completely.

Diana has no earthly idea what kind of attire she is wearing. Greek culture of the Classical Period (ancient Greece - 500 BC) referred to her dress as a *peplos*. Diana's peplos is a beautiful ivory-colored, full body-length outfit. An attractive, three-inch wide sash of finely stitched emerald-colored fabric encircles her slim waist. A gilded lightning bolt brooch fastens her garb at the shoulders. Athena, the Greek Goddess of wisdom, handicraft, and warfare, is often depicted in statues wearing a similar peplos. The Spartan women continued to wear the peplos later in history.

From her sitting position on the ground, Diana takes a few moments to look around at her surroundings. She is sitting on a lush carpet of verdant grass on the edge of a shimmering lake. She reckons it is Lake Vita. The lake is dyed a mysterious chocolate-brown. From across the lake where towering trees border the water's edge, she cannot hear a single sound. Nor are there any sounds in her vicinity.

The colorless looking glass glow of the lake mirrors neutral reflections of the far-off shoreline and silvery wisps of delicate clouds floating in the azure sky. Off to Diana's left a cluster of chubby, partially submerged rocks peppers the shoreline. Most of the rocks are the size of deflated, oversized bicycle tires. In her mind, she visualizes tiny schools of minnows playing hide and seek among the rock's countless hiding places.

She notices a baby stone nestled in the grass beside her. She picks it up to examine it. The flat stone looks like the offspring of one of the larger rocks. She gets to her knees and hurls the stone onto the lake. It stylishly skips seven times until it stops to sink into its final resting place. Not a single ripple radiates from where the stone skipped or where it came to rest. The lake's tranquil smoothness causes Diana to envision she could walk across the lake's surface to the far end without sinking.

She narrows her eyes to look askance very briefly at the honeycombed brilliance of the sun. It is nearly halfway to its zenith in the mid-morning sky, or so she thinks. The natural circle of light surrounding its cornea is a strangely intense golden color. The sun's radiance reminds her of the mythological Greek sun gods Apollo and Helios. She cannot help but smile as she imagines Helios in his chariot slowly pulling the daylight's gilded orb across the heavens.

Suddenly, she notices something very strange. She blocks the sun's cutting rays with the palm of her hand and narrows her eyes yet again.

She cannot believe what she is seeing. The sun's halo gives the impression of a golden Latin cross. Sun rays of peace, love, and harmony seem to emanate from the center of the crossbar. She stares hypnotized with wonder as an intense shaft of golden light appears from the bottommost portion of the crossbar. The light slowly moves down along the staff of the cross. It comes to an end at something odd that seemingly is floating in the heavens.

She strains her eyes to see what it is. It is a misshaped three-sided object blended with colors of blue, green, and white. The colors surely are water, flora, and clusters of pure-white snow on tall mountains. What she sees is a flourishing island floating in the sky!

Gathering her clothes mid-thigh, she manages to get to her feet. She tries to smooth the wrinkles out of her attire. It is then she notices she is barefooted.

"Well, this situation stinks," she whispers. "How am I supposed to walk around without shoes?" She glances around to see if she somehow lost her slippers where she came to rest on the ground. "Hmm, no shoes, slippers, flipflops, nothing. And where in the world are April and James?"

"I am here, love," April whispers. Diana spins on her heels.

"Goodness, you startled me. But I sure am glad to see you. I thought maybe the beam had swallowed you, that you were gone forever. Thank you for grabbing my hand in there. Your strong, encouraging words made me stronger." She notices April is holding footwear in her right hand. "Are those sandals mine?"

"Yes, dear, these are yours. They were misplaced somehow when Mendacium approached you in the beam. I was able to grab them before the beam shut. We do not call them sandals. They are called *carbatina*. They are leather, handmade. After you slip them on, you take the upper laces and tie them around your ankles." She hands the carbatina to Diana.

Diana bends to put the carbatina on her feet. As she fastens the laces around her ankles, she says with a smile, "Thank you, April. These are very comfortable. But tell me, where is James?"

The expression on April's face turns serious. She says, "James is still in the beam, Diana."

Diana cries out with a stunned tone of voice, "What! How can that be? He was supposed to accompany us all the way here, to the World Beyond. What happened?"

"When Mendacium appeared before you, he allowed you to see him actually as he is. He had temporarily cast off his indestructibility. He had temporarily weakened his potency. Consequently, he became vulnerable, so vulnerable that his wickedness had to latch onto another being so that he could regain his strength. That other entity was James."

Diana says, "I do not understand. Why did Mendacium have to latch onto another being, onto James?"

"Because you despised him. Because you attacked him. Because you enfeebled him. Since you strongly reviled him, and he had already shown his true self to you, you nearly destroyed him. So, he had to regain his power without delay. Otherwise, he was fated to remain in the beam forever."

April goes on to say, "Mendacium tried to latch onto me. However, I am too strong. I easily resisted his powers. On the other hand, James is not as strong."

She places her hands over her heart. With a deep sigh she says, "Quite frankly, Diana, I honestly think James sacrificed himself to spare you added agony." With a gentle smile, she adds, "Nevertheless, I think you could have handled the further pain from Mendacium without James' assistance. You made me very proud. You passed your first test with flying colors."

With a grief-stricken tone, Diana says, "No, I do not think that I did. Please excuse me for disagreeing with you. While I am thankful for your praise, I am unhappy James sacrificed himself for me, if in fact he truly did. I do not want anyone to be my sacrificial victim. That goes against everything in which I believe. I hope that you understand."

April replies, "Yes, I do understand. If James did, in fact, sacrifice himself for you, it was his decision and his decision alone. No one forced him to do so. He is a ghost, Diana. Whatever Mendacium has in store for him, he will not feel any physical discomfort. Then again, Mendacium may use James for nefarious purposes. On a more positive note, James may, in fact, return to us. Only time will tell."

Diana smiles with April's assertion that James may return to them.

In reaction to Diana's smile, April adds, with a sad expression on her face, "If James does return to us, we must be on our guard."

"Why, April? Why must we be on our guard if James returns?"

"Because Mendacium may have turned James against you, against everything good. Mendacium may have corrupted James' soul."

Diana replies, "Wow, that is terrible. I would not like that at all. In fact, I thought James was sweet, kind, gentle, and you know."

"Handsome?" April asks.

"Yep, I guess you could say that," Diana replies with a noticeable flush of red on her face. "Yep, James is handsome, I must admit, even if I could not discern the color of his eyes, hair, things like that."

April says, "Because he is a ghost."

"Yep, because he is a ghost. But, April, how is it I could see you plainly in my bedroom like now while I could not see James plainly?"

April replies, "As you know from your readings in the books on your shelf, I have enormous powers. But that is on earth, either on the Isle of Spardom or Surface Earth. We are now in my land, the World Beyond. I have no such powers here." She reaches out for Diana's hands.

"That is why you are here, my dear. Also, as you shall soon see, you have awesome powers and undeniable courage that far exceed that of youngsters your age. And, your courage shall surge over time."

Diana reaches to embrace April. As she does, her left foot catches on the hem of her peplos. April catches her before she tumbles to the ground.

She says, "Thank you. I do not think I will ever get used to this long dress. I keep tripping on it. I must not forget to gather it at my thighs or knees whenever I move and especially when I walk." She pats the right side of her buttocks. "My butt still hurts when I crashed to the ground upon exiting the beam. I don't want to trip and smack my butt again." She looks at April. "What's this dress called, anyway?"

"It is a peplos, a common garb of women thousands of years ago. You will get used to it soon enough. However, you will not wear your peplos too often, only during formal occasions."

"A peplos," Diana says thoughtfully. "That's a word I have never heard of until now. You said women thousands of years ago wore similar attire. So, am I like in an era of long ago?"

"Yes, you are in an era of long ago. In fact, you are in an era at least 500 years before the birth of Christ, around 500 BC."

Diana says with a giggle, "Well, as Dorothy had said in the Wizard of Oz, 'Toto, I have a feeling we're not in Kansas anymore,' I am fairly certain we are not in a place or era of my time.'" With a sincere smile, she adds, "Anyway, on a more serious note, you said I would not have to wear my peplos too often. What will I wear when, as you said, I am not wearing formal attire like my peplos?"

"You will wear warrior garb of the present age," April says with a smile. "Yes, Empress Diana, you will wear warrior garb most of the time for reasons you will soon learn."

"Too coolio. I like the idea of being a warrior. In fact, I draw pictures of female warriors. Two of the pictures I recently have drawn depict a female warrior holding swords and longbows. She is cloaked with a hood obscuring her face."

She pauses as she studies April's eyes. She notices they have a strange sparkle in them that she has not seen before now. She immediately knows something is up. She says, "Wait a minute, April, if you please. You just called me Empress, Empress Diana. What's up with that?"

April asks, "What do you know about Greek and Roman mythology, Diana?"

"Not too much. We learned a bit about Greek and Roman mythology in school, but I do not recall too much of it. I recall some Greek and Roman names such as Artemis, Apollo, Athena, Troy, names like those." She pauses, and then she says, "But, I did read some pretty cool books by Rick Riordan. He's an American author. The books were about Greek mythological fantasy."

April says, "Well, that is a start." She sits down on the lush grass and beckons for Diana to sit beside her. "Let me tell you a story. According to Greek mythology, there were four females called Diomede. One was the daughter of a King, Xuthus. Another was Lapith, a legendary creature, the daughter of Lapithes. Lapithes was the son of Apollo and his wife, Stilbe." She smiles. "From what you said, you already know a bit about Apollo. Apollo's wife Stilbe was a nymph. A nymph is a beautiful maiden that dwells in the mountains, forest, trees, and waters.

"Anyway, back to the Diomede. The third fictional Diomede female was a slave. The fourth was the wife of Pallas and mother of Euryalus. Euryalus fought at Troy. There was one other mythological youngster creature, a fifth Diomede, a heroine, that was yet to arrive. Given the foretold courage, heroism, and leadership skills of the youngster, the creature's name began with the syllable *Di*. Di is the Latin word for *gods*. Do you know who that youngster creature's name could have been?"

Diana replies, "Empress Diana? It is Empress Diana, yes?"

"Yes, Diana, you are correct. The mythological heroine yet to arrive is Empress Diana. According to legends, the brave youngster, Empress Diana, patiently waited for her moment to arrive in an era of a world yet to be. Can you guess what the world is?"

Diana cautiously replies, "This world, April? The World Beyond?"

"Exactly," April says. "The heroine youngster Empress Diana waited for her moment to arrive here and now, in the World Beyond."

Diana says, "Okay, I get all that. Empress Diana is a heroine, a mythological creature who is destined to arrive in a world yet to be, the World Beyond. She is the fifth female of Diomede. All of this sounds pretty cool. But what does all of this mythological stuff have to do with me?"

"Diana, there is an important variation to legends that speak of the mythological creature, the youngster Empress Diana. True, Empress Diana waited patiently for her moment to arrive in the World Beyond, a world yet to be. However, the legends also predetermined that the youngster would be a human being, not a mythological creature. She would be around five-foot-seven inches tall, have long brown hair and stormy blue-grey eyes that change with her moods. And do you know what else, Diana?"

Diana instinctively hesitates before she answers. For some strange reason, she feels oddly weird. Her knees are shaking. Her heart is racing nearly out of control, and her breaths are now coming in short gasps.

Her mouth feels parched. She licks her lips. They are bone dry. She somehow knows the answer before April will provide it.

In a halting, uncertain, whispering voice, she asks, "What else, April?"

"Her eyes seem to have little lightning bolts in their pupils whenever her mood changes to one of bravery or when someone or something tests her resolve."

Diana's eyes are wide open, and yes, telltale little lightning bolts are madly dancing in her pupils. She says excitedly, "April, by your portrayal of Empress Diana, you have pretty much portrayed *me*. But that is impossible. I am no heroine. True, I may be at this time in the World Beyond, and yes, I am wearing a lightning bolt necklace. Charles gave it to me, at least I think he did. And a lightning bolt pin is fastening my peplos at my shoulders. But honestly, I cannot be a heroine. Perhaps everything you have said is nothing more than mythological make-believe, a coincidence."

April says, "There is one more element of value that the legends foretold. The name itself, Diana."

"What does my name suggest in the legends' foretelling?"

"Before I answer your question, I must tell you something important. I do not know if you recognize this, but the name Diana signifies *heavenly or divine*. Diana was a Roman goddess of the woodlands, wild animals, and hunting. She had the magical power to talk to and control animals. She was comparable to the Greek goddess Artemis, protectress of the female child, typically pictured as a youngster or young maiden. She usually carried a longbow and a quiver of arrows. Over time, Diana and Artemis became fundamentally equal.

"A statue of Diana is in The Louvre, Paris, France. The statue shows Diana drawing an arrow from her quiver. She is wearing a knee-length maiden's dress, sandals, and a tiara." April chuckles delightedly. "As an avid fan of Harry Potter and an avowed member of the Gryffindor house, you will really like this. Diana's sacred animal, her patronas if you will, is a stag, a male deer. Diana in her statue is grasping the stag by the horns.

"Now, regarding your question as to what your name suggests in the legends' foretelling. The legends foretell that the youngster heroine

Empress Diana, who is to appear in the future, will have the earthly human name of Diana, middle name Jane. The given name Jane means "God is gracious."

April quickly moves to embrace Diana who is sitting motionless. She whispers, "Diana Jane, your arrival in the future of a bygone era has come at last. Yes, my dear, your quest to crush Mendacium and his evil allies begins from this day forward."

She gently pushes away from Diana to gaze squarely into her eyes. As she expected, the pupils in Diana's lovely blue-grey eyes are radiating excited silvery sparks of lightning bolts.

She says, "Certainly, Diana, in my heart I know that in your heart you recognize what I say is true. You are the courageous Empress Diana, the Youngster Heroine of the World Beyond."

*****

Part II: Hand in Hand at Last

April and Diana are standing near the shoreline of Lake Vita. April says, "Do you see the tall trees beyond the lake?" Diana nods her head.

"Yep. The trees look like they are a mile away, give or take, as the crow flies that is."

April says, "It is important for you to get to the trees before night-fall." She glances at the sun. "The sun will set fairly soon. It is not safe here. You will be much safer on the other side of the lake, near the trees."

Diana says, "What do you mean that the sun will set soon? The sun isn't anywhere near its high point. From its position in the sky, the time cannot be more than ten, maybe eleven o'clock in the morning at the latest."

"Not here in the World Beyond," April replies. "Here the day is very short and the nights are extremely long. In fact, I suppose the sun rose a few moments before we exited the beam. The beam never allows one to exit it during periods of darkness. It is too dangerous."

"Okay, I can accept that," Diana says. "Very short days and extremely long nights. How long are the days?"

"In a timeframe of which you are accustomed, I have no idea. We measure the time in the World Beyond by heartbeats. When one considers the atmospheric influences, the average day is around 4800 heartbeats. Naturally, it all depends on the individual."

Diana closes her eyes as she performs a quick division operation in her head. She suddenly exclaims, "Goodness, April, that is around sixty minutes' time, roughly one hour considering the average resting heartbeats are eighty beats a minute!" She looks across the lake to the forest. "We will never make it across the lake before the sun sets. While the far side is probably an hour away as the crow flies, to walk around the lake's perimeter will take us many hours, three or four at best! The sun will have already set before we get there. We will have to walk in the dark!"

April says with a confident tone, "I would not worry about it too much if I were you."

Diana says, "Well, okay, I guess I will have to trust you when you say that." She glances across the lake once more. "But I don't know about having to walk in the dark in a strange place. Anyway, how long are the nights?" She pauses a few seconds, and then she says, "About twenty-three hours in duration, give or take a few minutes. Am I correct?"

"No, Diana, I am afraid you are incorrect. Nights here in the World Beyond are, in your accustomed time, many days long. Again, in typical heartbeat time, nights are roughly 350,000 heartbeats in duration. Once again, it all depends on the individual."

Diana appreciates her next division operation will require loads of concentration. She closes her eyes yet again. She whispers, "Let's see, 350,000 heartbeats divided by the number of heartbeats in an hour which is 4800. No, let's say we round up 4800 heartbeats an hour to 5000. That will be much easier to compute." She taps her temple with her forefinger as she continues her math problem.

"Let's see, 350,000 heartbeats divided by 5000 heartbeats in an hour is sort of equivalent to the simple number 35 divided by five. That equals seven. Then I multiply that number by ten considering there is one more zero involved. That equals 70 exactly. So, let's see, 70 hours divided by 24 hours in a day is."

She does not complete her sentence. She stares at April, her eyes wide open in astonishment.

"My God, April, that is around three days. Are you telling me nights are three days long?"

April hunches her shoulders. She says, "I guess if your calculations are anywhere near correct, yes. All I know is nights here in the World Beyond are quite long, much longer than in the Real-world." She clutches Diana's hand. "But, as I said, I would not worry about it too much if I were you." She glances to her left and then to her right. "I think the shortest route to the distant tree line beyond the lake is to my right. Plus, there appears to be less undergrowth on which I have to navigate if I travel to the right."

Diana stares at April. The expression on her face is incredulous. She whispers in an uncertain voice, "What do you mean by with which *you* have to navigate? Aren't I going with you? Surely, you will not leave me behind. Before we departed the Real-world, you promised me that you would keep me safe."

April laughs as she says, "Naturally, I will keep you as safe as I can in the World Beyond. However, as I said, I have no magical powers in this place. But you do, or, you soon will have magical powers of your own."

Diana asks, "I have magical powers? What are they?" April does not reply. She takes Diana by the hand and leads her to the water's edge.

"Take a step onto the lake, Diana." Diana shakes her head disapprovingly.

"I would rather not if it's okay with you. We do not know how deep the water is. Besides, I would hate to get my peplos soaking wet. I don't have a change of clothes as you are well aware." She moves back a few steps and tries to release her hand from April's grasp. But she cannot. April's grasp is very strong.

April asks, in a sincere tone, "Diana, I thought you said that you trust me. Do you?

"Well, I honestly want to," Diana says as she looks into April's eyes. After a moment's hesitation, she nods her head. "Yes, I truly want to trust you. And yes, I do."

April says, "Then take a step onto the water." She giggles. "If you notice I said step *on* the water and not *in* the water."

Diana has no idea what April is trying to say. She takes a tentative step toward the water. She dangles her foot above the water's surface for the longest time. When she finally jabs at the water with her carbatina, she cries out, "What in the world? What I am experiencing cannot be happening!" She repeatedly tries to thrust her right foot into the water, but she cannot pierce the water's surface! A tiny bit of water on the lake's surface splashes onto her carbatina, but otherwise, her carbatina is nearly bone dry.

She jumps up and down excitedly. Then she rushes to April and hugs her tightly. She screams, "I cannot believe it. I think I can walk on water! My carbatina didn't get soaking wet!"

She moves away from April and dashes to the shoreline. She tries to dip her foot into the water. She cannot. At that moment she sprints onto the surface of Lake Vita and begins to glide back and forth. Although she can walk, or in this case, glide on the lake's surface, water still splashes onto the hem of her peplos. So, she has to gather a bit of the fabric in her hand to keep it from getting soaked.

As a talented roller skater, soon she is making wide circles on the water, spinning in place and gliding backward. All the while, with her arms held out wide like a professional figure skater, she is yelling over and over at the top of her lungs.

"I can walk and glide and skate on water! Yepity, yep, yep!"

She rushes to April and embraces her a second time. She whispers, "Is this one of the magical powers to which you alluded? Can I truly, honestly walk on water or is all of this a crazy dream?"

April can barely stop laughing as she replies. "Yes, dear, it would appear that you can walk on water. Since you were a child, you have always wanted to walk on water, at least in your dreams. In fact, Charles told me that you had once mentioned walking on water while you were visiting with your friend a year ago on Alabama's shoreline in the Real-world.

"You had said, 'Natasha, I wish Charles were here. He could teach us how to walk on water. I assume that he can. After all, ghosts can glide above the ground so they should be able to walk on water! It would be the coolest thing to walk on water, don't you agree?'"

April gently pushes away from Diana to look into her eyes. Her tone is serious when she says, "However, Diana, you must never take off your lightning bolt necklace or your lightning bolt bracelet. If you ever remove them, your magical powers will rapidly diminish. Your powers will not disappear entirely, but they will weaken greatly."

Diana looks with obvious surprise at her wrist. She whispers, "Oh, my goodness, April. It's a lovely macramé bracelet with gorgeous lapis-colored beads. And will you look at that? It even has my trademark lightning bold attached to it. This one is in glistening gold. But how in the world did it get there? I did not even notice that you had slipped the bracelet onto my wrist."

April says, "I didn't slip it onto your wrist." She gestures with her eyes to Diana's right. "He did."

Diana whirls around to her right. When she steps backward in disbelief, she releases the hem of her peplos which nearly causes her to stumble yet again. Standing by her side is the most handsome teenager she has ever seen in person. The attractive teenager appears to be about fifteen-years-old, maybe a little younger, maybe as young as fourteen. He looks like a dashing model straight out of a fashion magazine. His attire is a light brown, sleeveless tunic from the present period.

The teenager standing before her is slender and a bit taller than she is, perhaps five-foot-eight. He has Teutonic gold hair that falls to his collarbone. His crescent-of-moon eyebrows accent his mariner-blue eyes. An aquiline nose compliments his high cheekbones. While he stares at Diana with his full, ruby-red lips slightly parted in a sly grin, she can feel her heart racing. Her lips and throat feel dry like before. She resists the urge to moisten her lips, thinking that would appear quite inappropriate given the circumstances.

"Charles?"

"Hi, Empress Diana, the Youngster Heroine of the World Beyond, one of my dearest friends in the whole Universe. It is a pleasure, at last, to meet you in person finally."

He stares into Diana's tear-filled eyes. The pupils of her eyes are seemingly going crazy as silvery lightning bolts dance therein. He takes Diana's hand in his and gently kisses her hand three times.

Diana gracelessly trips one last time as she rushes forward to collapse into Charles' embrace. Tears of joy are streaming down her flushed face. She buries her face in Charles' shoulder and cries.

"Oh, Charles. Charles, Charles, Charles. I love you too!"

*****

Part III: In an Ethereal Way

Diana and Charles proceed across the lake. At first glance, their movements as two very close friends walking side by side seem entirely normal. However, if one were to look more closely, he or she would make out that the couple is anything but normal. Diana is walking on the surface of Lake Vita. She is holding her carbatina footwear in her left hand. Because droplets of water splash as she walks, she is grasping the hem of her peplos mid-thigh with the same hand. All the while, Charles is effortlessly floating mere inches above the surface of the lake. They are chatting nonstop as they proceed hand in hand.

Before the twosome is midway across the lake, the sun dives below the trees behind them. Dusk progressively settles over the lake and the surrounding landscape.

"Goodness," Diana exclaims, "it looks like we will have to continue in the dark. I surely hope my luck doesn't run out causing me to drop into the lake." She glances at Charles' shoeless feet. "On the other hand, you need not worry about falling into the water. If I were to go down beneath the surface, you would continue to float above it."

Charles replies, "Oh, I would not fret too much. April had said, as long as you wear your lightning bolt charms, you will be fine. Also, so that you know. If you were to plunge into the lake, I would continue to the other side as if nothing happened."

"What!" Diana exclaims. She brusquely takes away her hand from Charles'. She playfully slaps him on his shoulder. "Are you saying you would allow me to drown? That's not very nice of you, Charles."

Charles chuckles. "I am teasing you. Naturally, I would plunge deep into the frigid water to rescue you. There is no doubt about it."

Diana says, "That's better. But, honestly, Charles, you need not worry about falling into the lake. I assume, like me, you have magical powers. Am I correct?"

"I am sorry to say. I do not have magical powers. I am a humble ghost. So, I only can float in the air. I can go as high or as low as I want in the air, as long as I do not touch the ground."

"What happens if you touch the ground?"

"I will die. I will turn into powder and fly apart like fine particles in the breeze." With a loud laugh, he claps his hands together and shouts, "Then, *Poof!* No more Charles."

"That is not at all funny, Charles! But, I am curious. Why is it you will die if you touch the ground? I don't mean to embarrass you, but I thought you were already dead. Am I correct? You cannot die a second time, can you?"

Charles replies in a soft voice, "Yes and no. Yes, you are correct. I am deceased. Be that as it may, I exist in an ethereal way. Some describe it as a ghostly or otherworldly existence. In my ethereal life, although I am deceased, I am capable of serving the living. To answer your second question, unfortunately, you are incorrect. If I touch the ground, either purposely or accidentally, I will cease to exist in an ethereal way. As I said, I will die and disappear from the Universe."

"That is very sad to contemplate," Diana says with a sad tone. "I would not want you to die again, to cease to exist in your ethereal way. What would I do without you if you were gone?"

"You would go on, Diana. In time, you would forget all about me."

"No, I doubt I could ever forget you, Charles." She takes hold of his hand. "Charles, I know you are my friend. There is no doubt in my mind, and I can feel it in my heart. But tell me, do you have other friends? I think you must because you had said I was one of your dearest friends. Yes?"

"Yes, you are one of my dearest friends. In reality, you are my closest friend."

"Aw, you're just saying that because I am here."

"No, I am truthful, Diana. Ghosts cannot lie."

"Can you tell me who your other friends are? Please, Charles, do not answer if it makes you uncomfortable. It is not that important to me. I am curious. That is all."

"I am sad to say, many of my friends come, and then they go."

"What do you mean by your friends come, and then they go? Do I know any of them?"

"Yes, you know, or at least you knew of one. Ariel is her name. She passed away recently as you know."

Tears immediately well up in Diana's eyes. She feels like crying, but she resists. She must remain strong.

"Goodness, Charles. I am very sad about her passing. She was my friend. She was very sweet. Her passing was unexpected, very sudden. Everyone, teachers, staff, and students in my school were shocked when we learned of the news. She was incredibly young, my age. I, along with many others, family, and friends, will miss her. We will never forget her as well." She squeezes Charles' hand. "Was Ariel your friend for a long time?"

"No, sadly, I knew Ariel for a short time, in fact, for less than one day. Her death, as you know, was sudden, unforeseen, a tragedy. You see, Diana, I am called upon to comfort those who are close to death. They are the only ones who can see me. I sit with them, talk to them, hold their hands and, if they want me to, I hug them. I patiently listen and provide reassuring comfort as they recap their lives. I console them as they own up to their ups and downs, the good and, as you would expect, the bad of their lives. I give them comfort and respond as best as I can. We say prayers together.

"By the medical finding, Ariel was declared comatose. However, until the soul leaves the body, the living is not yet deceased. For that reason, I can continue to speak with them. Sometimes we have conversations for days on end even though doctors and visitors think those who are dying are unconscious.

"Most of the time they speak to me in their minds. However, now and then, they say things vocally. Naturally, I soundlessly answer them in a manner that makes them think they hear my words. Others cannot hear my side of the conversation.

"Diana, I must admit it is disheartening to watch as the dying cry out to live longer. Many will say or do anything to live for a few more days, for a few more weeks. They, understandably, do not want to stop living. But that is not always the case.

"I was by the side of an eight-year-old girl named Susan last week. Everyone referred to Susan as a superhero, Super Susan. Her infectious smile, her relentless courage, and her astounding love of life touched me. Susan decided for herself a couple of weeks ago that she would not continue the treatments to stay alive. She was diagnosed with cancer exactly three years to the day she passed away.

"Perhaps, if your government did more to research the causes and treatment of the evil of cancer in children, less precious children like Susan would die. Right now, only four percent of nearly five billion dollars of research funds go to research for childhood cancer. Children with cancer deserve as much as a chance to live as adults.

"Ghosts are unable to cry, Diana. Just the same, my soul wept for this amazing girl. When Susan's soul left her to go to heaven, visions of all my fears, sadness, joys, friends and my brother, and my hopes and dreams as a former living human passed in real time before my very eyes. All because of her and yes, because of Ariel's passing as well. Yes, my heart cried when Ariel passed away. I felt real pain, for you and all of your friends that I had befriended over the years as your ghost when Ariel passed away. In Susan's case, my heart mourned for her mother and father, her siblings, and all the thousands of people who loved her."

Charles firmly squeezes Diana's hand three times. Diana recognizes that he needs comforting by his gesture. She responds in kind with four squeezes of his hand with hers. Charles smiles.

"Thank you, Diana. That is why, as a ghost, I am blessed to have you as a friend in my ethereal way. You give me joy. You and your friends are indeed very funny. You make me laugh. I repay your friendship with silly pranks and mischievous tricks. You are always smiling, outgoing and constantly ready to help others, to give them emotional support. You study hard, read great books, and are involved in various sports. You act on stage, stay out of trouble.

"And you are respectful to your mom and dad and your brothers as well as to your friends. Whenever you see someone on the street that you know, whether she or he is an adult or a youngster, you go out of your way to say hello and to embrace them. You never shy away from those that you know, that you love. You are an excellent role model for others.

"In essence, Diana, you give me hope and a reason to continue. If it weren't for you, attending to those who are dying would be too much for me to bear. Without your friendship, I would give up." Clapping his hands together once more, he says, "Then *Poof!* No more me."

As they go on across the lake, Diana places her right arm around Charles' shoulder. He responds in kind by placing his left arm around her waist.

He says with an uneasy voice, "And so that you know, in a few days, I will depart the World Beyond temporarily. Susan's parents and hundreds of Super Susan supporters will release balloons in remembrance of her amazing life."

He grins. "I managed to acquire a few balloons to release in Susan's honor. I will give the balloons special handling that only a ghost who can float can achieve. I will drag the balloons up and down and back and forth in the sky. I will also make circles, draw squares with the balloons, who knows?" He giggles, saying, "It will be a spectacle to behold. Susan asked me to do it, to give the spectators something to remember for the rest of their lives. That was typical Susan. She was always thinking about others, finding ways to bring a smile to others' faces."

Diana is feeling low, and she wants to say something about Charles' planned departure. Suddenly, something in the sky catches her attention, erasing all thoughts of what she was about to say. She abruptly calls out, "Goodness, Charles, what is that?" She points to the sky. "It looks very pretty, and it is amazingly bright. I noticed it earlier, but I could not make out its beauty with the sun shining brightly."

"That, Diana," Charles says as he points to the sky, "is your destination. There is no moon in the World Beyond. The natural bright light of Domum, that is what we call it, illuminates the whole kit and caboodle after nightfall."

Diana laughs at Charles' description of the landscape being illuminated by Domum as the *whole kit and caboodle*. Charles' use of the phrase is his way of being clever as the habitual joker that he is. His fun nature is but one of the many reasons she loves him.

She says, "My destination? How in the world am I supposed to get up there?"

Charles says, "At this point, I honestly have no clue. I wish I did. But I do not. However, I promise you this. I will try to find out how you can get to the magical place of Domum."

"Can I use my magical powers? Can you tell me a bit more about them? I mean, can I fly up to Domum? It doesn't look that high in the sky. I expect there is breathable air up there." She laughs. "What in the world am I thinking. I cannot fly!" She glides across the water and flaps her arms. "See? All I can do is walk and glide on water." She laughs loudly adding, "But, that's enough for me!"

Charles says, "Once again, Diana, I have no idea what your magical powers are. Even if I did know, I would not tell you."

"Why not?" Diana asks. "Why would you not tell me?"

"Because Mendacium may be listening. In the World Beyond, Mendacium hears all. Mendacium sees all. Even so, we remain hopeful he does not know all. There is no point to risk giving him more clues for your purpose here."

Diana whispers in a downcast tone, "Well, that stinks. How in the world will I perform my tasks, whatever they may be if I have no inkling of how I am to perform them?"

Charles replies, "I am sorry, Diana. But again, I have no clue. I wish I could tell you more. But I cannot because honestly, I do not know. You will have to figure all of that out for yourself."

"Indeed I shall," Diana whispers to herself. "In reality, I must. Otherwise, I am destined to be here forever!"

CHAPTER THREE

THE LETTER

"Excuse me, Diana, you're wanted in the principal's office."

Diana's double is sitting at her desk in study hall at Rockville Middle School. She is working on her English composition, *The Mechanics of Writing Creative Fiction*. It is due this coming Tuesday. Diana has but a few more paragraphs to write, and she will have completed it. Her face flushes as she looks up at her teacher, Miss Williams.

I'm sorry, ma'am. Did I hear you correctly, that I must go to the principal's office? If so, do you know why?"

"Yes, you heard me correctly. You need to go to the principal's office. I should tell you this. There is no family emergency or anything like that. I asked. Since it is the last period of the day, you can go home after you're finished. So, pack up all your belongings. Hurry now. Your parents are waiting."

Diana gathers her papers and hastily stuffs them inside her backpack. She asks Miss Williams in an apprehensive tone, "Goodness, is everything all right? Am I in trouble or something? If so, I have no earthly idea why I could be in trouble! And why in the world would my parents be here, do you know?"

"No, Diana, I do not think you are in trouble. But, I do not know for certain. And, as I said, there is no emergency. That should be your primary concern. As to why your parents are here, I do not know. All I know is the principal's secretary said it has something to do with the ladies' championship softball game."

"Oh, I see," Diana whispers. "I bet I know what it is. It may have something to do with Mister Reynolds' questionable calls during the game." She frowns. "I sure hope that he is not in trouble. But surely, he can be grumpy at times. He also could use a new pair of glasses."

Diana's teacher flashes her a stern, judgmental look.

Diana hurriedly adds with a timid smile and a thumb's up, "But he is a nice man, once you get to know him. I like him. I like him a lot."

Miss Williams looks at her watch. She says, "Well, hurry along Diana. Whatever it is that is going on in the principal's office; I would imagine you do not want to spend too much time after school being in there." She glances at the window. "When you can be outside enjoying this great weather. After all, it is a three-day weekend." As she turns to return to her desk, she bends close to Diana and whispers, "Have a good one, Diana. Good luck in the principals' office, and stay safe. See you Tuesday."

Diana's best friend, Evelyn, who is sitting at the desk behind her, whispers as she adjusts her glasses, "What's going on, Diana? I could not help but overhear what Miss Williams said. It has something to do with the championship softball game, doesn't it?"

Diana nods her head and replies in a whisper, "I guess so. At least I hope that's all it is."

Diana and Evelyn go way back as best friends. Evelyn has fair, freckled skin. Like Diana, most of her freckles are on her face. She has jade-green eyes and dark brown hair that falls to the middle of her back. Every time she smiles, her straight teeth shine like ivory. Diana thinks Evelyn is one of the most attractive teenagers on the planet.

Evelyn whispers in a sarcastic tone, "Maybe the principal wants to join your team?" She manages to keep her laugh in check by covering her mouth. She adds, "Only kidding. You already have a water boy, don't you?"

"Yep, we do," Diana replies softly with an accompanying chuckle. "I'll tell you all about it when I get home if I can tell anybody what happened." With a long face of worry, she adds, "Or if I'm still alive." She flings her backpack over her shoulder and walks to the door. She turns around and whispers, "I'll see you later, Evelyn. Love you!" She watches as Evelyn replies with a soundless, "I love you too. Text me!"

When Diana opens the classroom door, she turns around briefly to glance at her classmates. Every one of them is staring at her with an expression of absolute jealousy. Diana imagines they think she has a good excuse to leave early, to enjoy a bit more of the late afternoon. As she waves at them, she thinks to herself, "If only you knew!"

She unhurriedly walks through the school corridors. She stops now and then to look at an interesting poster. The posters seem to cover every square inch of available space on the walls. She seldom has time to look at the posters in between classes. Most of the posters are pretty lame, but a few give a student reason to pause.

One of the posters, outside the counselor's office, is Diana's favorite. It shows a tiny, amazingly cute, red-headed, blue-eyed female elf holding a bunch of school books in the crook of her right arm. She is pointing the forefinger of her left hand at passersby. Red and yellow sparks flash brightly from her fingertip.

The caption in bold letters beneath the poster's picture reads, "You bully one of my classmates and *Yeow! You're toast!*"

As Diana slowly walks, her walking to the dreaded principal's office reminds her of something she once heard about an old movie called, *Dead Man Walking*. The title of the movie sounds ominous to her. That memory brings to her mind Stephen King's book, *The Green Mile*. She imagines how the prisoners in the movie and book must have felt, like the end of the line had finally arrived. For some reason, she feels the same way.

The dead girl is walking the green mile to the end of the line, to the principal's office!

She winces at the implication of what she just thought. She says in a soft whisper, "How ghastly is that?"

She figures there is no emergency and that she probably is not in trouble. She has not done anything wrong. Be that as it may, she is worried. Who wouldn't be? The principal has summoned her to his office! Being summoned to the principal's office without knowing the reason why is like the kiss of death.

Her legs feel strangely weak like they do not want to move. Her mouth is parched, and her lips are abnormally dry. If these anxiety symptoms aren't enough, her heart is racing like crazy. She is frightened, but she doesn't know why.

Little does Diana know, her other half in the World Beyond will experience similar anxiety symptoms very soon. And, while both

Diana's justifiably are nervous for well-founded reasons of their own, Diana in the World Beyond will soon find herself in a frightening world of hurt.

Diana stops outside the door of the principal's office. She wants to delay the inevitable as long as she can. She takes a deep breath and exhales every bit of air out of her lungs. Her protracted exhale makes her lightheaded. To make matters worse, she suddenly has the urge to visit the girl's bathroom. But, she supposes she has lingered long enough. She reasons she might as well face up to whatever awaits her on the other side of the door. Just as she is about to knock on the door, it opens wide.

"Oh, there you are, Miss Bower," the principal's secretary, Miss Gloria Hickman, says with a frown.

Miss Hickman never refers to students by their first name, always by their last name, such as *Mister So and So or Miss How do you Do.* In Diana's case, Miss Hickman likes to drag out her last name like she's howling at the moon or something like that. She speaks Diana's last name in her Southern twang with a long, four-second drawl, "Bowww-eeerrr." Diana knows that the drawn-out enunciation of her last name by Miss Hickman is four-seconds long exactly. Her classmates have timed it on more than one occasion.

Diana avoids Miss Hickman as best as she can. Try as she does, it is impossible to avoid her during the change of classes. She rigidly stands at attention like a Gestapo sentry outside of her office. With a hideous scowl on her face and her hands on her hips, she scolds and berates students that pass her by in the corridor. Some students have labeled Miss Hickman as the classic example of an adult bully.

Diana goes out of her way to be courteous to Miss Hickman. Even so, she disapproves of the secretary's abusive attitude. Most of the other students disapprove as well.

Howard Peters is the exception. He is a school bully. Despite his meanness, he is gifted, a straight-A student. And he is well-liked by most of the teachers. That is because he is the football team's star quarterback. His father is also a bigshot political official in town. Howard also volunteers to clean Miss Hickman and the principal's office at the end of the school day. His brown-nosing chores keeps him in good graces with the higherups in the school and out of harm's way.

"It's about time you got here, Miss Bower," Miss Hickman says as she yet again drags out Diana's name. She shakes her head disapprovingly as she looks at her watch. "We've been waiting for you for over five minutes now." She cocks her head to the side and frowns yet again. "I bet you stopped at the girl's restroom or deliberately dillydallied on your way here, huh?"

Diana has no clue what dillydallied means. But, considering Miss Hickman had said it, she rightly assumes it is not a compliment. She did not stop at the girl's restroom, but now she wishes she had.

She says in a sarcastic voice, "No, ma'am, I didn't do either."

Miss Hickman snaps, "Yeah, right, liar. Do come in, Miss Bower."

As Diana moves to the side to walk past Miss Hickman, she purposely gets in her way. She roughly bumps Diana's shoulder with hers, nearly causing Diana to stumble with the weight of her backpack. Then, she sharply smacks Diana between her shoulder blades with the palm of her hand.

She whispers in a nasty tone, "And, don't slouch, Sloppy Bower."

When Diana enters the principal's outer office, she winces. She knows from the get-go that something is not right in this room. Mister Reynolds' daughter, Regina, is sitting in a side chair. She is crying. She looks up and glares a hateful look at Diana. Her hateful look could melt an ice cube in a second flat on a cold, wintry day.

There are only two side chairs in the room, and Regina is sitting in one of them. Diana knows there is no way she is going to sit next to Regina, especially after that hateful look. She places her backpack on the floor and leans against the wall.

Miss Hickman says in a forceful voice, "Miss Bower, sit."

Diana replies politely, "I would rather stand if you please."

Miss Hickman growls, "I didn't ask for your input, Miss Bower." She glares above her horn-rimmed glasses and points to the empty chair next to Regina. "Sit down!" She sneers"Or do I have to go over there and put you in the chair myself?"

Diana says courteously, "Ma'am, I have been sitting all day. It feels good to stretch my legs. I prefer to stand." She rolls her eyes in Regina's direction. Regina is still sniveling. "Please understand what I am saying."

"Do you want to know something, Miss Bow-wow-wow-eeerrr?" Miss Hickman says, in a preposterously insulting, scornful voice. "I have never much liked you. You think you're all that. Did you know? There you are, standing in your typical, self-important attitude all pretty-like. Just because you're athletic, smart, and artistically talented doesn't mean you're anything special. I could whip your butt with my hands tied behind my back." She slaps the palm of her left hand with her right fist.

Diana is tempted to leap over Miss Hickman's desk to smack the woman senseless. But, she is not a violent person. However, no one, never in her fourteen years, has insulted her like Miss Hickman just did. She also has a strange sense that Miss Hickman is goading her on, that the slight woman ten or so years her senior is trying to make her do something that she will regret.

She stands up straight and folds her arms across her chest. She takes a deep breath and stares Miss Hickman square in the eye. Her expression is not hostile. Rather, it is one of disappointment for a young woman who probably doesn't even know she is disliked by so many. She shakes her head a few times for added effect. Her expression and non-verbal posture seemingly speak for themselves, at least in Diana's opinion.

"I feel very sorry for you, you poor, pathetic woman."

Miss Hickman does not react in response to Diana's comportment. All she does is stare at her. Because she does not respond, Diana decides it is imperative she speaks her mind. Failing to do so will make her appear weak. She knows that appearing to be submissive is the last thing one should do when bullied.

"Miss Hickman, why is it that you do not like me? You're always talking down to me, and I do not like, no, let me change that. I *detest* the way you pronounce my last name. It is demeaning. My name is Bower, Miss Hickman. Two easy, short syllables. Not a long-lasting, four-second long *Bowww-eeerrr!*"

She waits for a reaction from Miss Hickman. Not getting any and feeling strangely confident, she adds in a reproving tone, "Do you not know how much it hurts when you belittle people? You just belittled me, Miss Hickman, telling me to sit like I am a dog, threatening to force me into this chair in your typical bullying way. To make matters worse, you just said you do not like me and pronounced my last name in a very insulting way like you were barking or something. Is that the way a principal's secretary is supposed to act? I think not.

"Do you not know, when you yell at students for no reason, they feel miserable, ashamed in front of their classmates? How is it you manage always to find something wrong, anything to point out to them as improper conduct?"

Mimicking Miss Hickman's high-pitched voice, she says in a sarcastic tenor, 'Your shoelaces are untied! Tuck in your shirt! Stop talking so loudly! Don't you ever wear those tight pants to school again! Quit horseplaying in the halls! Are you wearing a bra?' Yep, Miss Hickman, you routinely say impolite things like that. Do you not know that we students do not appreciate your bullying attitude and impolite comments?'"

Miss Hickman seethes between clenched teeth, "How dare you, you insolent brat!"

She jumps up out of her chair. She pushes at her chair with so much force it slams against the wall with an earsplitting *Bang!* It teeters on its wheels for a split-second until it finally falls over on its side with a loud *Ca-lang!* She rushes from behind her desk to stand less than a foot in front of Diana. She points her forefinger mere inches from Diana's nose. Diana notices that she has her other hand clenched into a fist by her side.

She whispers, "Take that back, Miss Bower, or else."

"Or else, what?" Diana declares as she stares cross-eyed at Miss Hickman's finger. "Are you going to hit me? Go ahead, and our school will finally rid itself of its only adult bully." She wiggles her fingers on either side of her face. "Go ahead, ma'am. Smack me. I dare you." She smiles adding, "But let me warn you. If you even so much as touch my nose with that bony finger of yours, I will scream to high heaven!" Then, as she moves her clenched fists to either side of her face, she adds, "And, be assured. I will defend myself! As you know, I'm no easy pushover!"

Miss Hickman slowly withdraws her forefinger from Diana's nose. She curls her hand into a fist and slowly shakes it in front of her face. She says in a bullying tone, "I know where you live, Miss Bower. And I have friends. You know who I mean." She grins. "You have encountered them once before in your pitiful life."

Regina suddenly whispers, "Shut up, Miss Hickman! She is right. You *are* a bully. And, I will be her witness if you lay a hand on her." Regina slowly gets to her feet. She is tall for her age. She towers over Diana and Miss Hickman by at least six inches. She is also very powerful.

She says, "Not only that, I will beat you to a pulp if you even lay a finger on her." She sneers. "In self-defense, naturally."

Tears well up in Miss Hickman's eyes. She roughly pushes Diana to the side and rushes out the door.

Diana says, "Thank you, Reg. That was very nice of you to come to my defense. I honestly thought she was going to smack me. I wish she had. Then I could get revenge for the disgusting way she treats me, treats all of us."

Regina slumps into her chair. She buries her face in her hands and starts to sob. She says, "You shut up too. I hate you."

Diana stares at Regina with disbelief.

She says, "My goodness, Reg, what a terrible thing to say! Why would you say that? We are friends and teammates. What have I done for you to say such a horrible thing?"

Regina scowls at her. Tears are streaming down her face once more.

"Because you're going to make trouble for Daddy, that's why. About the softball championship game. How could you do such a thing? And all this time, I thought you were my friend."

Diana sits in the chair next to Regina. She whispers, "I am your friend, Reg. I haven't said a thing about your father to anyone in authority."

"See?" Regina cries as she looks up at her. She narrows the lids of her bloodshot eyes. "You just said, 'to anyone in authority.' See? You just admitted it. That means you have been talking about my father behind his back, behind *my* back! And, all this time, I thought we were friends.'"

"Now wait a minute, Reg," Diana says with an angry voice. She is getting irritated. Regina is falsely accusing her of gossiping. She takes a few deep breaths to calm her emotions, and then she says, "I told my parents I had questioned a few of your father's calls at the softball game. That is all. What's so bad about that? You tell things to your father that you don't tell others. You even told me on more than one occasion that you do the same thing. Confiding in one's parents from time to time is good. In fact, sometimes they are the only ones in whom you can confide and in whom you can trust."

Regina cries, "Then why are you here, Dynamite?" She wipes her tears with her shirtsleeve.

Dynamite is Diana's softball nickname. Her softball team players always refer to her by that name, both on and off the field. In fact, Diana is fairly certain that Regina doesn't even know her given name. She always refers to Diana as Dynamite.

Diana says in a whisper, "I have no clue why I am here, Reg. Honestly. Why are you here?"

"I cannot tell you, Dynamite. Mister Young made me swear I would not tell anybody." She stares at the floor glumly. "If I do, he will expel me. At least that's what he said."

Diana's heart sinks as she reasons to herself, "Is it possible you are here to intimidate me, Reg? That you are an unwilling character in a strange drama, someone else's stooge? That you're sitting here bawling your eyes out for real just so someone else can send me a message? If so, I'm not getting the message. And I will not be a part of this insaneness either!"

She whispers to Regina, "The principal made you swear to keep something secret, Reg? That doesn't sound good if you don't mind me saying. Faculty and teachers are not supposed to have secrets with students. It isn't proper, Reg. You know that."

Mister Young's door suddenly slams open. Diana and Regina bolt upright in their chairs.

"Miss Reynolds, you may leave," Mister Young says rudely. "Tell Miss Blair I said you could depart school early. I called your father. He is on his way. He will pick you up at the side entrance." As he puckers his lips in a scowl, he lowers his head and stares at Regina. "And I caution you. Remember what we discussed." He places his forefinger to his lips.

Diana flinches as her heart sinks even lower if that is possible. She does not like what Mister Young said. Nor does she like his non-verbal expression when he shushed Regina by placing his finger to his lips. It is obvious to her that Mister Young is warning Regina to remain silent about something. And whatever that something is, it does not appear to be on the up and up.

Regina looks at Diana. She opens her mouth to say something, but she does not. She stares at the floor. Tears begin to fall from her eyes once more. They make silent splish-splashes on the tile.

She mumbles, "Yes, sir. I will keep my mouth shut. I promise."

Mister Young says, "Good. You may leave." Then he cruelly gestures to Diana with the same forefinger that he used to shush Regina. He says, "You, come with me. Leave your backpack here."

Diana is taken aback by Mister Young's disapproving tone of voice and bad-tempered manners. He is usually very pleasant when he speaks to her. In fact, her father and Mister Young are on the same bowling team. Her father is also a member of the school board, so the two of them cooperate frequently.

Diana ponders, "Wow, whatever is going on, it surely doesn't look good for someone. But, no worries, I'm not in any trouble. At least I hope I am not."

She dutifully follows Mister Young into his office. She smiles when she sees her parents. As she bends down to hug her mother, she whispers, "What's this all about, Mom, do you know?"

Her mother replies solemnly, "Not now, Diana." She gestures to the empty chair beside her. "Please sit down."

Mister Young is drumming his fingers on his desk. His troubled look is giving Diana the creeps. He looks at her parents one by one. Then, he stares at her for the longest time. All the while, his fingers continue an annoying rhythmic tap dance on his unnatural-looking, perfectly organized, uncluttered desk.

Diana is growing impatient. As the seconds slowly tick by, she is feeling increasingly ill at ease. She says, "Sir, please tell me."

Mister Young waves his forefinger in the air before she can finish her sentence.

He says, "I think, Miss Bower, that perhaps you should not say anything until you read this." He pushes a sheet of paper across his desk. Diana notices it is a poorly reproduced Xerox copy of the original. "Please take your time to absorb its contents. After you have read it, you can talk freely."

Diana takes the paper from his desk. She begins to read the paper's handwritten words. As she reads further down the lines, her heart slowly sinks even further, and she begins to tremble with rage.

Wednesday, June 17

Dear Mister Young, Principal, Rockville Middle School,

Thank you for taking the time to read this letter. It truly pains me to inform you that Diana Jane Bower brutalized me at school the other day, Monday, June 15. She and I were alone in the female locker room. We argued, nothing serious, just girl's stuff. When I turned my back to her, Diana picked up a broom and hit me hard in the back of the head with the broomstick. As you can imagine, I was upset that my good friend and teammate would strike me from behind. Fortunately, I suffered no bruises or permanent damage. After conferring with my father, I chose to not press formal charges with the city police.

I did not retaliate, nor did I strike Diana in return although I wanted to. There are three reasons I did not strike back. First, she is my friend and teammate. Second, I would have beaten her pretty bad since I am much taller and stronger than she is. Third, I understand that fighting with a fellow student can result in expulsion.

Despite everything, I must admit that I did threaten Diana. I said, "Diana, I am going to tell the vice principal that you attacked me. True, we argued, but we have argued before, and we have never come to blows. What you did was uncalled for and cowardly." Diana replied, "If you report me, Regina, I will break all the windows in your house and beat up your little cousins, Christopher and Victoria! And then, I will spread rumors about you all over the school!"

Because of Diana's threats to me, my home and, more importantly to my cousins, I decided to write this letter to you rather than risk making an appointment with the vice principal, Miss. Walters. You know how students gossip. If they were to see me in Miss Walters' office, the word could get back to Diana.

Thank you for your time.

Sincerely,

//signed// Regina Ann Reynolds

PS - I hid the broken broom handle in the closet of the girl's locker room. In case you need proof.

Diana's reaction is one of outright indignity. She says in an annoyed tone of voice, "I do not believe anything in this letter!" She crushes the letter into a tight ball and tosses it onto Mister Young's desk. She looks at her parents and then, looking Mister Young squarely in the eye, she says, "This is outrageous. Not only do I not believe the letter's contents, but I also was never alone with Reg, I mean Regina, in the girl's locker room. Not once! Plus, I know that never in my worst mood could I strike someone with a broomstick."

She pauses briefly. "Especially when they are completely defenseless with their back to me! That is unfair, cowardly, and not the way I operate." Realizing that what she just said in anger could be misconstrued, she adds, "That is if I were to strike someone, which I swear I would never do for no good reason."

She scoops the crumpled letter from Mister Young's desk. She holds it high in the air.

"This is a setup. I have no idea who wrote this, but I do not believe Reg did. I have seen her written words. She doesn't think, talk, or write like this! Plus, she never refers to me as Diana. Never! To her, I am, and I will always be *Dynamite*. Her words, not mine! And, so that you know, I never call her Regina. I call her Reg when I speak to her.

"Someone is setting me up. Why? I do not know. Maybe it has something to do with the championship softball game. Then again, maybe not. All I know is that I never hit Reg with a broomstick." She tosses the letter onto Mister Young's desk. It rolls across his desk to land in his lap.

Mister Young frowns. He says with a firm voice, "Thank you for crumpling the letter, Miss Bower. Nice move." He reaches into his side drawer and produces another sheet of paper with handwritten words on it. "But no problem. I have the original." He thrusts the original letter back into the drawer. He says, "Miss Bower, I hope you know it is your word against hers."

"Yes, I understand that," Diana replies. "But you must believe me, sir. As God is my witness, I never struck Reg. In fact, I have never argued with her. We get along just fine. We're friends, teammates."

Diana's father says, "Jack, you know my wife and me. We do not condone violence. We brought up Diana and her brothers the same way, to look down on violence. To my knowledge, Diana has never been in a fight. Sure, she can be argumentative now and then." He looks at Diana and winks. "That is normal, especially for teens. So, I must protest. You have no proof that Diana assaulted this young lady, Regina. Besides, you said yourself it is Diana's word against Regina's and vice versa." He pauses, and then, with a questioning expression, he looks at Diana once more.

"Diana, you mentioned the softball tournament. Why do you think that the tournament has something to do with this?"

"Because, Dad, if you will recall, I confided in you and Mom that I had serious doubts about the umpire, Mister Reynolds' calls during the game. That included not calling me out. Mister Reynolds is Regina's father."

Diana's father nods his head. "Ah, I see. It never occurred to me that Regina is Mister Reynold's daughter. It all makes sense now."

Mister Young says in a sarcastic voice, "Please excuse me for interrupting your delightfully interesting family discussion. But, I do not think a ladies' softball championship game has anything to do with this letter." He picks up the crumpled letter and waves it in the air.

Then, with an angry scowl on his face, he lobs the letter at his wastebasket.

To Diana's delight, his aim is way off. The crumpled letter hits the side of the wastebasket and bounces. It rolls beneath Mister Young's desk to stop right in front of her chair. She reaches down to retrieve it. As she coldly stares at Mister Young, she slowly uncrumples it, and then she carefully smooths it flat on her thigh. She can hardly suppress a grin as she places the uncrumpled, wrinkled letter onto the front edge of Mister Young's desk.

Mister Young glares at her. He retrieves the wrinkled letter from where Diana had placed it. He holds it aloft and says in an angry tone, "This is the reason we are here. We are talking about an assault on one of my students not a stupid game of softball." He folds the letter in half and jams it into his middle drawer.

Diana's mother murmurs in a barely audible whisper, "We will have to wait and see about that." She raises her voice markedly adding, "So, Jack, what are your intentions. As you said, it is Diana's word against Regina's. I felt that you were leading Regina on when you asked her questions. It was almost like you were coaching her."

Mister Young replies incredulously, "Leading her on, you say? Coaching her, you say? What are you insinuating?"

Diana's mother stops Mister Young mid-sentence, saying, "Jack, I am not suggesting anything. And I am not accusing you of anything nefarious. I simply am telling you that the young lady, Regina, did not seem to follow the letter's script very well if you know what I am saying. Then again, perhaps she was overly excited, justifiably nervous."

"I do not agree," Mister Young says. "I think she did fine considering the circumstances, accusing her supposed friend, your daughter, of assaulting her. I would expect any young lady to act as she did."

Diana's father asks, "Okay, Jack, what do you intend?"

Mister Young replies, "As I said, it is Regina's word against your daughter's. However, in Regina's case, we have the handwritten signed letter. In Diana's case, all we have are her verbal denials."

"No, sir," Diana says in a strong voice. "What you have is a letter of lies. And you have my honest words." Her voice is shaking, not so much out of distress but because she is angry. "And let me say this,

Mister Young. I am appalled that Reg is not in here with her father. I should have the opportunity to face my accuser, am I correct? I mean, she was right outside your door when I arrived. You could have easily called her in to tell her lies to me in person."

Diana's thoughts are racing. What she wanted to say, but dared not say at this point is, "I bet you planted Reg outside your office to frighten me. And I bet you had someone other than Reg write that letter or someone dictated it to her. Also, I bet you sicced your secretary on me so I would get upset and tell her how I felt about her bullying. As for that, well, I probably blew it big time, but it felt good to get it off my chest. Even so, something tells me I will get my chance to say all these things at a later date."

Mister Young replies indifferently, "This is not a court of law, Miss Bower. It is a conference. I already have had a similar discussion with Miss Reynold's father. It occurred this morning. Naturally, Miss Reynolds was present during our discussion. I also talked to Miss Reynolds in private with Miss Hickman in attendance as a witness. I wanted Miss Reynolds to open up, to be truthful with me. She was very upset. You should know, in the circumstances such as these, I serve as an impartial arbitrator."

"I seriously doubt that," Diana thinks to herself. "You and Reg share a secret. The two of you have agreed to something dishonest. And, by your admission, Miss Hickman is in on the agreement. No wonder that detestable bullying woman hates me. So, I bet my bottom dollar that whatever that something is, that the three of you have agreed to, it has everything to do with me! And, you are more than an impartial arbitrator. You are the school's judge, jury, and executioner!"

Diana's father says, "Jack, I get all that. However, it is important to let Diana know, let us know what you intend to do." He calmly adds, "So, I must ask you yet again. What are your intentions?"

Mister Young says, "Considering it is your daughter's word against Miss Reynolds, I am going to go easy on Diana." He addresses Diana saying, "Young lady, I will not tolerate assault in this school, whether actual or threatening. Nor will I tolerate threats of breaking windows and promises to beat up anybody, especially younger cousins of my students."

He leans forward, his elbows on his desk. He interlocks his fingers and begins to twirl his thumbs slowly. His tone of voice is self-important as he says, "Miss Bower, I am putting you on notice, on probation for the remainder of the school year. If you step out of line one more time, I will suspend you for three days. And I will administer a week's detention. Likewise, if you cause any trouble for Miss Regina Reynolds, her father, her cousins, or even her friends and classmates, I will suspend you for three additional days. The suspensions will run concurrently, six days total. Any infractions after that will result in expulsion."

Mister Young points his finger at Diana menacingly. "And that includes during school hours any mention, gossip, or inferences about the championship softball game and Mister Reynold's performance as the game's umpire."

CHAPTER FOUR

DEAR FRIENDS

Part I: I Dunno

When the sun finally departs for its three-day slumber, the myriad of greens and browns fade into a colorless washed out khaki-gray. Diana is both relieved and pleased the luminosity of Domum is more than sufficient to navigate across the lake safely. She guesses Domum's brightness is two times more intense than a Real-world full moon on a cloudless night.

It takes less than an hour in ordinary time for Diana and Charles to walk across the lake. Unsurprisingly, Diana is clueless about the length of time it takes the two of them to traverse. That is because she is held spellbound by Charles' telling of facts and tales of the World Beyond. In turn, the two of them laugh side-splittingly at her puns.

When they arrive at the far end of the lake, Diana cries out, "Oh, look, Charles. Someone left a longbow, a quiver of arrows and, will you look at that! Someone also left a sword behind. Who in their right mind would leave such precious items lying around in full view on the shoreline, for someone to take?" She crouches down to examine the weaponry. She looks up.

"I see no evidence that someone camped here, do you?" Charles does not reply. She picks up the longbow to examine it.

"Wow, this looks brand new! I wish it were mine. I'd love to give it a try." She turns to look at Charles. He is standing next to her with his arms folded across his chest. He has an amused expression on his face.

"Why are you looking at me like that?" He hunches his shoulders in reply. He continues to grin.

"Geez, Charles, you certainly are acting weird." She right away refocuses her attention on the weapons. She pulls out an arrow from the rawhide quiver.

"Dang, Charles! The shaft is solid wood, and the fletching is genuine feathers. The arrowhead is pure iron, and the nock is artfully handcrafted." She balances the center of the arrow on her finger. "Perfectly balanced, and it is very light too. I bet these arrows are extremely accurate. I wish I could shoot one."

She cannot help but notice Charles still has not said anything. She looks at him questioningly. She says, "Goodness, Charles. Does a cat have your tongue?" He shakes his head.

She gets to her feet. She says with an excited voice, all the while lovingly staring down at the weapons, "Oh, Charles, I would do anything if these were mine. As you probably know, I have a compound bow at home. And, I don't want to brag, but I'm a fairly decent shot." She picks up the sword. The sword's scabbard is pure white leather. She slides the sword from the scabbard.

"This is gorgeous." She carefully slides her fingernail across the blade. "Surprisingly, the blade is dull, but the tip of the sword is razor sharp." She looks at Charles, saying, "I wonder to whom these belong?"

He responds softly, "They are yours, Diana, all yours."

She declares excitedly, "Mine? No, that cannot be. You must be mistaken. These carefully crafted weapons surely must belong to someone. I wonder who left them here?"

"I did," says a high-pitched, female's voice. "I did, yep, I did, yepity, yep, yep."

Diana whirls around on her heels. She demands, "Who said that? Where are you?"

"I did say that. I am here, Diana. Yep, I am. See?"

Diana's searches with her eyes above, within and under the trees. She does not notice anything of interest. Her gaze slowly moves along the shoreline until her eyes finally come to rest on Charles. She nearly trips on the hem of her peplos for the umpteenth time as she steps backward in amazement. Perched on Charles' left shoulder is an elegant creature. The creature is five or six inches in height.

Her eyes are enormous, perfectly rounded orbs of brilliant emerald green. They have a certain twinkle in them that speaks to the creature's bubbly nature. She has an avalanche of curly chocolate hair that cascades in waves to her waist. She has tucked a few locks of her hair behind her cute elf ears. She sports a tiny button nose and teensy lips. Her dress matches her hair. Unsurprisingly, she has four dainty, translucent wings!

"Hi, there, Diana! Do you like the stuff I brought you, yep?"

Diana gestures to the longbow, quiver of arrows and sword. "You brought all of this? How is that possible? You're very tiny, and all of this is, well, it is very large and probably very heavy too."

"I do magic. Not so hard if you know how. Lots of trips but I do it. Yep?"

"Well, you are one amazing fairy," Diana says. "What is your name?"

"No fairy am I, Diana. I am a pixie."

"Okay, you're a pixie," Diana says with a laugh. "Sorry. So, what is your name? What should I call you?"

"I Dunno, yep, I Dunno."

Diana asks incredulously, "You don't know? You don't know your name?"

"I know my name, Diana. I Dunno. Yep, I Dunno."

"So, what should I call you if you don't know your name?"

"I said, 'I Dunno.' I Dunno is my name, yep, sure is.'"

Diana and Charles roar with laughter.

Diana says, "Oh, now I get it. Your name is *I Dunno*. Am I correct?"

"Yep, my name is I Dunno. Daddy named me. When I was born, Mommy asked Daddy, 'What you want to name me?' He says, 'I Dunno.' 'Yepity, yep, yep.'" She curtsies gracefully, and then she says, "So, me I Dunno."

Diana cannot stop giggling as she says to Charles, "Have you noticed that I Dunno uses my favorite expression, *yep*, over and over as well as 'yepity, yep, yep?'"

"Yep, I know," Charles says with a chuckle. "It should come as no surprise to you. I Dunno is your protector pixie."

"What in the world is a protector pixie?" Diana asks with a bewildered expression.

Charles says, "Think of a protector pixie as a guardian angel. A guardian angel is assigned to protect and guide a particular person. Naturally, everyone assumes that angels are the only guardians in the Universe. Not surprisingly. It has been this way since antiquity. But the assumption is incorrect.

"You see, Diana, there are not enough angels in the Universe to assign one to each person. So, out of necessity, guardians come in all shapes and sizes and kinds. Some are fairies. Some are nymphs. And some are pixies. Your guardian angel, your protector creature, happens to be a pixie, I Dunno."

Diana says, "That is coolio, Charles. Thank you for explaining that."

She turns her attention to I Dunno. The pixie is hovering in the air a few feet in front of her. She says, "Well, I Dunno, I am thrilled to meet you. Thank you very much for giving me these weapons. You are too kind, and you are very pretty. And I thank you for being my protector pixie. I now know why I love people, animals, and nature very much. It is due to your kindheartedness."

I Dunno sets down on Diana's left shoulder. She whispers, "Diana is welcome. Now, I Dunno must sleep. Diana is correct. Weapons are too heavy." She lies down on Diana's shoulder. Then she closes her eyes and is in a deep sleep just like that.

Diana whispers, "Charles, will she be okay as she sleeps? I am afraid she will fall off my shoulder."

Charles retrieves a leather pouch from the tall grass. Diana had not noticed the pouch until now. She was too excited as she examined the weaponry.

He says, "She made it for the two of you to use. It is the best way to carry her when she is sleeping."

He gently scoops I Dunno into the palm of his hand. He carefully places her in the pouch and pulls the drawstring tight. He slips the strap of the pouch over Diana's head and onto her shoulder. Diana lovingly strokes the outside of the pouch with her hand as it hangs by her side.

She whispers, "How will I know when she wants to leave the pouch? Will she call out for me to open the drawstring?"

"Diana, please do not worry about I Dunno. As a pixie, she is charmed, so I expect she will figure out a way to leave the pouch on her own. She can sleep wherever, in the crook of the branch of a tree, in the grass, beside a rock, anywhere where she feels safe. Nevertheless, while you are with her in the World Beyond, she needs to be close to you in a physical way, even when she is sleeping. She also longs for your company. These are but two of the reasons she made the pouch."

He smiles. "I am confident you will find her company both reassuring and obliging. She will serve as your guide as well as your best friend as you journey. And I have a hunch she is the one who will teach you how to do magic."

*****

Part II: Gifts of Libum, Life Spirit, And the Death of Charles

"Charles, I am famished," Diana suddenly exclaims. She glances expectantly at their immediate surroundings hoping to see something edible. "Is there anything good to eat around here, something to munch on to curb my appetite? I'll eat just about anything right now."

Charles reaches into his rucksack. He withdraws an object roughly the diameter of a softball. To Diana, it looks like an uneven ball of leafy green vegetables.

She asks with a doubtful tone, "What in the world is it? It looks like a small clump of cabbage, but its leaves are much too dark, almost the color of spinach." With a disgusted look, she adds, "If it's cabbage, it's not exactly what I had in mind about something good to eat."

Charles laughs, and then he says, "It is not cabbage or even a vegetable for that matter." He tears off a piece of the greenery and hands it to her. "But, you are correct, these are leaves. They are leaves of the bamao plant. Bamao leaves are indigenous to the World Beyond. They are a natural preservative. You do not eat the leaves although they are edible when boiled. You eat what is inside the leaves."

He begins to remove the leaves carefully. After he unwraps the object, he hands it to Diana.

"Here you are. Try this. It is called *libum*. If you were at home, you could Google the name. Libum means cake in Latin. It is a pastry of ancient Rome. It is delicious, at least that is what others have told me. It tastes like cheesecake but much tastier."

She takes the libum from him. It reminds her of a cross between a slightly undercooked plump donut and a very large biscuit.

She asks, "What is this gooey yellowish-brown stuff on top?"

Charles replies with a chuckle, "It's honey, honey made by the World Beyond's bees. It's okay, Diana, give it a lick. It won't poison you."

Diana half-heartedly dabs at the honey with her tongue. The expression on her face instantly turns from one of uncertainty to complete delight.

"Wow! The honey tastes delicious, better than the high-quality honey Mom buys at the Amish farms." She splits the libum in two. "What is this creamy white stuff in the middle?"

Charles laughs again, as he says in a lighthearted tone, "For one who supposedly is famished, you surely ask a lot of questions. It is cheese similar to what you might find in the Italian dish lasagna. It has the consistency of ricotta cheese."

Diana gingerly bites into the libum. She licks her lips and rolls her eyes with satisfaction.

"Oh, my goodness! Libum is wonderful. Where did you get it? Do you have more?"

Charles opens his rucksack for her to look inside. He replies, "I have plenty." Diana peeks inside the rucksack. She counts at least a dozen softball-sized libum carefully wrapped in bamao. She takes another bite of her libum. She says, "Aren't you going to have some?"

Charles shakes his head as he replies matter-of-factly, "I do not desire food nor do I need it."

Diana says, "I see. I need to ask you a personal question. May I?"

"Yep."

"How did you, you know, how did you die?"

Charles says, "I was hiking a trail in Virginia. It had been raining for two solid days. The trail was a soggy mess, a river of rainwater. I slid on a slippery rock below the surface of the rushing water. The weight of my backpack was too much for me. I went over the cliff. They have yet to find my body."

Diana covers her mouth with her hand that is holding the piece of libum. Immediately, tears well up in her eyes. She reaches out with her other hand to take Charles' hand in hers. She says in a whisper, "Oh, my God, Charles, that is terrible. I am very sorry. I truly am. Knowing this makes me very sad. I wish I hadn't asked." She wipes the corners of her eyes. "And they have yet to find your body? That is terrible. Maybe they will find it, you know, they will find your remains someday."

"I doubt it, Diana. I was hiking alone. No one knew where I was. The only family I had was my brother James. And I hadn't seen him in years. He lived with foster parents across the continent. Sadly, James passed away one year after me. He has never told me how he died." He sighs. "And now he is somewhere in the tranquility beam, perhaps being held hostage by Mendacium. However, my brother is strong and very smart. Hopefully, he will find a way out of Mendacium's clutches.

"Anyway, I lived in an orphanage nearly all of my life. I had few friends at the orphanage. And, I think the staff of the orphanage could have cared less about me, whether I lived or died. I simply was another mouth to feed and one more deduction on their state-funded expense account. Besides, where I fell is remote and desolate with huge boulders surrounded by thick vegetation. I expect little remains of my living self. What is left of my body is probably scattered here and there."

Tears are now falling freely from Diana's eyes. She says with a grief-stricken tone, "Oh, Charles, once again I must say that I am truly sorry." She wipes the tears from her face. In between soft sobs, she says, "Did it hurt when you died?"

"Nope. My head must have collided with a rock when I slipped. I think I was knocked unconscious. I did not feel a thing nor do I remember anything but slipping with my arms flailing. I think I instantly died when my body impacted the boulders in the canyon. I estimate I fell two hundred feet, give or take."

Diana asks, "What was it like when you awoke?" She suddenly winces, saying, "Oh, I am sorry. I meant to say when you became a ghost." She pauses briefly, and then she says, "This is a bit awkward for me as you can imagine."

"When I awoke, for lack of a better word, I was floating a few feet in the air. I was staring with disbelief at my crumpled body lying on the ground. Surprisingly, I did not feel any emotion, no pain, no yearning for my now deceased former living self. I simply stared for a few moments. Then, I departed. Something in my soul told me I had the opportunity to go on, to help others in the world of humans. At first, I did not know what I should do or where I should go, but I eventually figured out my destiny."

Diana asks in a whisper, "How long has it been? You know, since you died?"

"It has been exactly fourteen years ago yesterday, June the 18th."

Diana exclaims in an astonished tone, "Oh, my gosh, Charles. June 18th is my birthday! And I just turned fourteen years old!"

Charles chuckles. And then he says, "Yes, I know it is your birthday, and I know you just turned fourteen. You see, Diana, a benevolent ghost, a ghost of a kind and caring human, is allowed to be the protective spirit of anyone he or she desires. But there is one stipulation. The person the ghost selects must have been born on the same day that the ghost died. You were born on the same day that I died. So, I picked you." He smiles. "And I am glad I did.

"So, even though I look like I am your age, if I were still alive today, I guess I would now be around twenty-eight, maybe a bit older or younger. And, Diana, so that you know, I have been with you since the day you were born."

Diana frowns. Shaking her head with uncertainty, she says, "I do not know if I like that, Charles, you passing away on the same day that I was born. It is disturbing to know that my very own ghost, my ethereal friend, died on my birthday." She looks at him with a sorrowful expression. "Do you understand what I am saying?"

"I understand. But, look at it this way. Although I perished on the day you were born, in essence, I also was reborn thanks to you. Because of your entrance into our wonderful world, I can now help others in need. I can comfort those who are dying as I did for Ariel and Susan. Otherwise, had I not latched onto you as your ghost, perhaps I would cease to exist in my ethereal way." He claps his hands together. *"Poof!"*

Diana nods her head as she takes another bite of her libum.

"Well, when you put it that way, it makes me feel a whole lot better. Still, it is a bit creepy. Whenever I celebrate birthdays in the future, I'll think of you alone amongst those boulders where you fell. Oh, well. It is what it is." She smiles. "So, what did you do when you were a kid?"

"I played softball at the orphanage and, like you, I played volley-ball too. But, my passion was hiking. I would venture alone in the woods as often as I could. I enjoyed the beauty of nature and its serenity. When I hiked, I imagined that I was my hero John Muir. Muir was an avid hiker and was best known for his nature quotes and as the *Father of the National Parks*. I recall a quote from John Muir that is relevant as to how I felt about hiking as a boy and the dangers of being alone."

I have never held death in contempt, though in the course of my explorations, I have often felt that to meet one's fate on a noble mountain, or in the heart of a glacier, would be blessed as compared with death from disease, or from some shabby lowland accident.

"Diana, as you can see from Muir's quote, my soul is at peace. I died on a noble mountain, not from disease or from some shabby lowland accident."

Diana says, "The quote by John Muir is beautiful, Charles. And your interpretation is very moving. I can now see why you are not upset about dying the way that you did."

Charles says, with a happy tone, "One day when I was hiking, I found an old backpack that was in poor shape. My discovery was almost as good as finding a wad of money. I patched the backpack with duct tape and spent hours redoing its seams. I was proud of my backpack. I would put it under my pillow at night and wear it every day as I went about my routine at the orphanage. If I hadn't, someone would have stolen it.

"I was pretty much a loner. I guess that is because I yearned for my parents. I never knew my parents. They were killed a few days after I was born. Ironically, they were killed in a car accident on their way to the hospital to take me home."

Diana whispers, "Oh, Charles! That is very sad. It makes me appreciate my parents and my brothers, Dan and Billy so much more. When were you born, what day, month and year?"

"I do not know. The hospital transferred me to the orphanage a few days after my parents died. Kids in orphanages often live lonely lives. No one ever told me my birthday. I missed not knowing about it when I was a kid, but I never asked. I was too afraid to ask. The staff at my orphanage was not too friendly. In fact, the reason I was hiking the day I died, I had run away from the orphanage. I could not tolerate being there any longer.

"When I think back to the day I died, I know that I was a teenag-er, perhaps your age, maybe a bit older. He smiles. "Naturally, I quit growing and maturing when I became a ghost. When I compare myself to living human teenage boys, I reckon I look the same age as some of them. As I said, maybe I was fourteen, fifteen, or even sixteen when I died. There is no way of knowing. But one thing is for certain. I was not yet eighteen years old when I died. If I had been eighteen, I would already have left that godforsaken orphanage."

Diana whispers, "What a remarkable but awfully sad story. You never knew your parents. You never knew when you were born. You do not know how old you were when you died. You grew up in an orphanage. And you died lonely on my birthday, the very day you were reborn into your ethereal world." She gobbles the remaining portion of her libum, and then she embraces him. She whispers, "And you are now my good friend, my lifelong ghost. I am tremendously thankful for that."

Suddenly, a gentle, high-pitched sound emerges from the trees.

Diana exclaims, "What is that? It sounds like the whinny of a horse. Do you hear it?"

"Yep," Charles says.

She notices he has the silly grin on his face yet again. She says, "You're up to something. I can tell. Tell me, if you please, Charles, what kind of mischief are you planning?"

He says in a joking tone, "Diana, how dare you insinuate such a thing!" He roars with laughter. "I would never make mischief. You know that. Look behind you."

Diana turns around.

While she hovers in the air, I Dunno, is leading a handsome pure white horse out of the forest by its reins. She is huffing and puffing as she struggles with the reins. She happily says as she points with her tiny finger, "Lookie here, Diana. I brings you a horsey. He is Diana horsey. Do you like?"

Diana cries, "Oh, my goodness, he is beautiful, I Dunno! Is he truly mine?"

"Yep, he is Diana horsey," Pixie says as she hovers close to Diana. She hands Diana the reins with a loud, grumbling *ungh!* "Glad to give Diana reins. Too heavy." She smiles excitedly. "Horsey name is Jayvyn. Means *Light Spirit*." She stretches her arms out wide and yawns. "Now I Dunno sleep some more." She flies to the top of her pouch. Diana quickly opens the drawstring and I Dunno slips inside.

Diana whispers, "Thank you, I Dunno, thank you very much." She can barely discern I Dunno's muted reply from inside the pouch.

"Diana welcome. Oh, goodness, I Dunno sleepy. Too much business today. Goodnight, Diana. You too, Charles."

Diana says, "Goodnight, I Dunno. And once more, thank you." She cocks her head to look at Jayvyn.

"You have a lovely name, and I like the fact that it means Light Spirit." She strokes Jayvyn's pure white mane. "It is a pleasure to meet you, Jayvyn. I have never seen such a gorgeous horse like you."

Jayvyn whinnies softly as he gently pushes against Diana's shoulder. Then, to her surprise, he bends his forearms at the knees and lowers his head until the nostrils of his muzzle are nearly touching the ground."

She shouts, "Oh, my goodness, Charles. Will you look at that! Jayvyn is bowing to me!"

Charles replies, "Not surprisingly. Jayvyn is honored to be the noble steed, the light spirit of Empress Diana, Youngster Heroine of the World Beyond."

*****

Part III: Charles Departs

After an emotional goodbye, Charles departed a few moments ago for the Real-world to release his balloons into the air as he had promised to Susan. Diana dreaded the thought of him re-entering the tranquility beam. She begged him not to leave.

She had said, "What if Mendacium snatches you like he did James? Who will take care of me? More importantly, I could not live without you as my ghost. It would break my heart."

Charles had replied, "You will be okay, Diana. I do not plan on being away for too long. Then again, something could delay me. I hope you understand. I must go. I have no other choice. I promised Susan. She will be looking down from heaven or, if she is in the ethereal-world like me, watching. I cannot disappoint her. A ghost's promise is his Word, his Pledge, his Bond. As I said earlier, ghosts cannot lie.

"So, even if I did not want to go, which I do, I would have to. Otherwise, I would violate my Word, which would be the same as lying." To Diana's annoyance, he had clapped his hands and softly whispered with a smile, *"Poof!* Then no more me."

Diana had scolded him. She said in a stern tone, "I wish you wouldn't be flippant when you talk about ceasing to exist. I dread the thought of you leaving my side. When you say the word *poof,* you sound very uncaring about your passing and my feelings."

Charles had replied, "Sorry." Then, to playfully annoy her, which ended up aggravating her even more, he said, "Maybe I should have said, 'Poofy?'"

Diana did not reply. She simply glared at him. Realizing she was not getting anywhere addressing her worries regarding Charles' welfare, she tried a different tactic. She pretended she was vulnerable, exposed, open to the elements.

"But, Charles, if you go, I will be defenseless. I haven't even learned to use my sword effectively. While I can shoot arrows well, I am not that accurate. What happens if Mendacium attacks me? What happens if some horrible creature creeps up on me while I am asleep? Worse yet, what happens if lots of creatures attack me at once?"

Abruptly, a thought had crossed her mind which completely changed the subject.

She said, "Charles, I am worried about April. Do you think she is okay? She should have been here by now, don't you think?"

Charles had replied, "I doubt April is coming, Diana. You see, she understands that you are safe. You have as your company I Dunno, and you have Jayvyn. If you need April in an emergency, I am certain she will respond."

"Goodness, and all this time, I thought she was going to accompany me on this journey. I feel bad, abandoned if you know what I am saying."

"Please do not feel that way, Diana. As I said, if you need her, she will be by your side in no time. Trust me when I say this."

Diana had said in an unhappy tone of voice, "Okay, I trust you. But, I still feel disappointed. I truly like April. I enjoy her company, and I will miss her too." At that precise moment, she tried another ploy to get Charles to stay. She glanced at the soiled hem of her peplos.

"I also need a change of clothes. True, I love my peplos. But, how can I go on with nothing else to wear?" A distressed, pitiful look appeared on her face. Purposely not looking at Charles' rucksack filled to the rim with libum, herbs and spices, she said, "Besides, I do not know how to gather food in this strange land. I could starve! Then, when you return, I will be nothing but bare bones!"

"You will not starve," Charles said with a laugh. He picked up his rucksack from the ground and handed it to her. "Here you go, my dear. There is plenty of food inside to last a very long time."

She tried a different tactic. She pretended to worry about her protector pixie.

"But, what about I Dunno?"

In a muffled, sleepy voice from inside her pouch, I Dunno mumbled, "What about I Dunno? You okay, Diana? I Dunno was sleeping."

Diana ignored her. She said, "Poor I Dunno. She will have nothing to eat either."

Charles laughed loudly as I Dunno said from within her pouch, "I Dunno not poor. I Dunno has Diana. And I Dunno has lots to eat. There grass, and flowers, and caterpillars, ants," she yawned adding, "and crickets, and beetles, and goodness." She paused for a moment as she yawned. Then she said, "I Dunno now hungry but still sleepy. Goodnight."

Charles said, "As you can see, I Dunno is quite capable of taking care of herself. As I hinted at earlier, she will teach you all you need to know about your weaponry. I suspect she also will teach you magic. As far as food goes, she will fetch your food. She knows how to gather edible grasses and herbs and other stuff in the forest. Also, she knows how to." Diana had waved her hand disapprovingly, stopping Charles midsentence.

"Hold it right there, Charles. If you think for one second that I am eating ants, crickets, beetles, and ugh! Just the thought of eating hairy caterpillars grosses me out enormously. You are one hundred percent wrong. No, Charles, there is no way I am eating that revolting stuff!"

Charles had said with a chuckle, "I Dunno does not eat insects raw, Diana. She cooks them in a soup filled with aromatic herbs and spices." He pointed to his rucksack that Diana had draped over her shoulder. "Some of her tiny bottles of spices are in there. Lots of other spices, herbs, and all sorts of cooking utensils are in her pouch. Others have told me her insect soup is tasty. Sometimes I have seconds." He chuckles. "I'm kidding of course. I have never tasted her soup. But I bet it is delicious. It sure smells delightful."

"There is no way," Diana protested, "no way I am going to eat soup filled with disgusting bugs! Yuck!" Then she said with a puckered brow, "See, Charles? I will lack protein. I will become weaker."

Charles said, "There is more than enough protein in libum." Then, with a chuckle, he added, "But, you must try I Dunno's insect soup. It truly looks like it is delicious and nourishing."

With that, Charles tightly hugged her. He whispered in her ear, "Diana, you will be fine. You are intelligent, innovative, courageous, and stubborn." He looked her in the eyes adding playfully, "Stubborn in a wonderful way. And you have a quest. For the truth. And I do not doubt that I Dunno will take loving care of you. After all, she is your protector pixie." He took Diana's hands into his, squeezed them three times, and then he quickly turned about and stepped onto the lake.

To say that Diana was surprised by Charles' abrupt departure goes without saying. She figured he probably was as sad as she was. She called out to him, "I love you too, Charles. Be safe and say hello to Ariel and Susan for me. Also, give them my love, if you please." She bent down to pick up her weapons from the ground. When she glanced up to look up across Lake Vita, Charles was gone.

As she gathered up her things, Diana reflected that something Charles had said continued to nag her. She couldn't get it out of her head.

"What was it that he said that is bothering me so much? Oh, yes, now I remember. He had said, rather quickly now that I think about it, 'Then again, something could delay me.'" She frowned. "I do not like the inference of that. Well, there is not much I can do about it now. He will get here when he gets here. It is what it is." She addressed I Dunno. "Okay, I Dunno, where do we go from here?"

I Dunno did not reply. That is because she was sound asleep in her pouch. Diana giggled as she listened with amusement to the whiny sounds of I Dunno's muted snorts, snuffles, and sniffs as she snored. She carefully slipped I Dunno's pouch from her shoulder. Then she sat down and rested her back against the trunk of a gigantic tree. She carefully placed I Dunno's pouch on her lap. After that, she placed her longbow and quiver of arrows by her side. She unsheathed her sword and placed it on her lap.

Jayvyn was standing over her munching on sprigs of grass. She whispered as she looked from her weaponry up to him. As she patted her weaponry, she said, "Just in case, Jayvyn, just in case."

She leaned her head against the tree trunk. She dreamily stared at the spectacular miracle of Domum floating like a three-sided diamond glistening in the sky. Lyrics from her favorite rock 'n roll band, AC/DC, suddenly swirled in her mind.

"See me ride out of the sunset. On your color tv screen. Don't you mess me 'round. T.N.T. I'm a power load. T.N.T. Watch me explode."

Dy-na-mite!

As quickly as her softball nickname flew in, and then out of her thoughts, she was fast asleep.

*****

Part IV: Whatnots from a Teacher

When Diana wakes up, she raises her arms high above her head and straightens her legs. She stretches her back to the left and the right. With a satisfied, lengthy yawn, she whispers to herself, "That felt good. I hadn't realized how tired I was after going nearly two days without sleep. At least I think it was two days. Since the sun is in the sky, but for one short hour in the World Beyond, there is no way of knowing. No problem. Even though I do not have a clue how long I was asleep, my sleep was refreshing and uninterrupted. I feel great!"

She gets to her feet and looks around. The illumination from Domum, while enough to light up the sky and the ground below, merely casts a shadowy dreariness over the land. Nothing has changed since before she fell asleep. Lake Vita is shimmering as usual, and the surrounding landscape is also unchanged. In fact, she has the strangest feeling that I Dunno, Jayvyn and she are the only things moving in an otherwise motionless photograph. Even her beloved lifelong ghost Charles is missing from the picture.

She says in a clear voice, "Hopefully, not for long."

She suddenly feels hungry. She reaches into Charles' rucksack to retrieve a ball of libum. As she searches with her fingers inside the pouch, she touches a cluster of bumpy, rubbery objects. They are on top of the libum. She immediately pulls out her hand in disgust.

"Oh, my goodness. What in the world are those rubbery things with bumps all over them? They feel strangely elastic. I hope they aren't some of I Dunno's insects. Or, worse yet, some nasty World Beyond creatures eating all of my libum!"

She cautiously peers inside the rucksack. On top of the libum is a heaping pile of fibrous strips of whatnots. At least that is the word that comes to mind when she sees the strips. Whatnots. They are a purplish-red and coated with granules that bear a resemblance to salt and peppercorn.

"Well, at least they're not moving. So, I guess whatever the what-nots are they must be dead." She gingerly seizes one of the strips with her fingers and carefully examines it. "Could it be? Could this be jerky? Then again, I don't know. It sure doesn't look like any jerky I've ever eaten." She raises it to her nose.

"Hmm, but it sure does smell good. God, I hope it isn't a dehydrated bug!"

She rips a piece of the whatnots from one end. She turns her head to one side and closes her eyes. She gulps air, and then she quickly stuffs the morsel in her mouth. As she chews, she abruptly exclaims, "Oh, my God! These whatnots are some form of jerky!" She starts laughing wildly. "Protein, yummy, delicious, all-too-familiar protein! And it isn't a bug! At least I hope it isn't! Yippee! I don't have to eat bugs for added protein."

She stuffs the rest of the whatnots in her mouth. Unexpectedly, she remembers something that she had dreamed as she slept. In her dream, she was hiking with Charles and John Muir. And get this. The three of them were happily tearing off strips of jerky with their teeth! Charles, who doesn't need to eat, called the slices of jerky whatnots. There can only be one explanation.

She calls out, "I Dunno?"

I Dunno is immediately at her side. As she hovers in the air in front of Diana, she says, "Yes, Diana. You okay?"

Diana replies, "Yes, I Dunno. I am fine. And very happy." She pulls another strip of jerky from the rucksack. She shows it to I Dunno.

"How in the world did you do this, I Dunno? How did you know?" I Dunno giggles.

"Me know because Diana know. I Dunno make good stuff I Dunno found in Diana dreams." She places her tiny hands over her heart and says in her squeaky voice, "I Dunno love Diana. I Dunno make Diana happy. Diana make I Dunno happy."

Diana cries, "Goodness, I love you too, I Dunno. With all my heart and my soul. And I thank you very much for bringing me this delicious jerky. Where did you get it? Is it found here in the World Beyond? What do you call it?"

"I Dunno no bring. I Dunno make magic. From your dream." She draws up her small shoulders as she says with a mischievous grin, "I Dunno call it whatnots like Charles say in Diana dream."

Diana laughs as she tears another piece of jerky, whatnots, with her teeth. In between chews, she says, "Okay, I Dunno, where do we go from here?"

"Diana, Jayvyn and I Dunno go to the forest. I Dunno teach Diana magic."

"Really? You're going to teach me magic?"

I Dunno replies happily, "Yepity, yep, yep. Diana must do magic. Very important."

She forms a triangle with her teeny fingers and thumbs. Then, as she slowly separates her fingertips, streams of bluish sparks that look like electrical current appear between them.

Diana says excitedly, "My goodness, I Dunno! That is very coolio. Are you going to teach me how to do that?"

I Dunno chuckles. "No, I Dunno just showing off. I Dunno teach Diana other magic. Fun stuff." She hops onto Jayvyn's head. "Diana mount Jayvyn please. Us go now. No time to dillydally."

Like her double back home, Diana has no clue what the word dillydally means. However, since I Dunno had said it, she knows it is not a rude word.

The first thing Diana notices upon entering the forest is how hazy it is beneath the trees. As one would expect, the luminosity of Domum does not penetrate the dense canopy. With a hint of worry in her tone, she whispers, "Goodness, I Dunno, it sure is dark in here. Are we going to be okay as we travel? Is it safe?"

"Must go. Sunshine too short. It safe for Diana. Jayvyn and I Dunno safe too. Very important we go."

Diana says, "Well, okay, if you insist. But, I wish the sunshine would stick around a bit longer. An hour or so of sunshine just doesn't cut it. I wish the long nights were much shorter than they are as well."

Jayvyn suddenly stops walking. Diana looks around anxiously. She says, "What is wrong, Jayvyn? Why did you stop walking?"

I Dunno says, "Me stop Jayvyn." She hops onto Jayvyn's back a few inches in front of where Diana is sitting. She looks up at Diana with her huge green eyes and says, "Diana, put hands like this."

Diana watches as I Dunno places her hands together palms up so that the outsides of her hands and pinky fingers are touching. With her thumbs resting tightly on top of her forefingers, she cups her hands.

I Dunno says, "Diana now say *lux magicae.*"

Diana repeats the words. Nothing happens. She says, "What is supposed to happen, I Dunno?"

I Dunno giggles. "Diana said it wrong. It *lux mag-ih-ca-e* not *lux mag-i-ca.*"

Diana says, "Oh, I get it. Instead of saying lux mag-i-ca I should have added a hard *e* when saying the words *lux magicae.*" She unexpectedly screams with delight. Her screams are very powerful. If they were buzz saws, they would bring down the surrounding trees in no time. She is screaming because a swirling ball of red and gold light has formed in the palms of her hands!

She whispers, "Oh, my God! I cannot believe this, I Dunno. I did magic. I did it! Thank you, thank you!"

I Dunno laughs. "Diana now throw magic up air."

"You want me to throw the magic ball of light into the air?" I Dunno nods her head.

While continuing to keep her hands pressed together, Diana gently tosses the swirling ball of light into the air. It comes to rest a half-dozen feet above and slightly behind of her head. It lights up the immediate surroundings with an intensity that is as strong as a camping lantern.

"This is terrific, I Dunno! Not only can I do magic, I feel much better now that there is light. Will the magic stay with us as we walk?"

As if to answer her question, Jayvyn resumes walking. The swirling ball of light follows along. It remains in a geostationary position above and behind Diana. She looks over her shoulder from time to time to stare at the light. Every time that she does, she whispers things like, "This is incredibly coolio. I made light. I cannot wait to tell Evelyn and all my friends."

As Jayvyn moves along slowly on a well-treaded path, Diana and I Dunno take turns dozing off. Unlike her prior catnaps, I Dunno curls up fast asleep in Jayvyn's thick mane. Diana is not sitting on a saddle. Fortunately, she has ridden saddleless many times before. As she naps, her hands are clasping the reins of Jayvyn's bridle like a pro. She looks like a fourteen-year-old cowgirl from an old black and white movie as her head gently bobs back and forth and up and down as Jayvyn walks.

When she awakens, she stretches as best she can. Her butt is beginning to hurt a little, so she knows she will have to dismount soon. She looks around. There seems to be nothing, but endless trees that are sprinkled here and there with tiny bushes. She is somewhat bored.

Her attention is drawn to I Dunno's pouch as it sways back and forth. She had tied it to the rearing rein swivel of Jayvyn's bridle. To break the monotony, she begins to speculate what I Dunno has in her pouch. She could peek inside, but she respects I Dunno's privacy. Plus, she is too embarrassed to ask I Dunno about the belongings in her pouch.

Just for fun, she envisions that, in addition to a fluffy handmade, gaily printed pixie pillow and a warm blanket, I Dunno's pouch surely contains super-cool pixie stuff. She imagines supple leather shelves brimming with vials of magic potions are lining the interior of the pouch. Maybe she has a book or two of magical spells.

She whispers to herself, "It could be I Dunno has disguises, so she can dress up to look like a leprechaun or a ghoul. She must have many changes of clothes inside her pouch as well. She wears different, lovely outfits throughout the day. I bet she even has a dresser, maybe even a bed! And oh, yes, I Dunno most assuredly must have pots and pans. Otherwise, how could she cook her gross insects?"

Her mention of food, not necessarily prompted by eating insects, causes Diana's stomach to growl. She reaches into Charles' rucksack. Much to her surprise, she retrieves a reddish, banana-shaped something or other. It is then she notices, I Dunno is staring at her as she sits in Jayvyn's mane. The pixie is grinning from ear to ear.

Diana says, "Well, hello there, sleepyhead. Did you have a good nap?" I Dunno nods her head. She points to the object in Diana's hand.

"Diana like?"

Diana replies, "Well, I dare say it is interesting. What is it?"

"A banapple, Diana. Charles says you need, how do you say, bunches of fruity?"

Diana laughs, and then she says, "It is called fruit, but I honestly think what you called it, fruity, sounds much better. And yes, Charles is correct. As nutritious as they are delicious, I cannot live solely on your whatnots, and libum. I need vitamin C." She giggles. "I need fruity!" She examines the object she is holding in her hand.

"So, I Dunno, this looks like a cross between a banana and an apple. I imagine that is why you refer to it as a banapple. It is shaped like a banana but reddish like an apple." She squeezes it. "And it is firm like a fresh apple. But, it doesn't have a peel like a banana. Can I eat the outer portion, the peel?"

"Diana eat the whole banapple. I Dunno eat some. It good."

Diana breaks off a small piece of the banapple. She pops it into her mouth. She mumbles as she chews, stating, "Um, this is good. Thank you, I Dunno. But, how did you come to make it? Is it like your very own creation?"

"Diana dream it. Two fruity. One ball. One curled." She laughs. "But I Dunno make oops magic. Fruity, how do Diana say, opposite?" She laughs again. "And two fruity become one fruity. But Diana like I Dunno mistake, yes?"

"Uh-hum," Diana replies. "This is the best fruity banapple I have ever tasted. Thank you." She licks her lips. "Can I Dunno make something from which I can drink water? You know, like the lake stuff, only less brown? I drank some of the water from Lake Vita. It tasted okay, but I don't want to get giardia or some other water-borne sickness from drinking unclean water."

I Dunno scratches her head for the longest time. Then, with a bright smile, she says, "Oh, I Dunno know what Diana say!" She leaps down from Jayvyn's mane onto her pouch. She squeezes into the opening. A few seconds later she scrambles out. She is holding a tiny leather waterskin.

She asks, "Diana mean like this?"

Diana chuckles as she says, "Yes, I Dunno, that is it exactly. But only larger. Yours is too tiny for me. I'd probably swallow it. Can you do magic to make me the same?"

I Dunno says, "Yes. I Dunno try to make." She closes her eyes and mumbles a bunch of unintelligible mumble jumble. Then, just as

Diana takes another bite of her banapple, a leather waterskin suddenly flops out of nowhere onto her lap. The waterskin is twice the size than Diana had expected, but it looks exactly like the one I Dunno is holding in her hand. Something inside the container splish-splashes from side to side as Jayvyn walks. Diana hopes it is water.

"Goodness, I Dunno, you are one amazing protector pixie. Thank you very much. You may have saved my life by giving me this waterskin full of water. It is water, yes?"

I Dunno says, "I dunno." She flies to Diana and hovers a few inches from her mouth. She carefully aims the neck of her waterskin toward Diana's mouth.

I Dunno says, "Diana mouth open."

Diana opens her mouth wide. I Dunno squirts a tiny stream of what tastes like water into her mouth. She licks her lips and swallows.

"That is perfect, I Dunno. It tastes exactly like water, like nothing. She points to her waterskin. Is the same liquid in that, in my waterskin?"

I Dunno replies, "Same. Now Diana stays happy like I Dunno."

Diana uncorks her waterskin. After swallowing what seems like a gallon of water, she says, "Thank you yet again, I Dunno." When she sets the waterskin in front of her, she notices that it resumes its former shape. In some way, I Dunno has magically refilled it! She says, "Wow, I Dunno. You must be the most talented pixie in all the world!"

I Dunno completely ignores her. She is happily jumping up and down on Jayvyn's head and pointing to a spacious meadow of verdant grass speckled with red and white blossoms. A row of lofty forest trees surrounds the meadow. The only opening in the trees that Diana can make out is at the far end of the meadow where the trail picks up again.

I Dunno yells in her tiny voice, "Diana, see? We go there! Yippee and a yepity yep yep!"

CHAPTER FIVE

CONFESSIONS OVER CREAM SODA

Diana and her parents just finished touring the local museum. They spent a little over an hour looking at the statues. It is a tradition for Diana and her friends to visit the museum and then walk a few blocks to a small café. Diana ponders that being alone with her parents is as good as hanging out with her friends, well, almost.

While they were touring the museum, Diana snapped a bunch of photos with her phone. She is scrolling through the photos right now. Of all the photos she snapped, her favorites are the ones of the statue of Artemis. The fact that she likes photos of Artemis, her mythological namesake, comes as no surprise.

She looks up from her phone. She says, "Both of you believe me, right? That I did not have anything to do with the accusations in that stupid letter?"

Her mother and father eye each other, and then, at the same time, they reply, "Of course we do."

Diana says lightheartedly, "I hesitate to say this. But it is obvious to me that your simultaneous, well-choreographed show of parental support is questionable at best." She laughs as do her parents. "But, thanks for saying it just the same. Saying you believe me makes me feel a whole lot better than I did a couple of hours ago. I would never lie to you. You know that."

Diana and her parents are sipping delicious Italian cream sodas at a quaint place called Café Cocos. Visiting Café Cocos when Diana and her friends are in the area is a tradition. Diana's sweet, good friend, Bonnie is their waitress.

Bonnie introduced Diana and her friends to the café. She is sporting her usual distinguishing hairstyle. She has her brown hair shaved on the sides. Today, her choice of dyed hair color on the top of her head is pink. She is in Diana's drama class. She recently performed in a play at their school. She and Diana strike up a conversation as she cleans the adjacent table.

She asks, "When can we hang out together? It's been like forever since we had some fun."

Diana replies, "I don't know. Things are a bit crazy right now." She pauses. "Wait a minute. Let's go to the zoo. I'm going next week Thursday. Are you off?"

"Matter of fact I am," Bonnie says excitedly. "What time do you want to meet up?"

"Come on over to my house say, around ten in the morning. We can go to the zoo, and then maybe hang out at the mall."

Bonnie says, "Awesomesauce! Let's do Panda Express. My treat." She giggles. "After all, I'm getting paid for," she looks around to ensure her boss is not looking, "to talk to my friends while I clean tables."

Diana says, "Sounds like a plan. I'll see if Evelyn, Edith, and Mary can make it."

"Cool," Bonnie replies. "And next weekend there's a fair in town. I'm off that weekend."

Diana types a note on her phone. "Okay, next Thursday we go to the zoo, then to the mall. Then we eat and eat some more." She laughs. "Lots and lots of orange chicken from Panda Express. Your treat! Then that weekend we head out to the fairgrounds. Evelyn, Edith and Mary are already planning to go."

"Okay dokie," Bonnie whispers. "I ought to get back to work. I'll be seeing you, Diana." She says to Diana's parents, "Nice to see you once again, Mister and Missus Bower. If you need anything else, please let me know."

Diana's father does not reply to Bonnie. Instead, he says to Diana in a serious tone, "So, Diana, tell us. What happened in Miss Hickman's office before you joined us in Mister Young's office?" He takes a sip of his soda. "When your mother and I were talking to Mister Young."

Diana winces as she thinks to herself, "Do they know? If so, how? It only happened a few hours ago."

She says to her dad, "Do I have to?"

"No, not if you don't want to. I am curious, that's all. We heard something bang against the wall and then we heard a loud crash. I could be wrong, but it sounded like a chair. Mister Young was about to go and investigate; however, fortunately, your mother stopped him." He looks at Diana's mother adding with a sarcastic-looking smirk, "Apparently, she did not want anyone or anything to interrupt our delightfully inspiring conversation with your principal."

"It was a chair that you heard," Diana replies. "Miss Hickman had pushed her chair forcefully against the wall when she stood up. She had become upset, and then she nearly leaped across her desk in anger."

Diana considers if she should say to her parents the thoughts whirling in her mind as it relates to Miss Hickman's bullying. She decides, "Why not? What's there to lose?"

She says, "Miss Hickman is a horrible woman, an adult bully. I do not like her. Nor do most of the kids at school."

Diana's mother says in a firm tone, "Diana, you know better than to call Miss Hickman horrible and an adult bully. If you do not like her, that's okay. But, calling her names is not nice. She is quirky. But, she seems okay." She takes a sip of her soda, and then she asks, "Can you tell us why she was upset, that is if you do not mind us knowing?"

Diana fully understands what is happening here as she noisily sucks on her straw. She is drawing into her mouth what's left of the delicious cream soda. Her parents are playing the *good cop, good cop* routine. That is what she and her younger brother, Billy, call their parents' questioning routine. Her parents never get angry when they cross-examine her. Diana sometimes wishes they'd play the *good cop, bad cop* routine instead. She could handle that much better than both of her parents being pleasant at the same time.

She appreciates that their questioning routine is their way of handling domestic issues in an affable manner. And she knows it is a whole lot better than one of them being the bad cop, being angry and yelling like other kids' parents. Just the same, the psychological make-up of their routine drives her crazy. She simply cannot say no to their questioning. Therefore, she nearly always gives in and she usually tells everything when the good cop, good cop ploy is in play.

She supposes, given all that has happened and Mister Young's threats to expel her, she needs more friends than enemies right now. Besides, her parents have supported her through thick and thin through, what she believed at the time, was the worst crisis of her young life. So, although she has the option of not discussing what happened in Miss Hickman's office, she might as well get it over with here and now. "Besides," she ponders, "they'll probably get wind of it eventually. Then the questioning will be more intense and the consequences less forgiving."

With a deliberate, long-lasting sigh, she unwillingly says as hurriedly as she can, "Miss Hickman and I got into it."

Much to her relief, her parents do not seem to make a big deal with what she just said. In fact, oddly, their expressions remain passive. They continue to sip their sodas nonchalantly through their straws. She thinks, "Yep, here goes the good cop good cop thingy. It's now in full swing." Her father nods his head for her to continue. She quickly summarizes the encounter she had with Miss Hickman.

"She called me a few names, threatened to beat me up. She talked to me like I was a dog, telling me to sit in a commanding, truly ugly voice. And then she bullied me. She said she would sit me in the chair forcefully if I did not comply. I wanted to remain standing. And, then, as if things could not get any worse, she threatened to punch me in the face." She adds, "Not with her words, but by her actions."

Stunned, but slightly encouraged by the continued passive expressions on her parents' faces, Diana quickly adds, "She nearly leaped across her desk to stand nose to nose with me. That is the reason you heard the loud bang. When she rushed from behind her desk, her chair hit the wall, and then it tipped over onto its side. As you know, the chair hitting the wall made one heckuva racket after Miss Hickman shoved it."

Her mother glances at her phone. She says, "Your brother, Billy just texted me. He wants to stay overnight with one of his friends." She looks at Diana's father. "I'm going to text him that it's okay if we do not have anything planned tonight. His friend's mother will drive him to the house to get his things." Diana's dad nods his head in agreement. As Diana's mother texts Billy, she resumes addressing her.

"So, Diana, we have plenty of time to hear you out. And we might as well do it here. This place is as good as any. As we just said, we believe you and, more importantly, we are here for you. As your parents, we need to know the facts, that is all. The more we know, the more you can tell us, the better we can support you."

Diana's father says, "And the better off you will be after all of this is behind you." With a serious expression on his face, he adds, "And I hope you realize you should not take Mister Young's threats of detention and expulsion lightly. Despite all that has happened up till now, something is nagging me. Something doesn't smell right. In my view, your principal overreacted and based his threats on innuendos in a letter supposedly written by one of your peers. That was obvious to me.

"We trust you and believe what you say is true. We know you can be mischievous at times." He puckers his lips and squishes his nose just as he smiles a playful smirk as he adds, "Be that as it may, your mother and I are one hundred percent certain you did not do the things mentioned in that letter." He looks at Diana's mother. She nods her head in agreement. "So, continue with your story about Miss Hickman if you please." He suddenly raises his hand to get Bonnie's attention.

"Three more Italian cream sodas over here, if you please. And another order of fries for Diana too. There is no rush. Whenever you get a chance is okay. Thank you, Bonnie."

Diana continues telling her side of the story, about the way Miss Hickman threatened her. She has not yet mentioned that she lectured Miss Hickman about her bullying. She wants to get all of Miss Hickman's scornful actions out at the outset. Better yet, maybe she will not have to mention how she goaded Miss Hickman on in the first place. She begins to summarize the most dramatic parts of the encounter.

After a few minutes, she says, "So, that's pretty much it. Miss Hickman had curled her hand into a fist and then she shook it in front of my face like this." She imitates Miss Hickman's threatening actions by shaking her fist a couple of inches in front of her nose.

"Then she threatened me again by saying that she knew where I lived, that she had friends. Miss Hickman ended her threats saying, 'You know of whom I'm talking. You know them from your former filthy life,' or similar words.'" She adds with a dismissive wave of her hand, "Obviously, I am paraphrasing here. I cannot recall her exact words. All I know is that they were very offensive."

Diana's mother says to Diana's father, "That's horrible. I have heard rumors from the other moms that Miss Hickman is somewhat of a bully, but I never dreamed she was that nasty." She looks at Diana, saying, "Well, it is your word against hers. We will have to wait and see what Mister Young does about the encounter you had with Miss Hickman, that is if anything comes of it."

Her father says, "Just the same, coupled with Mister Young's nasty attitude in his office and Miss Hickman's threats, something doesn't feel right." He taps his temple with his forefinger. "My noggin is telling me that something fishy is going on. None of this makes any sense." Then, as an afterthought, he says, "Too bad there weren't any witnesses."

Diana looks up from her phone. While the three of them were talking, she was randomly deleting unwanted photos from her phone that she took while they were at the museum.

She whispers, "But, Dad, there *was* a witness."

Her mother and father sit upright in their chairs. Once again, they look at each other just as they say simultaneously, "There was? Who?"

"Reg."

Her mother asks with an incredulous tone, "Regina was there?" She looks at Diana's father adding, "Why in the world would Regina be there in Miss Hickman's office? Her being there doesn't make any sense. Jack had dismissed her at least a half-hour before Diana joined us."

Diana's father hunches his shoulders. He says, "Beats me. But, it is quite strange to have Diana's accuser sitting right outside the door while you and I were in Mister Young's office." He looks at Diana.

"And while Diana was outside the principal's office. Diana, what do you think?"

Diana says, "Well, I did mention, while we were in Mister Young's office, that Reg had been in Miss Hickman's office. I guess you didn't hear me. Anyway, please give me a second or two to think about it."

Diana firmly believes that her parents suspect there is more to her story than what she has told them. And, of course, there is. She tries a delaying tactic. She hopes if she can delay long enough they will move onto another topic or something will occur to change the subject.

She nods her head as she looks around the café, pretending to be mulling over her answer to her dad's question. She tears off the end of the straw's paper wrapper and pushes a bit of the wrapper down the straw. Next, she puts the exposed part of the straw in her mouth and aims the straw at the napkin holder. She gently blows into the straw. When the paper wrapper hits the napkin holder dead on, she clenches her fist and whispers, "Gotcha!" She plops the straw into her second glass of cream soda.

She continues to pretend that she is pondering her father's question. She looks at the ceiling and then she examines the tablecloth. She even looks at the floor. She truly wishes all of this would go away, to disappear out the door like the handsome teenager who just exited the café. Regrettably, out of the corner of her eye, she cannot help but notice that her parents are staring at her. It is obvious they are patiently waiting for her to answer her father's question.

At last, she says, "Well, I have a theory. It could be far-fetched, but it is all I must go on at this point. You see." Before she can finish her sentence, her father interrupts.

"Sorry to interrupt you. A thought just occurred to me while you were doing everything under the sun to delay replying to my question. Earlier, you mentioned that Miss Hickman and you, as you put it, 'got into it.'" With a crafty smile and a few nods of his head, he adds, "So, for the two of you, as you said, to get into it, there must have been two sides of the conversation." He looks Diana squarely in the eye. "I do believe that you have left out an important part of your conversation with Miss Hickman. Perhaps you said something that angered her? Am I correct?"

Diana stares at the table in disbelief and thinks, "Darn, he's good!" She slowly nods her head. Then, she whispers a scarcely perceptible reply.

"Yes, Dad, there is, and yes, you are correct. I did leave out a few things. I am sorry to admit it." She looks up. With sad-looking eyes and her lips forming a pretend pout, she adds, "Promise you won't get mad?"

Her father does not reply. He crosses his arms over his chest. With a somber look, he says, "Okay, dear, spill the beans." He glances at Diana's mother and adds in a firm tone, "We're listening."

Diana begins to narrate rather rapidly what she had said that made Miss Hickman angry.

"I did not want to sit because Reg was balling her eyes out as she sat in the chair. As I mentioned earlier, I wanted to stand. The only available chair in that detestable, foul-smelling, perfume-infused office was right next to Reg's. Reg had already glared at me with hateful eyes. So, there was no way I was going to sit next to her.

"I was not certain what was going on. But I knew whatever it was that was happening, it had everything to do with me. After Miss Hickman insulted me, ordering me to sit in the chair like I was a dog, and threatening to push me in the chair if I didn't," Diana breathes in deeply, "I said a few nasty things to her."

She pauses a few seconds to catch her breath. She knows she is talking faster than normal, but she cannot help herself. She is nervous, not so much because she's afraid of restating what she said to Miss Hickman. The nasty woman deserved everything that she said to her, and more. She is nervous because she has never in her life insulted a grownup. And she does not want to disappoint her parents.

"After all," she thinks, "they brought me up to be respectful of others. And, up until today, I have."

"Go on," her father says in an understanding voice. "But, take your time." He smiles. "And try not to leave anything out. It could be important."

Diana inhales deeply, and then she exhales very slowly. With a nervous tone of voice, she says "Okay. Okay. I told Miss Hickman that

I hated the way she pronounced my name. She had said, 'Bow-wow-wow-eeerrr.'" Her mother interrupts.

"She said our last name like that, with a *bow-wow-wow?* Like a dog barking?"

"Yes ma'am, she did," Diana replies. "She always draws out our last name when she pronounces it. In fact, my friends have timed it. It's four seconds long." Tears well up in her eyes. "But that was the first time she had said it like she was barking like I had a dog's last name or something like that. I was stunned!" She wipes the corners of her eyes with a paper napkin. "And, as you can imagine, I was both upset and angry. I wanted to smack her!" She takes a few deep breaths to calm her emotions.

After a few moments, she says, "Okay, I'm good. Then Miss Hickman said that she did not like me, that I'm all that, trying to be pretty and all. Also, and I'm saying this as honestly as I know how, I did not yell, insult, or disrespect her at that point. I simply told her how badly I felt after she insulted me.

"I asked her why she did not like me. She did not reply. I asked her why she made fun of our last name when she pronounced it. She did not reply. Then, I thought of all my classmates who she had bullied over the years."

Diana hesitates for a moment, and then she says, "Then I mimicked her squeaky, high-pitched voice saying things like, and I'm paraphrasing here, 'Tie your shoelaces and stop talking so loudly. Don't fool around in the halls. Why aren't you wearing a bra?' I'm pretty certain I said other things like that. It's just that I cannot remember all of them. I was very upset. Then she called me a something or other brat and leaped from behind her desk to threaten me as I mentioned a few moments ago.'"

Diana's father says in a hushed tone, "Well, Diana, the fact that Miss Hickman scolds the students for being out of line, is no reason for you to scold her in return, to insult her. As a school employee, she has every right to scold students. If you think about it, although you do not like what she does, it is not your business to correct her. Do you understand what I am saying?"

Diana lowers her eyes, and as she nods her head, she replies in a whisper, "Yes, sir, she does have every right, and yes, you are correct." She slowly shakes her head as she looks up at her father. "But, Dad she is a bully. Sure, other teachers and staff scold us, but not in a mean way. Miss Hickman belittles us. She goes out of her way during the change of classes, before school and after school to insult us. Every. Single. Day. She likes to berate students in front of their classmates until they feel crummy. I avoid her as much as I can. I hate the way she messes with our last name!"

Her father says in a calming tone, "Yes, I know, and I am not defending her actions one bit. But, so that you know, it is not your place to tell her what she can or cannot do. She is an adult and in a position of authority. Scolding her and anyone else in a similar position of authority is wrong. You know that. You should have told your guidance counselor or your teacher." He looks at Diana's mother. "Or us."

Diana begins to protest. She stops as soon as her father shakes his finger at her.

"Don't get me wrong, Diana. I too am insulted by the way she treated you. I take it personally as should you." He looks at Diana's mother. "I bet your mother does as well." Her mother nods her head.

Her mother says in a whisper, "Yes, I take it personally, but I truly feel bad for you, Diana, that you were insulted by Miss Hickman."

Her father says, "Anyhow, I needed to get that out in the open. Miss Hickman had no right to insult you the way she did. More importantly, she was wrong to threaten you. In due time, your mother and I will address her threatening actions with the school officials. And while you were understandably upset, you should have come to us. The fact that you insulted her may have created more problems. I am thankful that your friend, Regina, was there as a witness." He pauses for a few moments in thought as he taps his lips with his finger. "Okay, tell us what happened after that."

Diana says, "Well, as she was pointing her finger a few inches from my nose, I looked down and saw that she had clenched her other hand into a fist." She exhales sharply. "So, I dared her to hit me." Much to her relief, her parents chuckle rather than getting angry at her.

Her father says as he continues to chuckle, "You dared her to hit you? That is too funny." He looks at Diana's mother. He says with a proud expression, "We admire our daughter with her courageous warrior spirit. Good for you for standing up to her, my brave warrior, Diana."

Diana's spirits seem to rise noticeably. A slight smile appears on her face.

She says, "Yes, and then, well, I insulted her yet again. I'm sorry that I did. I know I should not have done it. But I did. I told her if she even so much as touched me with her bony finger, I would scream bloody murder or words to that effect."

Her father says with a smile, "Well, I am glad you admitted that you insulted her." He laughs. "There's hope for you yet." He stares at his fingers as he wiggles them. With a chuckle, he says, "But, I have to say I agree with you. Miss Hickman's fingers are rather bony. So, come to think of it, maybe what you said wasn't an insult after all."

Diana's mother smacks him on the shoulder with the side of her hand. She laughs, saying, "Don't say that." Diana laughs as well. She sighs deeply as she silently thanks her dad for trying to inject a bit of humor into their otherwise depressing conversation.

Her father says, "Oops, sorry. I guess I should practice what I preach or, at the minimum, keep my thoughts to myself." He wiggles his fingers yet again and chuckles. Once he regains his composure, he says in a serious tone, "So, Diana, what did Regina do, what did she say, if anything, while you and Miss Hickman were standing toe to toe?"

Diana says with a smile, "I am pleased to say Reg came to my defense. Given the setting in the room, her crying and all and seeming to loathe me, and Miss Hickman bullying me, I was very happy that she did. I was also very relieved. While I could be wrong, Miss Hickman appeared ready to hit me. If she had, I would have had to defend myself, and for sure, they would have suspended me for fighting. Worse, she would have probably lied by saying I started the fight. I'm glad Reg stood up for me. She is powerfully strong." She giggles, saying, "After Reg threatened her, Miss Hickman ran out of her office like a dog with its tail tucked between its hind legs."

She thinks inwardly, "So, bow, wow, wow to you, Miss Hickman! Hah!"

Her father asks, "What did Regina do and say? How did she defend you?"

Diana says, "Literally, she told Miss Hickman to shut up. Then she supported me by saying that she agreed with me, that Miss Hickman *was* a bully. She stood up and stared down at Miss Hickman. And then she said to Miss Hickman, 'I will beat you to a pulp if you even lay a finger on her.' She had added, 'in self-defense, naturally.' That's Reg's favorite expression when someone ticks her off, beating someone to a pulp. She's one tough girl. She also said she would be my witness too.'" Diana pauses, and then she says, "That is if Miss Hickman were to hit me."

Her father asks, "Did she say anything else?"

Diana feels like she is going to burst into tears. But, she manages to hold her emotions in check. She looks at her father, and then she looks at her mother. As tears well up in her eyes, she says in a barely audible whisper, "Yes, Dad, Mom. Reg said that she hated me."

Diana's mother slumps back in her chair. She says in a soft tone, "Regina said that she hated you? Regina is one of your closest friends. She's your team's pitcher. You two seem to get along fine. I cannot believe she said that. I wonder what made her say such a terrible thing to a friend, to you?"

"That is what is so confusing," Diana says, "She and I do get along. And the fact that she came to my defense when Miss Hickman threatened to punch me seems to confirm that we are friends. But she said she hated me. It hurts to even think about it."

"Why would she hate you if you are close friends?" Diana's father asks. "Do you have any idea?"

As Diana considers her father's question, she fiddles with her straw. She places her thumb on the top of the straw. Then, she withdraws her straw from the soda and releases her thumb. She chuckles as the soda rushes back into her drink. After repeating her actions with the straw two more times, she looks up at her father.

"Well, I think it might have something to do with the softball championship game as I mentioned in Mister Young's office."

She suddenly sits up in her chair nearly knocking her cream soda onto its side. She manages to grab the glass before it falls over. She quickly dabs with her napkin at a few drops of soda that had splashed onto the tablecloth.

"It all makes sense now, well, sort of anyway. How Miss Hickman insulted me. How Reg seemed to hate me. The fact that she was crying like her heart was breaking. The fact that she even mentioned that I was going to say terrible things about her father, Mister Reynolds. She even touched on the softball tournament. The way Mister Young seemed to, as you said, Dad, overreact when he said he would punish me. How he had said that if I even mentioned the ladies' softball championship tournament and Mister Reynolds at school, I would be in trouble.

"And, you are not going to believe this. Just before Reg left Miss Hickman's office, Mister Young told her not to repeat something that the two of them had discussed in private! He even placed his finger on his lips to shush her, as if he was stressing that Reg should not talk about whatever it was."

She looks at her mother, and then at her father. "And, if you will recall, Mister Young even admitted when we were in his office that he had a private conversation with Reg. He said Miss Hickman was present as a witness."

"Talk about what?" her dad asks. "What was it that Mister Young told Regina not to talk about, Diana? Do you know?"

Diana plops down in her chair. "Talk about their secret, Dad. The two of them share a secret. And I bet Miss Hickman is in on their secret as well. I had told Reg that having a secret with a school official was not proper." She purses her lips. "And, I will bet my life on this. I bet that their little three-way secret has everything to do with the ladies' softball championship game!"

Diana's mother asks, "How's that?"

Diana replies, "Because, during the game, I was going to question Mister Reynolds' call when Sally, she's from the other team, slid into home. I thought she was safe. She had protested, and I was going to protest as well." She pauses, and then she says, "And if you will recall,

Mister Reynolds ejected Sally from the game. She is their star hitter. If she were to remain in the game, I doubt we would have won.

"And, as much as I hate to admit it, I think the pitch that the pitcher made when I was at bat, the one that came on the three and two counts, was a strike. I wouldn't bet my life on it, but it sure looked like a strike to me. I even started walking away from the plate thinking it was a strike. I was certain I had struck out."

Her father reaches out to pat her on the hand. He says, "If it helps to make you feel better, I think that the pitch you mentioned was a ball. It was close, but a ball. I'm sure of it. It was at least two or three inches outside the plate. And, I'm not saying this because you are my daughter. If it were a strike, I would have told you that. I wouldn't lie to you to make you feel good.

"Your mother and I were sitting almost directly behind home plate. We had an unobstructed view of the batter's box. Most of Mister Reynolds' calls were right on the mark. Yes, a few were questionable, but that's the way it is in softball, football, etcetera. The process by which refs and umps make calls is not a scientific process. We end up getting what we get unless, of course, there is visual proof like in video replays. Sadly, umpires and referees making mistakes and missed calls are part of the game. While the questionable calls may get team members and fans riled up, they add to the games' excitement."

Diana laughs as she says, "Yep, I remember. You and Mom were sitting behind home plate making me more nervous than usual when I was catching." With a sarcastic tone, she adds, "And gibbering about the umpire and opposing team's coach far too much for my liking."

Her father says with a laugh, "Sorry about that. But when I attend one of your softball games, I want to pretend I'm the ump too. As far as the gibbering goes, it's all part of the game. Even if us fans don't go out of our way to offend someone or to insult the players, I must state emphatically. Coaches and umps are fair game." He laughs. "Irate fans make the game even more fun. We want our team to win!"

Her father scratches his head in thought. He says, "And, yes, now that you mention it, I recall that you were pulling on Mister Reynolds' shirtsleeve after Sally slid into home plate. You were acting like you wanted to say something to him while she was protesting. But, Coach stopped you. I remember Coach was jumping up and down like crazy to get your attention. It is probably a good thing you did not protest. Mister Reynolds could have thrown you out of the game as well." He smiles, and then, with a twinkle in his eyes and a purposely slow wink of his right eye, he adds, "And who would have won us the ladies' championship softball game if Mister Reynolds had ejected its MVP?"

Diana says in a happy tone, "Thank you for saying that, Dad. It makes me happy knowing you think that way. And yes, some of it seems to make sense now. Mister Reynolds throws the game in our favor because his daughter is on the team." She pauses. "Or, Mister Reynolds does not throw the game, and he simply makes some questionable calls." She smiles. "After all, the poor man does wear the thickest glasses in the Universe.

"Then again, would Mister Young go to all these extremes to have a ladies' softball championship trophy in the cabinet outside his office? Honestly, would he try to coerce Reg and Miss Hickman to keep falsehoods?"

Diana purposely snaps her head backward as she slumps in her chair. She shakes her head and rolls her eyes. As she looks at the ceiling tiles, she says, "It is all too confusing to me. And it doesn't add up, doesn't make sense. I only hope Coach isn't in on whatever it is that is going on. But, one thing I know for certain, Mister Young and Reg have a secret between them. The two of them practically admitted it in my presence! And Miss Hickman may be in on the secret as well."

"Whew, that's a lot to digest," Diana's mother says. She looks at Diana's father. "What should we do about it?"

"I have no clue," Diana's father replies. He noisily sucks on his straw to finish off what remains of his Italian cream soda. He studies the check. Then he pulls three bills from his wallet and places them on the table. He covers the bills with the check.

He exclaims, "Nope, it is all too confusing for me to digest on an empty stomach. Let's go somewhere to eat!" He looks at Diana, and then with a hearty laugh, he says, "And Diana, let's splurge. Your mother's treating us!"

As they head toward the exit, Diana's mother winks at her as she silently mouths.

"No way!"

CHAPTER SIX

DEEP IN THE FOREST

Part I: Training Begins

Just as they enter the edge of the clearing, I Dunno exclaims with a broad smile, "This Diana practice place." She points. "See that over there? Diana shoots arrows there."

Diana looks across the vast expanse of the clearing. All that she sees are row after row of trees lining the perimeter of the clearing.

She says, "I'm sorry, I Dunno. But, I do not see any place that I can shoot arrows. All I see are trees. If I shoot my arrows at trees, I will not be able to remove them. Even if I could remove them from the trees, they would be unusable. You don't want me to shoot at trees, do you?"

"No shoot at trees," I Dunno replies. She points once more. "Over there, see?"

Diana narrows her eyes as she looks in the direction I Dunno is pointing. Way off in the distance, perhaps ninety yards away, Diana can barely make out a makeshift target. The target is a tight circle made of freshly picked green leaves attached to a heaping mound of dried grass. Two stubby rotten tree stumps are on either side of the mound of grass.

I Dunno struggles to pull an arrow from Diana's quiver that is leaning against a tree. Once she gets the arrow, she flies lopsidedly with the weight of the arrow to Diana.

Diana watches as her protector pixie fights to fly in a straight line. She says with a laugh, "What in the world are you doing?" She reaches out to grab the arrow from I Dunno. "Here, give that to me. It's much too heavy for you."

I Dunno hands the arrow to Diana. She mumbles in her pipsqueak voice, "Not too heavy like longbow and sword." She immediately turns in the air to retrieve Diana's longbow. Once again, with the longbow in her hand nearly touching the ground, she is flying lopsided as she tries to stay aloft. Diana rushes over to grasp the longbow.

She cries, "What in the world are you doing, I Dunno? I do not want to see you struggling like that."

I Dunno points to the improvised target way off in the distance. She says, "Diana shoot an arrow with Diana longbow. Hit that."

Diana laughs. "I am sorry to say this, but I cannot hit that target. It is too far away. I'll end up losing my arrow." She looks at the far-flung target, and then she says, "I'm not that good." She starts to walk slowly toward the target.

I Dunno flies from Diana's side to hover a foot or so in front of Diana's face as she walks. I Dunno stretches her tiny arm full-length in front of her with the palm of her hand facing Diana. She is gesturing for Diana to stop walking.

She whispers in her small voice, "No, no, Diana, no walk, please. Hit that." She points behind her to the target. Then, as she points to where Diana is standing, she says, "From here. I Dunno ask Diana nicely because I Dunno give Diana magic powers, good eyesight and wonderful hearing." As her tiny lips form a heartbreaking pout, she asks in a sad tone, "Diana trust I Dunno, yep?"

Diana quickly replies, "Of course I trust you." She looks at the target adding, "But, I seriously doubt I will get anywhere near the target. I'll lose my arrow in the trees for sure."

"Try, Diana, please? You do good. Arrow do good. I Dunno give you magic."

Diana sighs. "Okay, I Dunno, I will give it a try to make you happy. Please move aside. I do not want to hit you accidentally."

As I Dunno moves to hover to Diana's side once more, Diana carefully places the arrow on the bowstring. She sights down the shaft of the arrow to the faraway target. As she strains to see the target, she wishes that the light from Domum was a bit brighter. Just the same, shooting an arrow out here in the open is much better than shooting an arrow inside the forest. She'd be in a world of hurt if she tried to shoot an arrow accurately in the dim light of the forest. She breathes in deeply, and then she slowly exhales. As she lets the arrow fly, she says a silent prayer that the arrow will not disappear amongst the dense undergrowth of the forest.

She suddenly screams, "Oh, my God, I Dunno! I hit the target, a bullseye! I cannot believe this." She quickly walks to remove another arrow from her quiver. She is now standing at a twenty-degree angle from the target. She crouches down on her knees. After carefully sighting the arrow along the arrow's shaft, she lets the arrow fly. It is not another bullseye, but it is close!

She continues to shoot arrows at the target until she uses all twenty arrows in her quiver. Every one of her arrows had impacted the target dead center or just to the right of center. I Dunno flies to land on Diana's shoulder as Diana walks to the target. After she retrieves her arrows from the target and places them in her quiver, Diana sits on the grass. She rummages in her rucksack for something to eat. As she eats, she hands I Dunno small portions of her food. The two of them tell stories to pass the time.

I Dunno points across the field to where Jayvyn is grazing. She says, "Next shoot, you stay there. Jayvyn and I Dunno come here to get arrows. Too much Diana walk."

Diana replies, "It's okay, I Dunno, I do not mind walking. It feels good to be off Jayvyn's back for a while." She rubs the inner sides of her upper thighs adding with a grin, "Besides, my thighs and butt are sore."

She continues practicing with her longbow. After hitting the target spot-on forty more times, two full quivers worth, Diana exclaims, "I Dunno, I don't know about you, but I'm bushed. I need to take a nap. Do you?"

"No, Diana not sleep here," I Dunno replies. "Too unsafe. Diana must go there to the forest. Much safer in the forest."

Diana does not look forward to reentering the dimness of the murky forest. She says, "Well, perhaps we can wait a little while longer before we rest. I think I'll swing my sword a few times to get the hang of it."

Next, with I Dunno sitting on her shoulder, she walks to where Jayvyn is grazing. She breaks off a piece of her banapple and feeds it to Jayvyn. He greedily accepts it and immediately sniffs at Diana's rucksack for more. She opens her rucksack to get another banapple. She is pleasantly surprised to see that I Dunno has magically replaced the banapple she and Jayvyn just ate with a fresh one. She moves the fresh piece of fruit aside and takes the one below it. She removes the banapple from her rucksack, breaks it in two, and then she gives Jayvyn half. After he finishes his half of the magical fruit, Jayvyn saunters off to renew his grazing.

Diana has never handled a sword until now. So, she has no idea how to start practicing. She picks it up and immediately swings it in all directions. She looks like an overzealous Ninja warrior as she thrusts the sword up and down as she whirls in circles. It is as if she is fighting dozens of imaginary foes at once.

I Dunno hastily flies from her shoulder yelling frantically, "No, Diana. You get I Dunno and Diana killed. I Dunno show Diana sword stuff." She flies off to grab a tiny stick from the ground. She says, "Diana watch I Dunno. Diana do good. Sword do good." She laughs. "So Diana no kill us."

Over the course of the next several hours, I Dunno patiently shows Diana the different techniques for wielding a sword against a foe. First, she teaches Diana the most basic move, the lunge. The lunge involves what is called a feint. A feint is a tricking maneuver. It involves purposely lunging forward against an opponent. This purposeful action causes the opponent to attack first. This move often causes him or her to make a mistake or to be off balance. Diana practices the lunge and feint move against a make-believe opponent until she is very adept at employing them.

Next, I Dunno teaches Diana the disengage and circle-parry techniques. When practicing these techniques, Diana acts like she is going to attack a different make-believe target behind her. The pretending attack is the disengaging part of the procedure. Then, as she moves in a semi-circle arc, she attacks the original make-believe opponent with the circle-parry technique. Once again, Diana practices these offensive moves until I Dunno thinks she has mastered them sufficiently enough.

I Dunno also demonstrates defensive moves, such as the ripstop counterattack, lunge, and the circle parry move from a defensive perspective. The defensive circle parry move is employed to catch the top of the attacker's sword or weapon and deflect it. I Dunno says she doubts Diana will encounter an opponent with a sword. On the other hand, because someone could attack her with a stick, she wants Diana to know the defensive circle parry move. In retrospect, it is fortunate that I Dunno taught her this maneuver. We will discover why later in Diana's journey.

Diana's muscles are sore after hours of practicing with her sword. She is also sweating profusely. She drinks from her waterskin for the longest time. After she sets the half-empty container on the ground, she notices that it slowly refills with clean, fresh water.

As she tries to catch her breath, she says, "Goodness, I Dunno, you certainly are one amazing pixie." She points to her waterskin. "Not only can you refill my waterskin with fresh water, but you also replaced banapples I have eaten with fresh ones. You taught me how to make illumination and how to shoot accurately over a long distance. And now, you have just taught me how to defend myself using my sword. How can I ever repay you?"

I Dunno replies, "No need for Diana to repay I Dunno. I Dunno happy Diana can use longbow and arrow and sword." She chuckles adding, "Diana does not forget. Diana now can use sword offensively too."

Diana laughs. Then she says, "You are correct, I Dunno. I'm good with the sword. However, I do believe I'm a better archer than a wielder of the sword." Then, she ponders silently, "And look at you, I Dunno. Your vocabulary is quickly improving as time goes by."

I Dunno winks. She has read Diana's mind. She says, "Thank you, Diana. I Dunno trying to speak like Empress Diana. Only wish I Dunno voice was stronger." She laughs. "Like yours."

A little while later, the threesome reenters the forest. I Dunno flies ahead in search of a suitable camping spot as Diana leads Jayvyn along the trail. She is not yet ready to mount Jayvyn. Walking seems to help lessen the soreness she is feeling in her legs. After walking for what seems to Diana like an eternity, but was a little over an hour, I Dunno returns. She is yelling enthusiastically.

"I found it, Diana. The perfect sleep place for we."

Diana is about to correct I Dunno's grammar, but she decides not to. She believes I Dunno is quickly learning proper grammar on her own through the exchange of words with her. A split-second after she thinks this, I Dunno exclaims, "It okay, Diana. You teach me well." She pauses as she mulls over in her mind what she is going to say next. "Yes, the perfect place for us, not we, to sleep, right? See, I Dunno learn lots thanks to Diana."

Diana laughs, and then she asks, "So, where is this perfect place for us to sleep?"

I Dunno points along the trail. "Not too far. The cozy spot is next to large, how do you say, stones?"

Diana replies, "If they are very large like this," she stretches her arms out wide, "then they are called boulders. Itsy-bitsy boulders are called stones, like this." She makes a circle with her thumb and forefinger. "Rocks are assorted dimensions in the middle of boulders and stones in size. Does that make sense?"

"Yes, makes sense to I Dunno." I Dunno stretches her arms out wide. "They be much big than this. They are boulders!"

With an amused expression, Diana says, "If they are as big as the breadth of your arms stretched out wide, they are small rocks to me." I Dunno looks at her questioningly. She laughs. "I'm teasing you I Dunno because you are very small. It's a joke."

I Dunno ponders for a few seconds what Diana has said. Her eyes suddenly brighten with recognition. She laughs, saying, "I Dunno understands Diana's joke." She stretches her arms out wide once more. "My arms like this are boulders, but to Diana, they are small rocks." She makes a tiny circle with her thumb and forefinger. "And these to I Dunno are stones, but to Diana, they are, how do you say, pebbles?"

Diana roars with laughter. She beckons for I Dunno to set down in her cupped hands. She gives the sweet pixie a delicate, loving kiss on her forehead. She says in a whisper, "Yes, the size of your circle would mean they are pebbles to me. But, I must say, pebbles are adorable just like you. Because, as the saying goes, *good things come in small packages."*

After walking for a few minutes, they arrive at the camping spot I Dunno had selected. Diana figures this spot is as good as it gets. She compliments I Dunno for finding the perfect spot.

I Dunno says, "Thank you, Diana. But not too hard to find. It is along the trail. Diana could find it too."

A grouping of boulders ranging in mass from the size of wheelbarrows to small cars is set back in the forest. The boulders are about twenty feet from the trail. The setting will provide adequate shelter on three sides. It will also enable Diana and I Dunno to have a clear view of anyone or anything walking on the trail.

Diana says, "I like this spot. Maybe we can make a campfire. Then again, my magical light can provide adequate illumination." She contemplates what she just said. "Then again, maybe it's best that we do not allow others to know our location." She whispers, "I Dunno, how do I extinguish my light?"

"Oh, that easy," I Dunno replies. "Diana say *extinctus*. It old word for extinguish. Then to turn light on once more, Diana says lux magicae like before, but with the proper accent."

Diana says, "Extinctus." Her magical light disappears. Then she says, "Lux magicae." Nothing happens.

I Dunno giggles. "Oops. I Dunno forgot." She cups her hands. "Diana must do this with Diana's hands."

"Oh, that makes sense," Diana replies. She cups her hands and says again, "Lux magicae." Her magical light appears in the palms of her hands. She throws it up in the air where it comes to rest slightly above her head.

*****

Part II: Inania and Aegolius

While Diana and I Dunno eat, they discuss many topics. Diana tells I Dunno some of her best-kept secrets. Naturally, since she is Diana's protector pixie, I Dunno knows just about everything there is to know about Diana, her family, and her friends. However, unlike in the World Beyond, where she can read Diana's mind and interpret her dreams, I Dunno is unable to do the same on earth. So, unsurprisingly, I Dunno is spellbound with Diana's sharing of her secrets, a few of her most inner thoughts and intimate girl-talk topics.

After a bit of time, Diana says in an inquiring manner, "Okay, now, I Dunno. I told you some of my secrets. So, what about you and your secrets. Do you have any secrets you would like to share?"

"No, Diana, not really. I Dunno does not think about anything but how to keep Diana safe, both here and at home." She pauses for a few moments, and then, as her expression becomes unhappy and teeny tears well up in her lovely eyes, she says, "This is I Dunno's number one secret. Sometimes I Dunno cry for Diana. When Diana is sad, you know?" Diana nods her head in understanding.

She says, "Yes, I understand what you are suggesting. But, that's all behind me now. I am much stronger, wiser, and more self-confident, quick to recover from others' boorish slights. Never again will I allow others to belittle me, or to make fun of my friends." She scoops I Dunno into the palm of her hand. Then she tenderly tucks her into the crook of her arm. She lovingly looks at her protector pixie and says, "So, I Dunno, where were you born? When were you born?"

I Dunno's expression turns to one of deep thought. "You know, Diana, I Dunno is not sure. Perhaps, I was born when you were born. That makes perfect sense to me."

Diana abruptly cries, "Oh, my goodness, I Dunno. Did you notice what you just said?"

I Dunno shakes her head. She replies, "No, I did not notice. What did I say?"

Diana laughs happily, and then she says, "I am very excited and happy for you. You used the pronouns *I* and *me* when referring to yourself. You also used the pronoun *you* when referring to me. Your grammar is nearly perfect. That this is happening is very coolio!"

With a bewildered look, I Dunno whispers, "I did? Is it? I do not know what a pronoun is. But wait for a second here! Look, Diana, look at me. I just said *I* again and again and *me* too!" She giggles adding in a happy tone, "I talk just like you now." Then, with a made-up pout, she adds, "But, my voice is still falsetto, not nice to listen to like yours."

Diana kisses I Dunno on her forehead. She says lightheartedly in a singsong voice, "Golly gee, I love thee, my protector pixie!"

I Dunno blushes. She says in a likewise singsong voice, "Yepity, yep, yep! I love Diana too. Yep, I do!"

After a bit of ensuing frivolity related to I Dunno's grasp of proper grammar, I Dunno changes the subject. She begins to tell Diana what she knows about Mendacium and his wicked allies. None of what she knows is firsthand knowledge. Most of what she knows comes from tall tales and legends of the World Beyond. But what she knows will be enough to make Diana shiver. I Dunno starts off by narrating scary folklore stories about the terrible creature Aegolius.

To hear I Dunno describe it, the Aegolius essentially is an other-worldly creature. It is amazingly similar in appearance to a barn owl in the Real-world, except it is more than twice the size of the owl. It also does not have a true physical form. It is more like a shimmering apparition.

The Aegolius has unblinking yellow eyes that purportedly can see objects across far-flung distances. It can even see through rocks and trees. Legends claim that if one were to stare into the Aegolius' eyes for more than a glance, one would become petrified. Then, supposedly, the Aegolius would feast on the victim's body once it gradually began to return to its original state. All the while, the victim, although partially turned into stone, would be conscious the entire time.

With a scowl on her face and a disgusted tone in her voice, Diana says, "That is gross, and sickeningly tormenting for the victim. I hope we do not come across an Aegolius."

I Dunno says, "No, I Dunno neither. If Diana sees one, do not look into the Aegolius' eyes." She continues to describe other characteristics of the beast.

In addition to the Aegolius' evil eyes that can turn unsuspecting victims to stone, the beast is also astonishingly strong. Using its curved, foot-long, sharp talons, it can snatch the heaviest of prey and carry it to wherever it wants. Sometimes the beast carries the petrified victim to its offspring where the offspring will feast for days on end. More often, however, the Aegolius, particularly the males and females without offspring to feed, will carry the victim to Mendacium.

There, in Mendacium's devious lair, the King of Deceit and the Conveyor of Lies and Falsehoods will metamorphose the victim into an evil creature. Then, through careful encoding and indoctrination, the mutated creature will seek out others to prey on, to lie to or to double cross. Owing to the Aegolius' hatred for honesty and verity, and Mendacium's cunning ways, the cycle of mendacities, treachery and falsehoods spreads far and wide.

"Goodness," Diana says, "I knew from my experiences in my bedroom and the tranquility beam that Mendacium was evil. Charles, James, and April also cautioned me about his betrayal when dealing with honest people. But, I never dreamed Mendacium would transform the Aegolius' victims into hideous creatures to do his bidding."

I Dunno changes the subject to talk about legends involving an evil being called the *Inania*. Inania is a Latin word. In English, Inania means *the Thing*. The Inania, perhaps the most sinful of Mendacium's allies, is both cunning as well as deceptive. It is the evilest, hideous *cacodemon* in the Universe.

I Dunno says, "Just so you know, a cacodemon is an evil spirit, a demon." With a sly smile, she adds, "However, as I know from personal experience something amazing can counter the cacodemon." She curtsies adding with a broad smile, "It is the *agathodaemon*, the opposite of a cacodemon. An agathodaemon is a good spirit or angel." She continues to describe the Inania in detail.

The Inania can assume or replicate whatever it is about to attack. As an example, if it is seeking to attack a fox, it can transmogrify itself into the spitting image of the fox. As a result, the real fox becomes confused and lowers its guard. As soon as the fox puts its defensive instincts to rest, the Inania changes back to its original repulsive form. Then it attacks cruelly. With brute strength, the Inania tears its victim limb from limb until nothing recognizable remains of the victim. Like the Aegolius, the Inania is an unearthly beast, an apparition. Inania's are known to attack inhabitants of the World Beyond frequently.

I Dunno adds with a somber tone, "There is one other aspect of the Inania I should mention. While the beast usually returns to its original form before it attacks, it can also remain as the spitting image of its intended victim. Then, it has the strength, intelligence, even the voice mannerisms of its victim. Fortunately, however, these more advanced Inania are few in numbers."

Diana says, "The Inania is another beast I hope I never encounter. I do not know if I could strike something that looks just like me. That would be most problematic." She adds with a puzzled look, "I Dunno, your mention of other residents in the World Beyond is the first time anyone has mentioned such creatures. I assume they're creatures. Why haven't I seen any other creatures in the World Beyond to date?"

"The reason Diana does not see them, many are supernatural like Charles and April. They only allow Diana to see them if they want to. They are, how do you say, invisible?" Diana nods her head. I Dunno adds, "Nevertheless, there are other creatures, some good, some not so good. Perhaps Diana will encounter some of them as Diana journeys."

After a bit more of gossip, Diana reclines on a bed of dried leaves. It is not as comfortable as her cozy bed at home in the Real-world, but she is exhausted. So, anywhere halfway comfy to sleep on is better than nothing.

I Dunno hops in her pouch. She is snoring in no time. Jayvyn lies down nearby with his back to Diana. She recognizes from her readings about horses that Jayvyn's lying down on his side has one of three goals, maybe even all three at once. He may be on his side because he requires REM sleep after a long day. He may be doing so because he is protecting I Dunno and her. Then again, he may be lying on his side because he wants to feel comfortable or because he likes to.

Diana extinguishes her magical light. The radiance from Domum is barely adequate to illuminate their surroundings in the dense forest. She yawns, and then in a few seconds, she is fast asleep.

Vivid dreams enter her mind. In her dreams, she is a brave warrior fighting evil beasts created by Mendacium. She also dreams about her double at home. Diana's double is worrying about something, something to do with the championship softball game. Her double at home is also fretting about a letter that her good friend Reg supposedly has written. However, Diana in the World Beyond is unable to make out the contents of the letter.

After a while, perhaps five or six hours, Diana snaps wide awake. Something doesn't seem right to her. She feels odd in a strange way as if something is squeezing various parts of her body. She touches her forearm, her chest, and her shoulders.

She suddenly whispers, "I cannot believe this! I dreamed that I was wearing a warrior's outfit, and I am!" She is tempted to turn on her magical light, but she thinks better of it.

"Perhaps it is prudent I don't turn on my magical light. I don't want anyone or anything to know we are here."

The first thing she notices of her warrior outfit is her footwear. She is wearing mid-calf black boots made of leather. Her warrior clothing consists of a sleeveless, warm tunic of a blue-gray color. It falls to her upper thighs. A black sash with gold markings encircles her slim waist. Two black leather sashes run vertically from her right shoulder to the sash that encircles her waist. She has a fluffy black cape which will add to the outfit's warmth on chilly nights. The outfit also comes with a hood. She is wearing black leggings that hug her muscular legs. The warrior outfit is a perfect fit!

She begins to doze off once more. Then, just before all her senses slumber into REM sleep, she hears something in the bushes.

"What is that! It sounds like it is only five or six feet from us!"

She quickly cups her hands and creates her magical light. In a panic, she throws it in the air. At first, she does not believe what she is seeing. She silently watches in awe as the beast a half-dozen feet from her slowly develops from a shimmer of mist into its life-sized form. An unnatural chill in the air accompanies its slowly emerging form. All the while, it is whimpering like a lost child. Just one more deceiving untruth. From I Dunno's description a while ago, she immediately knows what it is.

It is an Inania, a hideous cacodemon born of Mendacium!

She screams out loud, "Oh my God. You are me, at least you look like me! I cannot believe this is happening!" For a brief instant, seeing her mirror image causes her to stare in awe. She instinctively grins as she notices that she is attractively stylish. She looks like a movie star resting comfortably on the bed of leaves. Her long, deep brown hair seemingly flows like a whisper in the gentle breeze. Her brand-new warrior outfit is chic. Its silver highlights are shining ever so delicately on its pitch-black cloths. Her blue-grey eyes are shining more brightly than usual. And there they are, her perfectly round pupils with lightning bolts dancing excitedly!

Unexpectedly, her debonair likeness begins to advance closer inch by inch. Then, the facial expression on the image slowly turns to a venomous look of hatred. Diana promptly realizes that its expression is mirroring her own. She has just met the beast this very instant, one of the evilest creations of Mendacium, and she already loathes it. The repulsed, echoing scowl on the beast's face looking back at her confirms it.

She and The Inania stare at each other for the longest time. Diana slowly unsheathes her sword. She scrambles to her feet. Just as she stands-up, the beast, having now assumed its original devilish form, lunges at her with its hideous, bony arms and hands outstretched threateningly before it.

She takes a step back, and then she whirls in place and lashes at the beast powerfully with her sword like I Dunno had taught her. Just as her sword connects with the nonphysical, spiritual beast, a putrid odor like rotten eggs fills the air. Then, with a look of revulsion accompanied by a horrifying scream of rage, the beast explodes into a cloudburst of pulverized grayish-white dust.

Diana, having met and defeated her first evil soldier of Mendacium, breathes a sigh of relief. She sits down, and then she abruptly starts to tremble. She has courage, with plenty to spare. She knows this. Even so, having met, if only for a few moments, and then killed, something that was her spitting image, was shocking to say the least.

I Dunno, who is wide awake, and who was watching the action from the opening in her pouch, calmly whispers, "One down. A million more to go." Then she slides back into her pouch and is sound asleep in a matter of seconds.

Diana wants to laugh by the way I Dunno coolly reacted to her having slain an Inania. However, she cannot. She still is unsteady from the experience. She decides to keep her magical light glowing. She figures, whatever it is that Mendacium is going to throw at her, she might as well see it coming. Besides, Mendacium's evil cohorts know the three of them are camping in this spot.

"What's the point in extinguishing the light if they know we are here? I feel safer with the light illuminating our surroundings. So, I am going to keep it lit."

Despite the relative ease with which she destroyed the Inania, she continues to tremble for the longest time. A horrid thought crosses her mind as she considers what happened. She whispers, "Goodness, I just killed something." But the awful thought lasts but a few seconds. She knows that the beast was out-and-out evil. It was either her or the beast that would go down, and she was certain that it was not going to be her.

She appreciates, not only was the beast disgusting to look at in its original form, it was as deceitful as I Dunno had said. Having to strike out with a deadly weapon against something that is the mirror image of yourself is, to say the least, incredibly scary. The only reason she did not hesitate to strike out at the beast is clear. She was scared out of her wits. And, when she swung her sword at the beast she kept reminding herself in her mind, "It is not me, it is not me, it is not me!"

She stares into the darkness beyond the gloomy, shadowy influences of her swirling light. She can barely make out two yellow-rimmed, half-moons reflected in the light. From I Dunno's description of the creature, she immediately knows what it is. It is an Aegolius.

She slowly retrieves her longbow from the ground. Then, she silently slips an arrow from its quiver. Having placed the arrow on the bowstring noiselessly, she carefully positions it on the longbow's arrow rest. She slowly draws back the bowstring.

She fully appreciates the misleading realism of twilight when shooting an arrow. Unlike the clarity of daylight, twilight plays tricks on one's depth perception. To further add to the problem, her magical light is casting weird shadows in the surrounding area. She unhurriedly breathes in and out through her pursed lips. Her slow, rhythmic breathing steadies her aim. Just as she is about to let the arrow fly, a voice enters her mind.

"Diana, no. What you are aiming at is an Aegolius. She is evil, almost as evil as Mendacium."

Diana remains motionless. She whispers, "Then, that is all the more the reason that I take her out."

124

"Trust me. Do not strike what you see. If you were to strike the creature and the creature was to die, everyone, everyone that you love and cherish would also die. That includes your companions, I Dunno and Jayvyn, and yes, your beloved Charles."

Diana releases her tension on the bowstring ever so slightly. She whispers, "My family? Charles? I Dunno? Jayvyn? All of my friends back home?"

The voice replies, "Yes, your family. And your friends. Everyone. Even your ghost Charles will vanish from your sight, forever."

"Who are you? How do I know you are not lying to me?"

She ponders what I Dunno had said earlier about the creature Aegolius. I Dunno never mentioned that if someone were to slay the creature, its death would cause harm to others. Then again, she reasons, perhaps I Dunno did not know that part of the legend as it concerns the Aegolius.

She says, "I seriously doubt what you are saying is true. Legends do not speak about the Aegolius' death causing the death of others."

The voice in her mind says, "Trust your instincts, Diana. If you shoot, and she dies, you are to blame for the penalties. If she lives, well, nothing will change. The choice is yours."

Diana slowly lowers her longbow. She says, "I will not risk my family, Charles, my friends and my companions, I Dunno and Jayvyn."

All of a sudden, the voice in her mind cackles mockingly.

"Hahaha, you are weak, Diana. While you may have won the first round, Mendacium has won the second. You and Mendacium are tied 1 and 1. Two more strikes against you and he will win! Hahaha!"

Diana raises her longbow once more. Her eyes search the forest for any sign of the Aegolius. But, the creature has disappeared into the shadowy depths of the forest.

She whispers, "Who are you? Who are you that is entering deceiving thoughts in my mind?"

Before the voice in her mind can reply, in some way she instinctively knows the answer.

James!

CHAPTER SEVEN

SELF-CONTROL

Diana in the Real-world is perched on the edge of her chair as she sits in her principal's office. Her principal is staring at her as he edgily drums his fingers on the surface of his desk.

"Well, Miss Bower, I truly dislike telling you this," Mister Young says, "but I am compelled to discipline you for your infractions as it concerns my secretary, Miss Hickman."

Diana's heart sinks. She begins to question in her mind what Mister Young has said.

"I should have known. I should have seen this coming. When I stood up for myself, I should have expected that I would be the one Mister Young would blame. And to think I thought Mister Young was going to apologize to me for the way Miss Hickman insulted me, threatened me. Why is it the victim always seems to lose?" Mister Young continues droning on in his monotonous voice.

"What you said to Miss Hickman, while uncharacteristic of your behavior, cannot be tolerated."

Diana remains impassive as she sits in the chair. Her thoughts continue to race.

"Well, this comes as no surprise. I should have known Mister Young would believe Miss Hickman's version of the story. Heck, he hasn't even bothered to ask me *my* side of the story! I should get to my feet and leave. And I should slam the door behind me for good measure."

Diana understandably is angry. And, she is disappointed. She wants to trust adults in positions of authority, but by the way Miss Hickman and Mister Young have treated her, she has second thoughts about giving them that trust. As her inner thoughts race in her mind, she is scarcely aware of what Mister Young is saying as his mind-numbing words continue to drone on.

"I run an orderly school here. I expect good discipline and manners always. I will not put up with students causing disruptions of this magnitude in my school."

"Disruptions that students cause? Can't he recognize the person at fault here is his bullying secretary, Miss Hickman? Her persistent bullying and her daily disruptions to peace and harmony in the school are to blame! And why doesn't he talk about the fact that she threatened me? When is he going to ask me about my side of the story? When? And why not? Because she never told him what she said and did to me, that's why not!"

"If I allow your indiscretions to go unpunished, it would be unfair to the other students. Despite your excellent school record, I must be fair and consistent. I would hope you understand."

Diana's thoughts immediately contradict what Mister Young just said.

"I'll tell you about unfairness! What is unfair is that Miss Hickman gets away with bullying every student in this school. Every. Single. Day!"

As she numbly pretends to listen as Mister Young harps on, Diana's conflicting voices of her conscience begin to question her mindset.

The tenacious, argumentative side of her conscience seems to say, "Dang, girl, why don't you speak up and tell him what you're thinking?"

The every day, easygoing, conciliatory side of her conscience immediately replies, "Why? Because he will probably punish you more, that's why! Besides, he will never believe your side of the story, so why bother?"

Mister Young finally concludes his critique.

"So, you leave me no other choice but to discipline you. I have taken your excellent grades and your involvement in extra-curricular activities, plus positive comments from your teachers, into consideration." He looks Diana squarely in the eye as he says, "Do I make myself clear, that you leave me no other choice but to discipline you?"

Diana does not reply. She stares back at Mister Young with an expression of bewilderment.

The tenacious side of her conscience commands, "Goodness, girl! When are you going to fight back? Once he utters his punishment words, it'll be too late. There will be no turning back once he reads the verdict. Fight back, Diana, fight back like you did when Miss Hickman was in your face!"

The easygoing side of her conscience counters once more.

"Why bother to fight back? Nothing is going to change. Mister Young will say yet again it's Miss Hickman's word against yours like he said it was Reg's word against yours. And once more, your word won't count!"

Mister Young glances at the pink-colored disciplinary paper on his desk. He adjusts his glasses.

"So, Miss Bower, what I have decided is this."

Diana suddenly stands up stopping Mister Young in mid-sentence. She wants to run away, run away as far from the principal's office and as quickly as her legs will move. She turns to reach for the doorknob, to escape the confusing madness.

Then, as her expression slowly changes from a look of dread to one of courage, she turns to face her principal. Although her knees are shaking, and she feels faint, she manages to control her emotions. What she has to say bursts forth like staccatos blasting from a vociferous trumpet.

"Sir, please allow me to set the record straight. Miss Hickman started it, not me. She is the one to blame, not me. She threatened me physically. I never threatened her. She called me names. I didn't call her a single name. But I should have. She is a bully.

"You of all people should know that, sir. She works right outside your door. Students have complained. You do nothing. Parents have complained. You do nothing. I am the victim here. Not Miss Hickman. Yes, I admit I should not have said the things to her that I did. But, she deserved it. She insulted me. She always does.

"Don't you know, sir? The woman shook her finger in my face. Then she made a fist and placed it inches from my nose. What kind of faculty member does that to a student? All the while I was standing with my hands by my sides. She threatened to sic unknown people on me. She said she knew where I lived. She said I could not escape her retribution. That she would pay me back for calling her a bully!"

Mister Young raises his hand to stop Diana. She cuts him off before he can even mutter a single word.

"You cannot hide from the truth, sir. And I'll be darned if I will take this and Miss Hickman's abuse and threats lying down. If you punish me, I will fight you to the hilt. I promise I will make our school, Miss Hickman's bullying tactics and the way you turn a blind eye to what's going on, a spectacle the entire town will relish." She looks Mister Young squarely in his eyes.

"I am not threatening you, sir. I promise you. My reputation, my class standing, my school records, my well-being are all at risk here. So, I. Will. Not. Take. This. Lying down! I will fight you till my last breath until you clear me of these deceptive falsehoods!

"As I said, I admit I was wrong for calling Miss Hickman a bully, but it was my way of defending myself. I never got physical. She did. I never clenched my fists. She did. I never pointed my finger close to her face. She did. I never shook my fist in her face. She did. Can you imagine how I felt when Miss Hickman, a school official I'm supposed to trust, threatened to punch me in the face? Can you?"

She pauses to catch her breath. She places her hands on her hips.

"I know what you're thinking, Mister Young. You are thinking yet again, like with Reg's letter, that it's Miss Hickman's word against mine. But, I beg to differ yet again, sir. When you think about it, it's Miss Hickman's word against the word of over fifteen hundred students!" With a sly smile, she says, "Besides, I have a witness. She saw and heard the whole thing."

With a respectful tone, Diana says, "Now, sir, with your permission, I would like to leave. I am very uncomfortable in your office without another person present."

As she turns to leave, Mister Young says in a soft voice, "Miss Bower, please wait." He takes the discipline paper from his desk and crumples it into a ball. He tosses it to the wastebasket. Diana is pleased to see that his aim is off yet again. He misses, and the crumpled paper ball bounces beneath his desk.

While she holds back a laugh, Diana sarcastically muses, "I'm glad you're not on our softball team. We'd never win! Evelyn was right. You wouldn't even qualify as our water boy. You're that pathetic!"

Mister Young says, "Diana, given your testimony here today, I have decided to give you one more chance." He smiles. "You and I can forget that this little meeting never happened. We can put all of it behind us. How's that sound to you?"

Diana shakes her head. She says, "No, sir. With all due respect, I must say this. I will not forget that this meeting has happened. And I will not put what was said, to include my headstrong words, behind us. As soon as I leave your office, I am going to phone my parents and ask them to come and get me."

Mister Young raises his hand in protest. He says, "Diana, I do not think that is necessary. There is no need to involve your parents. This incident never happened."

Diana replies in a firm tone, "Oh, sir, there is no way I am going to allow you to have a secret between us like you have with Regina Reynolds. This incident *did* happen."

Mister Young's inflexible look suddenly turns to one of worry. His voice is strangely weird-sounding as he whispers, "Regina Reynolds? What did Regina tell you, Diana?"

"She told me enough to know that you two, and probably Miss Hickman as well, share a secret. I do not know what that secret is. But, this much I do know. Secrets between faculty, staff and students are highly inappropriate. I know your shared secret is not immoral. Reg would never stand for that. Just the same, I do know it is improper."

With a scornful look on her face that could slay a giant, Diana adds in a whisper, "And with all due respect, sir, please do not call me by my first name. We are not on a first-name basis. I think Miss Bower will do fine. Thank you."

Mister Young places his elbows on his desk. He rests his chin on his hands. He stares at Diana for the longest time as he mulls what he is going to say.

"Wait a minute, young lady. Are you implying that I have a secret with Miss Reynolds? That's preposterous!"

"Sir, I am not implying anything at all. I am simply stating the facts. I'm just telling you what Reg told me. If it's true, that you two share a secret, fine. Have fun with that. If it's untrue, I am very happy for Reg. But, in my opinion, you're looking for trouble if you share a secret with a student, a minor who happens to be a female."

She looks Mister Young squarely in the eye once more. She says in a sarcastic tone, "Either way, it's your word against hers, isn't it?"

Mister Young contradicts what she has said. "I wouldn't trust what that girl says, Miss Bower."

"Oh? But you will trust *her* letter, her accusations against *me*? That sounds a bit hypocritical if you ask me." After a second's pause, she adds with a mocking tone, "Sir."

Mister Young leans back in his oversized, plush leather chair. He says, "Okay, I admit it. We do have a secret, an agreement if you will. I simply asked Miss Reynolds to not discuss with her classmates saying that she intended to beat you up."

Diana moves to sit in the chair. She says in a soft voice, "Beat me up? Why would Reg want to beat me up? We are friends. Besides, I haven't done a thing to her."

Mister Young pulls a sheet of paper out of his desk drawer.

"It's all about this letter, the one I had you read when your parents were in my office. It's the letter accusing you of hitting her with a broomstick." He shakes his head, declaring, "I told her that I would handle her accusations. I said, if she promised not to make trouble for you, I would forget that she threatened to beat you up." With a sickening smile, he adds, "After all, if you haven't noticed, Miss Reynolds is much taller and stronger than you."

Diana whispers, "Sir that doesn't sound like Reg at all. As I said before, she and I are friends. I seriously doubt she would tell you and others that she wanted to beat me up."

"Well, she did. As soon as I got wind of her threats, I called her in to speak with me." Mister Young quickly adds, "Obviously, I already had this letter in my possession. I discussed its contents with her father present."

Diana says, "I see. So, you had the letter in your possession before the two of you discussed her threats against me?"

"Yes, I did. I told Miss Reynolds what I told you. It was her word against yours."

Diana says with a dismissive tone, "But, as it pertains to the letter, you took her side, not mine. May I ask, did you threaten to punish her?"

Mister Young replies as he shakes his head, "I am sorry, I cannot disclose what, if any, disciplinary measures I took against Miss Reynolds. Student disciplinary records are confidential." He leans forward in his chair.

"Now, Miss Bower, why don't you and I agree to share a secret, for lack of a better word? Let's pretend this discussion never happened. If your teachers and classmates ask you what we discussed today, and they will, you can tell them I was concerned about your state of mind. How's that sound to you?"

Diana pulls her phone out of her front pocket as she stands. She has a serious look on her face.

"No, sir. I am sorry. I will not, cannot, and never will share a secret with you." She holds her phone up with its screen facing Mister Young. "You see, sir, I have been recording our conversation the entire time."

Mister Young declares angrily, "Why in the world would you do that? And without my permission, no less? I ought to expel you here and now, you, you, disrespectful, rude child! You have violated the law!"

Diana says in a soft tone of voice, "Go ahead, Mister Young. If you expel me, that is fine with me. I will take my punishment. Then, I will fight you tooth and nail for as long as it takes me to prove my innocence. I am confident the school district superintendent will exonerate me from any wrongdoings. As for you, sir, well, I cannot predict your future. But, based on what you have said here today, I doubt it will look very rosy."

She adds with a self-confident tone, "And, for your information, our state is what they call a *one-party consent* state. Laws of our state stipulate that it is not illegal to record a conversation if one part of the party consents to the conversation. Sir, I am a party to this recorded conversation, and I readily consent."

She hesitates a few seconds to consider if she should say what she is thinking. As if to justify what she is about to say, the tenacious side of her conscience says, "Aw, what the heck. You're already in enough trouble, so you might as well go for the gold. It's either boom or bust!"

Diana crosses her arms over her chest. She says in a critical voice, "While we are talking about laws, rules, and regulations, you sir, in my opinion, have violated the law, a school rule. You are supposed to have a witness present every time you speak to a student in your office. That is especially prudent when the student is of the opposite sex. You do not have a witness present right now. So, you may have compromised both of us, our reputations. Not to mention, I, as a minor female student, have felt uncomfortable being alone with you, an adult male, this entire time." She smiles. "You may thank God I have this recording. Otherwise, sir, what would people think?"

Mister Young mulls over what she just said. After a half-minute of not saying anything, he finally says, "Okay, at least tell me this, if you please. What do you intend to do with the recording?"

She is not surprised that he seemingly could care less about violating the rules about having a female student alone in his office. It is apparent. All he cares about is the recording and his hide.

"I am going to ask my parents to listen to it. Then, I will transfer it to my computer for safekeeping. Unless my parents force me to, I will not disclose its contents to anyone else. I give you my word." After a moment's pause, she adds, "However, sir, please let me assure you. I intend to use the recording as a basis for investigating what this farce is all about as it concerns me." She adds with a smile, "That is if you pursue disciplinary actions against me as they concern the dishonest lies in the letter and the lies told by Miss Hickman."

"So, now you are threatening *me*," Mister Young asserts.

"No, sir. I am not threatening you. I would never do that to you or anyone else. As I said, you are free to discipline me if you desire. You can even expel me for recording our conversation. While I must admit, I fear what course of action, if any, that you take, I will accept it. After all, you are the principal, and I am the student. I had no right to call Miss Hickman a bully and to mimic her voice. I know that now. So, I will accept the consequences as I should. However, I promise you this. No one accuses me of anything untrue and gets away with it."

She clicks off the recording feature of her phone. Then she moves toward the door.

"All I seek is the truth, Mister Young, the truth. Now, may I please be excused?"

With a glum expression on his troubled face, Mister Young nods his head.

When Diana exits the principal's office, she quietly closes the door behind her.

CHAPTER EIGHT

KINDNESS AND MENDACIUM'S MADNESS

Part I: Parva Draco

The sun has come and gone seven times since Diana encountered the Inania and Aegolius. She figures, if her calculations are anywhere near accurate, they have been on the trail twenty-one days, perhaps longer.

The total of sunshine each three-day cycle is noticeably lengthier. Diana had noticed that the longer periods of sunshine occurred after she destroyed the Inania. She estimates that a typical period of sunshine is now at least two or three hours in duration. Considering the increased amount of sunshine, her estimate of their days on the trail may be off by as much as one-half day. Without a way to tell time, there is no way of knowing for certain.

She longs for her parents and friends, her comfy bed and the finer comforts of home in the Real-world. Then again, her double at home is going about her business as usual while she, her persona's main Diana, is in the World Beyond. For this reason, she isn't longing for home as much as she would be under normal circumstances. But these are, as we know, anything but normal circumstances.

Even so, there are three things she does miss and misses very much. One of them is her delicious specialty, cheese-overflowing, omelet seasoned with her mother's herbs and spices specially designed for eggs. Her mother has a very cool business. The business specializes in rare combinations of herbs and spices normally not found in American cupboards. One of Diana's favorite dishes seasoned with her mother's herbs and spices is Spaghetti.

She is also craving for Chinese food and, without question, loads of golden-crisp French fries. Also, she would do anything right now if she could have a heaping plate of Panda Express orange chicken, rice, and noodles along with a super tall glass of fizzling cherry-flavored Coca-Cola.

She often dreams about her double's activities at home. What she perceives in her dreams is nothing like a play-by-play, up-to-the-minute lengthy affair. What she envisions is a summary of significant happenings in her double's daily life. Envisioning her double's goings-on reminds her of watching a trailer for an upcoming blockbuster movie. She doesn't get to see everything but obtains enough information to understand the gist of what is taking place in her double's activities.

She knows that her double in the Real-world is deeply troubled about Reg's alleged claims. She also envisioned the entire incidents when her double confronted Miss Hickman and Mister Young. She wonders if her own renewed courage in the face of physical danger here in the World Beyond is somehow making her double tougher. She isn't sure. But one thing she knows for certain. Before she arrived in the World Beyond, she is confident she would never have confronted Miss Hickman and Mister Young the way that her double did. She wonders if something in her spirit, what she is experiencing here in the World Beyond, is making her whole person stronger and more courageous.

Despite everything, what her double is doing concerns her greatly. She is worried that her double may be making things worse as it relates to Mister Young. Just the same, she trusts her, and she is silently cheering on her double. And she is hopeful that her double will prevail in the end.

"But, what do Mendacium and his evil allies have to do with what is going on at home? Could everything be caused by Mister Reynolds' questionable calls during the softball tournament? Did I hit the winning run? Or, did I strike out? Also, is what I am undergoing here in the World Beyond happening? Or am I imagining it? Could it be that what my double is experiencing at home is also a figment of her, my, our imagination? Once again, like the supposed longer periods of sunshine, I do not know."

Nonetheless, Diana in the World Beyond knows one thing is for sure as does her double at home. Whether imaginary, part of a dream or real life, she, Diana, in fact, both Diana's in both worlds, must learn the truth no matter the cost or how perilous the journey.

While Diana mulls over these extremely confusing thoughts in her mind, she is worried about I Dunno. I Dunno has been missing for, what Diana estimates to be, three hours. Her protector pixie had set off to find the Sana bush. The oil of the Sana bush berry has healing properties like tea tree oil in the Real-world. Diana had nicked her thumb while practicing with her sword. The wound is not infected but I Dunno thought it is wise to treat the wound just in case.

Diana says, "Gosh, Jayvyn, I wonder what happened to I Dunno? I hope she isn't in danger. Until she returns, I am clueless as to our next course of action." She glances up the untraveled portion of the trail. "I guess we could follow the trail, to see where it leads. But, perhaps it is better if we stay here and wait for I Dunno. I'd hate to leave just for her to find us gone when she returns. Then again, she probably can find me no matter where I am." She smiles happily adding, "After all, she is my protector pixie!"

Jayvyn is not a horse that talks like the talking horse *Mister Ed* in the sitcom by the same name. The sitcom *Mister Ed* was popular on television in the 1960's. All the same, Jayvyn is very observant. He appears to understand nearly everything Diana says. He gently pushes her right thigh with his muzzle. Then he thrusts his head back to his left. Diana has no idea what he is trying to tell her. He repeats his actions two more times.

Diana's eyes finally widen with an understanding of what Jayvyn is trying to tell her. She says, "Oh, I get it, Jayvyn. You want me to saddle up, yes?"

Jayvyn whinnies as he nods his head and kicks the ground with his hoof.

After gathering her things and hopping on Jayvyn's back, she notices that Jayvyn is heading in the direction from which they have already traveled.

She cries, "Wait for a second, Jayvyn. You are going the wrong way. We've already been in that section of the trail. You need to turn around." She points. "We need to go that way."

Jayvyn shakes his head back and forth. He continues walking in the same direction. Diana pulls hard on his reins, but he resists. He lowers his neck and strains on his bridle until Diana is forced to loosen her grip.

"Okay, Jayvyn, I give up. You win. I guess you know better than me the direction we should travel. After all, horses have instincts that we humans still do not fully understand." She laughs. "As the saying goes, Jayvyn, take me to our leader, to I Dunno!"

Jayvyn whinnies as he nods his head in agreement. Then he quickens his pace to a trot.

Even as Jayvyn continues trotting on the trail, Diana is becoming more concerned. There still is no sign of I Dunno. And, she doesn't recognize a single thing on the trail they had previously walked. Not a blade of grass is disturbed nor is a single twig broken off the bushes that line the trail. She looks at the ground. There are no hoof prints. She looks for telltale signs of something familiar, but she doesn't see anything.

She whispers, "This is weird. I should have seen something familiar by now, Jayvyn's hoof prints, anything." Abruptly, a tiny voice from up ahead calls out from the trees.

"Empress Diana, please help me! I'm over here, Empress Diana. Come quickly."

Diana yells, "It's I Dunno!"

She urges Jayvyn to quicken his pace by squeezing her legs against his sides. In a few moments, they arrive to see I Dunno is bound to the trunk of a small tree. Cords of rope made of vines are binding her wrists and ankles. She meekly smiles as they approach.

"Oh, I am sorry, Empress Diana." She glances to her left, to her right, and down at her tiny feet. "It would appear as if I am in a bind, no pun intended." She giggles.

Diana is surprised that I Dunno called her Empress. She also recognizes that I Dunno is trying to lighten up the moment, but she is in no mood to play along. While she removes the tangled vines that bind I Dunno's wrists and ankles she cries, "Goodness, I Dunno. You had us worried sick. I am relieved that Jayvyn knew to return to the trail on which we were previously. What in the world happened to you?"

I Dunno does not reply.

Once I Dunno is free, Diana gathers her into the palm of her hand. She cries, "Are you okay? Did they hurt you? Oh, what am I saying? You look fine." She looks around to see if anyone or anything is nearby. "Who or what did this to you?"

I Dunno replies, "I did."

Diana declares with a surprised tone, "You did? You did this to yourself? I don't understand, I Dunno. Why in tarnation would you tie yourself to a tree?"

I Dunno whispers, "Because I am not who you think I am, Empress Diana."

Diana's eyes widen as she stares at the small figure she is holding in her hand. With a hesitant tone of dread, she stammers, "Your voice, I Dunno, it's much deeper. It's almost as if it's a male's voice!"

She seems frozen as she watches, what she thought was her protector pixie, as it slowly transforms into a six-inch hideous looking creature. The creature reminds Diana of a mutated toy monkey. Except for its shaggy white hair on its head and shoulders, its entire body is pasty pink in color. Even its leering eyes surrounded by thick black circles are pinkish. As it snarls, its gaping mouth reveals a lower row of sharp teeth. Two fangs protrude from the top of its mouth just below its hideous nose. Its four gangling legs expose sharp, curved claws at their ends.

Diana screams, "Ick, what in the world are you? Phew, you stink!" She shakes her hand violently to dislodge the creature. It does not budge. It sticks like glue to the palm of her hand. She notices tiny drops of blood oozing from her palm.

With another scream, she declares, "You've dug your claws deep into my flesh! Yuck! Get off my hand! You are gross. Get off, I tell you!"

She punches the creature with her fist as hard as she can. Despite her forceful blows that hit the creature head-on, it remains stuck like glue. The more she punches it, the more it bounces back and forth like a toy punching bag. Worse, as she slams at it even harder, the deeper its claws sink into her flesh. Blood is now spurting out of the many punctures of her hand. All the while the disgusting, foul-smelling creature leers and laughs at her.

The ugly creature that she initially assumed was the gorgeous I Dunno, suddenly leaps from her hand onto the ground. Diana straightaway hops off Jayvyn. She angrily stomps at the creature with her boot. But it is too quick. It effortlessly avoids the stomps of her boot as it darts here and there and back and forth. She quickly realizes she is not getting anywhere with the nasty creature that hops around like it is dancing a Ukrainian Cossack Dance. She hastily draws her sword from its sheath. She repeatedly stabs and swipes at the creature with her sword. Once again, her efforts are in vain. The revolting, foul-smelling creature is too quick.

Unexpectedly, Jayvyn moves next to her. He lowers his hind hoof and stomps the creature to smithereens. The creature disintegrates into pulverized grayish-white dust. Jayvyn whinnies loudly with obvious satisfaction and joy for destroying the creature.

Diana feels as if she is going to black out from stomping her boot for so long and for the pain in the palm of her hand. She hastily rips a piece of fabric from her undergarment and wraps it around her bloody wound. She hugs Jayvyn's mane and says, "Oh, my God, Jayvyn, thank you. That was disgusting, unbelievably disgusting!" She stares at her injured hand that seems to have grown to twice its normal size.

"I wonder what in the world that creature was?"

A creepy, low-toned voice behind her states, "It was a *Parva Draco*, otherwise known as the Small Monster. Like me, Mendacium's esteemed creation, the Parva Draco can assume the form of any creature."

Diana whirls around. Standing less than five feet away is the mirror image of herself holding a sword! She immediately recognizes she is face to face with another Inania.

Her mirror image whispers in a mocking tone, "But, unlike me, who can only replicate a living form I can see, the Parva Draco can assume any form it desires. Dead. Or Alive."

The Inania laughs scornfully adding, "And I am very sorry to say this, Empress Diana. Your charming, infinitesimal protector pixie is no more. She is dead." The creature rears back its head and roars with laughter.

Diana shrieks with a voice that is bursting with hatred, "Nnnnnooooooooooo!"

She lunges at the Inania with her sword, and then she whirls around in a circle-parry. When she is facing the Inania once more, she can feel that her heart is sinking. Unlike the Inania she destroyed weeks ago, this Inania does not assume its original form. Instead, it raises its sword high above its head to deflect her blow. It is obvious to her that Mendacium has been watching her all these weeks as she practiced with her sword.

This Inania prepares to fight!

*****

Part II: Fight to the Death

Diana backs away slowly. I Dunno had taught her to keep a safe distance from an opponent when fighting with a sword. Keeping a safe distance by slowly retreating gives her time to assess her opponent's reactions without endangering herself. She is not sure how good the Inania is with a sword. Hopefully, the beast is not too talented. As for herself, she is the fifth Diomede, the Warrior Youngster of the World Beyond. Although she has trained sparingly, her natural instincts as a swordswoman are in her blood. Also, her protector pixie has bestowed her with magic that has enhanced the powers she derives from her lightning bolt necklace and bracelet. She feels confident that she can defeat the creature.

The Inania lunges forward slamming its sword downward. Diana reacts swiftly with a parry move, forcefully deflecting the creature's sword to its right. The Inania is pushed back but quickly recovers and whirls about in a complete turn. Diana backs away hurriedly. When the creature's sword slices through the air, her torso is but a few inches away from its blade, but thankfully, safely out of reach.

The Inania is now off balance. It quickly tries to regain its footing. Diana thrusts her blade to its midsection. The creature counters adeptly by strongly tapping the end of her blade with its sword. Its move causes her to lose her balance, but only temporarily. The Inania feigns a thrusting motion, and then it lunges forward. Diana quickly backs away and slams her sword into its sword. The Inania's sword rebounds to the creature's left.

The Inania seethes in a disgusted-sounding voice, "You're good, Empress Diana. But know this, swords have no place in the hands of a girl."

"I am not a girl," Diana counters in a hushed tone as she looks the creature squarely in the eye. "I am a female warrior. I am Diana, the Heroine Youngster of the World Beyond. And you're going down!"

The Inania lunges at her with so much force, that when their swords crash together, Diana collapses to the ground onto her back. She is now in the most precarious position possible. Thankfully, she keeps her sword in a vertical angle in front of her. It is the only defensive posture possible given her dire situation.

The Inania slams its sword downward. Its sword slams into Diana's with a tremendously loud *Clang!* The metallic sound of sword on sword reverberates in the forest like a tinny thunderclap until it weakens and fades away.

The creature whirls about clockwise to gain maximum momentum, to strike Diana with its second attack in response to her countering its first. It abruptly slashes with its sword to the left side of her head. She quickly brings her sword high above her head. She counters its strike with a flicking technique which bends its blade to the right. Then, as the Inania is forced to lower its sword, she slams its sword repeatedly with a beat attack. Her powerful wallops throw off its sense of balance forcing it to stumble backward.

Diana is on her feet in a flash. She lunges at the creature but misses. The Inania is off balance, but it quickly regains its footing and counterattacks with a parry as it goes on the offensive yet again. It lunges at her. She meets its lunge with so much force from her sword; she knocks the creature's sword out of its hand.

The Inania's expression turns to one of revulsion. It slowly moves to straddle its sword between its feet. The creature does not bend forward to pick up its sword. Instead, much to Diana's annoyance, it stretches its arms high above its head. Then it massages the back of its neck and shoulders. It stretches its legs behind its body and does a few shallow knee bends. The Inania is taunting her, trying to frighten her with its offhand movements.

Diana eyes the creature's sword lying on the ground. She demands with a scowl, "Pick it up. Quit stretching and acting like you're getting ready to run a marathon or something. You are not in a race. It's the battle for your very existence, you creepy animal. Pick up your sword. I want this to be a fair fight."

She positions her sword at a forty-five-degree angle in front of her body. She points the tip of her sword upward so that the sword's length runs from the bottom of her torso to the top of her head. This maneuver allows her to respond to the Inania's attack with reasonable speed. It also gives her many angles from which she can strike offensively.

She yells in a commanding tone, "I said, pick it up! Otherwise, you are nothing but a coward, a weak disciple of Mendacium's hateful treachery!" With a scornful laugh, she adds, "Who was it that said swords have no place in the hands of girls, huh?"

She looks to the Inania's sword lying on the ground between its feet, and back again to the creature. She taunts as she asks, "You're not scared, are you? Is the gutless follower of falsehoods and cock-and-bull lies afraid of a girl? Pick up your sword, you spineless chicken. I'm getting impatient!"

The Inania unexpectedly lets out a squeal heard for miles. Its high-pitched squeal is deafeningly excruciating. Diana hurriedly places her sword between her knees to cover her ears with her hands.

She yells, "Stop, stop screaming!"

The Inania unexpectedly retrieves its sword from the ground and lunges at her. She sidesteps its thrust causing her sword she had placed between her knees to crash to the ground. She does not have time to retrieve it before the creature readies to deliver another blow.

She quickly withdraws an arrow from her quiver. Just as the creature lunges at her a second time, she skillfully dodges its thrust. Now that the Inania's left leg is close to her right hand she forcefully shoves the arrow into the calf of its leg. She grimaces, a natural reaction caused by stabbing an arrow into a leg of something that is the spitting image of her likeness.

Surprisingly, the Inania does not vaporize. It sets its sword on the ground. Then, it lets out another loud, lengthy squeal as it slowly pulls the arrow out of its leg. The creature tosses the bloodied arrow to the ground with disgust.

Despite the booming pain pounding in her temples, Diana ignores the Inania's squealing. Holding her sword horizontal in front of her, with her elbows near her side, she readies herself defensively for its next move. It is then she remembers something I Dunno had said during a recent training session.

I Dunno had said, "Each opponent has a weakness, both physically and mentally. His weakness is your strength. Laugh, trick, joke, scold, insult. Do anything you must do to stir your opponent's emotions, so he makes a mistake. But, beware. An inexperienced opponent may be more dangerous than one that is highly skilled. You will not know what to expect from him." She went on to say somberly, "And always remember, Diana, a cornered prey is more dangerous than one who has the means to escape."

She yells, "C'mon you coward. Let's see if you have what it takes to defeat, how did you put it? Oh, yes, a girl who has no business holding a sword!" She begins laughing hysterically as she dances up and down on her toes, all the while holding her sword in front of her. Then, surprising even herself, she begins to sing at the top of her voice.

"She's somebody's hero, a hero to her with a skinned-up knee." The lyrics she is singing are from Jamie O'Neal's album *Brave*, "Somebody's Hero."

As soon as Diana begins to sing, the Inania quickly retrieves its sword from the ground. It ruthlessly attacks with its sword held high above its head. It thrusts downward brutally. Before its blade can strike her sword, Diana manages to grasp the blade of her sword with her other hand. Fortunately, the blade of her sword is dull. Charles had said the makers designed it that way to prevent her from injuring herself. She holds her sword horizontal with both hands above her head. As the Inania's sword impacts her sword, it ricochets cruelly off hers with a deafening *twang!*

Despite the intense pain resonating in her left hand and forearm, Diana counterattacks by thrusting her sword deep into the Inania's chest. It immediately drops its sword. As the creature gradually returns to its original form, it stares at Diana with a mixture of disgust and disbelief.

Diana says with a sardonic tone, "Oh, my goodness! Were you just destroyed by a girl who had no business with a sword?" She laughs. "Haven't you heard? A woman may someday rule the Earth!" She begins to sing softly once more.

"She's somebody's hero. A little kiss is all she needs."

The Inania snarls one last time. Then it vaporizes into a cloud of grayish-white dust to float without a sound in the forest's soft breeze.

*****

Part III: The Royal Family

Diana slumps to the ground in exhaustion. She is still keyed up from her death-defying battle with the Inania. She is also anxious for her protector pixie. While she was fighting for her life, all the while she was thinking about I Dunno. It is highly unusual for I Dunno to be absent for this length of time.

After resting for a few moments to catch her breath, she scrambles to her feet. She gulps down as much water as her stomach can hold. Her eyes well up with tears when she replaces the waterskin onto Jayvyn's back. Even though her magical protector pixie is nowhere in sight, her magic miraculously replaces the water she has just guzzled.

She picks up her spent arrow from the ground to inspect it. She decides that it is not damaged, and it is reusable. Nothing is evident on the arrowhead from its encounter with the Inania's leg, not surprisingly seeing that the creature is otherworldly. Just the same, she is grossed out even thinking about the arrowhead piercing the creature's body.

She thrusts the arrowhead into the ground and roughly twists it this way and that. She figures that if any evil remains behind on the arrowhead, cleansing it with good old-fashioned dirt will remove its immorality.

She wipes her sword with the end of her cape. Then she sheathes it and attaches it to the scabbard of the bridle cinch. As she gets ready to hop onto Jayvyn's back, a horde of Parva Draco suddenly appear from nowhere to surround her and Jayvyn. Three of the creatures begin tugging at her boots. Others begin climbing up Jayvyn's legs. A few more are merrily trying to catch Jayvyn's tail as it swings back and forth.

Diana lets out a scream as she rushes to unsheathe her sword. She plans to swing her sword in wide circles near the ground to thrash the creatures into pieces. But, for some strange reason, she hesitates.

She notices Jayvyn, unlike his encounter with the first Parva Draco when he smashed it to pieces, seems in high spirits. He is softly whinnying, and his tail is gaily swinging back and forth. He is also pawing at the ground with his hooves. As he does, he allows one or two Parva Draco to scramble up his legs so that they can climb onto his back. At least a dozen of the creatures is happily jumping up and down on Jayvyn's crest, shoulders, back, and loin.

She ponders, "Is it possible? Are these Parva Draco friendly?"

She scoops up one into the palm of her good hand. It had managed to crawl up her thigh. Unlike the first Parva Draco, this creature is smaller, perhaps four inches in height. And, unlike the scary features of the creature Jayvyn smashed to smithereens, this creature has friendly-looking facial features and stunning luminescent blue eyes.

His hair is much longer than the original Parva Draco she encountered. And, instead of his hair being ghastly white, it is chestnut brown. He is clothed which is sort of nice. There is nothing worse than looking at a naked creature that has the physical features of a human. His attire is a dull-brown, knee-length tunic. He has a black velvet belt around his waist. He has claws at the end of his human-like hands, but they are carefully trimmed. To Diana, he looks like a scaled down domesticated animal that a Greek god or goddess would have as a pet.

The tiny creature smiles as he looks up at her with his handsome blue eyes. She is pleased to see that he does not have nasty-looking teeth or ugly fangs like the other Parva Draco had. She is also relieved it doesn't sink its claws into her flesh. She smiles in return.

"Please tell me you are a nice Parva Draco."

The creature replies in a squeaky voice that closely reminds her of I Dunno's vocal sound. He says, "Yepity, yep, yep." He points to the other Parva Draco creatures. "All of us are Empress Diana's friends." He points to Jayvyn, saying, "See there. My lord wishes to speak with Empress Diana." He bows. "If you please."

Then he hops from Diana's hand and tumbles to the ground. As he lands, he summersaults acrobatically, and then he stands to brush the dirt from his tunic. Diana is relieved that he appears not to have injured himself from leaping so far to the ground.

Diana moves closer to stand next to Jayvyn to get a better look at, what the other creature referred to as, *my lord*. Between the ears of Jayvyn, on his poll, stands a handsome, dark-skinned Parva Draco clothed in armor made of rich leather. He is wearing a silver crown. Standing beside him is a gorgeous creature clothed in a bright red peplos with a sash of gold as a belt. A delicate golden tiara rests on her wavy auburn hair. By her dress, and the fact that she curtsies, Diana immediately recognizes this Parva Draco as a female. She correctly reasons that she is the wife of the handsome male.

Standing next to the female is a tiny youngster Parva Draco. He is sporting a blue, full-length tunic belted at the waist with a white sash. He is blond-haired.

The male bows deeply as does the youngster. He says, "Empress Diana, on behalf of your protector pixie, I Dunno, it is my sincere pleasure to meet you." Diana immediately notices that his voice is noticeably stronger and lower than the creature she held in her hand.

Before the creature can utter another word, Diana whispers, "I Dunno. Is she safe? Is she okay? What happened to her?"

The creature replies, "She is safe, Empress Diana. And she is well. She has, how did she put it? Ah, yes, she said she has a boo-boo. She said you would understand the word. She also said to tell you that everything is coolio and that she wishes you and Jayvyn well. She looks forward to seeing you soon." He bows deeply once more. "I will take you and your steed to see her shortly."

Diana breathes a sigh of relief. She says, "Thank goodness that she is okay. What happened to her?"

"She was injured on her wing by one of the hostile Parva Draco while she was seeking this." He bends over to pick up a brightly-colored purple berry from Jayvyn's thick mane. The berry is the size of a kernel of corn. He hands it to Diana.

"I Dunno said for you to squeeze oils from the berry of the Sana bush onto your wound. She instructed that you do so as soon as you receive it."

Diana examines the berry. With a lump in her throat and her heart breaking, she mulls over all that has happened to her protector pixie.

"My poor I Dunno. She received her painful injuries because of her devotion to me. Gosh, how I love her!"

Tears well up in her eyes. Even though tears cloud her vision, she sees that the creature is gesturing to the berry with his hands. He is impatiently telling her to squeeze the oils of the berry onto her thumb. He glances at Diana's bandaged hand. He says, "I urge you to attend to your injured hand as well." Then, with an impatient look on his face, he throws his tiny hands up in the air. It is as if he is saying with his non-verbal expression, "Hurry up!"

Diana laughs as she says, "Okay, okay, I get it. Here we go. The last thing I want to do is disappoint my protector pixie." She squeezes the berry between her good thumb and forefinger. As soon as the oil touches the cut on her injured thumb, the redness begins to disappear, and the throbbing lessens markedly. She removes the wrap covering her injured hand and squeezes oil of the berry onto her puncture marks. The redness immediately begins to disappear.

She says, "Sir, may I ask your name? You know my name, but I do not know yours."

As he takes a deep bow, the creature says boldly, "Empress Diana, I am Uvam, King of the Minima." He gestures to the throng of Parva Draco happily dancing and chattering away. "We, unlike the Parva Draco you encountered earlier are virtuous. They are evil, mendacious allies of Mendacium." He points. "This is my wife and Queen of the Minima. Her name is Saccharo."

Saccharo curtsies. She says, "It is my dear pleasure to meet Empress Diana, Youngster Heroine of the World Beyond."

Diana replies, "It is a pleasure to meet you as well, your Highness."

Diana is not very good at curtsying, so she deeply bows. She adds, "And if you do not mind, from now on I shall refer to you as Minima instead of Parva Draco. Those evil little monsters give me the creeps."

The Queen of Minima says, "That is preferable, thank you. And Milady Diana, call me Saccharo if you please." She flicks her thumb in the direction of the King of Minima. "And you can call him Uvam. His ego may not like it, but you, like us, are royalty. You deserve nothing less." She smiles cheerfully adding, "And this little fellow is our son, Eros."

Eros bows deeply, and then he says boldly, "It is my pleasure to meet you, Empress Diana." Then, with a mischievous smile, he casually says, "I know what your name means in our language. It means *heavenly, divine.* Do you know what our Latin names denote in your tongue?"

Diana giggles. "No, Eros, I have no earthly idea what Saccharo, Uvam, and Eros mean in my language. Can you tell me?"

"Yes, Empress. My mother's name Saccharo, my father's name Uvam, and my name Eros translate to *Sugar, Sour, and Peanuts!*" He roars with laughter. "How do you like that, Empress?"

Diana can barely talk as she says in between fits of giggles, "That is very cute, Eros. Who would have thought? Sugar, Sour, and Peanuts. I like it!"

CHAPTER NINE

JOURNEY FOR TRUTH BEGINS

Part I: Conflicting Words

"Your name is Diana Jane Bower, am I correct?" the School District's Superintendent, Miss R. Davenport says.

Diana replies self-consciously, "Yes, ma'am."

Miss Davenport says, "I am going to make a digital recording of our conversation, but only if you consent." She smiles. "If you do not consent, and that is fully within your rights to not consent, Miss Beach will take notes. She will use her notes to compile a transcript of today's proceedings to the best of her ability. Do you consent to a recording of our conversation?"

Diana says, "Yes, ma'am, I consent."

Miss Davenport glances toward Diana's mother and father who are sitting at the other end of the conference table. She asks Diana, "And these are your parents, yes?"

"Yes, ma'am, they are," Diana answers in a barely perceptible whisper.

"I'm sorry. I could not hear you. Please speak up, Miss Bower."

"Yes, ma'am, these are my parents," Diana says timidly in a much louder voice, and then she offers in an apologetic tone, "I am sorry, ma'am. I'm a bit nervous as you can well imagine." She clears her throat. "I'll try to speak more clearly."

"I imagine that you are nervous," Miss Davenport says with a smile. "I cannot blame you. However, please try to relax. This meeting is not an interrogation, nor will I decide anyone's culpability, if any, because of what we discuss at this hearing. It strictly is an administrative proceeding. It is a means to gather the facts, to obtain your side of the story. Do you understand?"

"Yes, ma'am, the fact that you say that makes me feel a bit better." She breathes in deeply. "Thank you for taking the time to explain the procedure to me."

"You are welcome, Miss Bower. It is important that you relax. Would you prefer that I address you by your given name, Diana? Would that help you to relax, perhaps making this procedure feel less formal?"

"Yes, ma'am, I'd like that," Diana eagerly answers with a meek smile, "if you do not mind."

"It is my pleasure, Diana."

Miss Davenport addresses her parents. She says, "Do you consent to me recording the conversation of your minor child, Diana?" Her parents nod their heads in the affirmative. Miss Davenport gets out of her chair to activate the digital recording device sitting in the middle of the table.

Speaking to her once more, she says, "Okay, Diana, for the record, please state your full name."

Diana says in a clear tone of voice, "My name is Diana Jane Bower."

Miss Davenport looks across the table. She says, "Do the parents of Diana Jane Bower consent to recording this conversation for administrative purposes?" Her parents say in unison, "We do."

She states clearly, "Let the record show that Miss Diana Jane Bower and her parents are present at this administrative hearing. They consent to the digital recording of a transcript of these proceedings. Also present is Miss Jacqueline Beach, the school counselor.

Addressing Diana, Miss Davenport says with a smile, "Diana, please tell me in your own words what occurred in Miss Hickman's office."

Diana pushes her chair from the table. She gets ready to stand.

"Don't I need to take an oath or something?"

"No," Miss Davenport says with a chuckle. "There is no need to take an oath. I know you will tell me the truth as best as you can. Start at the beginning, if you please. Take your time."

Diana says, "Well, I guess I should start when Miss Hickman and I met at the door." She inhales deeply and slowly exhales. "Okay, she was sort of angry when she first saw me. She accused me of taking my time on the way to her office. She purposely mispronounced my name like always."

"Did you take your time walking to the principal's office, Diana?"

"Yes, ma'am, looking back, I guess that I did. However, I only delayed for a half-minute at the most. I stopped briefly to look at a few posters on the walls." She frowns. "I never once had to see the principal since I've been in school. I was uneasy. As you can imagine, I wasn't looking forward to going there. I didn't run down the corridor if you know what I mean."

"Did you stop to use the restroom?"

"No, ma'am, I did not." She frowns. "But as things progressed, I wished that I had. I really had to go."

"You mentioned Miss Hickman purposely mispronounced your name. What did she say?"

"I'm pretty sure this is how it sounded. And I'm pretty much certain how long it was when Miss Hickman said it. That's because my friends have timed her saying it on more than one occasion." She scowls. "It takes four seconds."

Diana inhales deeply, and then, as she rolls her eyes, she says, "Bowww-eeerrr."

Goosebumps begin to crawl up her arms onto the nape of her neck. Just repeating her last name like Miss Hickman says it gives her the creeps.

"As you can imagine, ma'am, her pronouncing my name like that every time she sees me is very insulting." She shivers as the goosebumps begin to race down her spine. "And it hurts too. It hurts a lot."

"About how many times would you estimate Miss Hickman says that to you, Diana? As an example, one or two times a day. Please give me a number if you can."

"Ma'am, I would be lying if I said I knew for certain. But I can give you an estimate. Would that be okay?" Miss Davenport nods her head.

Diana stares up at the ceiling as she considers Miss Davenport's question. She notices that some mischievous student had, at one time or another, shot into the ceiling the paper wrapping of a straw with a pin attached to its end, so that the paper wrapping would stick in the ceiling tile. The pin and a bit of the yellowed paper are still protruding from the ceiling tile. She manages to stifle a laugh. Quickly realizing she needs to answer Miss Davenport's question, she looks away. As she looks at Miss Davenport, she can feel her face flush. To her surprise, Miss Davenport is looking to where she had been staring.

"Ah, I see you have found my memento," Miss Davenport says with a chuckle. "I keep it there as a reminder of one of my former students when I was a teacher, a few days before I became superintendent. My student and I had to see the former superintendent because her principal accused her of writing graffiti on the bathroom walls.

"Just before we departed this conference room, she shot the paper wrapping of the straw into the ceiling. The reason it's still there is to remind me, even though times can seem very challenging, there is always something we can do to laugh." With a tender smile, she adds, "And just so you know, the superintendent dismissed all charges against her. Another student confessed to the graffiti incident. But, I digress. So, Diana, please tell me how many times you estimate Miss Hickman purposely mispronounced your name each class day."

Diana says, "I pass her office three times in the morning and once in the afternoon during the change of classes. She's always outside her office when I pass, without fail. So, I'd have to estimate, on the conservative side, twenty times a week give or take."

"Does she mispronounce your name every time you see her?"

"Yes ma'am, without fail. Every. Single. Time. I often try to ignore her, but when I do, she usually repeats my name, generally louder than before. So, it's less stressful to wish her good morning or good afternoon. Sometimes I say hello. Then I hurry on my way."

"Have you ever once disrespected her in front of other students when you see her in the corridor? Have you ever corrected her for mispronouncing your name? Not that it's wrong for you to do so."

"No, ma'am. Never. I always figure Miss Hickman is the one that looks if you do not mind me saying, foolish when she makes fun of my name. I do not want to look foolish as well. As I have always said, 'It's better to ignore ignorance than to travel the path of foolishness.'"

Miss Davenport writes something in her notepad. She says, "I like that saying, Diana. Thank you for sharing it with us. Now, let's change the subject. Miss Hickman alleges before you two entered her office, when you were outside in the corridor, you said to her." She glances at her notes adding, "She alleges you said, and I am quoting here, 'Don't be so darned stupid Gloria, like usual.' Do you recall saying that to her?'"

"No, ma'am, I never said that," Diana replies with a puzzled look. "Who is Gloria, if you do not mind me asking?"

"Gloria is Miss Hickman's first name, Diana."

Diana replies, "Really? I never knew that. Not only did I not know her first name until now, I never call adults by their first names. The only exception is my friend Ed. He said it was okay that I call him by his first name. Everyone who knew him at the Skate Center called him by his given name as well. But, even in his case, I call him Mister Ed in front of others, unless I slip up." She shakes her head, stating, "I am sorry to accuse her, Miss Hickman, of saying something improper. But she is mistaken. I didn't say that."

Miss Davenport writes something in her notepad. "Okay, Diana, thank you. Continue, if you please."

Diana summarizes what transpired in Miss Hickman's office. Miss Davenport asks a few questions to clarify what Diana says. After twenty minutes, Diana ends her lengthy summation.

"After speaking with my parents, I now know that I should not have called Miss Hickman a bully or mimicked her voice. I should have told them, my parents, what happened, how Miss Hickman called me names and threatened me. I should have given them the chance of addressing my complaints. But, I was angry, angry at the way she made fun of my last name repeatedly. Yes, I was angry, and I was a bit scared when she threatened to hit me and sic unknown persons on me."

Miss Davenport says, "According to Miss Hickman, you are the one who threatened to hit her. In fact, Diana, she alleges that you rushed to her desk and kicked her chair causing it to crash into the wall. Mister Young substantiates these allegations. He claims he heard the commotion outside his office and went to Miss Hickman's office to investigate. He said he saw that you were standing next to Miss

Hickman's desk threatening her. He alleges you had your fist next to her face, threatening to punch her. He immediately told you to stop, and then he told you to join your parents in his office."

Diana says with a strong, disbelieving tone, "Ma'am, I have never before in my life accused an adult of lying." She looks at her parents. "I was brought up proper by my mother and father not to lie and not to accuse others of being untruthful. But I swear. Miss Hickman and Mister Young are lying. They are deliberately lying and conspiring against me. I never once threatened Miss Hickman. As to her chair, she is the one who caused it to bang loudly against the wall when she rushed from behind her desk to threaten *me!*" She glances at her parents.

"My parents can back up my claim. I'm telling the truth. They were inside Mister Young's office when the chair banged against the wall. Mister Young did not enter Miss Hickman's office until minutes later."

"I see," Miss Davenport says in a gentle tone. "Diana, I must ask you this. Are you completely honest with me when you say that you never threatened Miss Hickman?"

Diana raises her right hand. She says, "Ma'am, I swear. I did not threaten Miss Hickman. She threatened me. She was the one who pushed her chair, not me. As for Mister Young, by the time he entered Miss Hickman's office, she had already departed. She had departed four or five minutes earlier."

Diana takes a sip from the glass of water in front of her on the table while Miss Davenport writes lengthy notes in her notepad. Her hands are shaking. She is nervous, not because she is afraid or uncomfortable, well, maybe she is, but not so much. She is outraged at what Mister Young and Miss Hickman had said about her. She cannot fathom how two adults she is supposed to look up to could collude so evilly against her. How they could blatantly lie. She looks at her parents. Both are smiling. Her father gives her a thumb's up, and her mother blows her a silent kiss.

She ponders, "This entire charade ticks me off! Mister Young and Miss Hickman are conspiring against me for some reason. And they're doing it on the record! Is all of this about the softball tournament? If so, it sounds very trivial to lie about something as unimportant as a softball game! And how does it involve Reg? Should I tell Miss Davenport what Reg said to me? Or should I keep silent? Mom and Dad said not to ask questions. Dad also said I should only provide answers to questions that Miss Davenport asks me, that I should offer nothing else."

Miss Davenport looks up from her notes. She inquires, "Okay, Diana, I have one more question. There were no witnesses to the alleged confrontation between you and Miss Hickman." She glances at her notes. "Except for Mister Young, as he alleges, he saw you threatening Miss Hickman. Am I correct?"

Diana cannot believe what she is hearing. It is almost as if Miss Davenport had read her mind! She shakes her head vigorously.

"Oh, I am sorry to correct you, ma'am. But, there was a witness, my friend, Reg."

Miss Davenport consults her notes. When she looks up, she says, "When you refer to your friend, Reg, are you referring to the same Regina Reynolds who allegedly wrote the letter accusing you of striking her with a broomstick?"

"Yes, ma'am, she is the same, Regina. My softball teammates and I call her Reg. I am sorry I wasn't clearer when I referred to her."

Miss Davenport says, "There is no need to apologize, Diana, but," she glances at her notes, "according to Miss Hickman, there were no witnesses." She looks up and gazes briefly at Diana. Her expression is kind, understanding.

"Now, Diana, I want to ask the question I just presented to you in another way." She smiles. "I want you to be truthful as you can when you reply, okay?"

Diana nods her head, stating in a confident tone, "I promise I will answer truthfully."

"Good. Now, I must ask you, Diana. Was there a witness when you and Miss Hickman had the alleged confrontation in her office? Simply answer yes or no."

"Yes."

"Who was the witness, Diana?"

"Regina Reynolds."

*****

Part II: Text Me, Dynamite

"Dynamite, we need to talk."

Diana looks up with surprise. She and her brothers are eating Chinese cuisine at a local Panda Express restaurant. She almost chokes on a piece of orange chicken when she sees who has spoken to her. She places her chopsticks on her paper plate and jumps to her feet.

She says, "Oh, my goodness, Reg! What a pleasant surprise. It is very nice to see you." She reaches out to embrace Regina. Regina waves her hands at her sides as she backs away.

"Sorry, Dynamite. I'll hug you later. We need to talk." She looks around. "But not here. Too many people know us. Plus, some of our classmates are right over there." She gestures with a nod of her head to a group of six girls across the food court. They are engrossed in something one of them is saying. Diana notices that Regina is purposely facing away from the girls.

Regina says, "I do not want them to gossip about us. Even though school is out for summer break, they gossip about our classmates like it's nobody's business." She cringes "Then our business will be all over town, and I'll be in serious trouble." She bites her lower lip as she adds, "And, Dynamite, so will you." Regina pulls her phone from her back pocket.

"Do you still have my number on your phone?"

"Yes, I do, Reg," Diana replies.

"Text me, Dynamite. I'll see your number." She shakes her head as she stares at the tiled floor. "I'm sorry, I no longer have your number on my phone. My father forced me to delete it from my phone weeks ago. I won't text you back. My father might see your number on his phone bill. If he sees your number, that you texted me, that's okay. But, if he sees that I texted you back, that we're having a conversation, then, I'll be in a world of hurt."

"Okay, I'll text you," Diana says. "How have you been, Reg? You seem scared? Is everything okay?"

Regina's eyes fill with tears. "Not now, Dynamite." She glances over her shoulder at the group of girls who are now laughing at something humorous on one of the teen's phone.

"I must go before they see us together." She looks at Dan and Billy. She smiles and says, "It's good to see you two. Take care of Dynamite. She's the best."

She shakes her head, and then she whispers in a sad tone, "Dynamite, I'm sorry. I love you." Tears burst forth from her eyes like a dam. They spill down her face. Before Diana can reply, she spins on her heels and hastily walks through the food court out of view.

Her older brother asks, "Was that who I think it was? She seemed pretty upset."

Diana does not hear what her brother asked her. She is busily texting Regina.

Her text reads, "Hello, Reg. It has been a while since I saw you last. Just wanted to know if you can go swimming one of these days? I miss you. Love you too. Dynamite."

Diana looks up. She says, "I'm sorry, Dan, did you say something?"

"Yes, I did. Was that Regina? She seemed upset. I could not help but notice she was crying. I hope she is going to be okay."

Diana replies somberly, "Yes, it was Reg. I don't know what's going on, but whatever it is, she's scared out of her wits. Naturally, I'm also worried about what's happening, but Reg is deathly afraid of something. I'm worried about her."

Her younger brother, Billy, asks, "What did she say?"

"Sorry, Billy. But it's none of your business." She laughs, adding, "Just girl's talk, that's all." Then she says with a mocking tone, "Unless, of course, you want to know. If so, I can share all the juicy details with you."

Billy scoops a wad of rice into his mouth with his chopsticks. He mumbles, "Nope. None of my business. Girl's talk. Yuck!"

"So, what's up with you two?" Dan asks. "You were texting someone. I assume it was Regina, yes?"

"Yep, I asked her if she'd like to go swimming sometime."

Dan says, "That's a weird thing to ask given the circumstances."

"It's all I could think of when I texted her. I wanted my text to look as innocent as possible in case her father sees it. For some reason, she isn't allowed to text me back on her phone. I assume she's going to use Mary's phone."

Dan hunches his shoulders. "I don't think I know her."

Diana says, "Mary is one of our mutual friends. She is a very intelligent teenager who loves to read. She is my classmate. She is also Reg's next-door neighbor. I may be incorrect, but I think Mary's phone is new. So, she probably doesn't have my number."

"Sounds serious, Diana, that your friend isn't allowed to text you from her phone. I'm not going to pry nor am I going to give you advice. But, please be careful, okay?"

"Yes, I'll be careful."

Diana glances at the six girls huddled around their table. She's relieved that they are still in their little world of gossip. Her phone suddenly vibrates. She has received a text message. As she thought it might be, the text is from Mary's phone.

The text reads, "Dynamite! Look out the window toward the parking lot. I'm in the red car convertible next to the large white van."

Diana stares out the window to see Regina waving from the front seat of the red Mustang convertible that belongs to Mary's father. Mary is sitting next to her. Mary's father is in the driver's seat. Diana nods her head, acknowledging that she sees Regina.

Regina's text reads, "Mary's father has no clue what's going on. So, it's best that we not involve him. I told Mary that I'm not allowed to text you from my phone. She's sweet and not the least bit nosy. She didn't ask me a single question. I'll delete this string of texts as soon as I finish texting you."

Diana types, "So, Reg, what's going on? Are you okay?"

"I'll tell you later, Dynamite. It's too complicated to tell you what's going on via texts. Can we meet somewhere? Somewhere safe where no one knows us?"

Diana types, "You can come to my house. Would that be okay?"

"Are you sure your parents won't mind? I mean, after everything that has happened?"

"Reg, my parents know that whatever it is that you're involved in, it has nothing to do with something you caused. Like me, they suspect you're a victim in all this nonsense, whatever the heck it is."

"Cool. Your parents are the world's greatest. I wish my Mom were still alive. I could confide in her. Sure, Daddy is sweet, but he's in trouble. I don't want to get into it here. When can I come over?"

Diana replies, "Hold on a sec, Reg. I need to talk to Dan."

She says to her brother who is reading a news article on his phone, "Say, Dan, sorry to interrupt you. But, do you know if Mom and Dad have any special plans for tonight?"

Her brother replies, "What do you mean?"

"I mean, it being Saturday and all. I'd like to invite Reg over for dinner."

"Wow, Diana. Do you think that's wise given what she accused you of doing to her?"

"Dan, you and I both know that Reg did not compose that stupid letter. Someone forced her to write it. Or, maybe she didn't have a thing to do with it. Someone else may have written it. So, do you know of anything special going on tonight?"

"All I know is Mom and Dad said something about going to a movie."

Diana groans, "Shucks. Just my luck."

Dan laughs as he says, "Alone, Diana. They want to go out to see a movie and maybe go dancing or to dinner afterward. I think they need some good alone time considering everything that's been happening."

"Awesome!" Diana exclaims. "Totally awesome! I do not think Mom or Dad will mind if Reg comes over for dinner. I can whip up some burgers and fries or something else to eat."

Billy suddenly exclaims, "You are cooking?" He stuffs a glob of noodles into his mouth. As he purposely chews disgustingly on the noodles, he says with a full mouth, "Count me out."

Dan says, "I'm certain Mom and Dad won't mind if Regina comes over tonight. I'll be at home, so I can keep the two of you from exchanging blows if it comes to that." He laughs. "Promise me it won't come to that, Diana?"

Diana jokingly chides, "Oh, stop it, Dan! Reg is one of my good friends. I'm very certain we will get along fine."

"I was only kidding," Dan says with a sincere smile. "I'm sure you two will get along fine." He looks at his phone and starts to read the news updates.

Diana texts, "How about tonight, Reg?" Say, around six?"

Regina replies, "Are you sure your parents won't mind? I bet they're super mad at me."

"Nope, they will not mind. And they know, well, I won't get into it here. So, Reg, is six okay with you?"

"Yes, six is fine. Thank you."

Diana texts, "Are you going to tell your father? You should. I don't want to have you make this any more difficult than it already is if you feel compelled to lie to your father."

"Daddy has been distracted lately. He probably won't even realize that I'm not at home. But, no worries. He's going out for dinner tonight with his girlfriend, Kathy. He will assume I'm all alone at home which is usual these days."

Diana replies, "Well, I think I am going to tell my parents. That way some adults know where you are. You know me, I'm always trying to be safe and besides, I'd never lie to my parents." She adds, with an accompanying huge-eyed face emoji, "Well, not intentionally lol." Then, as an afterthought, she texts, "My parents will be out for the night on the town. Dan will be at home. So, not that we need one, but an adult will be present."

"Okay, Dynamite. Thank you. I'll see you at six. PS. Delete this conversation from your phone, please!"

Diana replies, "I will. See you at six. Stay safe."

When Diana and her brothers arrive home after shopping at the mall, Billy calls out, "Hey, you guys, Mom left us a note!"

The note Diana's Mom left on the refrigerator door reads, "Hey Kids. Your father and I decided to make a day of it. We are going shopping, and then we will see a movie, maybe go dancing, eat dinner, whatever. I made a fresh pot of Spaghetti. It's in the refrigerator. Enjoy. Love, Mom."

Billy cries as he yanks open the refrigerator door, "Yes! Now we won't have to eat Diana's nasty cooking. Yes!"

Diana sits at the kitchen table. She begins to text her parents about Regina's upcoming visit at six o'clock. But, she decides not to.

"Hmm, I see no need to bother Mom and Dad about this. Besides, Dan will be here. Naw, I'll leave them out of it and tell them tomorrow after the fact. I want them to enjoy their evening without worrying about what Reg has to say to me."

*****

Part III: Surprise Encounter

Diana's parents have just departed the movie theater across the street. They are waiting in the lobby for the maître d? to seat them at a table. Not surprisingly, the popular restaurant is busy on this Saturday night. Diana's mother is thankful that her husband made reservations. The wait for their table should not be too long.

Diana's mother tugs on her husband's arm and whispers, "Oh, look! There's Ray! On the far side of the restaurant near the wall. And he's with somebody. She's very pretty. I'm glad he's finally seeing someone after all these months. The two of them look very happy together."

"Yes, they do," Diana's father replies. "What's it been, eight months since his wife Denise passed away? What was she, thirty-one?"

"Something like that," Diana's mother says. "Her passing was very sad. I bet it must be difficult for Ray as a single parent."

"I bet it is, especially given the long hours he has to work at his auto shop. The last time I spoke with him was when he repaired my shorted-out taillight. That was a year or so ago. He said he was working ten to twelve-hour days six days a week to bring in extra mechanical repairs. He said he needed the extra hours to pay Denise's medical bills."

"It's sad when someone very young passes away," Diana's mother says, "but to have enormous medical bills after they are gone must be tougher." With a sad expression, she adds, "After all the time in the hospital and the money expended, she passed away just the same. It is very sad." She glances at her phone. "Ah, Dan just texted me." She quickly scans the text.

"Hey, Mom. I hope you two are having an enjoyable time. I was going to text you earlier, but I did not want to bother you while you were out on the town. Diana's friend Regina is here. After a bit of crying and hugging and all that other girl making up stuff, they're gossiping as if nothing has happened. Right now, they're eating popcorn as they watch a movie. No, they're throwing popcorn in the air and missing like crazy and making a mess! Lol. Anyway, just wanted you to know that Regina is here, and everything seems okay. I'm very glad they're happy and didn't have a fistfight. Lol. Have fun. Say hi to Dad. Love you!"

Diana's mother shows Dan's text to her husband. His eyes light up.

He exclaims, "Well, don't that just beat all. The two of them are making up. Maybe we will get some more answers as to what is going on."

"I hope that we do," Diana's mother says with a smile. "I am very happy for them. I know that it broke Diana's heart when Regina said that she hated her."

The maître d? approaches them. He says warmly, "Mister and Missus Bower?"

"Yes, that is us," Diana's father replies.

"Oh yes, thank you," the maître d? says. "I am sorry, there is a delay at your table. It would appear the former patron accidentally cut himself with his steak knife. Nothing too serious, thank goodness. However, I'm afraid the table is unusable temporarily while we, you know, remove it to the kitchen to disinfect it carefully. It is a necessary precaution. I hope you understand. These unfortunate incidents happen from time to time. If you would like, you may enjoy free cocktails at the bar. There is no limit. I am sorry for the delay."

As Diana's father glances at his watch, he says, "How long will it be?"

"About fifteen minutes longer," the maître d? replies. "I am truly sorry. Please follow me to the cocktail bar."

Diana's father says to his wife, "What do you think? Should we have a soda or two? They're free."

"No, I do not want to spoil our dinner by drinking carbonated soda." She glances across the restaurant. "Why don't we join Ray and his girlfriend? They appear to have finished their dinner and are drinking coffee. I bet they're waiting for dessert. Knowing Ray, he won't mind if we join them."

Diana's father says to the maître d?, "Would that be okay if we were to join that couple sitting beneath the Italian scenery picture?" He gestures with his eyes. "The one with the covered bridge? We know the gentleman quite well."

The maître d? looks to where Diana's father is gesturing. "Why of course, sir. And, by way of thanking you and your lovely lady for your understanding, both you and your friends will enjoy tonight's meal on the house." He adds with a smile, "For two couples, and that includes free after dinner drinks and dessert of your choice."

As he looks at his wife, Diana's father says in a happy tone, "Well, I'll be. How does Diana put it, coolio?"

Diana's mother laughs. She says, "Yes, she does. Indeed, our precious daughter does."

*****

Part IV: Perks and Exposés for Four

Diana's parents are standing beside the maître d? when he announces to Ray in a warm voice, "Sir, ma'am, this couple says they know you. Unfortunately, we cannot sit them at their table for fifteen minutes or so. With your concurrence, they would like to join you. If you agree, or even if you disagree, your dinner and after dinner drinks and dessert are on the house." He looks appreciatively at Diana's parents. "Our humble gesture is a token of our appreciation for your friends' understanding of this rather unfortunate situation."

Ray gets to his feet. He says, "It would be our honor to have them join us. They are friends of mine." He gestures toward his lady friend adding, "We are waiting for dessert. I must say, sir, our compliments to the chef. The meal was delicious. However, you do not have to give it to us free of charge. It was worth every penny, I assure you."

With a huge smile, the maître d? says, "Sir, with all due respect, I insist. It is the least that we can do to thank your friends, Mister and Missus Bower, for their understanding." He pulls out a chair from the table and gestures to Diana's mother. He says, along with a wave of his hand, "Ma'am, if you please?"

"Why thank you," Diana's mother says. After she sits, she extends her hand in greeting.

"Hello, Ray. It's been a long time, too long I'm afraid."

Just as Diana's father sits in his chair, Ray exclaims, "Oh, my goodness. Where are my manners?" With a genuine smile of joy, he introduces his girlfriend, Kathy to Diana's parents.

Diana's father asks, "So, Ray, how's business at the shop? Are you still working those long hours?"

"Yes, unfortunately," Ray says. "Those bills just won't go away." He adds with a puckered brow, "Because of the darned bills, the long hours I have to stay at work keep me away from those whom I love for too many hours of the day."

Kathy takes his hand in hers. She says, "Honey, it's okay. Regina and I understand. The bills won't last forever."

Ray says, "Thank you, Honey. I don't know what I'd do without you and Regina. Speaking of Regina, I hope she's doing okay. I don't like leaving her home alone. Maybe I should text her to ensure she's okay."

Diana's mother exclaims, "Oh, she's okay, I assure you, and isn't it wonderful? I am very happy, excited in fact that the two of them are now best of friends once more. Isn't it great?" She takes her phone out of her purse. "Here, Ray, look at this. I bet you'll enjoy reading this text from my oldest son. It's very uplifting." She types in the passcode and then she hands her phone to Ray.

Ray reads Dan's text. The expression on his face turns from one of joy to agony. Then his face turns ashen white. After he hands the phone to Diana's mother, he covers his face with his hands. He slowly shakes his head back and forth. When he removes his hands from his face, tears are welling up in his eyes.

He cries softly, "Oh, my poor baby. I never wanted her to get mixed up in all of this. Regina doesn't deserve all of this agony."

Kathy asks with a loving tone, "All of what? Please tell me." She looks at Diana's parents. "Or, if you prefer, it can wait until later."

Ray replies, "No, Honey, it's okay. What I have to say, what I've meant to say to you all this time is very embarrassing." He looks at Diana's parents one by one. "And, I'm afraid to confess, what I have to say has everything to do with their daughter, Diana."

"Oh, my," Kathy exclaims. "Is it something illegal, Ray? Please tell me it isn't illegal."

"No, I've done nothing wrong, nothing illegal. It's just that I have information about someone else who has done something illegal. And that someone has threatened to expose my past." He takes Kathy's hand in his. He looks her in the eye with an expression of genuine sorrow.

"You see, Honey," I was involved in the robbery of a gas station many years ago. It happened when I was a kid. I was sixteen. What I did was stupid. My parents were divorced, so I had no adult supervision. My mother was living with her boyfriend out of state, and my father was, well, let me put it mildly. He was gone every night of the week for years on end. I seldom saw him.

"I was vulnerable to peer pressure. That's no excuse, I know, but at the time I wanted to fit in. The gang, the thieves that regularly robbed establishments in my hometown, made me feel right at home. They welcomed me with open arms. I'm glad that no one was hurt when we robbed the gas station. One of my friends had a weapon."

"Oh, Ray, I am very sorry," Kathy says with a tone of sincerity. "That is terrible. But, Ray, you were a child. You didn't know better. I'm sure it pains you to recount your story."

Diana's father says, "Ray, I am sorry this happened. Kathy is right. You were young. We all made mistakes when we were teenagers. It's just that some of us made worse mistakes than others." He slides his chair back a bit. "If you'd like, we can leave you two alone to discuss this. It won't be long before our table is ready."

"No, please stay," Ray says with a smile. He takes a long sip of his coffee. With a mocking tone, he says, "Go figure. It's cold. Maybe I should take the maître d? up on his offer and get us more coffee."

He looks Diana's father squarely in the eye. "You need to stay. You need to know why I have been acting," he frowns, "why I have been acting crazy lately. Besides, what is going on involves your daughter, both of our daughter's. Your daughter, like Regina and yes, even I, are victims of someone's greedy charade."

Kathy asks, "So, Ray, what happened after you were apprehended?"

"I went to jail, juvenile jail, but it's all the same when you're a kid. Jail is jail, no matter what they call it, how they try to soften it up by changing its name. I spent two nights in solitary confinement. It was a nightmare. Since I had no previous record and I was doing very well in school with A's and B's, the judge cut me a break. He put me on probation until I turned eighteen. The judge sealed my juvenile records. But, for some reason, a person, whom I will not mention here, obtained a copy of them."

"That's horrible!" Diana's mother declares. "It is my understanding that authorities cannot unseal juvenile records unless the juvenile commits a crime as an adult and then, and only then, can the previous offense be used against him or her."

"Yes, you're correct," Ray says. "But sometimes people with influence can blackmail others with influence to serve their own immoral goals."

Diana's father asks, "So, was someone blackmailing you?"

Ray closes his eyes and nods his head. He whispers, "Yes, I was, or, I should say, someone is blackmailing me." He opens his eyes to stare straight ahead. "The person who is blackmailing me has threatened to divulge the contents of my juvenile arrest. If he does, it could ruin me. I've worked hard to build my automobile repair business from the ground up over the course of two decades. I've never cheated on my taxes. I've never been behind on my bills. I've never jilted a customer. I've lived an honorable adult life up until now."

He looks at Diana's father. Tears are welling up in his eyes once more. He removes his thick glasses and wipes them with his napkin.

Then he dabs at the corners of his eyes. As he puts on his glasses, he says with a serious tone, "You're a father. You know how it feels when it comes time for your children to have something special for their birthdays, at Christmas, or just because you want to show them that you love them. Like my Regina and me, I know you would do anything for your children. I know you can appreciate what I am saying."

"Yes, I can," Diana's father replies solemnly. "I would do anything for my kids." He looks at Diana's mother. "For our kids. They mean the world to us."

"It's the enormous medical bills," Ray says. "Their interest rate is ginormous. I pay them, even pay more than I owe each month, but I never can seem to put a dent in their balance. It's very depressing. I can barely pay the bills, mortgage, keep my business in the black, let alone give Regina allowance and buy the things she wants and put quality food on the table."

"Can you declare bankruptcy," Kathy asks. "Would that help?"

"Oh, sure, I could declare bankruptcy, but that would mean losing my house and probably my business. I do not know if I could deal with that and subject Regina to that embarrassing horror show. Then it would take me forever to get my credit score up to par. No, even though I've thought about it, bankruptcy is not an option, at least not yet."

"How about a loan," Diana's father asks. "Could that help?"

Ray laughs. With a somber tone, he says, "I doubt I could get a loan for one hundred-fifty-thousand dollars and change."

"Goodness," Kathy says, "that's a ton of money. Why didn't you tell me? I could help by giving you a couple of hundred dollars a month. It's not much, but it could help. And it wouldn't be a loan. You need not repay me." She squeezes Ray's hand. "That's what love is all about."

"That's sweet of you, Honey," Ray says, "but I'll keep on paying the bills until they're gone. It is the honorable thing to do, and Denise would want me to stay the course, to persevere. She was one tough lady, a fighting spirit until the end. Besides, they are hospital bills from procedures that kept her alive a few more years. So, it's personal."

The maître d? draws near to their table. He says with a happy tone, "Mister and Missus Bower, your table is ready. He gestures with his hand graciously. "If you will please follow me."

Ray says to the maître d, "If you do not mind," he looks at Diana's parents, "and if it is okay with our friends, I believe we would like them to remain here at our table." He looks at Kathy.

Kathy says, "I'd like them to stay too."

Diana's parents smile and say in unison, "We'd be delighted."

Ray says to the maître d? with an upbeat tone of voice, "I have some stories I'd need to tell them. But first, I have one request if you please. In fact, I have two. No, belay that. I have three requests."

The maître d? says with a chuckle, "I am at your service, sir."
"One, please take their order. Two, please check on our dessert. We ordered the brownies topped with vanilla ice cream." He laughs.
"Hopefully with extra chocolate fudge and lots of whipped cream. Heaps of pecans would be nice as well."

Then, Mister Ray Reynolds, in a noticeably better, upbeat mood, taps his coffee cup with his teaspoon, saying, "And that leads me to request three. Please fill 'er up. Something tells me that we are going to be here all night."

*****

Part V: Short and Sweet

Diana and Regina are playing an Xbox game when Regina suddenly throws her game controller to the floor and begins to cry. She says somberly in between sobs, "Dynamite, you're not going to believe this." She hands her phone to Diana.

The text on Regina's phone reads, "Regina, I'm going to make this short and sweet. So that you know, I'm with Diana's parents. Kathy is here. Hold on a sec."

Diana cries, "Oh, my goodness! Thank God I didn't tell my parents you are here. I was going to but decided it could wait until the morning. I certainly do not want you to get in trouble for being here. Talk about karma! Who would have thought your father and Kathy would run into my parents? The four of them together is unbelievable." She quickly hands the phone to Regina. "Here, he's sent you another text."

The text reads, "Sorry. I was talking to the waiter. Anyway, I know where you are."

Regina whispers, "Oh, no, Dynamite! He knows I am here." She shakes her head disbelievingly. "I am going to be in serious trouble. I'll probably be grounded for the rest of the summer if not worse."

Diana asks in an incredulous tone, "How in the world do they know you're here? I didn't tell them, Reg, I swear!"

"I believe you, Dynamite. Maybe one of your brothers texted your parents."

Diana says, "That must be it. One of them probably mentioned in passing that you're here."

Regina holds her phone at arm's length. She says with a tone of dread in her voice as she hands the phone to Diana, "He's sent me another text. I don't want to read what he said, Dynamite. I can't bear to read it. Please, you read it for me. Go easy on me when you tell me what my father says, okay?" She buries her face in her hands and sobs.

The text reads, "And I am happy you're with Diana, happy you two are back together once more. I've told Diana's parents just about everything. And I have more to tell you as well. Have fun, stay safe and always know. I love you with all my heart."

Diana hugs Regina as she screams, "Reg, it's okay! Not only does he know you are here, but he is also happy for you and me! Here, read what he said!"

Regina reads her father's text. She immediately begins to yell. "Yippee, this is wonderful! After nearly a month this nightmare will hopefully soon come to an end!" Tears of joy are streaming down her cheeks. She grabs a pillow from the bed and begins smacking Diana with it.

Diana grabs another pillow from her bed and smacks Regina in her face. As the two newly reacquainted friends begin a brouhaha pillow fight, Diana yells in a delighted voice, "Oh, you're going to regret messing with me, Reg Reynolds! Don't forget. I'm your number one pillow fighting nemesis. I'm Dyna-mite!"

Diana's phone tumbles out of her back pocket onto the floor just as she attacks Regina with her pillow. As the spirited pillow fight intensifies, Regina accidentally kicks the phone with her foot. It slides beneath the bed where it will remain unnoticed for nearly two hours. Also unnoticed is a message on the phone's note app.

"Diana. You and Regina are in serious trouble. We need to talk ASAP. Charles."

*****

Part VI: My Lucky Ticket

Mister Young is in the study of his three-story mansion on the far side of town, about one-half mile from Diana's home. He is relaxing in his easy chair as he reads the award-winning novel *Atlas Shrugged*. It is a 1957 novel by Ayn Rand.

Despite the book's intriguing plot depicting the dystopian United States of America burdened with over-regulated tax laws, Mister Young's mind is wandering. The intriguing story would normally keep him absorbed for hours on end. However, this is not a normal evening. Events to his loathing are unfolding.

The sudden ringing of his cell phone causes him to lose concentration even more. The caller has blocked his number. Just the same, Mister Young knows who it is that is calling.

He looks at the open the door to his study to make sure his wife, Marjorie is not eavesdropping outside of his study. He pivots his chair, so he is facing away from the open door. He whispers, "Talk to me."

The voice on the other end says, "You're not going to like this, Jack. The two girls are still together."

"Tell me something I don't already know," Mister Young snaps. "You told me that over two hours ago. Two teenagers hanging out together are of no concern to me. They're kids. What do they know? Nothing. Therefore, let me say this again. They are no concern to me." He looks at his watch. "If those two are anything like my daughters, they'll be chatting away and playing video games until well past midnight."

"Yes sir, I fully understand. But if the Regina girl tells her friend what her father knows, then it could spell trouble for you, for us."

Mister Young nearly barks into the phone. "I told you, they are of no concern to me. I made it quite clear to Ray that he is not to tell his daughter anything. Even if he does tell her, and she squawks, no one is going to believe her anyway. Kids lie all the time. They'll do and say anything to stay out of trouble. I know that from first-hand experience." He takes a sip of his iced tea.

"Besides, I made it very clear to the Regina girl. If she opens her trap, I will expel her. I also told the Diana girl, in the presence of her parents, that I would do the same to her. What else do you have?"

"Ray and her girlfriend are with the other girl's parents. Gloria told me they've been at the same table for hours. Ray is drinking cup after cup of coffee. According to Gloria, he is talking nonstop."

Mister Young nearly jumps down the throat of the caller saying, "What the? I told you, I did not want Ray meeting up with that girl's parents. They're friends. It complicates things." He slams his fist on the side table knocking the glass of ice tea to the lush carpet. "Darn you, Bob! Ray better not shoot his mouth off. I'll destroy him. Why did you allow this to happen?"

"Ah, sir, there is no way I can prevent four adults from accidentally bumping into each other in a restaurant."

"Are you certain it was an accident?" Mister Young asks. "You're supposed to be monitoring Ray's phone. That's why I'm paying you an extra six grand."

"Ray didn't call the girl's parents. It was a chance encounter. The only place Ray has called tonight is his shop. He talked for exactly ninety-four seconds. He also texted his daughter, Regina a few times. She never texted him in return. No, sir, I'm certain the four meeting up at the restaurant was a chance encounter.

"Well, fix it," Mister Young says.

"How do you want me to fix it?"

"Bob, use your head. Talk to Ray. Do not threaten him physically. That's not the way I operate. I'm not going to prison for the rest of my life for a measly one-hundred-seventy grand. Marjorie would never allow my daughters to see me. She's that cruel. And I cannot live without seeing my girls. Besides, I have already paid for our trip to France and Switzerland, including first-class round-trip tickets.

"Ask him what he told the girl's parents if anything. If he doesn't fess up, tell him I will release his juvenile arrest report, little by little." He grins. "Tell him that I know lots of important people in high places, and I'll make him squirm until he shuts his mouth." He adds in a mocking tone, "Or loses his shop."

"Okay, sir. I'll drop by his shop Monday. It's closed on Sundays."

"You do that, Bob," Mister young says. "You either fix it, or I won't pay you or Gloria your share of the money next week. Now, leave me alone until you have fixed the problem."

Mister Young grabs his billfold that is sitting on the side table. He pulls out a small ticket tucked in between hundred-dollar bills.

He stares at the ticket lovingly. With an evil snicker, he says, "You are my lucky one, my precious. Indeed you are. After all these years betting on the ladies' championship softball games and winning a trifling amount of money if anything at all, I finally struck it big. Thanks to you." He tenderly kisses his lucky ticket, and then he repeats the combination of letters and numbers over and over in his mind.

DJB06182003C

Little does he know, the significance of the letters and numbers on his *lucky* ticket will soon reveal his fate.

CHAPTER TEN

REVENGE OF MENDACIUM

Part I: Village of the Minima

Diana cannot talk with Uvam as the group proceeds to the Village of Minima. The lack of conversation is due to Jayvyn's quickened pace as he trots on the trail. While Diana is steady on Jayvyn's back, the Minima have to hold onto his mane for dear life. Occasionally, a few of the Minima slip from his mane. He must briefly stop so they can crawl back on. Thankfully, none that fall to the ground is hurt. That is because the Minima are athletic and flexible. They resemble miniature gymnasts as they flipflop in the air gracefully. They nearly always land on their feet. When they hit the ground, they purposely tumble head over heels. Their supple movements lessen their impact.

After a few minutes, the group arrives at the edge of a small clearing of flourishing verdant grass in the forest. Dainty blue and gold-colored flowers peek from between the tall blades of grass. The clearing is roughly two hundred yards in length and half the distance in width. Diana can see spacious vegetable gardens at the far end of the clearing.

Except for Uvam, his wife, and his son, all the Minima somersault from Jayvyn's mane to the ground. They race merrily through the grass to the cluster of beautifully manicured trees in the middle of the clearing.

Uvam says, "As you can see, they are happy to be home. Some of them have never ventured outside of this clearing in their entire lives. Plus, they must be famished. I know I am. We haven't eaten anything substantial since we departed the village a half sun ago. I am relieved it didn't take us as long to return to our village on your steed as it took us to arrive at your location in the forest."

Given what Uvam just said, Diana guesses it took the Minima around one and one-half hours to travel to where the Parva Draco and Inania attacked her. She is very happy they were there. Otherwise, without I Dunno to guide Jayvyn and her, she would have been clueless what to do next. Not to mention, she would have been scared senseless, left alone in the forest without a friend with whom she could have a conversation. She ponders if April and Charles purposely left her alone with I Dunno and Jayvyn to strengthen her resolve.

"Perhaps this is their way of forcing me to use my intelligence and talents to the best of my potential. Maybe they want me to mature as the purported Youngster Heroine of the World Beyond. There can be no other explanation. Thanks to I Dunno, I have remarkably adroit swordsman skills and expert archery abilities. And yes, thanks to her, I can create light to illuminate our way as we travel. So, I guess all of what I am experiencing is a test of sorts. Perhaps Charles and April's absence is to allow me to be myself, to see if I have what it takes to defeat Mendacium on my own."

Diana estimates there must be thirty-five to forty trees in the cluster. All the trees look the same. They are about ten feet in height. The chestnut-colored trunks of the trees are abnormally wide in circumference. So are the canopies with their broadleaf, brightly colored green and orange leaves. The dense canopies extend four to five feet on all sides of the trunk. The breadth of the canopies gives them a diameter nearly as wide as the trees are tall. The trees remind her of overgrown shaggy scrubs except they have all the features of trees, a trunk, branches, and broad leaves. She has never seen trees like these.

She jumps from Jayvyn's back to the ground. She scoops Uvam, his wife and his son from Jayvyn's mane into her hands one by one. She gently places them on the soft grass. Saccharo and Eros race toward the cluster of trees as they laugh loudly with excitement. Uvam remains behind. He stands beside her.

She gathers up her weapons and tosses her waterskin onto the grass. Then she removes Jayvyn's bridle. It is safer for him to eat without having the bit in his mouth. Otherwise, grass could get caught in his throat, and he could choke. He walks off to forage in the lush grass.

Diana scoops Uvam from the ground. She places him on her shoulder. She carries her things to the edge of the cluster of trees. Then she sets her belongings onto the grass and steps over a small three-inch high wooden picket fence that encircles the trees. When she gets closer to the trees, she is amazed at what she sees.

Barely controlling her emotions, she exclaims, "My goodness, will you look at that! There are bunches of tiny, thatched roof oval tree houses hidden within the branches, whole neighborhoods! Wooden stairways suspended by ropes connect each of the tree houses. This scene reminds me of the science class lesson Anna, and I had when we talked about the adventures of Swiss Family Robinson. Except for everything here is scaled down in comparison." As she looks at Uvam, she says, "Anna is a good friend of mine in the Real-world. She plays first base on our ladies' softball team."

She exclaims yet again. "Oh, my goodness! Check out that water-wheel. The force of the water in its paddles is causing it to turn slowly. And then it dumps the water into little buckets." As she points in another direction, she says, "And that is very cool. A pulley system is hauling the water buckets to that wooden reservoir up there. This water scheme is unbelievable! From where do you get the water, Uvam? I thought there were no open sources of water in the World Beyond except for Lake Vita."

With a tone of pride, Uvam says, "Empress Diana, we have a unique means of pumping water from an underground aquifer. Since we are very small in comparison to other creatures in the World Beyond, we do not use much water. I doubt we will ever run out of fresh water.

"The waterwheel and reservoir system services all the tree house neighborhoods in the village. There is only one system. It would be too costly to have more than one. The waterwheel and reservoir are undoubtedly the most important assets we have in our Minima Village. If something were to destroy the waterwheel and reservoir system, it would be a disaster. It took us many hundreds of sunlight cycles to construct it.

"The waterwheel and reservoir system serves two purposes. It provides fresh water to each of the tree houses via a pipe in the house's roof. It also is necessary for sanitary reasons." He points out a few of the tree houses. "If you will notice, Empress Diana, each of the tree houses has a wooden pipe protruding from its floor. The individual pipes link to the larger pipe in the middle of the tree house neighborhood. Water from the reservoir flushes the individual pipes and carries sewage to the main pipe. The main pipe ends in a culvert buried deep underground. That way, there is no chance of spreading disease." He laughs. "If only we had a similar sanitary system when we hunt or are in the fields attending to crops. Since we do not, we are forced to, you know, do our thing and bury our waste."

Diana frowns. She must do the same thing along the trail. It is the grossest thing she has ever done. She is glad that I Dunno had trained her how to do it properly. Plus, I Dunno had supplied her with absorbent leaves and plenty of handmade soap to ensure the unavoidable disgusting call of nature in the forest is as hygienic and tolerable as possible.

She suddenly cries out, "And oh, my gosh, will you look at that! Now that is super-duper coolio! It is an elevator pulley system designed to carry occupants from the ground up to the tree house neighborhood!" She scoops Uvam from her shoulder into the palm of her hand. As she looks down at the four-inch-tall Minima, she says excitedly, "Can you show me how the elevator works? Please?"

Uvam says with pride, "I certainly can, Empress Diana. And just so you know, every one of our tree neighborhoods has an identical elevator system."

Diana wants to laugh at Uvam's continual correctness by calling her Empress instead of Diana. But she thinks better of it. She considers, despite everything, he is the King of the Minima, so he can do and say whatever he wants.

Uvam jumps from her hand and somersaults onto the ground. He steps onto a platform made of what looks like intricately woven strands of wicker. The platform even has guard rails and a sliding entrance gate to enclose its riders safely inside. The platform looks large enough to accommodate ten or so riders. Uvam gives a tug of the rope, and the platform begins to rise slowly into the air.

Diana watches fascinated as an intricate system of wooden pulleys and cogs, belts made of cord, and springy sticks all work together to haul up the platform. The platform stops in the middle of the tree house neighborhood, just slightly below the level of Diana's eyes. Having the platform stop in the middle of the neighborhood allows for handy access for the residents, whether they live either above or below the platform's stop. After Uvam exits the platform, it slowly descends to the ground. It is then that she notices there is an identical elevator platform.

She says, "This seems very efficient. How does the other platform work? Is it the same as the one on which you just rode?"

Uvam says, "Watch this, Empress Diana." He hops onto the other platform and tugs gently on the rope. It immediately begins to descend slowly to the ground. By the time it reaches its destination, the other platform is already on the ground. He hops off the platform. It immediately begins to ascend.

He says, "You see, Empress Diana, one platform, the one I was on, is for those who wish to go down. This one," he points to the one he first rode, "is for those who wish to go up. That way there always is a platform up there." He points to the middle of the tree house neighborhood, "and always one down here. It eliminates the need to have two of the Minima manning the elevator system around the clock.

"It is far less time-consuming for the tree house neighborhoods' occupants and visitors as well. In the past, before we invented this two-platform system, our elevator control Minima's would often fall asleep due to boredom. It resulted in terrible elevator service." He frowns. "And we were paying them good salaries too. Ten holodi of a nighttime cycle."

Diana declares, "That makes perfect sense. But, what are holodi? Are they something like a barter system, a way of exchanging goods?"

Uvam says with a chuckle, "No, Empress Diana. Holodi is a part of our money system. There are fifty solodi to a holodi. Twenty holodi make a potanis. Most important, expensive transactions are made in potanis while solodi and holodi make up the majority of day-to-day financial transactions." He reaches into a tiny pouch he has hidden beneath his tunic. He withdraws two objects from the pouch. "Here, Empress Diana, look at these."

Diana sees he is holding two different colored objects. Each is the size of an eraser on the end of a wooden pencil yet very thin like a coin. But, instead of being round like coins, the objects are square.

Uvam says as he points, "This white one is a solodi. This brown one is a holodi." He pulls a dark, reddish-brown object out of his pouch. It is the same size and shape as the two other objects. "These are rare. Not many Minima have a lot of these in their possession. It is a potanis."

Diana notices that each of the square coins, assuming they indeed are coins, is made of wood. There is a symbol of a bird and the sun rays of the World Beyond's short-lived sun carved on each of the coins. The nearly white solodi appears made of wood like that of a pine tree. The brown holodi appears made of wood like that of an oak tree. The rare potanis appears made of wood like mahogany only it is much darker, almost black. Uvam continues discussing the money system.

"Also, Empress Diana, the holodi money system is universal throughout all of the World Beyond." He chuckles adding, "Of course, larger creatures handle money that is much larger in size than the Minima's money." He adds with a proud tone, "Naturally, all of the assorted sizes are transferable. The monetary value of the money doesn't change regardless of its size." He tosses the objects into his pouch.

Diana says, "Thank you, Uvam, for explaining your money system. And, I must say, your tree house neighborhoods are fascinating. I wish I could sleep in one of your tree houses. But I am much too large."

Uvam says, "Please pick me up and place me on your shoulder. Let us proceed to the rear of our Minima tree house neighborhoods. I have two surprises waiting for you."

Diana scoops up Uvam and places him on her shoulder. She steps over the fence and retrieves her belongings. Then she walks to the rear of the cluster of trees.

Uvam points to a large tree just inside the perimeter of the forest trees surrounding the clearing. "See that, Empress Diana? Your very own home for tonight or for how long you desire to stay. We Minima built your tree house exclusively for your Highness, Empress Diana, once we learned she was in the World Beyond. It is for Empress Diana and her very important royal guest."

Diana ogles at her very own, tailored-made tree house. She loves tree houses, and she always wanted one as a kid! She feels like freaking out. She wants to jump up and down like crazy and laugh and cry all at the same time. However, she in some way manages to maintain an air of dignity. She does not want to offend Uvam with improper, boorish conduct. After all, she is Empress Diana. She figures she can freak out and go crazy with bliss once she is inside.

The people-sized tree house the Minima villagers made for her rests within the wide branches of a tall deciduous tree. The tree house is approximately ten feet above the ground. A wooden porch surrounds it. A vertical wooden ladder affixed to the tree trunk allows access to the tree house via a square hole in the porch. A rocking chair and a small table are on the porch. A wooden vase on the table contains a bouquet of the blue and gold flowers she saw in the clearing. To Diana, this marvelous tree house looks like a home away from home only a heckuva lot better. Through the open window framed by white curtains, she sees the soft glow of yellowish light from inside.

Notwithstanding her eagerness to climb the ladder, she manages to maintain her decorum. With her heart nearly racing out of control and her eagerness ready to burst, she says to Uvam in a calm voice, "It is gorgeous, and it looks very comfy. I cannot wait to sleep inside. I welcome sleeping off the ground after all this time. I thank you and your fellow Minima for making this for me."

Uvam says with a grin, "The pleasure is ours, Empress Diana. You are welcome. Please stay as long as you wish." He turns to leave. As he does, Diana suddenly recalls something he had said a moment ago.

"Wait for a second, Uvam, if you please. You had mentioned that this tree house is for my royal guest and me. Who is my guest?" Uvam points to the tree house.

She looks to see where Uvam is pointing. On the porch, silhou-etted by the soft yellowish glow of the light flickering inside, a tiny figure is waving her small hand in earnest. She has an itty-bitty white bandage on her injured wing.

Diana throws her belongings onto the grass. As she scrambles up the ladder, she screams over and over with joy.

"I Dunno!"

*****

Part II: Tale of Duplicity

Diana and I Dunno spend considerable time telling each other the exciting stories of their frightening encounters with the Inania and Parva Draco. We already know how Diana's story unfolded. However, we do not know what happened to I Dunno and how it came to be that a Parva Draco had pretended to be her.

After searching for a long time, I Dunno had finally located the elusive Sana bush. She had recalled seeing the bush when the threesome passed it by hours before. She had thought at the time, "I should pick a few of these berries just in case." However, she became distracted and soon forgot about the healing berries.

When she saw the Sana bush once more, she was elated. She glanced around to ensure no creatures were nearby. Not seeing any, she reached to pluck a berry from the bush. Just as she did, she was astonished to see her spitting image staring at her. Naturally, for a moment, she was in shock as she sized up her image. Then panic swept over her as she realized that she was staring at an illusory Inania. The deceitful creature had mirrored her pixie form.

She began to panic. Unlike in Diana's world at home, I Dunno has no magical powers to counter evil in the World Beyond. The magic she does have is crude by protector pixie standards, creating water and foodstuffs, ordinary things like that. Therefore, she is very vulnerable, especially given her small size.

She immediately got airborne. In her haste to escape, she dropped the berry. She zoomed down to retrieve it. It was then a Parva Draco hiding underneath the Sana bush reached out for her. Its long, sharp claws ripped into her right wing causing her to plummet to the ground.

She struggled to escape, but she was no match for the creature. The Inania had joined in the fray. Its strength was equal to her own, so she was easily overcome. Since she was no longer able to fly, she was at their mercy.

She knew that Diana would worry that she was absent for so long, that she would look for her. So, she called out to Jayvyn in a means that she hoped only he could understand. In case Mendacium was somehow listening in, she was very careful not to disclose what had happened to her. She simply told Jayvyn that she was on the portion of the trail they had already traveled. Unfortunately, Mendacium had understood what she had said. He sent others to her location.

Then, the unthinkable happened. The Parva Draco bound her at the wrists and ankles. Next, he gagged her. Much to her alarm, she watched as the Parva Draco duplicated the bindings she had on her wrists and ankles and the gag covering her mouth. The Inania lifted the bound Parva Draco off the ground and tied it to a tree trunk. Then the creature removed the gag covering the Parva Draco's mouth so it could speak. The Parvo Draco instantly assumed I Dunno's look.

I Dunno immediately knew what was happening. They were going to use the Parva Draco that looked like her as a decoy. They were going to trick Diana and Jayvyn into thinking the Parva Draco was her! Meanwhile, the Inania would remain out of sight, presumably to assume the form of Diana when she arrived. I Dunno wanted to call out to warn Jayvyn. Because she had a gag in her mouth, she could not.

Two more Parva Draco arrived on the scene and rudely deposited her onto a cart. They set off to haul the cart to their village. As she lay struggling on the cart to free herself, I Dunno looked back in horror. The Parva Draco tied to the tree was speaking in a voice that sounded just like hers!

"Oh, our pretty, Empress Diana, beloved Youngster Heroine of the World Beyond. You are going to cease to exist very soon. And say goodbye to your protector pixie."

I Dunno's heart sank as she wept openly. She, the protector pixie of Empress Diana, had failed! The Parva Draco was going to trick Diana. And the Inania lurking in the shadows was going to attack her. And it was all her fault!

After a brief period, while they were walking in the thickness of the forest, one of the Parva Draco started yelling. "Abandon the cart and the pixie! The Minima are attacking!"

The pair of Parva Draco was too slow to escape. After a short-lived battle, the dozens of Minima overwhelmed them. She was safe!

She demanded that the Minima allow her to return to the location where the attack had occurred. However, the King of the Minima declined. He commanded five Minima to take her to their village and to tend to her wound. Meanwhile, he and the other Minima marched on to the location where her spitting image decoy and the Inania were lying in wait.

I Dunno sums-up her account of her encounter with the Parva Draco and Inania by saying, "I didn't know until a few moments ago that the Minima arrived too late, that you had to battle the Inania on your own." She smiles. "However, just so you know, Diana, I had full confidence in you. All along I trusted your instincts and skills to destroy the Inania if it were to come to that." She laughs. "Although I never imagined Jayvyn would pulverize the Parva Draco in the manner that he did. To be perfectly honest with you, I am delighted the Parva Draco's hideously evil life ended that way."

*****

Part III: A Breather of Sorts

After two comings and goings of the World Beyond's sun, I Dunno's slashed wing had sufficiently healed for her to fly short distances around the village. This is not to say that during her convalescent period, she was lazing around in Diana's tree house. On the contrary. She was very busy. Nor was Diana whiling away the hours aimlessly. The two of them were hard at work helping the villagers with their day-to-day chores.

Diana and I Dunno worked in the fields despite insistent protests from Uvam. Diana had explained to Uvam that, given her size, she could accomplish more than twenty Minima in one-tenth of the time. She went on to explain, as far as it concerned I Dunno, the pixie could assist farmers by using her magical powers. She had said that helping the villagers was a token of I Dunno's and her appreciation for the villagers' hospitality. It was also a way to say thank you for rescuing I Dunno from the Parva Draco and for building her tree house.

Even so, Uvam protested. He claimed that crowned heads toiling alongside common Minima was demeaning. He argued it would set a bad precedent. Diana and Uvam went back and forth in a friendly disagreement for the longest time. It was only after his wife, Saccharo intervened that Uvam relented.

She had said, "She's the Empress of the World Beyond, Uvam. She can do anything she desires." Uvam began to protest yet again. She stopped his words by raising her hand and stating, "You merely are the ruler of the Village and creatures of Minima." She made a circle with her arms spread wide. "While Empress Diana is the ruler of an entire world. She is the Youngster Heroine of the World Beyond. So, dear, please get over it."

Uvam had stormed off. However, much to Diana's joy, a while later he returned all smiles, a tiny rake in his hand. He was wearing a straw hat in place of his crown. As he marched off proudly to the fields, Saccharo and Eros joined him.

Diana had considered making a plow for Jayvyn to use. Nevertheless, after repeated attempts to draw up elaborate diagrams for a horse plow, she gave up. Instead, with the help of ladyfolk and Minima carpenters, Diana made a crude plow out of life-sized tree branches. The Minima weavers attached the plow to a curved fallen tree limb. The tree limb served as the plow's handle. Thus, the first human plow in the World Beyond came to be.

When Diana plowed the field, she pulled the plow by holding the tree limb behind her back. Dozens of Minima carefully enfolding stones between their feet provided the necessary weight to allow the blades to burrow deep into the ground. But, pulling the moderately heavy plow was far too draining for her. Although her hands were calloused from living on the land, oozing blisters formed on her fingertips. Plus, she unnecessarily was straining her back and forearms. There had to be a better way for a human to plow the fields.

The carpenters and weavers went to work once more. With a leathersmith's know-how, they drew up plans for a harness for Diana to use. Just before they began to work on it, a resourceful female Minima called Consilii designed a plow harness suitable for a horse. Consilii's coworkers marveled at her invention. The carpenters, weavers, and the leathersmith combined their skills and worked nonstop to make the crude device in no time. Thus, the Minima created the first horse-drawn wooden plow in the World Beyond. Jayvyn happily plowed all the fields in the village, in what Diana estimated to be, less than two hours.

Seeing as she was no longer needed to plow the fields, Diana raked weeds and dug up rocks. Digging up rocks that, to the small Minima, were the size of boulders, helped the farmers tremendously. She piled the rocks into cairns on every corner of the fields. Then she made a ten-inch high rock fence that surrounded the treehouse village. Carpenters tore down the old wooden fence. They used the lumber to construct six swinging gates to permit easy access into the village.

Diana also helped to repair the waterwheel and reservoir piping system. The Minima applauded and cheered as she re-tied ropes and pounded foundation poles into the ground. Naturally, they were excited the Heroine Youngster of the World Beyond was helping them. But, they were as happy they didn't have to climb the rickety ladders and scaffolding.

I Dunno was also busy. She worked alongside the farmers planting seeds and tilling the gardens. Using her magical powers, she created waterskins for all the farmers and kept them filled with clean, fresh water. And, while she was convalescing, she was a dinner guest of four treehouse families. In turn, Diana hosted several families in her tree house.

The six-day period was a fun-filled, enjoyable time with music, dancing, and delicious Minima hors-d'oeuvres. To Diana, it felt like a celebration during a Fourth of July holiday. Little would she know. An explosive, fiery, deadly scene was about to explode, the likes she, I Dunno and none of the Minima had ever seen.

We now return to the present.

It is the beginning of the third cycle of the short-lived sun after Diana arrived at the village. She estimates the sun's visit is now over three hours in duration. Diana and I Dunno are sound asleep in Diana's tree house. Suddenly, echoing cries pervade the tranquil sundown rudely awakening them. Pandemonium is sweeping through the village. Soldiers are yelling. "We're under attack! Proceed to your defensive positions! Take up the females and young to the underground shelters."

I Dunno soars to Uvam's tree house to learn what is happening. She returns moments later.

"Diana, numerous Parva Draco are attacking the village. A regiment of Inania accompanies them. The creatures are taking up the similarities of villagers to deceive the Minima. It is mass confusion out there!"

Diana shouts, "We must help them!" She dresses quickly into her warrior clothing and gathers her weapons. As she starts toward the ladderway opening in the porch, I Dunno shouts to stop her.

"There is more, Diana, more distressing news."

Diana declares, "What could be more distressing than an attack by many Parva Draco and Inania?" With a look of dismay on her face, she cries, "It is Mendacium, isn't it? He's here, I Dunno, yes?"

"No, Diana, not that I know of, at least not yet. What is out there is almost as terrifying. It is a flight of Malavem."

"Malavem? I thought the Malavem were extinct? They reportedly died out a millennium ago. Uvam told me the Minima destroyed the remaining Malavem during the Final War."

I Dunno states, "So, they thought. Mendacium must have resurrected them somehow." She pulls a face adding, "Uvam says his guards reportedly counted five of the frightening creatures. There could be more."

Diana says unemotionally, "Well, I have twenty arrows. That should be plenty enough." She smiles. "And you can always make more arrows using your magic, right?"

I Dunno says with a cautious tone, "Perhaps, I can. But, it'll take time to replace those that you use. Nevertheless, Diana, please bear in mind. When you strike a Malavem with an arrow, it will separate in two as it gives birth to its evil twin. You possibly could have dozens to oppose."

Diana smiles as she lowers herself onto the ladder. As she grabs the ladder rung, she looks up at I Dunno hovering over her. The expression on the face of Empress Diana, Youngster Heroine of the World Beyond, conveys her doubtless resolve. She states matter-of-factly, "Well, I'll have to make sure I strike the twin the exact moment its host creates it, won't I?"

*****

Part IV: Mendacium by Another Name

As soon as Diana drops from the ladder onto the ground, a dozen or more Parva Draco surround her. At the outset, she is hesitant to assault them. She is uncertain if they are truly Parva Draco or frightened Minima seeking shelter in her tree house. She does not want to strike a Minima by accident. Despite the brief confusion, she quickly notices that these creatures' eyes are pink. The eyes of Minima are blue.

Before she can strike at the beasts, two Parva Draco latch onto her right leg with their sharp claws. They sink their piercing upper fangs deep into her calf, drawing blood. Their bites are more painful than their eight sharp claws burrowing deep into her skin. She cries out in agony.

Tears of intense pain fill her eyes, clouding her vision. She quickly pulls an arrow from her quiver. She thrusts it with all her might. The single stab of her arrow pierces both bodies of the beasts at the same time. They fall to the ground moaning loudly and vaporize a few moments later. She slips the arrow back inside her quiver and begins to strike out relentlessly with her sword. Those creatures that do not run away to avoid her sword's reach, she impales with punishing jabs of the razor-sharp tip of her sword.

After the Parva Draco surrounding her are either destroyed or have dispersed, her first thought is to examine her aching leg. But, she quickly recognizes she does not have enough time to do so. She figures if she can stand she can fight. She bites her lips as she fights back the pain.

"Besides," she reasons, "it is what it is. I had comparable pain when I jumped over those shrubs last year in Ukraine and ungraciously landed in a rose bush. Well, perhaps, not as sharp pain as this. But, still, the thorn punctures were everywhere on my body!" She takes off running with a limp to the source of ceaseless, ear-piercing screams.

She arrives at the source of the screams a few moments later. She is standing just outside the rock fence that she finished building a day ago. Minima are engaged in hand-to-hand combat with either Parva Draco or Inania. At first, she cannot distinguish the Minima from the evil creatures. Within a matter of seconds, she can do so, at least as it concerns two of the creatures. The pair of Inania disguised as Minima immediately have mirrored her likeness. They instantly set upon her with swords held high above their heads.

Diana immediately assumes a defensive posture. She hastily backs away slightly and places her sword in front of her, parallel to her body. One of the creatures is in front of her, slightly to her right. The other creature is to her left. She quickly spins to her right and feigns an attack on the creature to her right. The intended victim backs away and falls onto its back. However, rather than assault the creature, she continues her spin past it. Her sword strikes the blade of the Inania to the left of her with a reverberating *Clang!* It expertly blocks her lunge. Then it counters by striking down severely hard on her sword.

She is knocked back a few feet with the power of the Inania's blow, but she manages to stay on her feet. The Inania rushes to her and strikes down hard once more with its sword. This time, she barely blocks its sword with hers. The sharp blade of its sword slashes her left forehead with a glancing blow less than an inch above her eye. Thankfully, the hard bone of her eye socket prevented the sword from piercing her eye and blinding her!

Blood immediately begins to flow from the gash into the corner of her eye. She does the best that she can with her reduced vision as she feigns a blow to the creature's right. However, instead of striking the creature on its right side, she immediately reverses direction. She spins around and strikes the second Inania at the knees. It immediately goes down on all fours. She runs her sword through its chest. It begins to vaporize as soon as it assumes its original form.

Diana immediately turns to confront the other Inania. However, much to her surprise, standing on the ground before her is I Dunno. The second Inania has disappeared. She assumes it ran off in fear rather than confronting her.

She yells with a tone of panic, "I Dunno, why are you here? You are defenseless. You need to seek shelter before you get hurt."

I Dunno says in a hurtful voice, "I must be close to you, Diana. You know that." She gestures with her thumb to her right wing. She begins to cry. With a miserable look on her face, she says in an unhappy tone, "I have reinjured my wing. Can you please lift me up onto your shoulder? I cannot fly."

Diana says, "Most certainly. But, I insist that you seek shelter with the Minima. You are in no condition to face danger." She bends over to lift I Dunno from the ground. To her disbelief, I Dunno's form immediately mirrors her own. She instantly jumps back and screams.

"I hate you, you horrible creature! I will kill you for assuming the mirror image of my beloved protector pixie! How dare you!"

She tries to step away to deliver a decisive blow to the creature. Before she can, the life-size replica of herself reaches out and trips her with its sword. As she falls, her sword slips from her hand. It cartwheels across the grass until it comes to rest well beyond her reach.

She sits on her backside staring up at the creature as it towers over her. She whispers with a tone of sarcasm in her voice, "So, what now, you miserable beast? Are you going to slay me? You don't have the guts!" She glances at her sword. She reasons if she is quick enough, she can reach it before the Inania can react. She knows that the Inania is not as agile as she is. She has proven that on more than one occasion.

The Inania kicks her sword further away from her reach. In a voice that sounds exactly like hers, which causes her skin to crawl, the wicked creature says, "No, Empress Diana. I am not going to kill you. I am going to take you as a Prisoner of Innocence. *He who is Unmerciful* awaits your presence."

Diana seethes between her clenched teeth, "If you mean, Mendacium, I doubt he wants me to be in his presence. He knows I will destroy him and end his deceitful ways before he realizes what is happening." She grins at the spitting image of herself. Then, as she looks hard at the beast, she says, "No, you will not take me to see, as you put it, He who is Unmerciful. I will not cower in Mendacium's presence. Period."

She quickly reaches her hand behind her back to extract an arrow from her quiver. She nearly screams in panic. Her quiver is empty! She anxiously looks about. Scattered here and there on the grass lay all twenty of her arrows. They must have fallen from her quiver when she was fighting. Like her sword, her arrows are too far out of her reach.

The creature says in a mocking tone, "Such a shame, Empress Diana, that your journey has to end this way. Just like your double in your other world, you will not change the course of destiny. Like you in the World Beyond, Diana, in your other world, how do you put it? Ah, yes, the Real-world. Diana in the Real-world also is in mortal danger and is unable to change destiny. She, like you, will fail miserably.

"You see, Empress Diana, humankind will someday bow to the supremacy of our noble ways. Even your world's leaders shall assume our scruples as they seek to mislead their peoples. You may call what we do as dishonest, trickery, duplicity, even unfaithfulness. There are many names. But we shall prevail in the end.

"As you know, Empress Diana, Mendacium rules the World Beyond. He could destroy your feeble Minima friends easily. However, he allows them to live so that they can appreciate his honorable charity. But know this, soon he will rule your Real-world as well. But first, he must destroy all remnants of you, the supposed Youngster Heroine of the World Beyond, as well as the double you left behind in the Real-world. Then, and only then can he conquer the Universe!"

The creature slowly raises its sword. The expression on its, or more precisely, Diana's mirrored face, is unadulterated hate. The creature sniggers as it prepares to strike. It whispers in Diana's voice, "Since you do not desire the honor of willingly joining the ranks of our noble leader, He who is Unmerciful, you give me no other alternative. I must hurt you." He laughs loudly in a disgusting manner. "I will not kill you. I will incapacitate you. My dear comrades will take you to Mendacium." The creature laughs as it looks to the sky.

Diana follows its gaze. High above in the sky, five Malavem are flying in a tight circle. The evil creatures that are circling overhead remind her of the scavenger birds she sees in the countryside of the Real-world. The Real-world scavenger birds loop round and round in the air over expired animals. Except Real-world birds do not kill for pleasure. These cruel birds do.

"Either way, Empress Diana, you are going to meet He who is Unmerciful, willingly or bloodied. The choice is yours."

For some strange reason, Diana is not frightened. She figures she should be shaking hysterically right now, pleading for mercy. She also considers maybe she should try to buy some time and agree to accompany the Inania as its prisoner. But, as she glances overhead at the Malavem, in her heart, she knows she cannot escape their clutches.

Something out of the corner of her eye catches her attention. It is flying lopsidedly. She purposely redirects her attention to her spitting image rather than look at whatever it is that is flying in their direction.

The creature says, "So, Empress Diana. What is your decision? Do you wish to go to He who is Unmerciful as you are? Or, do I have to maim you even more, so you are incapable of escape?"

Diana replies, in what she hopes is a courageous tone, because now she is shaking with dread from head to toe, "I will not go to Mendacium alive. You must slay me here." As the creature steps toward her with his sword ready to strike, she raises her hand. "But, before you do, I have one question."

The creature replies in her voice, "What is your question, Empress Diana?" It looks about. "I am afraid I do not have much time. It would appear your friends, the Minima, are triumphing after all. So, hurry if you please."

Diana says, "How is it you could assume the form of my protector pixie, I Dunno? To do so, she must have been in your presence. Unlike the Parva Draco, you were unable to assume her form unless she was nearby."

The Inania stares at her with a bewildered expression for the longest time. It slowly shakes its head back and forth as it dumbfoundingly ponders her question. Before it can reply, it instinctively leaps to its right as a high-pitched voice calls out.

"I'll tell you why! Because I Dunno was, and is, still here!"

Diana watches in awe as I Dunno lifts the arrow she is holding in her tiny hands to a horizontal position. Then she flies like a speeding rocket straight at the Inania. The creature is barely able to react as the tip of the arrow pierces its heart.

Diana leaps to her feet just as the Inania explodes into a million grayish-white pieces. With the help of I Dunno, she quickly gathers her arrows from the ground and places them in her quiver. She grabs her sword from the ground. She wants to scoop up I Dunno into her hands to thank her for saving her life. But, as she glances skyward, she knows there is no time for such pleasantries. The five Malavem that were circling overhead are diving toward them!

She screams, "I Dunno, get out of here. Now!"

*****

Part V: Malavem

The Malavem indisputably is one of the most feared beasts in the World Beyond. Malavem means Evil Bird. Its name comes from two Latin words, *malum,* and *aven*. In Latin, malum symbolizes evil, and aven means bird. Malavem.

Legends claim the Evil Spirit created the first Malavem. He supposedly bred the Malavem as a predator bird to hunt down large prey across the vast expanse of the Unforgiving Desert. The Malavem has brute strength and can carry weighty quarry in its five-inch talons. Legends also state that the Malavem can carry prey as large as a Real-world human. The fact that the Malavem can hunt, destroy, and carry large prey is largely noteworthy, given that it is relatively small when compared to other birds of prey. Its wingspan is a little more than three feet. Its overall length from head to tail is less than two feet. It also weighs much less than other birds of prey common in both the World Beyond and the Real-world.

Feathers of the Malavem are predominately mahogany brown, apart from a frill of bright red at the base of its neck. Its plumage is white. Its keen eyesight is comparable to that of an eagle of the Real-world. Once the Malavem sights its prey, it skyrockets through the air at a rate of speed equal to that of a Real-world condor.

When considered by themselves, the Malavem's remarkable eyesight, its speed of flight and its strength, the creature practically is comparable to other birds of prey. Other than its relatively smaller size, however, there is one amazing dissimilarity.

As I Dunno had said earlier, striking the Malavem with an arrow, or using any other deadly instrument, immediately results in the Malavem giving birth to a twin. As a result, whomever or whatever attacked the bird must contend with two vengeful Malavem! Then again, sometimes the first Malavem is so seriously wounded it dies. Only by striking the twin Malavem a few seconds after its birth can an attacker ensure the destruction of both creatures. When Mendacium created the Malavem, he included this phenomenon to ensure that the creature would never become extinct. In fact, without a doubt, it would proliferate even under the most difficult conditions.

Diana takes careful aim at one of the Malavem. Her aim is spot-on as she strikes the creature in its left eye. As she thought, it immediately creates a twin. She did not strike the twin shortly after its conception, so the Malavem she first struck continues to fly. She watches as her arrow falls from its eye. She limps over to where it fell. She retrieves the arrow from the ground and places it in her quiver.

Now, she has six Malavem with which she must contend. They swoop down at her in waves weaving in and out as they try to grab her. Unfortunately, they are not sacrificial beasts. They intentionally avoid the blade of her sword as she roughly swings it at them. However, try as she does, she cannot connect with any of the beasts. Trying to hit the fast birds with her sword is like someone trying to knock a flying bird out of the sky by swinging a stick at it. The beasts are too fast and agile.

Although they cannot, or intentionally will not, attack her directly, they besiege the helpless Minima on the ground. She watches in horror as two of the Malavem snatch eight or nine defenseless Minima in their talons. The cruel beasts fly high in the air, and then they let go of their hostages. The Minima, although they try to cushion their fall with their skillful acrobatics, crash to the ground with a disgusting thud. They die on impact.

Diana yells to the Minima in her vicinity, "All of you, get next to me now! I will try to keep them away as best as I can." Just as she says this, a Malavem swoops in on Eros. Diana scrambles to help him, but she trips over a mound of dying or deceased Minima.

She screams, "Eros, look out!"

Just as the Malavem picks up Eros in his talons, Saccharo stabs the beast in its breast with a long kitchen knife. A split-second later, the beast creates its twin. With a look of fearlessness on her face, only a loving mother can display, Saccharo screams, "You will not have my son!" She stabs the newly created Malavem in its neck. Then, for good measure, she once more stabs the Malavem that had attempted to seize Eros.

Diana watches in fascination as both creatures collapse to the ground. Then, just like the Inania, the creatures explode into a cloud of grayish-white nothing. Saccharo grabs Eros by his arm and dashes to the safety of the underground shelter. All the while, with tears streaming from her eyes, she is reprimanding him for, as she puts it, "Trying to be the stupid hero."

There remain but five Malavem. Diana crouches on her knees. She notices that her right calf where the two Parva Draco had bit her is more painful than before. She is tempted to look at her wounds, but she does not have time. She must ignore the throbbing pain. She says to herself, "Besides, it is what it is."

She removes two arrows from her quiver. She places one arrow on the bowstring of her longbow. The second arrow dangles from the pinky finger of her left hand. She takes careful aim at a Malavem that has just seized three Minima in its talons. She fires one arrow. It strikes the creature in its neck. Diana quickly places the second arrow on her bowstring. Just as the creature creates its twin, she shoots the arrow. Both creatures tumble to the ground. The freed Minima somersault safely to the ground and run in the direction of the underground shelters.

She whispers to herself, "Okay, one more down, four to go."

She places another arrow on her bowstring and dangles the second arrow from her pinky finger. She takes careful aim at a Malavem that is swooping down at a group of Minima soldiers. She lets go of the first arrow. It strikes the beast in the back of its head. As soon as its twin appears, she shoots the second arrow. It hits its mark. Both beasts begin to disintegrate as they fall to the ground.

"Two more down, three to go," Diana whispers to herself, "with sixteen arrows remaining. I'm in decent shape."

She repeats her technique of shooting two arrows one after another at her next target. While she hits the original beast, she misses its created twin. Once again, four Malavem are wreaking havoc in the village. Since most of the villagers have escaped to safety, the Malavem are now destroying the tree houses one neighborhood at a time.

"Still four to go, fourteen arrows."

Diana aims at one of the four remaining Malavem. Much to her annoyance, the beasts are adapting to her method of shooting. They cleverly avoid her arrows to the best of their ability. Nevertheless, they make mistakes as they crisscross in the sky. Because they were exposed when they were attacking the tree houses, they are now circling above her high in the sky. She assumes they will continue circling overhead since they have one purpose - to seize and then take her to Mendacium.

In brief time, she is down to five arrows with two Malavem flying overhead. She notices she is starting to feel lightheaded. She hasn't had anything to drink since before she slept. She assumes dehydration is causing her lightheadedness. The gash on her forehead is now starting to ache dreadfully bad. Added to that agony, she can barely move her injured leg. She must drag it behind her as she limps. She recognizes it is most likely infected. If things could not get any worse, her left eye has nearly closed shut.

"Well, I am in a dire mess here. I bet I have one heckuva, coolio black eye too. I cannot wait for Billy to see it. He will be very jealous!" While she sets her sights on one of the circling Malavem, she whispers to herself as she exhales deeply, "Steady, steady. Must not fail. Must not miss."

She lets her arrow fly. It hits the beast in its right side. It immediately creates its twin. Diana shoots her second arrow. It misses its mark!

"Oh, no," Diana whispers with a tone of dread. "Now there are three Malavem, and all I have are three arrows! The beasts have me outnumbered, and they know it. They're just waiting until I'm out of arrows before they swoop down to take me hostage!" She frantically looks around to see if she can see any expended arrows on the ground. She cannot see a single arrow.

Her left eye is now completely shut. Despite having only one good eye to sight the arrows, and the intense pain wracking her body, plus the sheer exhaustion and dehydration she is experiencing, she refuses to give up. She shouts in a loud voice, "But, I will win. I refuse to surrender! After all, I am Dynamite, the Youngster Heroine of the World Beyond!"

She takes careful aim at one of the Malavem. Just as two of the beast's cross paths, she shoots. The arrow passes through the neck of the nearest Malavem and continues into the breast of the other. She shouts, "Well, I'll be darned! Two for the price of one!" She quickly repositions the second arrow on the bowstring. Since the newly created twins are flying next to each other, she assumes she can repeat the tactic by taking out both twins with one arrow. All it will take is timing and, certainly, accuracy.

She yells with joy, "I cannot believe it! I just took out both twins with one arrow as well! Dang, but am I good or what?"

Diana's joy is short-lived. As she reaches with her hand to her quiver, she recoils in dread. Because of her excitement of killing four Malavem with two arrows, she forgot. She has but one arrow remaining! If she shoots accurately, one arrow will take out the remaining Malavem, but it will not die unless she takes out its twin. Then she will have two Malavem with which she must contend. Her only hope will be her sword. She looks around. A miserable expression of inescapable worry creeps onto her face.

"One arrow left, and I have no means of escape. Unlike the Minima hiding in their shelters, I am completely at the mercy of the Malavem. Sure, I can fight them off with my sword, but I will eventually tire. Then I will be theirs."

Sensing that she has lost, the remaining Malavem circles lower and lower until it is less than twenty feet above Diana's head.

She screams as she stares with hatred at the creature, "Well if I'm going to go down, I'm going to go down fighting!" She places her last arrow on the bowstring. She is about to shoot when a familiar voice in her mind tells her to hold fire.

"Diana, my dear friend, trust me. Do not shoot until you retrieve the remaining arrow I Dunno's magic just placed in the quiver. Be careful, take your time. Don't miss."

As Diana reaches into the quiver for the arrow I Dunno made for her with her miraculous magic, she senses something invisible squeeze her hand three times. She can hardly control her emotions. She wipes away the tears from her right eye with her bloodied sleeve. As she holds the second arrow in her pinky finger and repositions her other arrow on the bowstring, she whispers.

"I know you are far away, but once again your loving spirit is close by, never but a whisper away. I thank you, my dear friend. And, I love you too!"

She takes careful aim at what she hopes is the last Malavem she will ever see. She hits the swooping Malavem head-on. It creates its disgusting, evil twin that she quickly destroys. Just as the two beasts vaporize, wickedness heard throughout the World Beyond pervades the scene of destruction.

Diana's first impulse is to cover her ears as the thundering words jab at her temples. She knows the speaker of the words, so she is determined not to show any emotion. She is barely able to stand upright. But somehow, probably due more to her tenacious audacity than physical strength, she remains standing. The heroic expression on her face could rival that of history's most beloved warrior heroines.

The voice screams, "Empress Diana, you have destroyed my cherished resurrection, the only Malavem in the Universe! Mark my words, so-called Empress. I will destroy both of you, here in the World Beyond and your Real-world! I promise!"

Diana collapses to the ground. She is sitting amongst the distressing wreckage of combat. Her legs are stretched before her as she hangs her head, her chin resting on her chest. She looks up briefly to glance with her one good eye at her surroundings. She sees that she is alone. All the Minima are either in the underground shelters or dead. She is hopeful I Dunno heeded her command and is also bunkered safely in the shelters. But, even her concern for her protector pixie does not seem to arouse her interest. She is exhausted and hurting from head to toe.

Without warning, a huge raging fireball explodes from the heavens. It slowly grows in intensity until it is hurdling at lightning speed toward the ground. It strikes the Minima's waterwheel and reservoir with tremendous force that is accompanied by a thunderous, crackling explosion. The complex wooden machinery splinters to smithereens. Diana's expression remains emotionless as fragments of blazing wood and waves of water rain down on her. She doesn't even bother to look up.

A bulky chunk of the burning wooden reservoir lands a few feet to her right throwing shards of wood in all directions. She barely flinches as a jagged inch-long shard of wood lodges in the muscle of her right upper arm. She indifferently glances at the splinter sticking out of her skin. Then she expressionlessly stares at the ground in front of her.

After a few moments, she reexamines the bite and claw marks on her right calf. The wounds are deep to the bone. And they look like they are infected as they ooze deep red blood. She rips three strips of cloth from the tunic of her underclothing. Her calf is throbbing wickedly. She nearly blacks out as she carefully wraps it with a strip of cloth.

She dabs at her forehead with the end of another strip of cloth. Like her calf wounds, the gash on her forehead is also oozing blood. She wraps the strip of cloth around her forehead to cover her left eye. Then she jerks the shard of wood out of her upper arm. Blood immediately trickles out of the laceration and cascades in dark red ripples as far down as her wrist. She wraps the wound on her upper arm, seizing the end of the cloth with her teeth to tie a knot.

It is then she notices many blood-oozing puncture marks in the palms of both of her hands. She reckons the wounds were caused by the tips of the arrows when she frantically positioned the arrows on her longbow. She presses her bleeding palms into the blood-stained cloth covering her upper arm.

Her eyes are welling up with tears. She looks at the devastation and death that surrounds her. She shakes her head over and over as she whispers in a gloomy tone.

"So many dead. So many innocent Minima killed. Because of me!"

Then suddenly she screams.

"And Mendacium's hatred of *me!*"

She sits silently for a few moments. She has no idea what to do next. She closes her good eye and nearly falls asleep while sitting up.

Gradually, her characteristic tenacity to never allow a fight to go unchallenged wins over her unemotional state of mind. She makes a heroic effort to get to her feet. But her attempt is pitifully unsuccessful. Her bloodied, aching leg will not support her weight. She tries to kneel on her knees, but the shooting pain in her calf muscle is too much for her to bear. Try as she does, she cannot bend her aching leg. She collapses on all fours. Her throbbing leg is stretched full length behind her.

At long last, using both her longbow and sword as leverage, she finally manages with great difficulty to get to her feet. Her longbow slips from her trembling hand nearly causing her to fall yet again.

Once she is standing, she can barely remain upright. She must support the weariness of her sore, bloodied body with her sword. Mixed tears of triumph and sadness are flowing down her dirt-smeared, battle-worn, bloodied face. Her heart is breaking as she glances yet again at the destruction all around.

She continues to stare for a few moments longer at the devastation Mendacium and his evil creatures wrought on the Minima village. She absentmindedly begins to count the mutilated little bodies lying near her. She stops at forty-seven and bursts into tears.

She remains completely still, staring straight ahead for the longest time. Then, little by little, a frightful scowl of relentless determination begins to appear on her face. After a few moments of gazing up at the sky, she triumphally pumps her fist in the air. She suddenly yells in a threatening tone.

"You will not win!"

With a challenging expression on her bloodied face that reflects her unwavering courage and pounding tenacity, she raises her sword high in the air and shouts to the heavens.

"I will come to destroy *you*! I promise!"

CHAPTER ELEVEN

ROCKS AND STONES
AND FLAT TIRES

Diana and Regina's raucous pillow fight continues for about five minutes longer. Diana's spirits are soaring now that she and Regina are back together as good friends. It bugged her all these weeks knowing that Regina was sore at her. Regina even went so far as to write an incriminating letter about her, and when she had said she hated her. But now, as the pillow fight continues, Diana knows in her heart things are going to be okay. After all, Regina told her everything from the beginning to the end. And Regina was as forthright and honest as possible. Well, maybe not the end, because the deceitful saga is still ongoing.

There still are her principal Mister Young and the bullying secretary Miss Hickman with whom Diana must contend. More importantly, she must figure out why all the ridiculous deceitful schemes are happening in the first place. Regina told her she doesn't know for certain the reason behind all the madness. All she knows is that her father is in trouble of some sort. She is confident he hasn't done anything wrong but that someone else is causing the trouble for him. Whatever it is, she is worrying herself sick about it.

When Diana smacks Regina hard with her pillow, it explodes at the seams. She is allergic to animal dander, so her pillows are hypoallergenic. Therefore, instead of feathers flying everywhere, tiny bits of nearly impossible to vacuum up, rubbery stuff spread out all over her bedroom.

"Un-oh," Regina says with a frown as she looks around the bedroom. "Look at this mess. Your parents are going to latch on to you."

She laughs as she adds, "But, knowing how easy-going they are, they'll probably laugh it off."

Diana replies, "Well, I seriously doubt they'll laugh it off. However, once they learn that it was your fault, I'll be off the hook."

Regina giggles as she asks in a questioning tone, "My fault! Why is it my fault, Dynamite?"

"Because, if you hadn't written that stupid letter," she chuckles as she pretends to frown, "that you deny writing, you wouldn't be here right now. And we wouldn't have had this fun pillow fight. And the pillow with which you were smacking me wouldn't have split open at the seams." She bends over to pick up a few of the larger pieces of the rubbery stuff from her bed. She forces the pieces into the pillowcase, but most of it pops right out to land on the floor.

She laughs as she says, "So, it's your fault. Am I right? You know I'm right, Reg."

Regina reaches out to give Diana one of her crushing bear hugs. As we know, Regina is very muscular. Since she towers over Diana and has the rare strength for a female teenager, she usually hugs Diana tightly around her shoulders until Diana cries, *Uncle.* As a rule, Diana can only withstand her friend's powerful bear hugs for a few scant seconds.

Regina says in a whisper, "Dynamite, you and I will always be the best of friends. I am truly sorry that I said I hated you when we were in that dreadful women's office. Had she laid a hand on you, I'd still be in juvie lockup for smacking her. I would have hit her that hard. That's how much I care for you." She laughs, and with a shake of her head, she adds, "And they'd probably throw away the key."

Diana squeaks out in a whisper, "Okay, I get it. Uncle, Reg, uncle. You're crushing me. I can't breathe."

Regina releases Diana from her embrace. She says, "Oops, sorry. Sometimes I don't know my strength." With a serious tone of voice, she asks, "So, what now?"

Diana places her hands on her knees and bends over. As she gasps for breath, she says, "We clean up this mess as best that we can. But, before we do it, let's raid the refrigerator, grab some cold cream sodas and sit outside for a bit. It's a nice night, not too hot or humid. Maybe throw a few balls beneath the lamppost. It's a bit dark, but we can see well enough."

"Sounds good," Regina says. "Let's do it."

After grabbing some fruit and two bottles of cream soda from the refrigerator, Diana and Regina are sitting outside. Regina is tossing a softball a few feet into the air and catching it with Diana's catcher's mitt. Both girls seem to be in their private worlds. They are silent for many minutes.

Diana is munching on an apple. As she does, she has the sudden craving for a banana as well. In between bites of the apple, she whispers, "Reg, don't look now, but to the right and left of us are two cars I've never seen on this street before. I have this weird feeling something is about to happen. Maybe we should go inside." She adds with a whisper that is less audible than usual, "I could have sworn Charles was whispering in my ear, or his thoughts were trying to enter my mind. It was almost like he was saying something like, 'The two of you go inside, Diana, now!' But, I probably imagined it.'"

She shrugs her shoulders, and then she says with a serious tone, "And you know what, Reg? Lately, I've been having these weird visions, sometimes in my dreams, and sometimes even when I'm awake. I know it sounds crazy, but it's like I can see myself shooting arrows and fighting strange beasts. In my visions, I'm constantly on the edge like I'm surrounded by danger, never knowing what is going to happen next."

She rubs her right calf muscle. "And do you want to know something else, Reg? My calf has been aching since last night." She touches her forehead. "And I have this stinging pain on my forehead. It's like I bumped my head or something. But, for the life of me, I cannot remember doing it. As far as the calf muscle issue is concerned, I probably pulled my muscle during the softball game."

She looks at Regina.

"Weird, huh? It's almost like I'm in two places at once. I am here at home putting up with all this confusing garbage, deceit and lies. While somewhere else, I'm doing all that I can to stay alive." She shakes her head as she takes another bite of her apple. "I have been told I have a vivid imagination. I guess that's true."

Regina glances up and down the street. She says in a confident voice, "Yep, you do have a vivid imagination. I've read some of your fiction. It's darned good." She adds with a sarcastic tone, "Dynamite, don't be a worrywart. They're just random cars. Besides, I don't see anyone inside them. The drivers are probably visiting your neighbors."

Diana replies doubtfully, "I'm not very sure, Reg. Two strange cars parked a couple of dozen feet apart. Two different visitors to two different neighbors. Why not park in their friends' driveways? Plus, I thought I saw someone in the car to the left of us. I think it was a woman's head that I saw. It's gone now.

"Oh well, Reg, you're right. I'm probably mistaken." She swallows the last bit of her apple and stuffs the core into the front pocket of her jeans. "Let's throw a few. I'll race you to the lamppost! The last one who touches the lamppost is a weed."

The two girls race each other to the lamppost. As usual, Diana is the first to touch the pole. She is much faster than Regina.

Regina cries, "You may be fast, Dynamite, but I can do a ton more push-ups than you!" She drops to the asphalt and begins doing push-ups. Diana gets down on her hands and knees beside her. She stretches out in the push-up position and starts counting as she slowly lowers her body. "Nineteen, twenty, twenty-one."

Regina laughs in between breaths, and then she says, "You're cheating, Dynamite! You just started."

"Naw," Diana jokingly replies as she fibs. "I'm counting yours. You believe me, right? Thirty-six, thirty-seven, thirty-eight."

Suddenly, a familiar voice cries out from nowhere. It causes Diana's heart to sink.

"Hello there, Miss Bowww-eeerrr! Miss Reynolds."

Diana and Regina quickly get to their feet.

With a sharp look that is boiling with rage, Regina seethes between clenched teeth, "What in the world are you doing here, Gloria?"

Diana notices Regina is clenching her fists by her sides.

"I've come to visit you. Someone told me you two were together tonight. I see you've made up, am I right?" She glares at Regina adding, "And Regina, don't call me Gloria. It's Miss Hickman to you. You may not like me, but I'm your principal's secretary. I can make or break your next school year. I can do things to your school record, things that you wouldn't believe I'm capable. Don't you forget it."

Diana says in a self-assured tone, "What we are doing together is none of your business, Miss Hickman." She smiles. "And, although I promised my parents I wouldn't do so, you force me to say it again. You're a bully. You just threatened Reg with your holier than thou bullying words. Your bullying arrogance seemed to say yet again, 'I'm gonna getcha.' Don't you forget it.'"

She continues to stare at Miss Hickman. "Now, please get out of here before I call the police." She reaches into her back pocket for her phone. She is startled it is not there. She looks at Regina and says, "Reg, I must have dropped my phone during the pillow fight. Do you have yours?"

Regina is staring fixedly at Miss Hickman. If the piercing looks from her narrowed eyes were barbed arrows, they would pierce Miss Hickman's soul many times over. Regina seems not to have heard Diana's question. She takes a few steps closer toward Miss Hickman.

"I'll call you anything I want to call you, Gloria. And I doubt there is anything you can do about it. Am I right? After all, you and I and Mister Young have a secret pact." She laughs at Miss Hickman's worried reaction.

"Yes, I see that my saying that causes you a bit of discomfort, doesn't it, Gloria? Certainly, you're not threatening me of all people. Maybe I'll spill the beans if you make me angry enough."

Diana tugs on Regina's sleeve.

"Reg, let's go inside. I don't want you to be in any trouble." She glances at Miss Hickman and adds in a disgusted tone of voice, "She's not worth it."

Regina seems to be ignoring her yet again, so Diana says once more, "For the second time, Reg, do you have your phone?" Then, as she roughly grabs Regina by the shoulder, she says, "Let's get out of here. She's nothing but a troublemaker, a bully."

Regina commands in a sturdy voice, "So, Gloria, leave now. Or do I have to force you to leave?" She glances sideways at Diana and whispers, "We don't need a phone, Dynamite. This woman is trespassing, and it'll be her word against ours." She grins adding in a confident voice as she looks at Miss Hickman straight on.

"Besides, why would the principal's secretary be on your street after dark during our summer break? And how does she know we were together? Is she spying on us? Does she intend to threaten us? Does she intend to bully us? If so, I am not going to stand for it!" She takes a few more steps toward Miss Hickman. Now, only four or five feet separate them.

Suddenly, a male's voice says in a stern tone, "No one is trespassing, Miss Reynolds. We are on public property. Or, are you too stupid to recognize that a street is public property? And, let me warn you, missy. If you take one step closer to Miss Hickman, I will break both of your arms."

Diana and Regina turn around slowly. Standing before them, about five feet away, is a huge, overweight, dumpy man in his late forties. A wrinkled, ill-fitting blue suit hangs from his sloped shoulders and outlines his graceless, hourglass-shaped torso. His white polka dot bowtie is cock-eyed and stained with something that looks like ketchup.

He has an unpolished-looking goatee and a fat pimply face covered with hideous-looking black zits. His slovenly appearance reminds Diana of the revolting movie character Peter Pettigrew. Peter Pettigrew, sometimes referred to as Wormtail, appears in the Harry Potter series of novels. The character standing before Diana and Regina is as repulsive as Wormtail with, as you would expect, a gross-looking goatee for added ugliness.

The man says, "Now, don't get all upset, ladies. Miss Hickman here has a few things she would like to say to you." He sneers which causes his goatee to bunch into an unsightly mass of grayish-black whiskers around his mouse-like lips. "After all, you two are our insurance policy of sorts." He places his arm around Miss Hickman's shoulder. "Ain't that right, Sweetheart?"

Suddenly, out of nowhere, a rock is soaring through the air. It hits the man in the back of his head with a stomach-turning, forceful, *Thunk!* The man cries out in pain as he rubs the back of his head with his hand. He turns about and shouts angrily, "Who did that?"

Just as he says this, stone after stone after stone begin to soar in the air. Diana and Regina duck for their lives. But, even as they shy away by stooping low beneath the volley of stones flying in the air, they quickly realize the stones are purposely targeting Miss Hickman and the man. More amazingly, the stones pummel the two adults unmercifully as well as very accurately. And, by the direction from which the stones are coming, they appear to come from Diana's rock garden located on the side of her house.

Diana and Regina swiftly turn to run to the safety of Diana's house. At the same time, Miss Hickman and the man turn to run to their respective cars. Despite their intentions, a barrage of stones strikes them in their faces, their heads, their torsos - everywhere! What is more, try as they do to return to their cars, the stones are forcing them to scamper further away from their cars. They turn to run side-by-side after Diana and Regina, probably because they realize that nothing is assaulting the teenagers. But, an enormous volley of much larger rocks stops them in their tracks.

After a few more seconds of being pelted, the adults are forced to lay on the asphalt. They bury their faces in the asphalt and cover the back of their heads with their hands. Now and then they try to clamber to their feet. Whenever they do, a fresh barrage of rocks forces them to lay back down on the asphalt. Then, the occasional larger rock flies to land inches from their faces. The well-placed rocks stop them from getting up from the asphalt and running toward their cars. The rocks are like ominous warning volleys of cannon shots across the bow of an enemy ship.

You move. You get pelted!

When Diana and Regina reach the doorway of Diana's house, Regina says with bated breath, "Dynamite, do you have your phone on you? We need to call the police!"

Diana replies with a hearty laugh, "Reg, I seriously doubt we need to call the police. Those two clowns aren't going anywhere anytime soon. Besides, I don't have my phone. It must have fallen out of my pocket when we were messing around upstairs." She glances at Regina's back pocket. "Yours is in your back pocket, Reg."

Regina smiles. "It's dead, Dynamite." She points to the street. "Just like those two characters, well, not exactly. But if they move another inch, they're toast."

In reaction to Regina's comment, the two girls look at each other and begin to roar with laughter. They realize what is happening. The two of them suddenly shout at the same time as they watch each other's lips.

"Charles!"

Miss Hickman suddenly cries out as she eyes the man lying beside her. "It's a ghost I tell you. Look! There is no one out there! No one is throwing the rocks and stones at us. Be that as it may, they are coming from the side of the girl's house! Something is haunting that girl, I tell you!"

She stares at Diana and Regina, her eyes blazing with a combination of terror and hatred. She screams, "And those two stupid girls are free and in the clear. Whatever it is that is throwing rocks and stones at us is not bothering them!"

The man shouts, "Something is haunting this whole city block. It ain't natural! Let's get out of here while the stones aren't coming!"

He scrambles to his feet. As he begins to run, a jagged, ornamental rock the size of a softball lifts from Diana's flower garden. It soars through the air and strikes the man dab smack in the middle of his kneecap crushing it. He immediately goes down on all fours and grabs his knee with both of his hands as he cries out in excruciating pain.

Despite the pain wracking his kneecap, the man begins to crawl slowly on his belly toward his car, but he suddenly thinks better of it. That is because larger rocks are landing just inches from his face just daring him to move another inch. Like before, the flying rocks are precisely placed to prevent him from getting to his car.

Unexpectedly, all the theft alarms of the few cars parked along the curb and those parked in driveways begin to activate. The unrhythmic blaring of the car alarms resonates up and down the street. Then, from off in the distance, perhaps a few blocks away, the telltale echoing scream of police sirens is heard. In a matter of seconds, porch lights of neighborhood houses light up. Then, Diana's neighbors begin to gather outside of their open doors to gawk at the noisy commotion on the street.

Dan opens the door wide and commands, "You two get in here now!" He glances at Miss Hickman and the man lying in the street. "Something weird is going on out there!"

Diana says in an unconcerned tone, "It's okay, Dan. Charles has those two crooks lying low, no pun intended." She laughs as does Regina.

Regina says, "We are safe, Dan, thanks to Diana's ghost, Charles. If it's okay with you, we'd like to remain here to watch. The police are on their way." She tilts her head to the left. "You do hear their sirens, yes?"

Dan nods his head. He folds his arms across his chest and stares at the two adults lying in the middle of the street surrounded by rocks and stones. He says to Diana, "Diana, isn't that Miss Hickman, your school principal's secretary?"

"Yep," Diana replies. "It's pretty coolio I dare say! As Dad would say, 'paybacks are,' well, you know what I mean.'"

Dan asks with a laugh, "Who's the idiot with the ugly bow tie that is lying next to her?"

"I have no clue. However, the man must be a good friend of Miss Hickman." She looks at Regina. "He threatened to break Reg's arms. The two of them are sort of like two nasty peas in a bully pod." Diana's spontaneous allusion to nasty peas in a bully pod causes the three of them to roar with laughter.

Diana says, "That's coolio if I do say so myself. I'm going to use that saying the next time I see two or more bullies together at school. Nasty peas in a bully pod."

Regina says, "Yes, it's pretty ironic now that I think about it. Miss Hickman, the classic adult bully, hanging around with a geek who threatens to break feeble and defenseless girls' arms." She flexes the huge bicep muscle of her right arm. With a nasty tone of voice, she declares, "Ha! I'd like to see him try. I'd run little circles around him for less than a minute, and then he'd collapse with exhaustion." She smashes her right fist into the palm of her left hand. "Then *Pow!* He's toast. I'd beat him to a pulp. I mean, will you look at him now? Sniveling and shaking like a wet poodle."

Miss Hickman suddenly shouts, "Let's make a run for it! There are too many people, too many witnesses! Let's get to the cars now, before it's too late!"

Before she can even rise from the asphalt, she hears the unmistakable hissing sound of car tires being impaled one by one by an unseen sharp object. The betraying sound of air rapidly escaping from the first tire is followed by a second, and then a third, and so on. *Pssst! Pssst! Pssst!*

In less than thirty seconds, all eight tires of Miss Hickman and the man's cars are as flat as a board. Then, as if to add insult to injury, the hood on Miss Hickman's car pops up all by itself. The engine's radiator cap suddenly appears from beneath the hood. It is tossed onto the asphalt and rolls into the storm sewer. Six spark plug wires ripped from the engine follow the radiator cap. They are flung one at a time far and wide onto the street.

Next, the hood of the man's car pops up all by itself. What follows is the radiator cap, and then the spark plug wires of his car tossed high in the air. Then the passenger side of the car slams open. MiscEvelynneous papers fly from the glove compartment to scatter on the asphalt. One piece of paper that, by its rectangular shape, resembles a vehicle registration form, floats in the air. It lands on the asphalt mere inches from the man's head. Then, miraculously, a stone lands on top of the form to keep it from blowing away in the brisk nighttime summer breeze.

Lastly, a pistol appears from inside the man's car. The pistol floats for seconds in midair! Then, Diana, Regina, and Dan, plus everyone else who is witnessing the weirdness on the street, stare with amazement as something empties the pistol of its six bullets. After that, the pistol and its bullets speedily slide one after the other across the asphalt to vanish into the sewer. It is almost as if some angry, invisible force is kicking them.

What just happened is obvious to all the onlookers, especially to Diana and Regina. The two adults lying in the street aren't going anywhere, at least not in their vehicles. What is even more obvious, and very disturbing, the man cowering on the street had a loaded pistol in his car!

Diana, Regina, and Dan are roaring with laughter with what happened to the vehicles and the pistol. Meanwhile, Miss Hickman and the man stare flabbergasted at their disabled cars. They shout swearwords repeatedly, shockingly vulgar words that are not worth echoing here.

Regina says, "He has to teach me that trick." She glances at her watch. "How your ghost, Charles, can pierce eight tires, strip two engines, open a car door, empty a pistol, and accomplish it all in less than a minute flat is nothing short of astonishing." Then, as she glances around at Diana's wide-eyed neighbors gawking and snapping pics with their cell phones, she says, "And, if I had to bet money, I would bet that what everyone just witnessed by Charles is going to make tomorrow's front page in all the newspapers!"

Diana replies in a whisper, "Well, for certain, I'll never tell. Charles is my ghost and I ain't sharing."

Regina whispers into Diana's ear, saying, "Dynamite, it's better that you don't tell anyone. If you do, you'll be in the looney bin for the rest of your days." With a chuckle, she adds, "Especially after telling me you feel as though you're in two worlds at once." With a huge grin, she adds, "But, you must admit, what just happened was undoubtedly the coolest thing in the world."

Suddenly, all the car alarms cease their bellowing just as a man cautiously approaches Miss Hickman and the man lying on the street. The man is Diana's neighbor, Officer Meadows. Officer Meadows is carrying his sidearm at the high ready position, about eight inches in front of his nose. Both of his hands are on the firing grip with the muzzle of the weapon at a 70-degree angle. He's ready to shoot if necessary but, since he's in a neighborhood filled with onlookers, he is extra careful as well. He has not released the safety on his sidearm.

Officer Meadows is a metropolitan police officer. Presently, he is off duty. He was about to have his son whip his butt for the second time this night as they played Xbox video games. Then the commotion on the street began. When he first stepped outside onto his porch, Officer Meadows immediately knew something wasn't right. He reentered his house to retrieve his sidearm from his gun safe. Then, as he cautiously cast an eye up and down the street, he slowly strode toward the two strangers lying on the asphalt.

Officer Meadows drops his weapon to the low ready position. As he stands over the man, he picks up the vehicle registration form from the asphalt. After he studies it for a few seconds, he says, "Well, look what we have here. Don't this just beat all? I cannot believe my good fortune. It is none other than *Crazy Face* Bob Studeman lying prostrate on my street." He looks around at his gawking neighbors and adds with a grin, "And in front of all my neighbors no less.

"I saw your mug shot just this morning before my shift began, Crazy Face. It seems like you violated parole and are wanted for grand larceny as well." With a laugh, he adds, "And wouldn't you know it? There's a two-thousand-dollar reward for your capture from the proprietor that you robbed. Guess you hauled off a lot of money and goodies during your robbery, eh? Not to mention, you must have ticked off the victim royally.

"Yep, thanks to you, Crazy Face, it seems like today is my lucky day. There are two thousand clams as reward money to be had for my wife, kids and me." He nods his head up and down a few times adding with a smile, "Yes sir, looks like we're going to Disney World during the kids' summer break. Thanks, pal."

Then, with a stern look on his face, he asks in a serious tone, "Are you carrying, Crazy Face? Don't mess with me, man. If you're carrying, I'm not going to be nice anymore. If you're carrying, be gentle like and toss whatever it is in front of you. Easy now."

Crazy Face indifferently replies as he stares at the sewer where his pistol vanished, "I had a pistol, but something invisible stripped it of its bullets. My pistol is in the sewer." He moans, "So, no, I'm not carrying, but I wish I were."

"Well, just in case you're lying to me, you lay there real still like and don't move a muscle. You can breathe and talk but nothing else. I don't want any trouble from you. Are we clear, buddy?"

"Yes, officer, crystal clear. Please make sure no one throws any more rocks at me. A huge rock crushed my kneecap, and I have a splitting headache to boot! I must have been hit in the back of the head twenty times!" He gestures with a nod toward Miss Hickman. "She was hit too. But, her injuries aren't as serious as mine. At least I do not think they are. Look after her if you please."

Officer Meadows pulls his handheld police radio out of his pocket.

"Hey, dispatcher, make certain paramedics are on their way as well. We have some injuries, not life-threatening. But one of the suspects has a crushed kneecap. I'm going to look at the other suspect." He looks at Miss Hickman who is lying face down on the asphalt. She is afraid to look up for fear a barrage of stones will pummel her yet again. He adds, "I'll report back if her medical condition warrants."

Addressing Crazy Face, Officer Meadows says, "And, just who is this charming young lady, Bob? Is she your girlfriend? She's a bit young for you, don't you think?" He chuckles. "Most of the ladies you hang out with are, well, there's a lady present, so I won't say the nasty word you know that I'm thinking."

He reaches down to touch Miss Hickman's shoulder. She glances up at him momentarily. Then she rests the side of her head on the asphalt. As he offers his hand to her, he says, "You okay, Miss? I will permit you to sit up if you would like to. I am Josh Meadows. I'm a metro policeman. I'm off-duty. What is your name?"

Miss Hickman looks up at Officer Meadows. She says in a weak voice, "My name is Hickman, Gloria Hickman. And, I do not want to sit up if it's okay with you. If I sit up, I'm a bigger target. I'm afraid of getting hit with all those rocks and stones. It's a ghost I tell you, a ghost." She rests her head on the asphalt once more.

Officer Meadows looks about him. Rocks and stones are encircling Miss Hickman and Crazy Face's bodies. To Officer Meadows, the placement of the rocks and stones strangely appear like the chalk lines forensic experts draw to trace around homicide victims lying at the scene of the crime. There is no sign outside of the ring of a single misplaced rock or stone or even a pebble. He cannot wait until on-duty officers arrive to take pictures. Otherwise, folks at the precinct will not believe what he is seeing.

He says to Mis Hickman, "Yeah, I was going to ask Crazy Face there about all of these rocks and stones. Looks like you two either ticked off someone and they had more than picture-perfect aim, or you are members of a cult or something. I mean, the rocks and stones are without a flaw in their placement. They symmetrically surround your bodies right up to the shape of your arms and legs, even your heads. Any idea who threw them at you?"

With a smirk, he adds, "Or, can you tell me why you're purposely lying within a perfect outline of rocks and stones? Either way, all of this is strange if you were to ask me. Ain't ever seen anything like it in all my days. And I've been on the force twenty-nine years. I'm eligible for retirement in four months."

Miss Hickman cries out, "It's a ghost I tell you. Something is haunting that girl. She's a freak. She's probably a ghost too. A ghost tossed the rocks and stones. Lots of them." She points to the back of her head caked with dried blood. "Hit me right there at least ten times. Thought I would pass out. Hurts bad." She looks down the street and begins to cry.

"And look what that ghost did to our cars! I just bought that car on an IOU with the money I have coming to me. The money I probably won't ever get to see. All because of a ghost. Gosh, how I hate ghosts! Never did like them even as a kid. Used to haunt my grandmother's house when I visited her. Ghosts and stewed cabbage and putrid cat litter. Just thinking of the scary ghosts and nasty cabbage and litter smells make we want to gag. No, ghosts are not good."

She pauses a few moments, and then she looks up at Officer Meadows. The tone of her voice sounds contrite as she whispers.

"Evil ghosts like those of my past are as bad as bullies. Maybe what has happened tonight is fate's way of paying me back for being so mean to people." Tears begin to fall from her eyes. As she shakes her head, she looks at Diana. She silently mouths the words, "I am sorry." Then, as she looks up at Officer Meadows, she says, "Maybe what happened to me tonight is Diana Bowers' compassionate ghost, if there is such a thing, telling me I screwed up." She glances at Diana once more.

"I bullied that poor child. I threatened her. I caused much pain for her and her friend Regina. And now, look at me. I am very sorry." She rests the side of her face on the asphalt and continues to mumble to herself. The words ghost and bully appear at least once or twice in each sentence as she sobs.

The expression on Mister Meadows' face is sad. He stares at the back of Miss Hickman's head. As he slowly shakes his head, he says in a reassuring, soft voice, "Well, you just lay right there quiet like Miss Gloria Hickman. Everything is going to be all right. Soon you'll be in a safe, noiseless place where your ghosts will not getcha. I promise."

He thinks to himself, "Well, maybe not. Inmates tell me ghosts can walk right through the bars of a jailhouse cell. I suppose they can get into padded cells as well."

CHAPTER TWELVE

PREPARATION FOR THE FINAL BATTLE

Part I: The Reawakening

The nightmares do not seem to stop. What is more, the horribleness of their perplexing scenes is almost too much for Diana to bear as she tosses and turns on her sleeping mat. Nevertheless, her unconsciousness focuses intently on each nightmare's scenes despite the merciless fever wracking her exhausted body.

Her nightmares are recreating about every aspect of the confusing deceit that is negatively affecting her double in the Real-world. All the while she is reliving in her mind her actual life-threatening nightmares in the World Beyond. The evilest of creatures imaginable, the constant pain of deceit and trickery, the senseless death of innocent Minima and indescribable destruction.

The worrying visions Diana suffers in her nightmares are like watching a marathon session of scary movies that constantly keeps you on edge. All the while your heart races out of control. In her nightmares, she watches in panic as her Real-world double undergoes heartbreak after heartbreak. Mister Young lying for Miss Hickman, Miss Hickman lying for Mister Young. Miss Hickman bullying her, physically threatening her. Then actually stalking her and Regina. And Regina! Regina is stating that she hates her, her sharp words nearly breaking Diana's heart in two.

Fake accusatory words in a forged letter. The school superintendent, Miss Davenport asking all sorts of probing questions. Mister Reynolds being blackmailed by persons unknown because of something he did as a child. Diana is not certain, but she suspects Mister Young is the blackmailer. The strange man, Mister Crazy Face Studeman, carrying a loaded pistol in the glove compartment of his car. And Charles throwing stones and rocks and tearing apart car engines, slicing tires, miraculously tossing the loaded pistol in the sewer after emptying it of its bullets. His noble actions surely saved Diana and Regina from harm or a worse fate.

The raging fever that is attacking Diana's body is causing her nightmares. She does not know this, but the saliva of the Parva Draco mutants is highly toxic. The creatures' toxicity is one more evilness created by Mendacium so that the evil creatures can wound their prey coldheartedly. When the two Parva Draco bit her on her right calf, they infected her with their poison. Fortunately, her fever seems less severe.

While she is experiencing physical and emotional agony as she dreams, her knowledge of what has come to pass in the Real-world has its benefits. She now has more information of the treachery that she faces in both worlds. More importantly, as she dreams nightmares of both worlds, she desperately is trying to communicate with her double in the Real-world. She is confident that some of what she is experiencing in the World Beyond is now discernible to her double.

Mendacium is causing the grave treachery she is experiencing in the World Beyond. She is certain of this. And, by reliving the deceit her double has undergone, she now knows that Mendacium also is creating the deception in the Real-world that involves many people. Her family. Her friends. Those that she cares for deeply and loves with all her heart.

Given the treachery of both worlds, that she and her double are experiencing, Diana knows in her heart that Mendacium is causing it. She also knows that for some reason Mendacium, the King of Deceit is afraid of her. She does not yet know why. However, she is confident that she will soon learn the truth.

She suddenly has the sensation that something is walking on her chest. She imagines it is a bug of some sort. Maybe a spider. She hates spiders! Her first impulse is to knock it away with the swipe of her hand. But, something in the back of her mind is telling her not to swipe at whatever it is.

"Are more nightmares coming?" she ponders. "I do not think I can stand more scenes of what's happening to me in the Real-world. What's going on here is bad enough."

She suddenly feels something cool and refreshing on her forehead. She realizes that someone is dabbing her feverish forehead with a cool cloth. She opens her eyes.

"Oh, my God, it's you, I Dunno! I am so glad you're safe! Here, kiss me!"

I Dunno shouts in her high-pitched, squeaky voice, "Hey everyone, Empress Diana is awake! Come look!" She is teary-eyed as she plants a loving kiss on Diana's cheek.

"We were worried sick about you. You had a high fever but thanks to the Sana berry potion I made, you're much better. You need to lie still for a bit longer. Then soon enough, you'll be as fit as ever!"

Diana replies in a weak voice, "Thank you for taking care of me, I Dunno. You truly are my protector pixie. I love you."

"I love you too, my brave warrior Empress," I Dunno says with a shout. "You are the true Heroine Youngster of the World Beyond!"

"I don't feel like a heroine," Diana says glumly, "since I could not stop Mendacium's creatures from killing so many Minima." Tears well up in her eyes as she adds, "And Mendacium's destruction of the village and ruin of the waterwheel and reservoir. So much senseless pain and ruin. Why?" Suddenly, she feels someone has planted three kisses on her forehead. She looks up.

"Charles!"

She sits up in bed and reaches behind her.

"Give me a squeeze if you please!"

As Charles moves to embrace her, she whispers, "I thought you had abandoned me on the battlefield, Charles. Really. That was until I felt you squeeze my hand three times when I reached for the miraculous second arrow I Dunno had created."

Diana forms a kiss on her lips and pretends to blow it to I Dunno. I Dunno, who is sitting on her chest, pretends to catch it with both of her hands. Then, she clutches her hands to her heart.

Diana resumes whispering into Charles' ear. "I knew then you were with me all along."

"And I will be for the rest of your life, Diana. I swear."

Diana says, "And then I saw you in my nightmares. I saw that you had texted me, my double in the Real-world, warning me, us, that we were in danger. And then you hurled all those stones and rocks at those two bullies." She laughs loudly adding, "It was incredible, amazingly incredible."

As she shakes her head disbelievingly, Diana adds with a laugh, "And then you stripped their engines and flattened their tires. Flattening their tires was coolio. How did you do it? I didn't see a knife or a screwdriver. What kind of sharp instrument did you use?"

Charles laughs. "I didn't use anything sharp. I didn't have time to get a knife or anything from your kitchen. I knew they were going to escape. I couldn't allow that to happen. So, I bit the stems off the tires, one after the other, as hard as I could.

"I was very angry, Diana. And I knew Crazy Face had a loaded pistol in his car. And I knew he intended to use it as a warning to you and your friend, Regina." His face turns to beat red. "I refused to let that happen." He looks Diana squarely in her eyes. Her pupils are dancing excitedly with dark blue lightning bolts. His face turns serious as he says in an angry tone, "Nobody, I mean nobody messes with my Diana and her friends!"

With a worried look on his face, he says, "My Supreme Lady may be angry with me right now. However, I am sorry. I will not let anyone in the Real-world hurt you." He looks at Diana. "My Supreme Lady is the ghost who decides who goes where and what they will do when they get there. If she gets angry enough," he claps his hands together with an accompanying laugh and says, *"Poof!"*

"Thank you, Charles. Not only are you mischievous, but you are also the most wonderful ghost in the world, my hero. Thank you for giving me the courage here in the World Beyond so that I could destroy the last remaining Malavem. If you hadn't reached out to me with your thoughts, I would not have known about the second arrow."

Charles says solemnly, "And you would have perished, Diana." He looks at I Dunno adding, "Thanks to I Dunno's magic you are still with us."

Diana asks, "What would have happened to me if the Malavem had seized me?"

Charles replies in a sad tone of voice, "The Malavem would have taken you to Mendacium. Then the corruption in all the worlds, both here and in the Real-world and many other worlds out there would be debased. Deceit, treachery, treason, and betrayal would pervade our Universe until deadly conflicts result. Then everything that we love, everything that we cherish, everything that is good and wholesome would vanish and be lost forever."

Diana asks with a shocked expression, "All that because of me?"

Charles says somberly, "Yes, Diana, all the worlds would change for the worse over time, if Mendacium, the King of Deceit had you as his prisoner, his *Prisoner of Innocence*. We cannot allow that to happen." He says softly, "You are special, Diana."

Diana says in a questioning tone, "I'm confused, Charles. What does all of this have to do with me? I'm just an average teenager. In the Real-world, I play softball, volleyball, go roller skating, attend school, hang out with my friends, eat Chinese food. Sure, I'm a bit different because I read a lot, I like to draw and act in plays, and do other things many teens my age do not. But why, Charles? Tell me. What makes me so different, special as you say, that Mendacium would want me as his Prisoner of Innocence?"

Charles hesitates a few moments before answering. He knows that Diana does not like a lot of attention focused on herself. Nevertheless, he believes she must know all the details of why she is here in the World Beyond. She must also know the remaining facts of her very important purpose in life that he has yet to reveal.

"Because you are the *Favored Child*."

Diana asks in a disbelieving tone, "I'm the what? April told me I was the fifth child of Diomede, but she never said anything about being the Favored Child. What in the world is that?"

Charles says, "If and when, and I must stress *if,* you defeat Mendacium, your journey will not end. Destiny will call upon you to face other challenges. You will encounter other vile creatures of the supernatural, creatures eviler and more threatening than Mendacium. As the Favored Child, you must prevail."

"Whew," Diana says with a long sigh accompanied by a puckered brow. "Looks like I'm going to be busy for a while. But, Charles, you still have not answered my question. What in the world is the Favored Child?"

Charles replies, "As you know from mythology, Diana is the Goddess of the Moon and Hunting. She can talk to and control animals. I do not think you know this, but Parva Draco, Inania, and Minima are animals. So is your protector pixie, I Dunno. You and only you can converse with them. Also, that is why Jayvyn responds to your commands easily. He knows what you are saying." With a smile, he adds, "And you also know that in mythology, Diana equates with Artemis. You and I know you have felt an uncommon closeness to the Goddess Artemis your entire life."

Diana says, "Yes, Charles, you are correct. I have. It is almost as though Artemis and I are the same if you know what I mean."

Charles nods his head knowingly. With an honest smile reflecting his love, admiration, and profound respect for Diana, he reveals the true meaning of the word Favored Child. This revelation also reveals why she can never be Mendacium's Prisoner of Innocence.

He pronounces in a strong voice, "My dear friend, Diana. You are the Favored Child, the reincarnated, reawakened, all-powerful Goddess Artemis-Diana!"

*****

Part II: Paulavis

Diana is fascinated by one aspect of being close to death's bed. While I Dunno and others attended to her, they also prayed. Before Diana arrived in the World Beyond, I Dunno and the Minima did not know the power of prayer. However, as they watched and listened when Diana said her prayers every night, they learned the truth. Prayer is good.

Diana has completely recovered from her wounds. Her right calf where the Parva Draco bit her is still sore, but the leg has complete mobility. Lying in bed with a raging fever as I Dunno and Minima healers attended to her wounds sapped her strength. I Dunno told her she was unconscious for two cycles of the sunshine.

Given that Diana had slain additional Inania and destroyed Malavem, the days have become noticeably longer. Even though she has no way of knowing for certain, she estimates the period of sunshine is now over twelve hours. The period of darkness is also twelve hours, give or take. She figures she was unconscious for over three days.

The increased periods of sunshine are refreshing. Wildflowers, the likes that the Minima have not seen in generations, are flourishing. The leaves on the trees seem to be more vibrant. The forest animals seem to be livelier than before when the sunshine remained in the sky for an hour. Once again, the forest echoes with the miraculous sounds of Mother Nature's laughter.

Also, not only are the lengthier days of warm sunshine more cheerful, but the Minima seem to be over the moon with happiness. Their happiness is surprising given the destruction of their waterwheel and reservoir, and extensive damage to their tree houses. Uvam told her that the Minima can now grow a higher quality of crops and an increased variety which makes them very happy, especially for the youngsters.

Diana spends many hours of the day exercising. She sprints back and forth across the clearing to strengthen her leg muscles. She also jumps against tree trunks to toughen her back and stomach muscles and to better prepare her for the harshness of physical combat. She does tons of push-ups to build up her shoulders. Push-ups also serve to strengthen her right arm that was pierced by the shard of wood. Although, she has come to realize that she is favoring her right arm.

The injury to her right arm has caused her some slight problems. She is right-handed. When pulling back on the bowstring, she feels a twinge where she was injured. It is not enough to hamper her accuracy, but her arm hurts enough to remind her that a long shard of wood pierced it. Fortunately, when she thrusts with her sword, her right arm feels fine.

Probably the coolest thing she has experienced since regaining consciousness five or six days ago is her interaction with animals. It is the strangest thing. She is allergic to animal dander. When she gets on a horse, pets a dog, messes around with a cat, her allergies kick in like crazy. She sneezes, wheezes, and her nose runs like it's off to the races. That is in the Real-world. But here, in the World Beyond, she suffers no symptoms.

What is even more interesting, wild animals routinely come up to her. Certainly, they are tentative at first and a little shy. That is undoubtedly due to their instincts. She has no way of knowing, but she assumes many, if not all, have never seen a human being. Certainly, they have seen ghosts like Charles, but here in the World Beyond, ghosts cannot harm them. And yes, they have seen Parva Draco, Minima, and Inania, and other creatures, but these creatures are also animals.

Right now, a small darling bird of vivid gold and blue colors alights on her shoulders. She tests what Charles had said about her ability to talk to animals as the reawakened Artemis-Diana. What transpires is nothing short of amazing.

"Hello, little bird. My name is Diana. What is yours?"

The bird does not reply in a manner that Diana has expected. Unlike made-up talking animals in movies, its beak does not move. Nor does it bow, curtsy, shake its head. It does not look at her. Rather, it looks across the clearing as it stands on Diana's shoulder. Then, she senses the bird's reply in her mind.

"Hello, Empress Artemis-Diana. I am called Paulavis. My friends want to meet you, but they are very shy. But then, I am not shy. That is why I am here."

"It is a pleasure to meet you, Paulavis. That's a very pretty name."

"My name means Little Bird."

"Do you have many friends, Paulavis?"

"Yes, Empress Diana. Would you like to meet some of them?"

"I certainly would. Where are your friends?"

Paulavis whistles a shrill singsong toot that completely catches Diana off-guard. She had expected that Paulavis would fly off and then return with his friends. Suddenly, scores of birds of all shapes and sizes sail from the forest. Diana is relieved that they do not try to land on her shoulder. Instead, they fly in looping circles a few dozen feet above her head. The diverse types of birds fly in groups of their kind.

There are Paulavis' gold and blue-feathered friends. They are flying the lowest. Above them fly birds with bright green feathers. These larger birds remind Diana of parrots. Then there are birds of blue, birds of orange, and birds with bright yellow feathers that look like the feathers of canaries.

High above all the various kinds of birds soar very large birds. They swoop here and there as if they are diving for prey. They look like eagles but lack the telltale plumage of America's national bird, the bald eagle. Their feathers are pure white, except for their plumage which is a dark blue color. The birds' wingspan is enormous, perhaps fifteen or twenty feet in length, many times lengthier than Real-world eagles' wingspan. Diana estimates their length is ten to twelve feet. The birds have eight-inch-long, bright red talons that are tucked close to their bodies as they fly.

If the incredible sight of so many birds flying above her is not amazing enough, the birds do not chirp, sing, or twitter. They remain silent!

Paulavis' thoughts are in Diana's mind once more.

"These are but a few of my friends, Empress Artemis-Diana. Now, with your permission, I shall ask them to return to the forest."

Diana replies, "Please do, and I thank you for bringing them to meet me."

After a series of high-shrill toots from Paulavis, the birds fly in groups to hover briefly before Diana, and then they disappear into the forest. Paulavis remains perched on her shoulder.

"I am happy to tell you, Empress Artemis-Diana. My friends have just chosen me as their leader. Whenever you need us, please call my name. Perhaps I shall be out of sight, but I will remain nearby and come to you when you call. I promise I will never be far from you."

"Thank you," Diana replies. "I am thrilled to have met all of your friends. Those larger birds, what are they called? They look like predator birds."

"They are called *Aquila*. It is a Latin word for a bird with which you are familiar, the eagle."

Diana says, "I am familiar with the word, Aquila. Not only does it represent the Romance word eagle, but it is also a name of a constellation on the celestial equator. But how is it you know the word eagle."

"Because you described the eagle in your mind, Empress Artemis-Diana. It is the same as Aquila. The Aquila will protect you like no other bird in the World Beyond."

"That is encouraging," Diana says. "I can use all the help I can get. But, I have a question, Paulavis. Can you read my mind? If you can, that is amazing."

She reads Paulavis' thoughts in her mind as he replies, "I can read your thoughts when I am on your shoulder or nearby. Otherwise, you need to call my name out loud. Only then, if I am far away, will I hear you. Now, with your permission, I request your leave. It is feeding time."

"Yes, of course, Paulavis, please feel free to fly away. And I thank you. Please enjoy your meal."

Diana hurries to her treehouse shouting, "I Dunno, I Dunno, you won't believe what just happened! A bird that calls himself Paulavis and I just had a conversation! It's true, I Dunno. It's true! I am the reawakened Artemis-Diana!"

CHAPTER THIRTEEN

THERE ARE WORSE THINGS THAN EXPULSION

"Good morning, everybody," Miss Davenport says. "I am glad you could make it on time." She glances at the gloomy scene outside the rain-streaked window panes. "Considering how ugly the day is. Hopefully, this week-long period of rain will end soon." She glances at Diana, Regina, Sarah Cousins and Sally Turndle. They are sitting side by side on her left.

"I know you girls are anxious to get back on the softball field." With a sincere smile, she adds, "With a bit of luck, you'll be practicing soon. Considering each pair of you is on opposing teams, I am confident you will give your practices everything that you have."

As everyone around the table looks at her anxiously, Miss Davenport looks from her right to her left, saying, "For the record, we have with us today, the following individuals. All have consented to a live digital recording of today's proceedings by signing an authorization form. I'll go around the table and introduce everyone.

"Closest to me on my right is Miss Beach, our transcriber. Sitting next to her, across from their daughters, in this order from left to right, are Mister and Missus Bower, Mister Reynolds, Mister Cousins, and Missus Turndle. At the end of the table are Mister Young and the School District Union Leader, Miss Smith. To the right of Miss Smith is Miss Hickman."

She smiles once more at the four girls in attendance.

"To my left, in this order, are Diana Bower, Regina Reynolds, Sarah Cousins and Sally Turndle." Miss Davenport motions with a nod of her head to the left and right of her. "Seated behind me to my left is Mister Vanderbilt. Behind me to my right is Miss Williamson. Mister

Vanderbilt and Miss Williamson are two of our school board members. They were unanimously selected by their peers to serve as witnesses during today's proceedings."

Miss Davenport laughs as she says, "Okay, now that we have all of the introductory requirements over with, please allow me to say a few things. Once again, I thank each of you for being on time. Second, I sincerely appreciate your cooperation over the past several weeks. Third, I need to remind you that today's proceedings are formal. Although I will not administer oaths, that you will swear to the truth, I expect that you will be honest and forthright." She smiles. "After all, we are recording our proceedings.

"Lastly, we will take ten-minute breaks approximately every hour so that everyone can unwind. Free coffee, sodas, and snacks are in the corridor." She nods her head. "I almost forgot. The restrooms are down the hall to your right. If anyone needs to visit the restroom, we will break for a few minutes. Simply interrupt me by raising your hand. Thank you."

Miss Davenport addresses Miss Beach by saying, "Miss Beach, please read the memo that outlines the reasons we are here today."

Miss Beach pulls a green folder from the middle of a four-inch stack of multi-colored folders. She puts her glasses on and reads from the memo.

"The purpose of this proceeding is to allow participants to provide, in front of their accusers and other interested parties, answers to questions posed by the School Superintendent, Miss R. Davenport. Based on her findings during the proceeding, the School Superintendent will, if deemed necessary, administer disciplinary action to any or all student's subject to the School District's laws and regulations. Also, if the School Superintendent finds any or all student's innocent of pending or actual disciplinary charges against them, made before these proceedings, the School Superintendent shall expunge charges from their records."

Miss Beach glances at Mister Young and Miss Hickman. "Additionally, if the School Superintendent finds that any or all faculty members of the school committed offenses contrary to the laws and regulations of the School District, she will forward her recommendations to the District School Board for disposition." Miss Beach looks at Miss Davenport. "Signed Missus Martin."

"Okay," Miss Davenport says with a serious look, "there we have it. Are there any questions?"

Diana raises her hand.

"Yes, Miss Bower."

"Ma'am, I have a question. What happens if someone here," she glances to her left toward the end of the table, "says something contrary to what one of us knows is true? Can we, you know, raise our hand or something, to protest?" With a smile, she adds, "Or, conversely, if we feel we need to clarify or add to something that is the truth, can we do so? Thank you."

Miss Davenport replies, "That's an excellent question, Diana." She looks at each of the girls one-by-one. "Is it okay if I refer to each of you by your first name?" She smiles at Diana. "I think it may help to make you less nervous and to ease the tension. May I?"

Each of the four girls nods their heads in the affirmative.

"Okay then, I thank you. Diana, to answer your question. If anyone of you four girls, or anyone else for that matter, disagrees with something someone has said, raise your hand. I may acknowledge you by saying your name and asking you to speak. Please notice I said I *might* and not I *will* acknowledge you. If I acknowledge you, then, and only then, may you speak your mind." She glances around the table.

"However, I caution everyone present. I will not tolerate the raising of voices, cursing, displaying anger or speaking out of turn. And, I must say this explicitly. If I feel you are getting out of hand with your statement, I have the prerogative to cut you short." With a chuckle, she adds, "I will endeavor to do so as graciously and with as much civility as I can." She looks at Regina.

"Okay, Regina. I would like to begin with you. Are you okay with that?"

Regina is trembling. She looks like she is about to cry. She does not reply as she stares at the table.

Diana places her hand on Regina's arm. She whispers, "It's okay, Reg. Tell Miss Davenport the truth." She looks across the table at Mister Reynolds. His expression is sad. She notices tears are welling up in his eyes. As she smiles at Mister Reynolds, she says softly, "Tell the truth, Reg, even if it hurts."

Regina says, "Thanks Dynamite." She looks up at Miss Davenport. "Yes, ma'am, it is okay. I'm ready."

Miss Davenport looks away from Regina for a moment as she pretends to study her notes. She wants to give Regina ample time to regain her composure. The last thing she wants is one of the students losing control of her emotions. She breathes in deeply as she prepares to begin the official part of the proceedings. Then she looks at Regina. She is pleased to see Regina appears calmer. She notices that Diana is holding Regina's hand.

"Regina, did you write the letter accusing Diana of striking you with a broomstick when you weren't looking? The incident allegedly occurred in the girls' locker room at your school." She glances at Miss Beach who hands her the original, signed letter. Miss Davenport hands the letter to Diana.

"Diana, please give the letter to Regina so she can refresh her memory." Diana places the letter in front of Regina.

Regina shakes her head over and over. She looks away from the letter like it is poison.

Diana says, "It's okay, Reg. Tell the truth. Look at the letter. It won't bite you."

Regina looks at Diana, and then she stares at the letter. She nods her head.

"Yes, ma'am. I wrote the letter."

Miss Davenport says, "Thank you, Regina. I know this is hard for you, but I must ask you to answer me truthfully, okay?"

Regina replies, "Yes, ma'am. I will tell you the truth." Her eyes remain fixed on the letter.

Miss Davenport says softly, "Regina look at me if you please." Regina slowly raises her head to look at Miss Davenport. Tears are streaming down her face.

Diana hands Regina a tissue from one of the four boxes of tissues that are on the table in front of each of the girls. Diana wants to laugh at the irony of it all but quickly thinks better of it.

Her mind ponders, "Goodness, Miss Davenport expected lots of tears today. But, four full boxes of crying towels? Goodness, how tough is this proceeding going to be on us? Today's proceeding is worse than a crybaby movie!" Her fixation on the boxes of tissues suddenly is broken by Miss Davenport's next question. Her undivided attention is now on what Miss Davenport is saying.

"Regina Reynolds," Miss Davenport says in an enquiring tone that strikes Diana as very stern, "did the incident happen? Did Diana Bower strike you with the broomstick?"

Regina shakes her head. "No, ma'am. All of it's a lie." She looks at Diana. "It's a stupid, stupid, horrible lie."

Mister Young blurts out, "A lie? Then you lied to me! How dare you!"

Miss Davenport says in a stern voice, "Sir! Mister Young! I must caution you. I will not tolerate you or anyone else speaking out of turn. Nor will I tolerate accusations. Please calm yourself, or I will ask you to leave. Do I make myself clear?"

Mister Young unhappily replies as he continues to stare at Regina, "Yes." Then, as he looks at Diana, he adds, "Well, Miss Bower spoke out of turn when she was speaking to Miss Reynolds."

With a look of total disbelief on her face, Miss Davenport says, "Really, Mister Young? Really?"

Diana cannot help but notice that Mister Young's fingers are noisily drumming the table like he did when she was in his office. She also ponders whether he needs to attend anger management classes. She is certain something is unhinging the angry man for some strange reason.

Miss Davenport says, "Regina, I am not going to ask you any more questions for now. Instead, I want you to tell me everything about the letter, how it was that you wrote it, who, if anyone, told you to write it and why you wrote it. Take your time." She stares at Mister Young. "I do not want anyone at this table to interrupt her. If you have something to say, raise your hand."

Regina looks across the table at her father. She shakes her head back and forth. It is obvious she does not want to say the things she knows she has to say. She tilts her head as if asking him if it is all right.

In response to her non-verbal expression, her father says in a whisper, "It's okay, Regina. It'll be okay. Tell the truth. Everything."

Regina stares straight ahead as she begins to talk. Not once does she change her expression, even as Diana occasionally squeezes her hand. Her tone of voice is monotone and void of any emotion.

"A month or so ago, a couple of weeks before the school year ended, I was called into the principal's office. Miss Hickman was present. Nobody else was in the room. I thought it odd that, one, I was there because I hadn't done anything wrong. And two, that Miss Hickman also was in Mister Young's office. I haven't had any dealings with either one of them since I've been at the school."

Regina hesitates for a few moments. Then, as she looks at Mister Young, she says in a confident voice, "Mister Young said that he wanted me to throw the ladies' championship softball game." She looks at Miss Davenport. "I don't know if you know this, ma'am. I am the team's pitcher."

Mister Young raises his hand to protest. Miss Davenport shakes her head as she says, "Not right now, sir. You'll have your chance." She looks at Regina. "What do you mean, Regina, when you say," she glances at her notes, "that Mister Young wanted you to throw the championship game?"

"He told me I should throw lots of strikes and fewer balls. He stressed that I shouldn't make it too obvious. Otherwise, as he said, the coach would replace me with another pitcher. He said I should try and throw the game toward the end. Doing so earlier would be too noticeable." She glares at Mister Young adding matter of factually, "He also said that I should throw the game earlier if the opposing team were ahead."

Mister Young is waving his hand high in the air.

Miss Davenport says, "Not now, sir. Be patient." She addresses Regina once more. "Continue, if you please."

Diana perks up her ears when she hears Mister Young say under his breath something that sounds like, "Stupid Woman." How she can discern his mumbled words when no one else seemed to notice what he said fascinates her. Over the past several weeks, she has noticed that her hearing, as well as her eyesight, have changed. She can hear and see things never noticeable. She looks around the table. Regina has everyone's undivided attention.

Regina cries, "I refused. I stated flat-out there was no way I was going to throw the game." She looks at her father. "My father taught me better than that. He raised me to be truthful at all times. Throwing the game would be like lying, cheating, robbing my friend here, Diana, and all my teammates of something they worked hard for all season. Throwing the game would be unfair to Sarah and Sally and all their teammates as well. They would forever question in their minds if they had won the game fair and square." She hesitates a few seconds, and then she says, "Or if somebody like me had deceived them." An angry scowl crosses her face as she recalls her reaction.

"I got up from my chair and started to leave. I was angry. And I was confused. Why my principal, a person to whom I should look up to, would want me to cheat was shocking." She looks at Miss Hickman. Miss Hickman's face is strangely blank as she stares at the table. She has a cloth bandage on the back of her head where the stones had struck her. She also has a small band-aid on the bridge of her nose.

"Miss Hickman grabbed me by the arm and steered me to Mister Young's empty desk. Mister Young had departed the room a few seconds before. She said something to the effect, 'You may want to listen to Mister Young, Miss Reynolds. He hasn't told me what is going on. But, one thing I know for certain. You better listen to what he says, what he tells you to do. Otherwise, he can cause you a lot of harm. He can make things difficult for you and your father. He told me that you would have to quit school and move out of state. He said your father could lose his business. So, whatever it is, it must be bad. Your father will be very disappointed in you.'"

Regina dabs at the corners of her eyes with a tissue. "I cannot affirm that those are Miss Hickman's exact words, but I bet I'm pretty accurate." As she breathes out deeply, she adds, "Obviously, I sat back down. There is no one in the world whom I love more than my father. He has been with me through thick and thin, and he is the only person with whom I can confide after my mother passed away. I was confused. I was to throw the game. I didn't suspect it at the time, but my father was to throw the game as well." She looks at her father adding, "But, like me, he didn't. He also refused to do anything that would look deceitful. He is a much stronger person than I am."

Diana places her arm around Regina's shoulder. She whispers, "You're doing good, Reg. Real good. Stay strong." She glances at Mister Young. "Don't let him bully you."

Regina says, "Thanks, Dynamite. I needed that." She continues telling her story.

"And then, since they know Dynamite, I mean Diana, is my good friend, for some reason they went after her. So, there I was sitting in Mister Young's chair. I had to make a choice. Miss Hickman said that if I didn't write the letter, Mister Young would do something nasty to me and embarrass my father. Or, he could do something nasty with Dynamite. As it turned out, they threatened and hurt Dynamite as much as they hurt my father and me. I never intended to write the letter. All of what it says is a lie." She looks at Diana. "Dynamite and I would never hurt each other. Sure, we argue from time to time, but that's natural I guess."

Miss Davenport says, "Why do you think they threatened your friend, Diana, Dynamite as you refer to her?"

"Because she has eyes like a hawk. She is the catcher and as honest as the day is long. Besides, she seldom misses a call. She's almost as good, no I should say, she's better than an umpire. That's because she's the one catching the ball in her mitt or scooping it up from the dirt. When we practice, Dynamite is the one who makes the calls at home plate, a ball, a strike, you're out, etcetera. She is very honest, even when she is at bat. If someone calls a ball on her and she thinks it's a strike, she'll say so.

"Also, Miss Davenport, Diana had told her parents that she thought my father had made questionable calls during the softball tournament. That information somehow got back to Mister Young. I have my suspicions how that happened that I'll address in a minute. Diana's father, Mister Bower, is a member of the school's board as you know. Maybe someone was worried Mister Bower was going to tell others on the board. Then there could be trouble, investigations, that sort of thing."

Miss Davenport says, "Let the record show that Mister Bower is not present today in his capacity as a school board member. He is present, along with his wife, in support of his minor child, Diana Jane Bower." She looks at Regina. "Continue if you please. Say whatever it is you have to say, whatever comes to mind. Take your time."

Regina states, "So, there I was. I was sitting at Mister Young's desk. It was only Miss Hickman and me. Miss Hickman dictated the letter's contents to me." She glances at the letter that is on the table. "As you can see, there are smudges on it where my tears splashed on the letter as I wrote it. I was upset. I hated doing it. I hated the things, the outright lies, that I was forced to say about Dynamite."

She glances in Miss Hickman's direction. "There is something I must add, Miss Davenport. Although Miss Hickman dictated the letter's contents to me, she kept stressing over and over that she had no idea why Mister Young wanted me to write the letter about Dynamite. She seemed confused as to why she was telling me things that I was forced to write. I do not think she knew anything about anyone trying to blackmail my father." She cringes, and then she suddenly looks at her father. Her eyes are welling up with tears once more.

"I am sorry, Dad. I didn't intend to say that."

Her father says, "That's okay, hon." He nods his head for her to continue.

Regina says, "I've since learned from my father that someone is blackmailing him. He knows who it is, but he will not tell me. However, he told me this much. He had a conviction as a juvenile. He and his friends robbed a gas station. There was a handgun involved although, thankfully, my father did not have it in his possession. Thank God no one was hurt. Naturally, they caught my father and the other kids. The authorities punished my father, rightly so. Then, they sealed his records because he was a juvenile with a clean slate up until the robbery."

Tears are streaming down Regina's face once more. She wipes them with a tissue.

"What he did was wrong, I know that, as does he. But it was many years ago, nearly a decade before he met my late mother. I do not know this for a fact since my father hasn't told me. However, I'm a very smart girl." She glares at Mister Young.

"I suspect Mister Young was going to use my father's juvenile arrest record against him if he didn't throw the game. I don't know this for certain. But, now it all makes sense. I was to throw the game. Since I refused, they went after Diana and my father."

Miss Davenport is tempted to tell Regina that she must strike what she just said from the record. That is because Regina levied accusations against Mister Young. However, she decides not to reprimand Regina and to strike her accusations from the record. She will make her reasoning clear in a few moments later during the proceeding.

"Regarding my father's juvenile arrest, sure, when he told me, I cried, not so much because my father was in trouble as a kid but because someone was blackmailing him. Had I known then what I know now, I would have told Mister Young to go," she hesitates for a few seconds, and then she says, "I won't say what I am thinking out of respect for everyone here." She smiles meekly. "But I think you can guess what the following words are when I say go." She dabs the tears with a tissue that Diana hands to her.

"What is even worse, two weeks ago my father took my phone to the cell phone company where we bought it. It was acting strangely. Although he bought it for me four months ago, it kept turning itself on and off, even when I wasn't using it. While we were at the cellphone company, the technician asked to see my father's phone. After examining both of our phones, he said that he suspected someone had compromised our phones using external software. He said someone was listening in to our conversations. He asked for permission from my father to dial a special number on both of our phones. Then he said he was certain someone was listening to our conversations and reading all our texts. It was horrible to think someone had invaded our privacy. We went to the police. As far as I know, they're still investigating."

Mister Young raises his hand. He waves it back and forth like an impatient second grader who knows the answer to the teacher's question.

Miss Davenport says, "Give me a few more seconds with Regina if you please. I have a couple more questions to ask her. Then, you can have your turn. Thank you."

Mister Young's face turns bright red. He is not used to being ignored or to be asked to wait by anyone.

Diana discerns his mumbling words that sound like, "I'm going to kill that stupid woman."

She thinks to herself, "Do I imagine his words? Or, am I somehow hearing his thoughts! His lips were not moving!" She shakes her head. "Dang, I must be going crazy." She refocuses her attention on what Miss Davenport is saying. Miss Davenport is addressing Miss Hickman.

"Miss Hickman, do you have anything you would like to add to Miss Reynolds' words, her statement?"

Miss Hickman replies in a strong voice, "No, ma'am. What Miss Reynolds said is the truth." She looks at Diana and Regina.

"Regina, I did not know about the blackmail or your father's conviction as a juvenile. I swear. I was kept pretty much in the dark about what was going on. Others told me I had to play along with everything. If I did, I would get a ton of money. If I didn't, school officials would fire me for incompetence.

"I am very sorry this has happened to the two of you. I know that I cannot change anything in the past. But, I can affect the future by saying I am very sorry, and I apologize, and that I will work to regain your trust and respect.

"And Regina, maybe you should have pummeled me when you went to Diana's defense in my office. Then, perhaps, I would have been reminded how much it hurts to be hurt by another. I am forever sorry that I dictated that letter to you. For your information, I have passed a polygraph. It confirms that I did not know anything about the blackmail attempt against your father. All the same, what I made you do was unforgivable and unprofessional. You were supposed to trust me, and I violated that trust. Please, please find it in your heart to forgive me." Miss Hickman looks at Diana.

"And Diana, I also ask you to please forgive me. You were right. I am, or at least I was a bully. I realize that now. After what happened, when I was outside your house that night, after whatever it was that hit me with stones, my bullied past flashed before my eyes. I envisioned the bullies of my past throwing stones at me as I ran, calling me names, taunting me, and striking me with their fists. They called me horrible things. But one of their favorite bullying actions was to call me *Gloria the Boria*, probably because I was boring, and I had no loyal friends. That's how I came to insult your last name. When you think about it, Boria and Bowers, both names begin with the letter *B*.

"That night, as I lay on the street surrounded by those weirdly-placed rocks and stones, I realized that my past should not dictate my future. I am proud to say I am now in counseling. I can only hope and pray that I can be a better person." She presses her two hands together in a gesture of prayer and forgiveness. "I am truly sorry. Please forgive me. I pray you will find it in your heart to do so."

Diana gets out of her chair. Miss Davenport almost tells her to sit back down in her chair. But, her heart tells her this is a moment for which breaking the rules is permissible.

Diana walks up to Miss Hickman. She places her arm around Miss Hickman's shoulder. As she chokes back tears, she looks Miss Hickman squarely in the eyes. She whispers, "Miss Hickman, I accept your apology, and I forgive you. I honestly do. And I will pray for you tonight and every night that your counseling is successful. What you said here today took guts. My respect for you as a strong-willed, highly intelligent, honest woman begins this day going forward."

As Diana returns to her chair, she looks at Miss Davenport and declares, "Give her a second chance if you please. Others bullied me when I was younger. Without question, I know how much bullying hurts. But, I forgave those who bullied me just like I would like to have others forgive me if I were to hurt them in any way. When you think of it, we're only human. As humans, we sometimes are not in control of what our brains tell us to do as it concerns others.

"Saying 'I am sorry,' like Miss Hickman just did, concerns but three words. However, it's meaning implies so much more. When you say you're sorry to someone, you place another's feelings above your opinion of yourself. What Miss Hickman said today emphasizes that. Her saying she's sorry reflects her regret just as she casts her ego aside.'"

Regina looks at Miss Davenport. She does not speak aloud. She nods her head and mouths silently, "I agree."

Miss Davenport, her facial expression melancholy, says, "Whew, Diana. I could not have said it any better. Well said, child. Well said." She sighs deeply, and then she says, "The interaction between the three of you was something else. I wish we could have made a movie of it. What a remarkable teaching and an anti-bullying tool it would be for your fellow students. I want to thank the three of you for being forthright and, it would appear, honest. I commend the three of you." She looks at Mister Young with a disgusted look that could start a war.

"Mister Young, do you have anything you would like to add?"

Mister Young looks at his watch. He says, "I think it's time for a break, don't you? Besides, I need to use the restroom. I'll have my say when we return." Then, he sarcastically adds, "In case you didn't notice, you went over your promised allotted time of an hour."

Miss Davenport says, "Okay. Let's take a twenty-minute break. We went over our time by twenty-nine minutes as Mister Young so aptly pointed out, so an extra ten minutes is warranted." With a laugh, she adds, "I don't know about the rest of you, but I'm hungry. My secretary told me there are glazed donuts out there just waiting for us to devour them!"

Diana is unable to control her emotions when it comes to delicious food, especially snacks. She declares, much louder than is appropriate given the solemn situation, "Yes, I love, love, love donuts, especially glazed donuts!" As everyone rises from their chairs, she smacks Regina on her shoulder. "Let's go, Reg. I'll race you to the donuts. The last one gets the donut hole."

It is more than thirty minutes later that the proceedings restart. The delay was due to a heated discussion in the corner of the conference room between Miss Davenport and Mister Young.

Diana and Regina each have a plate of donuts before them. The other girls do as well. Diana had asked if it was okay if they brought their donuts into the conference room. Miss Davenport said that she did not mind as long as they did not make a mess. She knows that it is important for the girls to be as comfortable as possible. She has more tough questions to ask. Something in her heart tells her it is going to become more heated in the room as well.

Miss Davenport starts off the next session with Sally Turndle.

"Sally, can you please tell me why Mister Reynolds ejected you from the game?"

Sally replies, "Will I get in any trouble if I tell you the truth?"

"Well, just so you know, Sally, I have statements from others including a statement from your mother. The statements will either corroborate or contradict what you have to say. Then it is their word against yours. However, I would encourage you to tell the truth. It's the proper thing to do as you know. As far as your question is concerned, if you will be in any trouble, let me say this. After speaking with your mother, I think you are already in enough trouble. Your mother told me she grounded you from just about everything but softball for the rest of summer break. So, what do you have to lose?"

"I do not want you to expel me," Sally says in a whisper.

"Oh, I do not think expulsion is warranted unless, of course, there is something you say that I don't already know." Miss Davenport smiles. "So, what do you say?"

Sally says in a soft voice, "I handed Mister Reynolds a note."

"What did the note say, Sally?"

"It said, 'You know I will get on base if I do not hit a home run. Either you call me safe, or I'll tell everyone you kissed me in the dugout.'"

"Was the accusation that Mister Reynolds had kissed you the truth?"

Sally shakes her head. "No, ma'am. It was a lie. I made it up. Mister Reynolds always respects the girls. We don't always like his calls, but he has never said or did anything improper to any of us, at least not to my knowledge."

"When did you give Mister Reynolds the note," Miss Davenport asks.

"I think I gave it to him before the game. I was quite nervous, so I cannot be certain. Maybe I gave it to him sometime during the game. I'm sorry. I don't remember exactly."

"Do you know when Mister Reynolds read the note?"

Sally shakes her head. "I'm not certain, but it must have been when I was running the bases or just as I started protesting that he had called me out." She looks at Mister Reynolds. "I'm sorry, sir. I shouldn't have done what I did. I truly regret it, and I ask you to forgive me for my stupidity."

Mister Reynolds looks at Miss Davenport before he replies. She nods her head.

He says, "It's okay, Sally." He glances at Missus Turndle adding, "After talking with your mother, I think you have learned your lesson. If I were a betting man, I'd bet you will never do anything like that again."

As she nods her head, Sally states, "Yes sir. What I did was wrong. I didn't realize it at the time, but if someone else had seen that note, it could have caused you a lot of trouble. I knew you were dating, that you had lost your wife recently, and I figured I could get at you that way. I wanted to do anything to win the game. However, now I realize that winning a game through bribery or threats isn't winning. Trickery and dishonesty can only make things worse." She smiles meekly. "I shouldn't have protested the way I did. I embarrassed you in front of both teams and the fans. You had every right to eject me from the game. I am sorry for my actions, and I apologize."

Mister Reynolds says, "I didn't eject you from the game solely based on your objections. I ejected you to teach you a lesson. Coaches, players, and officials have no business trying to influence a game's outcome. It is deceitful. Your objections simply made my decision to eject you much easier." He smiles and says, "Your mother and I had a very long conversation concerning that note. At first, she was angry with me for ejecting you. Once she had read the note, she, as we say in softball, was my greatest fan."

Everyone, including Sally, laughs at what Mister Reynolds says. Mister Young is the only exception. He has his eyes closed and is shaking his head back and forth nonstop.

Miss Davenport says, "Sally, it appears that you have learned your lesson. And I am happy that you have. You are correct. That incriminating note in the wrong hands could have destroyed Mister Reynolds' reputation more than you'll ever know. It also could have been very embarrassing for your friend, Regina. Despite everything that you have said up to this point, I have one additional question. Why were you protesting?"

Sally says with a confident tone, "Because I was safe. Diana's tag missed me. I slid under it."

Miss Davenport says, "Are you certain you were safe, that you slid beneath Diana's tag?"

"Yes, ma'am. I am certain." She looks at Diana. "Diana told me the next day that she thought I was safe, that Mister Reynolds may have made a bad call. She didn't say anything to accuse Mister Reynolds of anything improper. However, I thought that she agreed with me, that Mister Reynolds was mistaken when he called me out at the plate.

"Also, she had no idea why Mister Reynolds ejected me from the game. She, along with others, assumed he ejected me because I am the best hitter on my team. Naturally, only Mister Reynolds and I knew about my nasty note." She breathes in deeply and says with a sigh, "Wow, I screwed up. I'm sorry."

Miss Davenport says, "Well, perhaps it will clear up any doubt when I say this. You were out. We are certain Diana tagged you." She looks at Diana. "So, both of you were incorrect. Mister Reynolds made the right call. Sally was out. Diana tagged her fair and square."

Diana blurts out, "How can you be so sure?" Then, realizing she spoke out of turn, she says, "Sorry. I should have raised my hand."

Miss Davenport says in a stern voice, "Again, I caution everyone. Do not speak out of turn. If you have something to say or to add to our discussion, raise your hand. This proceeding is not a debate. There are more than a dozen people here. Speaking out of turn will result in mass confusion."

Diana, with a glum look on her face, raises her hand and says, "Sorry."

"It's okay," Miss Davenport says. "But, just so you four girls know, the entire game was recorded. We record every championship softball game, ladies, and men alike. Every single play, every single hit, every single ball, strike, and so on, are recorded for posterity. We do the recordings, so we can show clips of the highlights of the games to recruit new ballplayers."

She looks at Sally and says with a sad tone, "For the record, I might as well state this. We have reviewed the recording as it pertains to the note you gave to Mister Reynolds. You handed him the note just as a small, two-engine plane flew somewhat low over the field. Everyone's attention focused on the plane. Everyone's attention but yours." She glances at her notes. "It was right after you received the first ball. Mister Reynolds kept the note in his left hand. He finally read the note when you were running the bases."

Diana wants to jump up and down and scream, "You have a recording, a recording of the entire game? That Miss Davenport has a video recording is too coolio. I must ask. I have to ask!" She raises her hand to get Miss Davenport's attention.

Miss Davenport smiles at Diana. She says, "Not now, Diana. I know what you want to ask me. But, now is not the time. It can wait for later." She looks at Sarah.

"Sarah, you volunteered to attend this proceeding. Can you please tell the others why you and your father are here?"

Sarah says, "Because I know something that someone doesn't know that I know."

"And what is that something? Can you tell us?"

Sarah looks at her father. She asks uncertainly, "Should I, Daddy?"

Her father replies after obtaining Miss Davenport's permission to speak. "Only if you want to. Miss Davenport already has my statement, so what you say is not a surprise to her." He glances around the room. "But it will be a surprise to others." He crosses his huge, tattooed, muscled arms over his enormous chest. He says, "Don't worry. No one is going to hurt you. I promise."

Sarah says, "Okay, Daddy. Thank you." She looks at Miss Davenport.

"I was at Mister Young's house one day. I was with my best friend, Missy. Missy is Mister Young's oldest daughter. She and I go way back, all the way back to kindergarten." She interlocks her forefingers. "We're like sisters. We're this close." She reaches for a tissue as she begins to cry.

Miss Davenport says, "You do not have to say anything else if you do not want to. I do not want you to feel ill at ease." She glances at Miss Beach who hands her a folder. "I have your father's statement right here in this folder. You need not say anything during this proceeding."

In between sobs as she wipes her eyes, Sarah says, "I need to say it even though I know it will break Missy's heart. I only hope she will forgive me. I know she'll be angry with me for a while. But, best friends are best friends forever. She'll eventually forgive me.

"I was at Missy's house. She and I were standing outside the door to Mister Young's study. We were about to play a trick on him, to scare him with some Halloween masks we found in the attic. We noticed he was talking on the phone. Missy had said, 'Oh, let's go. We'll scare him later.' Then she ran off to use the bathroom.'" She abruptly looks down at the table. Her face flushes.

"I stuck around outside of Mister Young's study. I know I should not have eavesdropped, but I heard him mention the ladies' softball championship game between our team and Diana and Regina's team. So, I listened in. I'm not proud that I did. However, in retrospect, I am glad that I did. This way I can clear up some of the confusion surrounding my friends." She looks at Diana, Regina, and Sally with teary eyes. "My friends who are here at this table."

"What did Mister Young say?" Miss Davenport asks in a quiet tone as she taps the folder with her pen. "What did he say that upset you so much you had to tell your father?"

"He, Mister Young, said, and I'm fairly certain this is close to word for word, 'We must do anything to win the ladies' championship game. And tell Reynolds we are going to destroy him if he doesn't play along. Do anything you have to do short of breaking his legs. Go after his daughter. I don't care. I intend to win big when I place my bet. You win, we all win. Yes, I know it's cheating, but I don't care. Make it happen! Now leave me alone!'"

Mister Young suddenly blurts out, "This is a charade! A kangaroo court I tell you!" He stands up and shouts at Miss Hickman as he points his finger at her. "You are a sniveling little weakling. I knew you were worthless the day you started working for me!" He points to

Sarah. "And you, you little brat! You are a liar. Admit it. You're going to cost me my job, my reputation. I never said the things you said I did. I dare you to prove it!"

Mister Cousins is up out of his seat in a flash. He has his clenched fists at his side. He does not say or do anything but glare at Mister Young. His muscular, huge, six-foot-three-inch frame is intimidating.

Miss Davenport yells, "Sit down, Mister Young. Sit down, or I will call security." She calmly says to Mister Cousins, "You too, Mister Cousins. I don't want anything violent going on here. There are minors present. I refuse to subject my students to violence. Period."

Mister Young says between clenched teeth, "You're all conspiring against me. I will have my day in court. You'll see. Then all of you will learn the truth." He slumps down in his chair and glares at Miss Davenport.

Miss Davenport says calmly, "Perhaps you shall have your day in court, Mister Young. Perhaps you shall." She turns around to look at the school board officials sitting behind her. The look on her face is solemn. Diana and the other girls cringe. They instinctively know it is time for her to dole out punishments if any.

Miss Davenport says, "I have made my decisions regarding disciplinary actions as they concern the four students in attendance today." She looks at Sarah.

"Regarding Miss Sarah Cousins' actions, since she is a voluntary witness and has done nothing wrong, I commend her." She looks at Miss Beach. "Please write up a letter of commendation for Sarah. Naturally, leave out the details discussed here since they remain a matter of adjudication. What Sarah said today, as Diana had so aptly put it, took guts."

Mister Young shouts in a commanding tone, "What the heck do you mean they remain a matter of adjudication? What in the world is that?"

Miss Davenport declares with a commanding tone, "Sir, I will ask you for the last time. Please do not speak out of turn. Thank you." Then, she adds, "Besides, Sarah doesn't even attend your school. So, what I do or say is none of your concern."

Turning her attention to Miss Beach once more, Miss Davenport says, "About Miss Sally Turndle's actions, I award the following." She looks at Sally.

"I award Miss Sally Turndle one hour's detention after school for two school weeks for a total of ten hours. She will perform her detention when classes resume in the fall. Her incriminating note was uncalled for and reflected poor judgment. I'm glad no one else saw her note. I'm tempted to discipline her more severely. However, I fully support her mother in this regard and realize that Sally's punishment at home is severe enough given the infraction. Besides," she looks at Sally's mother, "I know in my heart that Sally recognizes what she did was dangerous. I know she has learned her lesson. And, Miss Turndle, I support your disciplinary actions one hundred percent." She looks at Sally once more whose hand is in the air. Miss Davenport nods her head.

Sally says, "Yes, ma'am. I learned my lesson. I am sorry. And I thank you for going easy on me. I know you could have expelled me for my stupid actions. Nothing like this will ever happen again. I promise." Miss Davenport says, "Thank you, Sally. I believe you."

Miss Davenport looks at Regina. She says in a quiet but firm tone, "Always remember to trust your instincts. Do not allow others to force you to do anything you know is wrong. Most of all, and you may quote me on this as you spread the word to your classmates, never have a secret pact with a teacher or a faculty member. Period. If someone in authority asks you to do so, tell your school counselor and your parent or parents without delay."

Miss Davenport consults her notes. She looks up at Regina once more. "Regarding Miss Regina Reynolds. Given the circumstances of her case, there is no need for disciplinary action."

Diana exclaims, "Yes!" Realizing she yet again spoke out of turn, she says, "I'm sorry, ma'am. I'm happy for Reg."

"As for you, Miss Diana Bower," Miss Davenport states rather briskly, "I order that any reference by Mister Young regarding disciplinary action in your case, to include detention and expulsion, be expunged from your school record." She adds, "That includes the fake letter regarding allegations that you struck Regina with a broomstick."

Regina claps her hands, and then she pumps her fist high in the air.

Miss Davenport gives her a disapproving look that could freeze a tall glass of water in a second flat. She focuses her gaze on Miss Hickman. Her voice is soft and her tone sympathetic when she speaks.

"As for you, Miss Gloria Hickman. I have spoken at length with your counselor. I have also spoken to your fellow faculty members. Many of your peers have come to appreciate and respect your intelligence, diligence, and accuracy as the school's primary secretary to the principal.

"However, I must tell you, none, and I mean absolutely none, respect you for your bullying attitude. You do not know this, but I have already received many complaints about the way you treat the students at your school." Miss Beach hands her a folder. Miss Davenport opens it, and then she pens a few notes. She looks up at Miss Hickman.

"In fact, while there is no way you could know this, I had scheduled your dismissal hearing for ten o'clock next Friday. I fully intended on recommending to the school board that we terminate you." She smiles, and then, in an affectionate tone, she says, "However, I know it was very difficult for you to say the things that you said today. I am pleased that you apologized to Diana and Regina. That you asked for their forgiveness also moved me. What I am about to say was also influenced by Diana's moving comments today. That Diana got up from her chair to embrace you and say the things she said made my decision much easier."

She looks at Diana. "Thank you, Diana, for your display of compassion. Your empathetic actions and forgiving words reflect the strength of your character as well as your courage. After everything that Miss Hickman did and said to you, you still found it in your heart to forgive her and to say that you respect her. That, my dear, in your own words, takes guts. You, Diana, are, by far, the most courageous youngster I have ever had the pleasure of knowing."

Miss Davenport addresses Miss Hickman once more.

"So, Gloria, here is what I am going to do. I am going to recommend to the board that you continue as a secretary but not as the principal's secretary. You will join the school's office secretary pool. You are talented, intelligent, and adept at what you do. However, I want you to schedule with the school counselor, Miss Beach, a date and time when you will address all the students at your school in an assembly. I want you to address bullying, bullying by adults and students alike. And, if you desire, and I strongly recommend it, I think you should tell how you, the bullied, turned out to be a bully.

"You admitted to me that others bullied you as a child and the bullying became second nature to you. Bullying others was your way of escaping your childhood nightmares. Those are your exact words you said to me over the phone when we scheduled your appearance at these proceedings.

"I also took into consideration that you are in counseling with, as your counselor says, excellent potential. I also considered the fact that you passed a polygraph regarding the attempted blackmail issue, that you had no knowledge it was ongoing." She writes something in the folder. Then she says, "I am putting you on one year's probation. I expect results. Am I clear, Gloria?"

"Yes, ma'am, you are clear. I will do all the things you ask and more. Thank you."

Mister Young blurts out, "Well, don't that just beat all." He roughly pushes his chair behind him as he stands up. "I've had enough of this. I'm sick of all this sniveling and apologizing and lies and scandalous bull, not to mention less than adequate punishments."

Miss Davenport stands up. She says firmly, "Sir. If you, please. I have one more announcement to make. Please give me the satisfaction of making the announcement."

"Yeah, go ahead," Mister Young shouts. "I don't want to hear it, but what the heck." He glances around the table. "You're all full of bull anyway. It ain't going to hurt me to listen to you as you fling more dung."

Miss Davenport calmly says, "I adjourn this proceeding."

As Mister Young turns to leave, she says, "Mister Young. Please hold on. There's one more thing I'd like to say. You're going to like this."

"Yeah, what is it? Are you going to tell everyone you are going to recommend to the school board that you want to terminate me?"

"Oh, no sir. I am not going to say that. I will not recommend to the school board that they should terminate you."

Mister Young says with a surprised tone, "You aren't? Oh, I thought you were. I am sorry." He sits in his chair. With a fake smile, he says, "Please, Miss Davenport, do continue." He adds in a sarcastic tone, "I'm all ears."

Out of the blue, a man's commanding voice from Miss Davenport's adjacent office calls out. "I see you have adjourned your proceeding, Miss Davenport. May we enter?"

Miss Davenport says, "Yes, officer, we have adjourned. Please come in."

Mister Young stares with a bewildered, shocked expression as two uniformed officers enter through the open door of Miss Davenport's office. One of the officers is none other than Officer Meadows. He smiles at Miss Hickman and gives her a thumb's up.

As the two officers approach Mister Young to handcuff him, Miss Davenport says, "The other thing I wanted to say was this. Mister Young, you're under arrest." She chuckles, and then, with a serious tone, she says, "It appears your good buddy, Crazy Face Studeman spilled his guts for the promise of immunity in your case. He's going to testify against you. Isn't that grand?

"The officers will provide you with your Miranda Rights and the reason they're arresting you. Knowing the details that I do, I'm certain your charges will include blackmail, extortion, money laundering, illegal gambling, multiple violations of privacy standards, tampering with evidence and, most seriously, threats to a minor child." She grabs Diana's phone from the table. As she waves it in the air, she adds, "Not to mention your attempted corruption of the morals of a child as documented in this phone's recording!"

As the policemen walk Mister Young out of the conference room, he turns his head and glares at Miss Davenport. His lips silently form two cuss words.

Miss Davenport exclaims, "Same to you, sir. And oh, by the way. You're fired, terminated. And, I'm very pleased to say, you won't be back!"

CHAPTER FOURTEEN

THE BATTLE BETWEEN TRUTH AND LIES

Part I: The Staircase

Diana is visibly annoyed as she glares at the creepy, dilapidated, winding spiral staircase before her. Despite the beautiful cobalt sky and blazing buttery sun, and all the kaleidoscopic natural beauty of the World Beyond behind her, the staircase is out-of-place. Charles had described it to her the day before. But, she never expected something as revolting as this.

Charles had said, "It's called the Sine Fine Staircase. It leads to Mendacium's inner sanctum. At least that is what legends say. It is there where you will find him as he awaits you. If you wound him in some way or manage to defeat him, you will climb on to the gates of the wondrous Kingdom of Domum in the sky. Once again, I must state, that is what legends say. Afterward, you will return here for one last visit, to say goodbye to all your friends."

Charles' look abruptly had turned serious which caused tingling shivers to run up and down Diana's spine.

"However, Diana, if you do not wound him in some fashion or defeat him, you shall be his Prisoner of Innocence. Then deceit, treason, and betrayal will pervade our Universe. After that, everything that we love, everything that we cherish, everything that is good and wholesome in our worlds will vanish forever."

Diana had replied, her bated breath making it difficult for her to talk lucidly, "Does that mean you, Charles? Will you vanish?"

Charles had replied in a somber tone, "Yes, Diana, sadly, yes, I would cease to be."

As tears welled up in her eyes and she quickly reached out to embrace her lifelong ghost, Diana simply cried out, "Nnnnnoooooooooooo!"

Now, as Diana stares with loathing at the decrepit staircase, she has a heavy heart. If she fails to defeat or wound Mendacium in some way, everything that she loves will vanish, to be lost forever. Then half of her being, this one in the World Beyond, will become Mendacium's Prisoner of Innocence. And her loving ghost, Charles, I Dunno, Jayvyn and the Minima will cease to exist. Although Charles did not say it, then a part of her would remain in the World Beyond forever. Or, and she hates to even think of it, the whole of her, both here and in the Real-world could also cease to exist.

She knows she has no other choice but to ascend the staircase. She also knows she must win because failure is not an option. But, now that she is here at the foot of the staircase, for some strange reason, she is hesitating. She feels more afraid than she has ever felt in her life. If she fails, she loses everything. And what she will soon face, unlike what her double must face in the Real-world, is much more than winning a ladies' softball championship game and trying to wind her way through the chaos. What she is about to face, what she is experiencing here and now could mean the difference between life and death.

She suddenly cries, "Ugh! This baluster is wobbly. Charles, please come here and look at it. It can hardly stand by itself let alone support the handrail." As Charles moves next to her, she kicks with her foot at something on the first stair tread.

"Yuck, it's a huge spider!"

She seizes a bit of the dense spiderweb that is enveloping the baluster, handrail, and newels.

"And look at this. This stuff is super sticky. If I were to get stuck in a huge spiderweb made of this stuff, I'd never get free!" She makes a face as a tingling shiver rushes across her shoulder blades. "Then, the nasty critters would eat me alive."

She crouches to get a better look at the staircase. She brushes the thick layer of dust and cobwebs from the first stair tread with her hand. A spider scurries from beneath the dust. She quickly jumps back. She looks up at the second and third stair treads. With a disgusted tone, she says, "There are hundreds of the turn your stomach creatures crawling out of cracks in the stair treads and risers. I hate, I hate, I hate spiders!"

Charles says matter-of-factly, "Oh, Diana, there are not hundreds of spiders. I see less than a dozen. After battling Inania and Parva Draco and eradicating the last Malavem from the Universe, don't tell me you're afraid of spiders."

"Not afraid," Diana replies coldly. "They're disgusting to look at."

She kicks at another spider that scurries from a hole in the riser. It crashes against the closed string, the sideboard of the stair tread, and then it flips upside-down. All eight of its two-inch-long legs wildly thrash in the air as it tries to regain its footing.

"I mean, look at them, Charles. They are sneaky little critters that only come out at night to feed on the unsuspecting. And they have the nastiest hairy legs." She swats at another spider with her hand. "And they're huge! I bet they're as big as the average field mouse in the Real-world! If these are baby spiders, I can only imagine what their mommies and daddies look like!"

Charles laughs. "Well, I think you can overcome them. After all, Diana, you are the Favored Child, the fearless warrior Artemis-Diana. Don't let a few hairy-legged creatures bother you."

She replies grimly, "A few you say, Charles? I've already smacked more than a few, and that's just on the first stair tread!"

She takes a tentative step onto the first stair tread. It loudly squeaks as she steps on it, and it sags a little too much for her liking. She grabs the handrail for support. The portion of the handrail between the baluster and newel snaps in two. It falls to the ground creating a cloud of dust. She leaps backward. She gives Charles a dirty look.

"Charles, isn't there any other way? I know I must do this but come on." She picks up a piece of the decayed handrail. "This thing is falling apart. And, I haven't even gotten past the first riser! Tell me I don't have to climb this staircase, Charles? Please!" She vigorously shakes her head. "I'll be lucky to make it past the first ten risers before I tumble through the decayed wood to the ground. There must be another way!"

Charles replies glumly, "Diana, I cannot, nor would I, force you. Whether you ascend the staircase or not is entirely up to you. However, if you do not, you will always wonder if you have what it takes to defeat or wound Mendacium." He places his hands on Diana's shoulders and gently turns her body, so she is facing him. He firmly squeezes her shoulders.

"Do you trust me, Diana?" She nods her head.

"Well, if you can have trust in me, have trust in yourself. I know you. I've known you for your entire life. There is nothing you cannot do if you put your mind to it." He takes the piece of handrail from her that she is holding in her hand.

"This, my dear friend, is nothing more than decayed wood. But, it once was strong, resilient, unbreakable, able to withstand the test of time and yes, the clutching hands of countless others who depended on its support as they tread upon the staircase. Over time, Mendacium purposely caused it to decay, to waste away, just like his deceitful existence, just like everything his lying ways touch." He hands the piece of handrail back to Diana.

"You, my beloved friend, Artemis-Diana are strong. You are resilient. And you are unbreakable. Do the honorable thing you feel in your heart, that which you know is noble. Breathe life into the legacy of the handrail, the staircase risers, balusters, landings, stair treads, all of it." He turns around to look at the breathtaking views in front of them.

"The World Beyond was gradually dying, Diana. Then a miracle happened. You arrived."

With a sweeping motion of his hand, he says, "The forests are leafy once more. The verdant grass is tall once more. The animals sing in their unique way as they happily prance within their respective kingdoms once more. The Minima are confident once more. All that you see before you are flourishing under a reinvigorated, warm sun. Diana, you made the sunshine longer and the dimness of nighttime shorter by defeating many creatures born of Mendacium's hatred." He turns around to face her and the staircase. He takes the piece of the handrail from her yet again.

"Perhaps you can do the same to this piece of handrail, to the entire staircase. Perhaps you can make the staircase new and whole once more as the sole means of connecting the World Beyond with Domum. However, if you choose not to ascend the staircase, I shall support your decision. You will not disappoint me. You never could. On the other hand, if you choose to ascend the staircase, know that I anxiously will await your return with open arms."

Diana stammers as she says, "Wait a minute, Charles! Are you saying that you are not going with me? Please tell me you are not going to leave me alone up there!" She glances up at the gloomy staircase encased in spiderwebs and generations-old dust. She cannot help but shiver at its hideousness together with its foreboding cheerlessness.

"I am truly sorry," Charles replies. "I cannot ascend the staircase. As I said before, I have no powers in the World Beyond. Like my brother James, Mendacium surely will seize me. Then, as I suspect he did with James, he will turn me against you. If Mendacium turns me against you while you are on the staircase, I fear you will not have a chance. Your strength would rapidly diminish. Then you will pass away." He kisses Diana on the cheek. "Yes, ultimately, our love as lifelong friends will serve to be our undoing. You will perish, as will I."

Diana gasps as she whispers, "Are you telling me that you and I will die if Mendacium seizes you?"

"Yes, Diana, we must die. You and I are the nearest and dearest, inseparable souls. It is inevitable. If one dies, the other dies. And our souls will never again be as one."

Diana collapses to her knees. She buries her face in her hands and sobs uncontrollably. Her entire body is shaking. She hates to appear weak, to cry. But, in this situation, she cannot help herself. The awareness if she were to die, that her passing would cause Charles' death, is inconceivable, unimaginable. Her demise would bring an end to his noble and compassionate ethereal healing for the poor children who are on death's bed.

"And," she whispers in between sobs, "I would lose you, Charles. I cannot live without my dearest friend, my ghost."

Charles bends to help Diana onto her feet. Once she is standing, he embraces her affectionately.

"Oh, Charles," she whispers, "I love you very much. I cannot allow you to die because of me. So, I do not want you to accompany me."

She looks at him. Charles gently wipes her tears with his fingertips. "But tell me this, Charles. Say I were to die a natural death like in an accident in the Real-world or when I grow old. Would you also die?"

"No, Diana, I would continue in my ethereal way. I would probably latch onto another human who has all your fine attributes. Only if Mendacium were to seize me, and your strength diminished, would I perish. As I said, ultimately, so would you."

Diana whispers, "Okay, as much as it scares me, I understand what you are saying. But what about my double, the other me, Diana, in the Real-world. Even if I were to perish at the hands of Mendacium, as would you, you'd still live on in her, in my life, in the Real-world, yes? You would still be with me, my other self?"

Charles expression becomes even more miserable. "Diana, as I said, I would cease to exist. In this world and the Real-world, you call home. While the other you, your Diana double would live on, she would have to go on without me."

Diana wipes her tears from her face with the back of her hand. Then she brusquely moves from Charles' embrace. She picks up her quiver and places its strap over her head to position the quiver on her back. She retrieves her longbow and sword from the ground. The sudden, transformed look on her face is astounding! It is an expression of outright resolve. She reaches to kiss Charles on the cheek. Then she rapidly walks to the staircase.

"I refuse to allow Mendacium to hurt you, Charles, to hurt me! You must stay here. I will meet him face-to-face. If it's the last thing I do, I will have him cowering, begging me for mercy in no time!" She takes a deep breath and steps on the first stair tread.

Charles reaches out to grab her firmly by the shoulders. He says, "Not so fast, my dear warrior. There are a few things I need to tell you." He picks up Diana's waterskin and rucksack from the ground. "You forgot these." Diana notices that he did not pick up I Dunno's pouch. She rightly assumes I Dunno will also stay behind.

"I won't need them," she declares. "It'll be over with before you can say 'Mendacium is gone.'"

Charles shakes his head. "Slow down, Diana. It's not going to be that easy or that quick. There are a few things I need to tell you." He hands the waterskin and rucksack to her. She slips their fastenings over her shoulders.

"Okay," Charles begins. "There are a few things you must know. First, the winding staircase continues for three-hundred twenty-two stair treads until it reaches the first landing. At least that is what legends say. You must rest before you reach the first landing."

"Why?" Diana asks. "I'd rather stretch out on a landing than," she glances at the staircase, "on those godforsaken rickety stair treads."

"Listen to me carefully," Charles says. "Rest before you even get close to the first landing. Drink plenty of water. Eat. Take a nap if you must. Three-hundred twenty-two stair treads of a surprisingly steep spiraling staircase are nothing to take for granted. I hope you know that. Having to climb that many stair treads easily will tire you."

"Okay, I get it," Diana says with an impatient tone of voice. "But why can't I just wait until I get to the first landing to recuperate?" She smiles. "After all, I'm in very good shape. Having to climb a few hundred stair treads is nothing compared to fighting a sword battle."

Charles says in an offhand tone, "Because it is there, at the first landing, you will encounter your first challenge."

Diana stares at him for the longest time. He returns her stare. He jokingly backs away, pretending that he fears that she is going to strike him. The thought does not cross her mind. It never could, and it never will. All the same, he cannot help but notice that her expression is not a happy one. Undoubtedly, he has aggravated her.

When Diana replies to Charles' mention of the challenges she will encounter, she deliberately talks to him in halting sentences. With a narrowing of her eyes, she says in a disbelieving tone, "Charles. What. Do you mean? When you say. My first challenge?" She takes a few steps toward him and playfully jabs his chest with her finger. "You never told me anything about challenges. And, if you're talking about my first challenge, there must be more than one challenge. Is my assumption correct?"

She takes a step closer to him. Now, less than two feet separate them. Charles smiles as he takes a few steps backward. He knows that Diana is angry because he never mentioned the challenges. It is also obvious to him that she is upset because he is making light of her anger.

He says in a sheepish tone of voice, "Well, Diana, I was going to tell you sooner than later. It's just that I forgot."

"Oh, really," she replies sarcastically. "You forgot. And when were you going to tell me about my challenges, Charles?" She looks him straight in the eye. She suddenly laughs.

"Oh, now I get it. You wanted to soften me up first, to tell me how you and I would die together like Romeo the ghost and Juliet the warrior, yep?" She sets her longbow and sword on the ground. "Well, now is the later time, Romeo. Please tell me all about the challenges." She adds with a genuine scowl, "And please quit fooling around. What is happening here isn't the least bit funny."

Charles playfully pretends he is afraid of Diana as he moves past her, all the while he looks her in the eye. He sits on the first stair tread of the spiraling staircase. As he does, he is very careful to make certain his feet do not touch the ground. If they were to touch the ground, he would vanish. He motions with his hand for Diana to sit next to him. At first, she refuses. Then, with a playful air of rebelliousness, she crosses her arms over her chest. She shakes her head over and over as she stares at him. She silently mouths the word, "No."

In reply, Charles puckers his brow, as he asks, "Please, my dear Diana?"

Suddenly, Diana begins to laugh. Charles laughs as well. As she sits next to him, she takes a swig of water from her waterskin. She purposely offers Charles her waterskin knowing that he will refuse it. In the back of her mind, she wants him to feel awkward like she is feeling right now.

"You know I do not need water, Diana," Charles says with a tone of discomfort. "But thanks anyway."

"Yes, I know that," Diana says softly. "I didn't mean to embarrass you, to make you feel uncomfortable." She smacks him on his shoulder. "Like I'm feeling right now! And, oh, I am sorry. Like you, I had forgotten. You're a ghost. And I'm flesh and blood, a sixty-percent water human. So, my dear ghost friend, tell me, if you please, everything I need to know about these challenges." With a wry smile, she adds in a cynical tone, "What do you say we start with the challenge I will encounter on the first landing, huh?"

*****

Part II: The Promise

Diana takes another lengthy swig from her waterskin. She sets the waterskin on the stair tread and then she pulls out a piece of whatnots from her pouch. She stuffs the entire piece in her mouth. As she gnaws on the delicious whatnots, she begins to massage her aching calf and thigh muscles.

She lets out a long groan as she whispers to herself, "Dang, Charles was correct. Climbing these stair treads is tiring! I have no idea what tread I am on. Maybe I'm on two-hundred something, or I could be on three-hundred something. I quit counting after two-hundred-fifty something. All I know is having a swordfight is nothing compared to climbing stairs for hours on end."

Diana had to take her first rest break on stair tread ninety. She took another break on stair tread one-hundred forty. Her goal was to climb fifty stair treads, take a break, then climb another fifty stair treads and so on. Her plan did not last long. She began to take short breaks every thirty stair treads, give or take. Then, she was taking longer breaks every twenty or so stair treads. Now, she is stopping to take a break every fifteen or so stair treads that she climbs.

She is very tired, and her muscles are aching, particularly her right calf muscle. Because of her fatigue, she had to climb the last ten stair treads on all fours, one arduous, muscle-aching, exhausting hand over hand step at a time. Although she hates to admit it, her grievous injuries took a greater toll on her body than she had assumed.

She is profusely sweating as she climbs the staircase, so she must drink ample amounts of water to stay hydrated. However, every time she draws from the waterskin, the amount of water she drinks is immediately replaced by I Dunno's magic. Unlike a hiker that drinks as she hikes, which results in her water container getting lighter with each succeeding mile, thereby quickening her gait, Diana does not have that luxury. Her waterskin remains the same weight. And, if you will recall, the waterskin I Dunno created for her is much larger than she had expected. The waterskin is so heavy, on one occasion, she had considered chucking it. The reason is obvious. It is too darned heavy. Fortunately, she thought better of it.

She also adjusted the straps, so now she can drag the heavy, never-emptying waterskin behind her as she climbs the stairs instead of carrying it on her back. While the waterskin's loud, annoying plopping and gurgling noises grate on her nerves, pulling, instead of carrying, the heavy waterskin is considerably easier.

She briefly stands to look up at the next gradual bend of the spiral staircase. She counts the stair treads that are within her sight. She tallies fourteen stair treads. She reasons, "Good, like all the others, I can see the next fourteen stair treads. The fifteenth stair tread disappears around the bend."

She is also relieved to note there is no landing in sight. For that reason, she believes there is no need to worry about encountering her first creature. What worries her more is she has no clue on what stair tread she is resting. She leans her head against two of the staircase spindles. She is fast asleep in no time.

Diana does not know she has fallen asleep on stair tread three-hundred six. The first landing is but sixteen stair treads away. What is more, Charles had told her that all the creatures she would encounter had to remain on the landing before they could attack her. Although Charles had said that the first evil creature she would encounter would be a basilisk, he had no idea of the basilisk's length. The basilisk, "Caverna Reguli," has a length that encompasses more than twenty stair treads! It effortlessly can slither twenty stair treads in either direction on the staircase while its tail remains on the landing.

Diana awakens with a scream. Staring at her, its gaping mouth less than four feet away from her astonished face is the basilisk Reguli!

From legends' descriptions, Charles had described Reguli to her in detail. The basilisk has a forked tongue and six-inch fangs like a serpent. Its limbless, cylindrical-shaped body is very supple. It has scaly skin predominately of a rich golden color. Its underbelly is a deep brown. Unlike a serpent, Reguli has features one would expect to see in mythical dragons. He has two, ten-inch curved, pointed thorns that protrude from his forehead. Six additional three-inch thorns are behind the two longer thorns, three each on either side of his head. Like many mythical dragons, Reguli has spines that run the length of his back. Five, razor-sharp one-foot-long spikes are on the end of his tail. He uses the spikes to lash unmercifully at an opponent thereby slicing it to pieces. The basilisk's reptilian stare is fixed on Diana as its dark tongue flits less than a foot from her face.

At first, Diana is unable to move. While Reguli stares at her with its red eyes, she suddenly has the urge to vomit. The basilisk's wide-open, yawning mouth is dripping blood. At first, she imagines the blood is hers. On closer inspection, she determines that the source of the blood comes from dozens of spiders. The basilisk must have grabbed the spiders on his way down the staircase.

She wants to scream as she notices that those spiders still alive are the size of hairy-legged softballs! Every time the basilisk opens and closes his mouth, he squishes spiders between his fangs. Grotesque spider blood squirts everywhere as a result, including onto Diana's face.

In a mind-boggling panic, she hastily unsheathes her sword as she scrambles to her feet. She quickly raises her sword high above her head to thrust it into Reguli's head. Before she can dole out the deciding blow, Reguli rapidly withdraws from the stair tread. Her downward thrust angrily connects with nothing but air.

Diana is scared out of her wits. Like the basilisk, she also wants to retreat as quickly as she can, but in the opposite direction, down the staircase into the waiting arms of Charles. However, she is shaking violently, and she is unable to move. Then, the terrifying, thundering voice she has come to know all too well echoes within the snaking confines of the desolate staircase.

"Greetings, Empress Diana. We meet another time. I see you have met my comrade, Reguli." Mendacium scornfully laughs at the top of his voice, and then he says, "You cannot attempt to slay my comrade, Reguli where you stand, nor can he slay you. The two of you must battle on the first landing. Your feeble ghost, Charles told you that. Am I right?

"Thus, Empress Diana, do carry on. He, I, we, beseech you. For your nemesis here in the World Beyond and the Real-world, the place you call home awaits you with his open arms. Likewise, Empress Diana, do not tarry. If you diddle-daddle, you lose. I promise."

*****

Part III: Rules of the Game

Diana knows that she desperately needs sleep. She also knows she needs to take it easy on her weary limbs. Or else, she risks pulling a muscle or worse. One misstep on the unstable stair treads and she is a goner. Twice she has fallen hip-deep between rotted out cracks in the stair treads. Both times she had to cling to the staircase spindles to keep from plunging to whatever it is at the bottom of the staircase. While the baluster splintered with her weight, the spindles held. Despite her drowsiness, she knows she will not be able to sleep no matter how much she needs to. As she massages her calf and thigh muscles, eats and drinks, she ponders her next move.

"If I retreat down the staircase a few stair treads, I should be out of harm's way as it concerns Reguli. Then again, I do not know how long he is. He could be dozens or even a hundred stair treads longer than what I saw of his body. The last thing I want to happen is he will attack me while I'm napping. However, Mendacium did say that he, I guess both Mendacium and Reguli, await me. So, maybe it is safe enough here. The stair tread seems strong enough." She stomps at the stair tread with her boot. Droplets of fresh spider blood splash onto her legs. She immediately cringes and frantically wipes her legs, hands, arms, and face with the cape of her tunic.

"On the other hand, maybe I should ascend the staircase and face the inevitable." She opens her rucksack to retrieve a banapple. As she looks inside her rucksack, she notices a bright green object on the very bottom. She immediately recognizes it as an *industa*. The industa is a spiritual type of fruit used by the mythological gods that gave them energy before battle. I Dunno had tried numerous times to create the industa using her magic. Each time she had failed. However, by the looks of the oblong, bright green object in Diana's rucksack, she must have succeeded.

Diana begins laughing crazily. She shouts, "Yes, I Dunno, yes! I hadn't noticed it before now, but it must have been in my pouch from the very beginning of this part of my journey. Thank you, my lovely, super magical protector pixie, thank you!"

She grabs the industa from her rucksack and immediately takes a small bite. She instantly spits out the piece she has bitten.

"Dang, I Dunno was correct. This stuff is disgusting, a combination of sour and bitter and outright gross. It tastes like boogers, although I've never actually *eaten* boogers, at least not on purpose. But, I Dunno had warned me. The first bite will taste horrible. The second bite even more so. Then, as my taste buds get used to it, so will I." She frowns. "But it has to be the most sickening thing I've ever tasted. Yuck!"

She takes a second bite and immediately spits it out. Then, as I Dunno had instructed her, she licks her lips. Surprisingly, what she licks from her lips is not as foul-tasting as the first and second bites.

"Well, so far, so good. I Dunno must be on track with this disgusting junk. I should be happy because she said the fouler it tastes the better its quality." She raises the industa above her head and shouts, "Way to go, I Dunno! This stuff is unbelievably horrible, so it should be of the finest quality imaginable!"

From what I Dunno had said to her, if she, I Dunno, was able to create industa, all it would take was for Diana to take a small third bite to create the magic in her body. And the best thing, the industa would never go bad.

"Never go bad," Diana says to herself. "Heck, this stuff will outlast humanity. Anything this gross will last longer than tons and tons of Styrofoam waste in landfills at home."

She pinches her nose with her fingers, and then she takes the third bite. As she closes her eyes tightly as I Dunno had instructed her, she swallows it. She gets to her feet briskly and begins to jump up and down in place. As she does, the entire staircase shakes violently. But, she cannot help herself from jumping up and down. As the small portion of industa travels down her throat into her stomach, it feels as if her esophagus and stomach are on fire. She suddenly doubles over with astonishingly painful cramps. Then, as quickly as the tormenting sensations had appeared, they vanish.

She shouts, "Oh, my goodness!" She stretches her legs and her arms, twirls her hands in the air, flexes her feet at the ankles, and begins to do the first of twenty-knee bends. "I feel so much stronger, almost unbeatable! And miraculously, the aches and pains are gone. Plus, I do not feel as sleepy as before. Thank you, I Dunno, thank you!"

She picks up her waterskin from the stair tread. She takes a long draw from it, and then she readjusts the sling to its normal length. She slips the sling over her head and positions the waterskin on her back. She picks up her quiver and rucksack and does the same. Then, with her longbow in hand, she bolts up the staircase, two steps at a time.

In less than twenty seconds, she spots the first landing beyond the curve of the staircase. The landing is very wide, many times wider than the stair treads, perhaps twenty-feet from end to end. Its length appears twice as long. There, coiled in a huge ball, ready to strike, is Reguli. His gaping mouth is open. Blood continues to drip from the roof of his mouth. His red eyes flash a vile combination of hunger and hate.

Diana knows Reguli cannot strike her until she steps foot on the landing. Likewise, she cannot strike Reguli until she also is on the landing. Suddenly, something I Dunno said to her many weeks ago crosses her mind.

"When the prey is very large, consider using two arrows instead of one. Place them as far apart on your bowstring as necessary. The distance between the arrows depends on how far away the prey is. The further away from the prey, the closer the distance between the arrows. The closer the prey, well, you can place the arrows, so they touch each other. By using two arrows instead of one, the tips of the arrows will inflict two wounds instead of one wound. With luck, you will hit a vital organ or artery killing or severely injuring whatever it is at which you are shooting."

Diana kneels on the stair tread. One more step and she is on the landing. Then, presumably, the battle between Mendacium's creation, Reguli, and her will begin. She slowly retrieves an arrow from her quiver. She carefully positions it on her bowstring. Reguli blares the hideous sound from his nostrils. Diana's first reaction is to cover her ears from the deafening sound. Instead, she grins as she removes the second arrow from her quiver. She carefully positions it on the bowstring, an inch below the first arrow.

Reguli blares another earsplitting sound. His eyes widen as he stares straight on at Diana's longbow.

Diana grins a second time. Then she reaches behind to her quiver and positions the third arrow on her bowstring. She places the arrow a bit further down the string, a few inches from the second arrow. In response, Reguli moves his head away from the edge of the landing. His eyes remain focused on her longbow.

She grins with a look of hatred in her eyes. As she stares at Reguli, she reaches to her quiver. She withdraws the fourth arrow. Without taking her eyes off Reguli, she positions the fourth arrow a few inches above the first arrow. The spiral staircase suddenly sways back and forth as Reguli uncoils his body and thrashes from place to place on the landing. Suddenly, Mendacium's voice is shouting so loudly it causes Diana's temples to throb.

"Empress Diana, you cannot do that! Your action violates the rule of warfare. You may only use one arrow or your sword. To do otherwise is dishonest. Others will refer to you as a charlatan!"

Without taking her eyes off Reguli, Diana yells, "Who is calling who a charlatan, a fake, a swindler? You of all creatures, Mendacium, with your deceit, lies, evil posturing and scheming hate, calling me a fraud? You, the so-called King of Deceit calling me a pretender? While all this time, on both worlds that I love and cherish, you have been hurting innocent people with your falsehoods and duplicitous schemes! How dare you!"

Mendacium replies in his thundering voice, "There are rules. You must follow the rules in this noble game of life and death. Violating the rules is cheating. If you cheat, you are not the Empress Artemis-Diana as others have claimed. As I said if you violate the rules, you are a charlatan!"

Diana leaps onto the landing. As she does, Reguli springs at her from the far side of the landing. His huge, gaping mouth widens. His fangs dripping venom are ready to strike her dead.

She calmly stands firm as she carefully aims for the roof of his mouth. When his grotesque, spider-filled gaping mouth is less than three feet from her, and ready to strike her, she lets her arrows fly. His head viciously snaps back from the force of the arrows impacting the roof of his mouth. Then, as he lets out a final earsplitting scream, he slowly begins to desiccate.

Diana watches with a sardonic grin as Mendacium's prized basilisk unhurriedly breaks up into countless shards of grayish-white debris. The debris cascades like a superfluous cloud of dust as it gradually falls onto the landing completely covering it in chalky debris two inches deep.

She triumphantly raises her longbow high above her head.

"You have not told me of any rules in this supposed game of yours, Mendacium. Even if you had, it doesn't matter. From this point going forward, I, Artemis-Diana, make up the rules."

*****

Part IV: Diana's Worst Fears

After her brief, one-sided, second encounter with Reguli, Diana scrapes some of the basilisk's chalky debris from the landing with her boot. This is the spot where she will sit to relax for a spell and, as she hopes, take a nap. She is not tired, but the respite will give her a chance to consider what lies ahead.

Charles had said that legends told of something unknown is awaiting her at the next landing. He had said he had an inkling what it was. However, he was reluctant to tell her his hunch for fear she would not be up to the task if she knew. No amount of sweet-talking, light-hearted threatening or flattering from Diana would convince him to convey his hunch to her. Therefore, the simple fact that Charles was worried about her next challenge, and he would not tell her what he thought it would be, sets her nerves on edge.

She turns her waterskin upside-down to wash all visible remnants of the basilisk debris from the floor where she will sit. She smiles as she sets the waterskin on the floor. It immediately begins to refill. Then she walks around the landing, kicking the debris with her boot to find the four arrows she shot into Reguli's mouth. She can only find three of them. She reasons the fourth arrow probably embedded itself in the upper portion of the staircase, or it fell over the side. She examines the three arrows carefully. The tip of one of the arrows is ruined as is its fletching. She discards the arrow. The other two arrows are in perfect condition. She tosses them into her quiver.

Next, she removes her cape. Using the tip of an arrow, she cuts three long strips from the cape. She tucks what remains of her now unusable cape into her rucksack. She moistens a strip of cloth with water to wash the spider blood from her face. Then, using a second strip of cloth moistened with water, she wipes her arms, legs, and lastly, her hands. She throws both cloths onto the floor and kicks them into a corner. Finally, she saturates the last strip of cloth with water and wipes the floor of the landing where she will sit. Once it is dry, she sits down to relax.

"Okay, whatever it is at the next landing had Charles particularly worried. He said it was not Mendacium waiting for me at one of the upcoming landings. He is certain of that. So, I can only speculate on what it might be. I wonder. Could it be? Naw, that is impossible." Stretching her arms out wide and yawning, she adds, "Oh well, it is what it is. There is no sense worrying about something I cannot change." She leans her head against the spindles and falls asleep.

When she awakens, she anxiously looks around. Her heart is racing, and she is perspiring. She had a dream that Reguli was sneaking up on her. Her dream seemed vividly real, so real in fact; she had grasped her sword in her sleep. Quickly comprehending that she is, for now at least, safe, well, as safe as she can be on a rickety spiral staircase, she begins to calm down. She opens her rucksack to get a banapple. After eating it and chewing on some whatnots, she takes a bite of the industa. To her surprise, this time it does not tingle her taste buds. She reckons that is good. She is not in the mood to undergo a fire in her stomach and severe cramps for a second time.

One of the strangest things she has noticed is the lack of spiders. She assumes that Reguli ate all the spiders on this part of the staircase.

"Hopefully the enormous bugger of a basilisk ate all the spiders on the next portion of the staircase as well. If I never see another spider in my life, I will have realized at least one of my dreams come true. And spiders the size of softballs. How gross is that?"

She slowly gathers her things, and then she walks to the other end of the landing. She hops onto the first stair tread and begins the steep climb once more. This time, however, thanks to I Dunno's magic, she is much stronger. Plus, the nap helped. She is invigorated and raring to go, ready to face whatever it is Mendacium will throw at her.

Some time ago, when she was struggling through the first phase of her climb, she forgot what Charles said about the number of stair treads to the second landing.

"Was it six-hundred-something that Charles said? Or was it something six-hundred? Naw, there cannot be over sixteen-hundred stair treads. But, then again, the distance from the ground to Domum looks to be very far away. Ah, what the heck. I cannot remember, and there is nothing I can do about it anyway. It is what it is."

Out of the blue, she hears a soft cry. It sounds like a child is crying. She dashes up the staircase. She stops one step short of the landing. When she sees what has caused the child-like crying, she is in shock. Sitting in the middle of the expansive landing is a human baby! The baby appears to be seven or eight months old. There is no way for her to know for certain. Also, there is no way for her to know if the baby is a boy or a girl. That is because the child is wearing a cloth diaper, pinned at his or her hips with two oversized safety pins. A plastic baby bottle lying on its side is next to the baby. Diana cringes when she sees that the bottle is empty.

As soon as the baby notices Diana, who is kneeling on the stair tread, he, or she, cries out with its chubby arms stretched out wide.

"Momma, momma."

Diana does not dare to move. She searches the landing from end to end, corner to corner. She does not see anything out of the ordinary. The baby calls out yet again.

"Momma, momma."

She remains motionless. She does not make a sound. She purpose-ly slows her breathing like she does when she is going to shoot an arrow. In return, her heartbeats should slow as well. However, they do not. They are racing out of control because of what she is witnessing on the evil landing!

The baby begins to howl. In between sobs, and with a look of complete bewilderment and sadness on its tear-streaked face, it cries out a third time.

"Momma, momma, momma!"

Still, Diana does not dare to move. Her heart is breaking as she stares at the baby. Tears begin to well up in her eyes.

"Oh, my God, please give me the strength and knowledge to think this through. How is it a Real-world baby is here in the World Beyond? Did Mendacium kidnap it from its mommy in my world? If so, he is much eviler than I thought. Or, could it be an Inania or a Parva Draco in disguise? If so, how in the world did the creature assume the baby's mirror image? There are no humans in the World Beyond, at least not to my knowledge. And how in the world did a plastic baby bottle get here?"

She wants to run to the baby, to hold it in her arms, to cuddle it, and to dry its tears that are now flowing from its eyes like torrents of water from a burst dam. But she cannot move. Something in the back of her mind is telling her to stay put. Maybe it is intuition. Then again, maybe it is outright common sense. Either way, she does not approach the landing.

"The first Inania I encountered said that the Parva Draco could assume the spitting image of something even though it is not in its presence. Okay, I buy that. But how in the world did a Parva Draco know what kind of image to mirror? There are no human babies in the World Beyond!"

She slowly gets to her feet. She puts an arrow on her bowstring. She purposely keeps her longbow pointed downward. She does not want to strike the baby accidentally, that is if what she sees is a real baby.

The baby suddenly teeters and falls with a thud on its side. It begins to wail even louder. Then it slowly crawls to the empty baby bottle. It grabs the bottle with its two chubby hands. Then it stuffs the nipple of the bottle into its mouth. Diana winces as the baby begins to suckle on the empty bottle. She watches horrorstruck as the plastic lining inside the bottle begins to contract little by little. Soon, the baby's eyes snap wide open. As it looks at Diana with a confused expression, it roughly pushes the bottle from its mouth. Then it screams. Its ear-piercing screams echo throughout the staircase.

Diana must cover her ears from the tormenting screams. She places her longbow and arrow onto the stair tread. Then, she raises her head in prayer.

"Oh, God, please help me! I know a baby cannot be here in the World Beyond. There is no way! But, its screams are tormenting me. I cannot stand it. Its crying sobs seem very real. And yes, the baby looks real enough as well. And it is hungry. But how can I feed it? I have nothing but water!"

Water!

She scrambles to her feet. She quickly jumps onto the landing and rushes to the baby. Just as she reaches out to grab the baby, it disappears before her very eyes! She collapses to her knees in shock. Then, as she quickly regains her right mind, she hastily turns around and crawls to the stair tread where she left her belongings. Once she is safely on the stair tread, she immediately buries her head into the palms of her hands. She begins to cry, her uncontrollable sobbing intensifying with each breath that she takes.

"Oh, God, how did he know? How did he know that a helpless, crying baby is one of my main weaknesses? Oh, God, please help me! Help me through this. I beg of you! Before I go insane!"

She rests her head against a few of the rickety spindles. Just as she is about to close her eyes, a familiar voice calls out from the landing. She immediately covers her face with her hands as she vigorously shakes her head back and forth.

"Empress Artemis-Diana, my love. Help me, please. Please put me out of my misery. There is much pain, Diana. Help. My God, Diana, look at me! Please!" After a pause, the familiar voice shouts, "Diana! Uncover your face. Please. I need your help! Trust me, Diana, trust me! Why won't you look at me?"

Diana whispers, "Oh, my God, it's I Dunno! Please tell me it's the real I Dunno I am hearing and not some imposter or horrible illusion in my mind."

She slowly moves her hands from her face. As soon as she sees what is on the landing, she screams once again. She fears that what she sees on the landing will rip her aching heart to shreds. She whispers, "I take that back. Please allow what I see to be nothing more than a figment of my imagination! Please!"

I Dunno is lying on her side about ten feet from the edge of the landing, just beyond Diana's reach. She is staring at Diana with her enormous green eyes. The look in her eyes is one of extreme pain. Streaks of blood and horrible black and blue bruises completely cover what was once her pretty, pale face. Her delicate wings are nothing but shredded slivers of their former glorious selves. Her tattered green dress is streaked with mud. Blood flows freely from a deep gash in her left leg. A two-inch Minima arrow is sticking out of the small of her back.

Diana is forced to look away. She covers her face with her hands yet again. She begins to sway back, and forth as uncontrollable tremors begin to wrack her body.

"Oh, my God, no! Not I Dunno. If what I am seeing is fake or if it's real, I cannot stand this torment any longer!" She lifts her head to the heavens in prayer. "Please, make this scene go away. I beg of you!"

The voice of her beloved protector pixie cries out once more. Her voice is much weaker.

"Diana," She gasps. "I do. I do not." Gasps. "Not much time. Help me, Diana. Help me." Gasps. "Please, I." Gasps. "Much time."

As Diana continues to stare at her protector pixie, she feels as if her heart is breaking in two. She wants to run to her. But she does not. Something seems to force her to remain on the stair tread. Still, she must do something, especially if what she is seeing, what she is experiencing is real.

"Oh, my God, I Dunno. I don't know if you are real or if you are one of Mendacium's illusions. I want to come to you. But, I'm afraid."

"Real, Diana," I Dunno manages to whisper. She wheezes as rose-tinted blood burbles between the lips of her tiny mouth. "Real. Here. Catch this, Sana bush. Berry." Wheezes. "Hurry. Please."

With a heroic effort, she somehow manages to toss her pouch in Diana's direction. It lands short of the stair tread on which Diana is kneeling. She leans on the landing. As soon as her hand touches I

Dunno's pouch she knows that it is genuine. She has handled it hundreds of times before.

She screams, "Where is the berry? Where?"

I Dunno does not reply. She has shut her eyes, and her breathing is labored. Diana recognizes she is dying.

Diana cries in a frantic voice, "Please I Dunno, you cannot die. Stay with me! Talk to me, I beg of you! I Dunno, wake up! Wake up now!"

I Dunno whispers as horrible rattling sounds emanate from deep within her chest. Her shuddering, panting breaths are less frequent. She manages to whisper, "Bottom. Diana. Bottom. Hurry."

Diana sticks her hand into the pouch. She searches for the evasive berry. She cannot feel it among all the miraculous things I Dunno has in her pouch. She turns the pouch upside-down. Her sweet pixie's belongings spread out everywhere on the landing. Dozens of books, cooking utensils, vials and jars of all sizes filled with liquid and powdery herbs and spices, a tiny table and chair, a bureau made of wicker, and what appears to be a hundred changes of pixie clothes. And there, at the bottom of I Dunno's possessions scattered on the landing, she spots three Sana bush berries.

She glances at I Dunno. I Dunno's breathing has stopped. The blood that was bubbling from between her open lips is now frothy, dark red. She knows in an instant that her beloved pixie protector is dead. She begins to weep openly. She wants to rush onto the landing to cradle her beloved pixie, but she is too afraid.

Certainly, she has witnessed death before in the World Beyond. Although she is somewhat immune to its dread, she hates seeing it just the same. But then, she has somehow managed to cope with seeing death. But, not this time. Not this time. This time she has witnessed the death of her friend, her beloved protector pixie.

She cries, "Oh, my God, I Dunno. I am very sorry. It's just that I was afraid. Afraid you were another illusion like the baby, a terrible figment of my thoughts, a nerve-wracking deception in my mind. Please forgive me, I Dunno. I am very sorry. I love you, my sweetheart, with all my heart and soul."

She remains immobile. She is kneeling on the stair tread with her arms spread-out wide on the landing. All the while she is clutching the three life-saving, miracle Sana bush berries in her right hand. As she weeps, she says over and over in a whisper.

"I could have saved her. I could have saved her. I could have saved her."

At long last, she regains her composure. As she stares at her now gone but not forgotten lovely protector pixie, she prepares to say a silent prayer in honor of I Dunno's life. As she gets ready to fold her hands in prayer, she withdraws her arms and hands from the landing. Once her hands are beyond the edge of the landing, the Sana bush berries she clutched in the palm of her right hand vanish. She angrily cries out at the top of her lungs.

"You hideous monster! I hate you, Mendacium! I truly despise you and your deceitful, cunning, lying ways! I want you dead!"

She does not bother to look at where I Dunno had lain. She instinctively knows that her protector pixie, like the Sana bush berries and I Dunno's pouch and its many belongings, were nothing more than a ghastly illusion.

She whispers, "Okay, Mendacium. You have won these two rounds with your little shop of horrors. I now know that the purpose of this landing is to torment me, to strike at my heart and soul with things that I love and cherish. To drive me insane as slowly as you can. Well, your trickery isn't going to work a third time. I will not strike out."

She quickly gets to her feet to gather her belongings. She takes a long drink from her waterskin. She watches with satisfaction as it slowly refills and resumes its original shape. She flings it over her shoulder.

"Hah, I Dunno lives on, you miserable beast. See? She just refilled my waterskin!"

With that, she hops onto the landing. Then she slowly saunters across the landing as she sings at the top of her lungs a familiar theme from the musical *The Sound of Music*.

*****

Part V: The Power of Prayer

As Diana climbs the staircase, she notices that her entire body is still trembling. Her knees feel weak. She realizes that the last landing's incidents took more out of her than she would have expected.

"I guess what they say is true. Mental anguish is sometimes more demanding on a person's body than physical exertion. I guess that's because, when something tasks you physically to your limits, adrenaline kicks in to help you out. On the other hand, when it comes to mental suffering, there is nothing to tap into but brainpower and courage.

"I think I should take a load off my mind and eat some of I Dunno's delicious grub." With a hint of sorrow in her tone, she says, "To celebrate her wonderful life." She sighs deeply. "Thank God she's still alive."

After a brief time eating, drinking, and desperately trying to clear her mind, she sets off to the next landing. She is not sure if the previous landing, the little shop of horrors, as she refers to it, was the one that had disturbed Charles so much. She figures it must have been because it involved her seeing I Dunno in the worst shape imaginable and then watching her die. Then again, she supposes she could be wrong.

She considers that the next landing may have a challenge that is a walk in the park, at least as it concerns her ability to defeat whatever she will face. Then again, it could pose a difficult challenge. Or, it could be the landing after that, if there is one, that had Charles so riled up. At this point, she does not care. When she gets the opportunity to battle Mendacium, that will be good enough for her. She reckons that everything else is a minor hindrance along the way.

Her magical light unexpectedly douses. She cries out in the dark, "Lux Magicae!" Nothing happens. She cries out a second time, "Lux Magicae!" Again, nothing happens.

She whispers, "Darn it all. What now?"

She crouches down and slowly climbs up the staircase on all fours. As she climbs, she carefully places her hands on each succeeding stair tread as she comes to it. She does not want to crawl onto the next landing by accident. As fate would have it, five or six minutes later, she discovers that nearly her entire body is on the next landing. Her feet are the only things touching the stair tread. She breathes a sigh of relief.

"Whew, that was close. I should know better than to allow my mind to wander." She chuckles. "Go figure. As soon as my magical light extinguishes itself, I find myself in the dark in the worst situation imaginable with my entire body on the landing except for my feet. Thank God my feet are touching the stair tread. Otherwise, I'd be in a world of hurt."

She gradually backs away from the landing. As she does, she intently listens for any sign of movement in front of her. Soon, only her upper body and her outstretched arms remain on the landing.

"Just a few inches more, and I'll be safe!"

Just as she thinks this, she cries out in panic. The staircase she just climbed begins to break free as it crumbles beneath her feet. Then the staircase collapses as it implodes within itself. It breaks apart and loudly plunges into the abyss below. Now, the lower part of Diana's body is dangling precariously over the edge of the landing!

She desperately clutches with her fingertips onto the landing's splintered wood. But she instantly realizes that her feeble attempts are in vain. The weight of her weapons and waterskin are slowly dragging her over the side. She strains with all the strength of her fingertips, arms, and shoulder muscles to hang onto the landing. By the shooting pain in her fingers, she knows that she rapidly is losing ground. She imagines that uselessly clawing at the decaying, splintered wood of the landing is ripping her fingertips to shreds.

She cries out, "Oh, God, please help me! Tell me what I should do! I cannot hold on much longer! The shooting pain on the tips of my fingers is unbearable!"

As her upper body continues to inch gradually to the edge of the landing, she thinks to herself, "Shooting. Tips." She suddenly shouts, "Arrows!"

She takes a deep breath. Then, as she exhales sharply, she reaches behind with her right hand to pull an arrow from her quiver. Now, since only her left hand is clawing on the landing, her upper body is sliding across the landing more quickly than before. Despite the nagging pain of her fingers, she shoves her fingertips deeper into the splintered wood.

By using her thumb and forefinger of her right hand, she slowly works the shaft of the arrow to cause it to slide in her palm. Once she feels the tip of the arrow is between her thumb and forefinger, she carefully flips the arrow upside down. She encloses the shaft of the arrow tightly inside her fist. Then, by using her thumb as leverage, she slides the arrow in her fist until two inches of the shaft and the tip of the arrow are exposed. Suddenly, she cries out in panic when she realizes that the elbow of her left arm has reached the edge of the landing. She is but a few seconds away from falling into the abyss.

She hurriedly reaches with her right arm over the landing as far out as possible. With all the remaining strength she has in her arm, she jabs the tip of the arrow into the rotting wood. Much to her relief, it holds. However, she is unable to pull herself onto the landing. Her arms are too tired. She realizes she needs more leverage than she now has. She needs another arrow. She must repeat the process.

While she clutches the shaft of the arrow she jabbed into the landing with her right hand, she grabs another arrow from her quiver with her left hand. After she retrieves it, she repeats the process. Then she jabs the arrow deep into the splintered wood. Thankfully, it holds. Using the two arrows as leverage, she gradually pulls herself onto the landing.

"Thank you, God. Thank you. I owe you one."

Once she is safe and sound on the landing, she scrambles to her feet. Out of the blue, her magic light begins to shine once again. She immediately unsheathes her sword. She looks around the landing, but she sees nothing. She looks at her fingertips. Just as she expected, they are not injured.

She yanks her arrows from the splintered wood. After she examines them, she places them in her quiver. Then she uncorks her waterskin and takes a long drink.

"Well, I think I finally understand what is happening here. Not only am I being tested, but Mendacium is measuring me." She laughs, and then she yells with a mocking tone, "Yes, Mendacium, I see what mischief you forced me to suffer.

"First, you wanted to see if I have staying power, the courage to meet a challenge head-on rather than retreating. Well, I did demonstrate courage, didn't I, when I followed Reguli to his landing rather than retreat down the staircase to safety.

"Then you wanted to test me to see if I have what it takes to adapt to unpredictable, seemingly unwinnable situations." She laughs. "Well, once again, I did prove myself adaptable, didn't I? I killed your pitiful, overrated, prized basilisk, Reguli. And of course, with four well-placed arrows into the roof of its hideous mouth. Pretty smart of me, huh?

"Next, you wanted to see if I had the nerve to face what I feared the most. The vulnerability of the weak, defenseless, those that I love, those things I fear that are hidden away deep within my psyche. Yes, Mendacium. You had me going with the fake crybaby. And yes, you scared the bejesus out of me with the I Dunno illusion. But, not only did I recover from those horrible scenes, I saw through your ruse as I nonchalantly walked across the landing. How'd you like that, huh? I wasn't in any hurry as you can tell." She walks back to the landing and peers over the side. She laughs.

"Just as I expected, Mendacium, so-called King of Deceit. The staircase is intact. As rickety as it is, it's still here, dust, cobwebs and all. Once again, I must commend you. You made me think, made me feel as if the staircase had collapsed into the abyss. That was clever of you." She chuckles. "But, after all, you are the King of Deceit, the architect of falsehood, hoodwinks, and lies, aren't you? I would expect nothing less of you.

"But, Mendacium, you must admit. Once again, I did not give in, did I? I proved my cunning, my strength, and my ability to overcome the worst that you could dish out at me. So, Mendacium, you creep. What do you have in store for me now? Have you analyzed my strengths and weaknesses sufficiently enough to quench your thirst for fun at another's expense? Are you ready to meet me, my dear sir? Or do you still desire to test me, to gauge my abilities?"

She quickly retrieves her belongings. As she rapidly walks across the landing, she shouts with obvious revulsion in her tone of voice.

"See you on the other side, Mendacium. That is if you have the guts!"

*****

Part VI: Gift of Undying Love

When Diana reaches the next landing, she does not hesitate to jump right onto it. She has no idea how many landings she must go before all of this will end. But of one thing she is certain. She wants to get this horrible experience over with as soon as she can.

She immediately notices that this landing is much larger than the others. She can barely discern where the far side of the landing ends. As she stares into the dimness, she notices that something is moving in the shadows to her right. She fixes an arrow on the bowstring of her longbow. Just as she is about to shoot an arrow at whatever it is, James jumps in front of her.

He yells, "I thought I told you that it is unwise to slay her!"

He roughly grabs Diana's longbow from her grasp. Then, with brute strength, he crudely pushes her to the floor of the landing. As she lies on her back, she reaches for her sword. James forcefully kicks at it. It careens across the landing and falls over the edge onto the staircase. She listens as it clangs down the staircase treads. She counts five stair treads. She thinks to herself, "Well, at least it didn't go too far or over the side."

She yells, "James! It is me, Diana. What in the world are you doing? I am your friend, a friend of your brother, Charles!"

James stares at her as he whispers, "I thought I told you that it is unwise to slay her!"

"Yes, James, you told me that. But, I honestly had no clue what it was that I was going to shoot. All I knew is that it probably wasn't going to be very nice, whatever it was." She pauses, and then she says, "Nothing on this horrible staircase is."

"I thought I told you that it is unwise to slay her!"

Diana jumps to her feet.

"James, listen to yourself. You sound like a robot or something."

He roughly pushes her to the floor of the landing a second time. Then he backs away as he continues to stare down at her. He says again, this time in a softer tone, "I thought I told you that it is unwise to slay her."

Diana scrambles to her feet. As she expected him to, James immediately lunges at her. She quickly sidesteps him. He stumbles. Before he falls face first on the floor of the landing, he reaches out with his hands to catch his fall. As he does, Diana grabs her longbow from him. When he looks up at her, James is staring at the tip of an arrow. It is less than six inches from his nose. She had hastily placed an arrow on the bowstring of her longbow while he was turning over onto his back.

She yells, "You will not push me to the floor of the landing again, James!"

He swipes at the arrow to grab it. But Diana is too quick. She hops back a few steps, all the while continuing to point the arrow at his face. She is now standing three feet from him. He lunges at her again. She steps back another foot or two.

She is trembling from head to toe, but she is resolute. She knows Mendacium has turned James. She may love James as Charles' brother, as a friend, but she will destroy him if she must. Just the same, she must try to talk some sense into him. She lowers her longbow slightly and loosens the tension on the bowstring.

"I am going to say what I have to say one time, James. So, listen very carefully. I do not want to hurt you."

James reaches out to grab the arrow once more. In reply, Diana draws back on the bowstring and aims the arrow at James' chest.

"But, I promise, as God is my witness, James, I will destroy you if I have to. You do not have any magical powers here in the World Beyond. You are just as vulnerable as me. I love you, James. Charles loves you. Don't you remember? And April, your good friend, she loves you too. But I will destroy you if I must. After all, you are a ghost, so you're already dead. For this reason, I will take some comfort in knowing you will not suffer."

James shakes his head slightly. As tears well up in his eyes, he slowly whispers, "I thought I told you that it is unwise to slay her."

Diana detects some awareness in his tone of voice. She thinks that perhaps he is coming to his senses, recognizing who she is.

She says, "Slay who, slay what? What are you talking about when you say that? And why do you keep repeating those words? Are you in a trance? Has Mendacium brainwashed you?" Suddenly, something to her left catches her eye.

James scrambles to his feet. He yells, "I thought I told you it is unwise to slay the Aegolius, Empress Artemis-Diana!"

Diana whirls about just as the Aegolius flies at her. She shoots an arrow at the creature, but her aim is off. That is because James once again lunged at her causing her to stumble. She immediately places another arrow on the bowstring, but her action is futile. The Aegolius is hovering in midair about twenty feet in front of her. The creature is staring into her eyes. She tries to resist its stare. But she is unable to. She stares back. She begins to scream as she feels her body is changing. She tries to move her feet, but she cannot.

"Oh, my God, she is turning me to stone, petrifying me!"

Diana is now completely helpless as she stares into the yellow eyes of the Aegolius. The longbow and arrow drop from her grip as her hands begin to turn to stone. She wants to scream, but her lips cannot form words. Suddenly, she is unable to breathe as her lips and nose gradually turn to stone. She knows that it will be but a matter of seconds before her entire body is encased in stone as she is petrified. Then the Aegolius will snatch her up to take her to Mendacium as his Prisoner of Innocence.

Suddenly, Charles appears out of nowhere. He immediately jumps in between Diana and the Aegolius. She watches in terror as Charles' feet and legs begin to turn to stone just as her body gradually returns to normal. She wants to move, to push Charles out of the way, but her legs and arms will not budge. They are still petrified.

As soon as her lips are back to normal, she screams, "Charles no, no! Do not sacrifice yourself for me! I would rather die than live without you. Think of your ethereal mission and all those dying children that you love. They need you, Charles! Think of everyone that loves you, those that need you!"

She stares horrified as the grayish color of stone gradually creeps up his torso. Then, she thinks she will surely die from unbelievable, heart-stricken emotion as Charles slowly moves the forefinger of his left hand. He taps his thigh three times with his finger. Then, a split-second later, his entire hand is encased in stone.

She screams, "Oh my God, I love you too! Hang in there, Charles. I will save you!"

Suddenly, a booming voice echoes on the landing.

"Ah, Empress Diana. I had wanted you as my prize, but I will settle for your beloved ghost, Charles. Besides, I will have you soon, I promise. Even as you struggle, you cannot do anything to help your pitiful ghost. It takes three times as long for the effects of the Aegolius' petrifying magic to reverse itself than it does to enact its wonder. It is only a few more moments before the Aegolius will claim your beloved ghost.

"Then she will bring him to me. I will cherish having him in my ranks. In that matter, I can better haunt you and your double just as I watch your heart break in two." He begins to laugh loudly. Abruptly, his laughter stops. He suddenly cries, "No, you cannot do that. You are my vassal! I forbid it!"

By now, although her legs are still petrified, Diana can move her upper body. She turns to her left. James is standing beside her. He says, "My dear friend, Diana. The Aegolius cares not who or what she takes as her victim. All she knows is that she has a purpose, to petrify a victim and to take it to Mendacium." He smiles as he repositions a curl of hair on Diana's left cheek.

With a somber tone, he says, "I have something to confess to you. When you were in the tranquility beam, I purposely sacrificed myself for you. Would you like to know why?"

As tears freely fall from Diana's eyes, she says, "Why, James, why?"

"Because, Diana, the moment I met you, I was jealous of my brother. For he, as your Protective Soul, is very lucky. You are beautiful and very intelligent. You are kindhearted. You are outgoing. And you are courageous and tenacious." He tenderly touches Diana's cheek once more.

"Please think of me often. For, like my beloved brother, I also love you. Take care and stay safe, my precious Youngster Warrior of the World Beyond, Empress Artemis-Diana."

Before Diana can reply, James steps toward Charles. He tousles Charles' hair a bit, and then he kisses Charles on the cheek. He turns around one last time to look at Diana. As he nods his head, he smiles and silently mouths the words, "Goodbye." Then he steps in front of his brother.

Many moments later, even as Diana and Charles' bodies continue to return gradually to their original selves, the Aegolius carefully lifts James' petrified body from the landing. Then she flies off.

After a lengthy period, Diana and Charles are back to normal. Charles appears devoid of emotion at the loss of his brother for the second time. All the same, Diana knows that deep inside his ethereal, ghostly body, his heart is breaking in two. He takes her by the hand to retrieve her sword from the staircase. Then he walks with her to the far side of the landing.

"Once again, my dear Diana, Mendacium has shown he is no match for you and those of us who love you. Thanks to the gift of undying love and our dedication to you, our beloved Empress Artemis-Diana, Mendacium has once more gained nothing."

Then, as he kisses Diana on the cheek, he vanishes.

*****

Part VII: It's Going to End My Way

Diana does not have to climb the staircase much further before she sees the next landing. As she cautiously approaches it, she fixes an arrow on her bowstring. She figures if anything is going to spring out at her, she might as well have the advantage of distance over the surprise.

She sits down on the stair tread just below the landing. She occasionally places her hand on the landing. She wants to see if anything appears. Nothing does. She does not see anything of interest on the landing but a few softball-sized spiders that scamper here and there. Seeing the spiders causes her to wince with disgust.

"God, I hope this landing doesn't have super huge spiders on it. I can handle just about anything but creepy, hairy-legged spiders. I wonder if this landing is supposed to be like the previous landings, full of illusions. If it is, perhaps Mendacium has given up knowing that I can now see my way through his dishonest, mind-altering ruses. He certainly must realize that I am cleverer than he thought." After pondering what she just thought, she adds, "Well, it may have taken me a couple of illusions to figure out his deceitfulness, but I am a quick learner. He won't deceive me a third time."

She leans her head against a few of the spindles. As she nibbles on whatnots, libum, and a banapple, every so often she places her hand on the landing. Again, nothing happens. She figures that maybe she needs to have more of her body on the landing. So, she moves from her position on the stair tread to sit on the landing. To be safe, she keeps both feet firmly planted on the stair tread. Again, there is no reaction.

"Okay, this is getting to be mightily boring. I cannot sit here and wait for something to happen. I guess I need to go to Mendacium because it's obvious Mendacium is not coming to me."

She reaches down to retrieve her belongings from the stair tread. As she does, she plants one foot on the tread and the other foot on the landing. She gets to her feet. As before, nothing happens. With her sword at the ready, she quickly moves to stand on the landing with both feet. Once again, nothing happens. She crouches in the ready position with her sword in front of her, parallel to her body. She carefully looks from corner to corner and at the far end of the landing.

"Well, it looks like nothing's going on here. Charles did say that it is possible a landing may not contain any challenges. Well then, I guess I'll have to see what's in store for me at the next landing."

She quickly walks across the landing. To her surprise, she notices that this landing is much wider than the last one. It appears to be at least a football field in length. When she reaches the far side of the landing, she immediately stops.

"Oh, my goodness! The staircase ends here. And what is this? I can see the ground! And there's Lake Vita. I can also see the start of the staircase far below. Can it be? Have I reached Domum? Have I defeated Mendacium?"

As she peers down at the beautiful scenery of the World Beyond, her mind is racing at full speed. She quickly starts to have doubts about what she is seeing.

"Or is this one of Mendacium's illusions? Is he trying to deceive me yet again, forcing me to believe that I am at the end of my journey?" She removes a banapple from her rucksack. She tosses it over the side and watches as it tumbles out of sight toward the ground.

"No! What I am experiencing cannot be happening! It's not supposed to end this way! How do I get from here to there? From Domum to the World Beyond or my home in the Real-world?" Tears suddenly well up in her eyes. She drops onto all fours and stares at the magnificence of the World Beyond. She cries out.

"God, please tell me what I am supposed to do? I know I haven't defeated Mendacium, at least I do not think that I have. But, then again, by destroying his basilisk and overcoming the horrors of watching I Dunno die and seeing the baby crying, perhaps I have defeated him! Especially after James stepped in front of the Aegolius sparing Charles' and my lives.

"On the other hand, perhaps he has defeated me! After all, I struck out three times with those hideous illusions. Three times! Sure, I overcame illusionary challenges on two separate landings, but there was a total of three illusions! Have I lost? If so, what is to become of me, the Favored Child? Am I now stripped of all of my innocence?" She abruptly buries her face in her hands. She refuses to cry, although she knows that she wants to.

"I must think this through. This point in time cannot be the end of my journey. It is too anti-climactic. Mendacium would want me to suffer more than this. I'm certain of it!" She clasps her hands together in prayer.

"Dear God, please give me the knowledge to understand what is happening here. I appear to be stranded. Thank you."

She suddenly jumps to her feet. "Perhaps if I start all over from the stair tread I was just on, I can begin the process anew." She races across the landing to the other side.

When she reaches the other side of the landing, what she sees is like a shock wave to her disbelieving eyes. The staircase that she had ascended has disappeared. All she sees is the same breathtaking scenery of the World Beyond. She races to her left and then to her right. Every time she gets to the edge of the landing, she peers over the side. She sees nothing but the World Beyond far below. She throws a banapple over the side. As before, it slowly falls to the ground until it disappears out of sight.

"Oh, my God! I'm on a decrepit wooden island floating in the sky! But, this cannot be Domum. Domum is enchantingly beautiful when one looks up at it from the ground. This platform is nothing but splintering, rotting slabs of wood, a drab, uninteresting staircase landing. What I am seeing cannot be happening!"

She collapses onto the landing. She removes her quiver and her waterskin from her shoulder and tosses them in front of her with disgust. Then she throws her rucksack on top of them. She sheathes her sword and tosses it onto her belongings.

"This cannot be happening! I am supposed to battle Mendacium, the King of Deceit, lies, falsehoods, trickery!" She looks around at the dismal scene of decaying wood. "And all this time, legends have spoken about the wondrous paradise of Domum." She screams at the top of her voice, "It's all a lie, a deceitful, hideous lie! Domum doesn't exist at all." She kicks at the rotting wood with her boot. Then, with a scornful laugh, she says, "And all this time Charles, I Dunno, the Minima, and I have believed that Domum exists. Domum is nothing but a dilapidated wooden platform in the sky! And it looks like I'm stuck here forever!"

Suddenly, an inexplicable thought enters her mind. She tilts her head to the side while she ponders what she is thinking. She perceptively nods her head up and down. A devious smile gradually begins to appear on her face. She shouts at the top of her voice.

"Well, Mendacium, I ain't going down without a fight. If this is going to end, it's going to end *my* way, not yours!"

She scrambles to her feet and quickly retrieves her belongings. After she slings them over her shoulders, to include her longbow, she sprints to the far side of the landing. As she runs, Mendacium's angry shouts reverberate.

"No, no, no! I know what you are thinking! You cannot do this! It is wrong, unfair, deceitful. You are supposed to remain here on the landing. You are supposed to die slowly, utterly alone as I hunt down your ghost and protector pixie. You are supposed to lose!"

As she continues to run across the wide expanse of the landing, Diana shouts, "Promise me, Mendacium, you will not harm the Minima any longer. Promise me!"

"I promise, Empress Diana. I give you my Word. Do not do what you are planning to do. That is all that I ask."

Diana triumphantly waves her sword high in the air as she continues to run.

"Thank you, Mendacium, thank you! Like me, Empress Artemis-Diana, the Heroine Youngster of the World Beyond, I know that your Word is your Bond. You cannot violate your Bond. Otherwise, you will cease to exist."

As she closes in on the edge of the landing, she increases her stride. She says with a hearty laugh, "Don't you recall, Mendacium? I told you, for now on I make the rules, not you! And know this, while I did not defeat you, you have fallen. You have fallen from honor. Cheerio!"

Then Diana leaps from the platform into the sky and quickly falls toward the ground.

CHAPTER FIFTEEN

TOGETHER AS ONE

Part I: Play it Again

Diana in the World Beyond is in a very happy mood. She had a peaceful sleep. Without a doubt, she also had one of the best dreams of her life. For a reason we will soon learn, she also is hankering after Chinese orange chicken like nobody's business. Despite her craving for one of her favorite foods, Diana is happily chewing pieces of I Dunno's fibrous whatnots. She alternates bites of the whatnots with mouthfuls of a delicious banapple.

In her dream, Diana saw herself, her Real-world double, sitting at Miss Davenport's conference table. The school was still out of session for summer break. Miss Davenport had asked her secretary to bring back lunch for Diana and her. Diana was ecstatic when she saw what was for lunch. There, enclosed in a Styrofoam carryout box, was a huge, double portion of orange chicken from Panda Express! Nestled within the box alongside the aromatic chicken were a scoop of white rice, green beans sautéed in a delicious sauce and a crispy, sugar-coated donut! Unsurprisingly, Diana dug into the tasty food like it was going out of style.

Just as the mouth-watering lunch had appeared, Miss Davenport began to replay video highlights of the ladies' championship softball tournament. To Diana, in the World Beyond, as she dreamt, the softball tournament she had participated in seemed like it had occurred eons ago. After all, since arriving in the World Beyond, she has had her share of life-threatening challenges. She battled evil creatures, watched in horror as the Minima's village nearly was demolished, confronted a basilisk, and almost was destroyed by Mendacium. As she absentmind-edly rubs the scar on her forehead, she thinks, "Not to mention me nearly being slain by hideous Inania and Parva Draco and then nearly dying from their poisons."

As she saw herself while she dreamt, she also knew in her heart that her double in the Real-world had to endure challenges of her own. Bullying, threats, innuendoes, secret pacts, and nightmarish episodes of confusing turmoil were but a few of her double's challenges. When she takes both parts of her personae as a whole, Diana cannot fathom how she, her double, the two of them in worlds apart, were able to carry on in the face of diverse challenges beyond description.

In last night's dream, she perceived with great interest what her double in the Real-world was seeing as Miss Davenport replayed the best parts of the championship game. Miss Davenport rapidly skimmed through the first five innings of the video recording. She stopped here and there so Diana could watch exciting plays. During the first five innings, there were a few hits here and there, some errors, and lots of great catches. The whole time, the score remained tied nothing to nothing. Then, in the top of the sixth inning, with one out by the visiting team, the real excitement began. That is when Miss Davenport played the video recording at its normal speed.

With a disappointed expression on her face, Diana silently watched the video as Sally handed Mister Reynolds her threatening note. Sally did so a split-second before she stepped up to the plate. Sally's slipping the note into Mister Reynolds' hand probably was unobserved by everyone because of a low-flying, two-engine plane that was overhead. But, the video camera didn't miss a thing. It recorded for prosperity Sally slipping the note into the hand of a surprised Mister Reynolds.

Then, Diana watched as Sally Turndle slammed the line drive over the center fielder's head. By all accounts, it looked like Sally would score an inside-the-park-homerun. With her head down low, her long brunette hair sailing behind her like crazy, and her arms pumping madly, Sally ran the bases like there was no tomorrow. As she was heading to third base, the center fielder threw the ball to the second baseman.

Diana in the World Beyond watched as her double in the Real-world nearly fell out of her chair as she watched the next terrifying scene unfold. She groaned along with the videotaped sounds of the home team fans' loud moans and groans. The second baseman was turning to throw the ball to home plate before she even had the ball in her mitt! As a result, she bobbled the ball and nearly dropped it. Then, a split-second before Sally started to drop into a slide at the home plate; the second baseman threw a lightning bolt strike right into Diana's mitt.

Miss Davenport played the subsequent footage in slow motion. From the slow-motion account, it was evident that Diana tagged Sally at least two seconds before Sally's right shoe touched home plate. A cloud of dust that traveled alongside Sally as she slid obscured Diana's ability to see the play. Plus, Diana had fallen face first to the ground with the force of the much larger girl's colliding slide. Naturally, because of her obscured vision, she wrongly assumed she had missed the tag. On the other hand, Mister Reynolds', who was standing to the right and slightly behind the plate, clearly could see the tag. He properly had called Sally out. Unbeknownst to Diana at the time, the base umpire confirmed it as he snapped his thumb in the air.

Unsurprisingly, Diana asked Miss Davenport to play the scene in slow motion a few more times. The fact that the cameraman had zoomed in on the action as Sally slid into home plate left no doubt about the play. Diana had tagged the runner. Sally was out. Mister Reynolds had made the right call.

As she watched the replay for the final time, Diana felt mixed emotions. On the one hand, she was happy she tagged Sally. After all, that is why she practiced tagging aggressive runners sliding into home plate. On the other hand, she was disappointed she incorrectly assumed she had missed the tag.

Regarding Sally's note, it wasn't until she was rounding the bases that Mister Reynolds had unfolded the note that he held in his hand. He did not watch as Sally rounded the second base and headed into the third base. That is the role of the base umpire. He simply shook his head with a troubled look of disappointment as he stared at what Sally had written on the note. Only after Sally rounded third base did he look at her as she ran. Then, expecting that she would continue to home plate, he moved to the right of Diana who was blocking the plate.

After Sally slid into home plate, the unruly scene Sally exhibited was extremely difficult for Diana to watch. Mister Reynolds stood straight-faced as Sally berated him in front of hundreds of people. She was in an agitated state of mind. Her hands were on her hips, and she had positioned herself close to Mister Reynolds. Her face was mere inches from his. Then the video camera caught her in action as she pointed to the note Mister Reynolds held in his hand. She said something that the camera could not discern.

We now know that what Sally had said. She said, "You have the note. Either call me safe or else!"

It did not take Mister Reynolds more than a few seconds to respond to Sally's unruly manners. His face visibly flushed, and then he shouted, "I said you are out!" He pointed his thumb to Sally's visiting team stands and said at the top of his voice, "Out of the game! Ejected! Please leave the field now!" The camera had caught every word that he had said.

As it concerns the calls on the next batter, Sarah Cousins, Diana could not confirm or deny that Mister Reynolds made the correct calls. That is due to the gentleman videotaping the game from the scoreboard accidentally tripping over the video camera cord. Because of his clumsiness, the camera was unplugged from its electrical source. Consequently, at least thirty seconds of the game were unrecorded. Therefore, any question about the correctness of the call must fall to the umpire's truthfulness.

Knowing what she now knows about Mister Reynolds' upstanding deportment, Diana decides she will let the matter rest. Even so, deep in the back of her mind, she still believes Mister Reynolds made the wrong call by calling Sarah out on strikes.

Playback of the videotaped recording revealed that the seventh and eighth innings were pretty much like the first five innings. There were lots of hits, a few errors, and some fantastic plays, but no runs. The first half of the ninth inning was pretty much the same. Then, as it concerns Diana's final at-bat, with the bases loaded and the score tied nothing to nothing, Diana in the Real-world was on the edge of her seat once more as she watched the video replay.

There were two outs, and the count against Diana was full, 3 and 2 with three balls and two strikes. Mister Reynolds had announced that if the game were scoreless after Diana's at-bat, the game would end in a tie. Diana recalls that, at the time, she was as nervous as a long-tailed cat in a room full of rocking chairs.

Miss Davenport changed the video playback to slow motion once more. Diana watched as the pitch, the one she had disputed in her mind, was thrown. She had thought the ball had caught the corner of the plate. She had thought she was out! She had begun to walk from the batter's box to the dugout. However, once again, the video recording did not lie. Nor was Mister Reynolds' call incorrect. The pitched ball was at least three inches outside the plate. Diana had misjudged the call yet again, this time as a batter! The count was 3 and 2. She still had a chance to win the game for her team!

Diana nervously watched the video replay as Mister Reynolds walked between the pitcher's mound and home plate. She heard his words loud and clear. Because of the weather, he would call the game even if there was no winner. The game would end in a tie. Then he looked at Diana and yelled, "Batter up!"

As she sat even closer on the edge of her seat, Diana relived the remaining heart-stopping moments of the game replayed on the screen. Her eyes were wide open as she watched with nervous anticipation. The pitcher had placed her mitt beneath her armpit as she rubbed the ball between her hands. She popped her chewing gum as she glared at Diana. In reply, Diana took two slower than usual practice swings. She bent over to pick up a handful of dirt. She rubbed it in between her hands. Then she tossed some of the dirt to the ground in front of the plate. She could not help but smile as she watched the wind catch some of the dirt and deposit it at the feet of the pitcher.

Then came the pitch. Diana had been correct. The pitcher had thrown a curveball. But, instead of widely swinging at it, Diana had hit it! The line drive sailed between the shortstop and the third baseman. It was high enough in the air that neither could field it. Nor could the outfielder field the ball since it stopped in the grass ten feet or so in front of her. Diana had hit in the winning run! The ladies' softball championship was theirs!

Miss Davenport had ended the refreshing lunchtime session with words of wisdom.

"As you can see, you won the ladies' championship softball game for your team, for your school. You should be justifiably proud. However, please remember, never doubt yourself, because you never know what the future may hold. Naturally, if you find you have made a mistake, always remember this. 'To err is human, to forgive, divine.' Whether on the field, in a play, in class, and in this conference room, you repeatedly have shown that you live by that decree. I am very proud of you, Diana, and I am duly respectful of your moral compass.'"

To Diana's amazement, Miss Davenport handed her a plastic straw. A pin was attached to the twisted end of the straw's paper wrapper.

Diana looked at her questioningly, the expression on her face wordlessly seeming to say, "Really, do you want me to do this?"

Miss Davenport had replied with a laugh, "Yes, Diana. Please do. Like my former student who shot that," she points to the remnants of the yellowed scrap of the paper straw wrapper with its pin stuck in the ceiling, "I never want to forget your performance in this conference room."

Diana stood. She took a deep breath. Then she placed the plastic straw to her lips. She blew hard on the straw. She shot the paper wrapper and pin into the ceiling where it remains to this day. It is a constant reminder, a teaching tool of a youngster's amazing courage and unyielding tenacity in the face of adversity.

*****

Part II: Scars of Innocence

Diana, Charles, and I Dunno are relaxing on the porch of Diana's tree house. Except for a few broken shingles on the roof, the tree house was unscathed during Mendacium's vicious invective.

Charles replies to a question Diana has just asked him.

"Yes, Diana, you are correct. All this time we assumed that the rickety spiral staircase that you climbed was the original staircase that led to Domum. We now know it was nothing but a deceptive hoax by the King of Deceit. Like the misleading horrors he had placed in your mind when you saw the human baby and I Dunno in distress, and when you thought the staircase had collapsed, the staircase was imaginary. I should have seen through Mendacium's subterfuge, but even I was fooled. Thanks to you wounding Mendacium, weakening him, the authentic spiral staircase that leads to Domum is known to us. That makes me very happy. I would not want the legends of our glorious World Beyond to be untrue."

Diana asks, "So, Charles, do you honestly think I wounded him, weakened him?"

"Yes, Diana, with your courageous misleading actions, by refusing to end your journey his way, you wounded him. You wounded him enough that decency in the World Beyond prevailed in the end. And yes, because you defied him, you weakened him as well. Your actions as Diana, both here in the World Beyond and in the Real-world, proves that he is not invincible." He glances up at the sun.

"And, I must say this. Every kind creature in the World Beyond owes you a debt of gratitude. We can now measure the period of sunshine in hours instead of heartbeats. And the period of semi-darkness can now be measured in hours instead of days. Your harsh destruction of the Malavem and many of the Inania and Parva Draco made it happen."

Diana declares, "Yes, regarding what you said about me seriously wounding Mendacium is true. That proves he is not invincible." She breathes in deeply. When she speaks once more to Charles, sincere emotion is evident in her tone of voice.

"I have to admit. I was frightened. Yes, I was dreadfully frightened, Charles. Even so, I felt as though God had answered my prayer when I asked Him to give me the knowledge of how to escape the spiral staircase. But, even as the method of the escape entered my mind, I still had reservations. I mean, what if I had made a mistake on how to end the battle, I would not be here today. Fortunately, I was correct. So I lept over the side, hoping with my heart and soul that I would end up on the ground in one piece, which I did."

She shakes her head adding, "I trusted in my God, and I trusted my instincts. But, after I lept from the edge of the landing, I suddenly realized I stupidly had not thought about what would happen after I lept. So, as I watched myself speedily fall to the ground, I started to cry. Then, as God had told me to, I called out to Paulavis. As Paulavis had promised me, he was not far away. He called the other birds to save me."

With a big grin, she says in an excited tone, "And then I saw them. A beautiful flock of the most graceful, powerful birds in the Universe, a dozen of the Aquila, the World Beyond equivalent to the Real-world eagle. One of them caught me in midair, and after flying for a while, she gently lowered me to the ground. The other Aquila had accompanied her just in case she missed me as I fell. I had at least eleven backups!" As she throws her hand high in the air, she laughs, "And here I am, safe and sound and as feisty as ever!"

Charles says, "And that you are, my dear friend, Empress Artemis-Diana. That you are."

"Charles, I must also say this. The dreams I had of my double in the Real-world also proves decency and truth can prevail over corruption and deceit. I am very happy Mister Young got what was coming to him. However, I must not gloat. His devious, greedy actions all for the sake of money have wounded others. His daughter, Missy and her little sister, Ruth, will suffer because of his poor decisions." With a frown, she adds, "As will Miss Hickman."

Then she says in a cheerful tone, "On the other hand, I am very happy, despite everything that happened, Miss Hickman is in counseling, that she will become a better person. It's just a shame that she had to subject others to her incessant bullying before she came to her senses, sought counseling and asked forgiveness." She indirectly glances at the sun as she breathes in deeply to sample the refreshing fragrance of the morning dew.

"And, I must agree with you, Charles. The longer period of sunshine is very refreshing. The breeze is more prevalent. The animals are happier. And, the Minima's crops are flourishing, even though they are still tiny seedlings."

I Dunno uncharacteristically has remained strangely quiet while Diana and Charles have been talking. She excitedly blurts out in her squeaky voice, "Speaking of Miss Hickman, I met her guardian angel a couple of days ago. Her name is Dimittetur Illi. She is a lovely angel. Our Lord appointed her just the other day because her former guardian angel was not doing a very good job. Dimittetur Illi specializes in reversing personality quirks that make a person less than pleasant to others. I credit Dimittetur Illi with helping Miss Hickman to seek counseling." She giggles. "Like me, she was at the proceeding with Miss Davenport, your parents, and the others. I didn't know who she was at the time. But I had fun, especially when the policemen arrested your principal."

I Dunno flies from the table to hover close to Diana's face. She plants a kiss on Diana's cheek.

"I am very proud of you, Diana. Your words of compassion for Miss Hickman were wonderful. And the way you asked Miss Davenport to go easy on Miss Hickman was very moving as well." She smiles. "Dimittetur Illi was a bit jealous, I dare say!"

Diana says with a smile as I Dunno lands on her left shoulder, "I thank you, I Dunno. That is very sweet of you to say."

She looks at Charles. "Mister Young and Crazy Face were manipulating Miss Hickman. She didn't know it at the time, but those two were bullying her, saying that Mister Young was going to fire her if she didn't play along." She shakes her head. Then, with a sad expression, she says, "A bully was bullying others while being bullied by bullies. How ironic is that? When will it stop? Will it *ever* stop?"

Charles says with a straight face, "Unfortunately, Diana, you and I Dunno, and I recognize that bullying in the human world will not stop. In fact, it is more rampant now than ever before as it hides from public view on social media. Hopefully, with continued education of the human youngsters and their parents, it will diminish or go away entirely. Perhaps, over time, it will die a well-deserved, natural death."

Diana says, "That would be nice if it were to go away entirely. But, I doubt it will. Even if it doesn't die a well-deserved, natural death like you say, education will serve to help the bullied people to seek help."

She glances across the clearing to the newly constructed Minima waterwheel and reservoir. A smile crosses her face. She is happy that the Minima have recovered from the devastation of the battle. Crops are flourishing, ruined fences and storehouses mended, and every single tree house restored. Naturally, she helped to speed the recovery process by working long days to assist the Minima. She places her hand on Charles' arm. She whispers, "So, Charles, what is to become of me?"

Charles replies, "What do you mean, what is to become of you?"

"You had said I was the Favored Child. You had mentioned that after I, the Favored Child, defeated Mendacium, which I did not, my journey would not end. You also said I would have to battle other supernatural creatures. You said some of those creatures are eviler and nastier than Mendacium." She looks at Charles straight on. With a long face, she says, "Charles, Mendacium and his evil conspirators were difficult to fight. I dread thinking about having to face even eviler and nastier creatures." With a look of troubled concern, she adds, "What's more, I must ask you this. It has been bothering me for some time now. Will I have to battle Mendacium yet again?"

Charles says in a somber tone, "Yes, Empress Artemis-Diana, I am confident you will face Mendacium again. As you know, he is not defeated. Yes, he has fallen thanks to you, but he is going to return. His devious influences will not go away. You know that is true. When he returns, he will be stronger than ever. I suspect he will have by his side even more wicked creatures than the basilisk, Malavem, Parva Draco, Aegolius, and Inania."

Diana says in a firm voice, "I do not want to appear impolite, Charles, but I must ask you yet again. What is to become of me?" She rubs her right calf. "My calf where the Parva Draco bit me still hurts." She traces the scar above her left eye with her forefinger.

"The scar on my forehead still hurts as well. Surprisingly, the wound where the shard of wood pierced me on my upper arm has healed. And, unlike the scars on my calf and forehead, it does not hurt. Will the scars on my calf and forehead heal completely?"

"Yes and no," Charles replies. His tone is sad. "The pain may diminish over time. But the scars will never go away. They will remain with you forever, just like the puncture marks in the palms of your hands caused by the tainted blood of the Parva Draco on the arrow tips. They may fade a bit over time, but they will never disappear."

Diana shakes her head and softly asks, "Why, Charles? Why won't the scars go away?"

"Because, my dear Empress Artemis-Diana, they were brought about by evil. When the Parva Draco bit you, they left an indelible mark on your innocence. Their bite marks are the same as the puncture marks on the palms of your hands. They will remain with you forever."

"But, Charles, that does not explain the nearly straight-line, vertical scar on my forehead." She once more traces the three-inch scar with her finger. "The Inania did not bite or scratch my skin. The creature hit me on my forehead with its sword."

"The Inania's sword, Diana, was an extension of the creature's being. As the Inania mirrored your image, its sword was part of its evil body. When the blade of its sword nicked your forehead, it was no different than if the creature had scratched you with its fingernail."

Despite the morbidity of what Charles has said, Diana manages to laugh.

"I guess that makes sense when you put it that way. So, I should learn to live with my scars forever. I hope my parents do not discover them and ask me a lot of questions. I would have an extremely tough time explaining these scars, no less how I could be in two places at the same time. They will think I completely have lost my mind."

"Oh, Diana, I would not worry about your parents discovering your scars. Like the nightmarish scenes you've witnessed and the battles you fought here in the World Beyond, your scars are yours and yours alone. Your scars and the suffering in your heart are yours to bear and nobody else's. Just like your memories, your scars will be invisible to others. Your family and friends will not see them."

Diana states, "That doesn't make sense. Why is it I should see my scars and others cannot see them? It's not like I want to show off or anything like that, but it seems unfair if you know what I'm saying. It's like I must live with my memories by myself. It's scary when I think of it. I feel lost in a way, alone." As she shakes her head, she says, "Why, Charles, why must it be like this?" Charles takes her hand in his. He firmly squeezes her hand three times. She squeezes his hand four times in return.

"My dear, sweet friend, Empress Artemis-Diana, as I have said many times, you are the Favored Child. Mendacium's cruelty by having his evil mutated creatures leaving an indelible mark on your body is his way of making a small part of you his Prisoner of Innocence."

Diana cries, "Wow! That stinks. So, Mendacium is reminding me that I too am vulnerable. It is his way of saying that, by leaving permanent scars on my body that only I can see, I too am not invincible. Am I correct?"

"Yes, you are correct," Charles offers. "And, in Mendacium's twisted mind, a part of you, albeit a small part of you, makes you his Prisoner of Innocence for life. It's his way of reminding you that even one of the most virtuous, pure, and good creatures in the Universe, Empress Artemis-Diana, can be soiled."

Diana says in a whisper, "So, I guess what you are saying is this. By leaving me with scars that only I can see, it is his way of winning, even though he lost the battle and is now much weaker."

"Yes, it is Mendacium's evil way of reminding you that he has not finished with you, that he will be back." Charles adds with a troubled look, "He may have fallen, but when he returns, his power will be huge, far beyond our imaginings. You must be ready at all times, always on your guard."

*****

Part III: A Closing I Love You

Having to say goodbye to I Dunno and Jayvyn undoubtedly is one of the hardest things that Diana has ever done in her life. Thankfully, Charles will return with her to the Real-world as she reunites as one with her double. Naturally, I Dunno will remain by her side forever. It is just that in the Real-world Diana and I Dunno will be unable to carry on a conversation. And, while I Dunno can see her, Diana will be unable to see her loving protector pixie in return.

Saying goodbye to the Minima is as difficult for her as saying goodbye to I Dunno and Jayvyn. However, as good luck would have it, Uvam arranged for a special festival, both to thank Diana for her honorable deeds in the World Beyond and to send her off in style. In this fashion, she can say goodbye to the entire village at once.

The Minima carpenters had built a special platform, a stage of sorts. Diana sat in front of the stage while Minima performed skits and sang ballads in front of her. The Minima wives and husbands baked and cooked all sorts of delicious delicacies.

As she watches the Minima sing traditional Minima songs and perform tricks and funny skits on the stage, she is munching on a *crustulum*. The wholesome snack is one of her favorite Minima foods. The Minima had placed at least a dozen of the delicious snacks before her on the makeshift stage.

The crustulum was a favored food of the Romans as humble nourishment for soldiers. Its ingredients consist of flour, a vinegary, non-alcoholic liquid in place of white wine or mead, olive oil, apples, raisins, and nuts. The crustulum's shape is like a pancake. The Minima bake it on hardened wood, so there is a charcoal fire taste to it.

After the Minima complete their skits, Diana gets ready to make a short speech. Charles had said that it would be appropriate, that the Minima would appreciate it very much.

"In fact," he had said, "The Minima may even quote some of your words and inscribe them on their Holodi coins."

With tears welling up in her eyes, she begins her speech. She must whisper since many of the Minima children are fast asleep in their mother's arms. She does not want to wake them. She motions for I Dunno to alight on her shoulder. The hundreds of Minima form a semi-circle before her on the stage.

"First off, on behalf of I Dunno, I must thank each of you for saving I Dunno's and my life. Without your love and attentive healing skills, I doubt we would be here today to enjoy your company."

The Minima get to their feet and cheer. Their robust cheers immediately wake the sleeping Minima. However, much to Diana's surprise, not a single child whimpers or calls out.

"Second, I wish to thank you from the bottom of my heart for constructing my tree house. As many of you know, I've always wanted a tree house, and now I have one. Thank you!" She blows silent kisses to the throng. They get to their feet and cheer once more.

"Third, as you know, Mendacium has not been beaten, but he has fallen. He is not as strong as he was." She glances at Charles adding, "However, someone told me he would someday return, perhaps even stronger than before. But, I promise you this, if the King of Deceit returns, I shall also return to you. And when I do, I guarantee not only will he fall a second time, he will become extinct in the World Beyond!"

The Minima scramble to their feet. Before they can cheer a third time, Diana holds up her hand to stop them. With surprised looks on their faces, they sit back down.

"But know this, mighty Minima of the World Beyond. If Mendacium is somehow able to return before I return, fear not his evil. For I have his Word, his promise. Neither he or any of his evil creatures will ever strike down a Minima. And you can quote me on this. I believe righteousness will prevail over evil and truth will always win over lies. For, in the end, those of us with unswerving veracity and unwavering honor will someday rule the Universe!"

The Minima get to their feet and cheer a third time.

"So, now, my dear friends, I must leave you. But, please, before I go, I would like each of you to pass by me on the stage so that we can touch each other's hands. While I cannot give each of you three squeezes of your hands, which you know is my custom, I can say it." She gets to her feet. As she places her hands over her heart, she exclaims, "I love you!"

The Minima immediately break out in song. At that moment, as they continue to sing, they form a curved line. As they pass by her, one after another, they lay a hand on her outstretched forefinger. Much to her surprise, all the Minima squeeze her finger four times.

After the very last Minima passes her by on the stage, she gets to her feet. She waves goodbye. Then, she hops on Jayvyn's back. I Dunno alights onto Jayvyn's head. With Charles floating next to Jayvyn's side, the foursome disappears into the forest.

A few hours later they arrive at the threshold of the bona fide spiraling staircase. Diana kisses Jayvyn on his forehead.

"I love you, Jayvyn. Thank you for carrying me over these long distances. And thank you for plowing the Minima's fields. But most of all," she breaks out with laughter. "Thank you for smashing that Parva Draco to smithereens."

Then she enfolds I Dunno into her arms.

"I will see you in my dreams, in my heart, and in my writings, my sweet, tiny protector pixie." She kisses I Dunno on her forehead three times.

I Dunno replies, "I love you too, my sweet Empress Artemis-Diana, Youngster Heroine of the World Beyond. I am very proud of you, Diana, very proud." She hugs Diana with her tiny arms. "I will be by your side forever." She crosses her heart adding, "I promise to God."

Diana abruptly turns around and reaches out for the handrail of the actual spiraling staircase that will lead her to Domum. She is both happy and sad at the same time. Her happiness comes from knowing that she will soon be whole once more. She will be in her comfy bed, hugging her parents, eating her favorite home-cooked and fast foods, bugging her brothers, and hanging out with her friends. She also is happy the World Beyond is nearly normal once more. Just like the sparkling newness of the actual spiraling staircase, she is about to ascend, the World Beyond is fresh, wholesome, newborn.

She is also very sad. While she suffered tremendously, both physically and mentally, while she fought Mendacium's evil, she will miss her Minima friends. And yes, she will miss the excitement of battle, of doing something moral to help those in need. Nevertheless, something is telling her that she will return to the World Beyond. Whether she likes it or not.

She takes Charles' hand in hers, and then she steps onto the first stair tread. Within a few seconds, she and Charles disappear around the first bend of the staircase.

CHAPTER SIXTEEN

DIANA, CHARLES, AND FRIENDS

Diana, Edith, Bonnie, Anna, and Mary are sipping sodas at Coco's Café. Diana, as you might expect, is on her second glass of Italian cream soda. She seems distracted as she busily dips an extra-long, crispy French fry into a dab of ketchup on the side of her plate.

She and her four friends are sitting at a table for six. The one, apparently unoccupied seat, has a glass of Italian cream soda resting on the table in front of it. The glass of soda is half-full.

Edith cries in a whisper, "How in the world does he do that? It is simply remarkable. Look. There he goes again!"

The others stare in amazement as the plastic straw in the half-full glass of Italian cream soda slowly swirls. Then, something invisible draws soda into the straw. Next, to everyone's amazement, the straw miraculously lifts from the glass to float in the air. It carefully moves in a horizontal position until it stops at the edge of the tabletop.

Bonnie shrieks, "Oh, my goodness, he's going to sip the little bit of soda from the straw!"

Diana glances around the nearly empty café. She says, "You guys be quiet. We don't want anyone to see what's happening. Charles is my ghost, well, he's our ghost and we ain't sharing! So, shush!"

Anna whispers, "Look, there it goes! He sipped the soda out of the straw!" Just as she says this, something plucks the maraschino cherry from the top of her soda. She covers her mouth to stifle a scream of delight as she watches as the cherry floats in midair above the table. Then it disappears. As the others break out in barely audible hysterical laughter, she cries, "No, please tell me he didn't do that!" She looks at Diana. "He didn't do that, did he?" In reply, Diana nods her head and stuffs another French fry into her mouth.

Bonnie stares at the back of the empty chair where Charles is sitting. She says in a hushed whisper, "Diana, how did you know he likes Italian cream soda? Did he tell you? And where does the soda go after he, you know, drinks it?"

Diana states matter-of-factly, "He told me he would like to try an Italian cream soda." She leans across the table to whisper. The others lean across the table as well.

"He doesn't need to drink or eat. He's only doing this for you, to prove a point. He loves me, and he wants for you to believe me, to believe everything that I told you about the World Beyond." She smiles. "As far as where the soda is going, I guess it's going into his stomach. Since he's invisible, so must the soda be invisible once it touches his lips."

Mary whispers, "I didn't know he could leave your house. That he's here with you, with us, is nothing short of amazing."

Diana replies, "I guess he has become stronger after everything that happened in the World Beyond." She looks at each of her friends one-by-one adding, "You guys do believe me, yep? Everything that happened is true. You know I would never lie to you. Lying stinks. Given everything that I just went through, I can attest to that firsthand."

Edith says as she looks at the others, "Of course we do, Diana. Even if we didn't believe you, which we do, watching Charles in action proves that anything is possible."

"Yeah," Anna says as she playfully cradles her soda on the table in between her forearms. "Anything or I should say, anyone that can pluck a maraschino cherry from my drink has to be real." She hugs her drink even closer as if she expects Charles will take a sip from her straw.

Diana replies with a big smile, "Thank you, Edith, Anna. That means a lot to me. It truly does." She notices Mary is shaking her head. "What's with you, Mary?"

"Well, I don't know, Diana. I'm still skeptical." She raises the soup bowl containing the last bits of her chicken noodle soup to her lips. After swallowing her soup and wiping her mouth, she says, "I want to believe what I see here at our table. But, I wonder if it's only an optical illusion. Then again, I know you would never lie to us, and I truly, honestly, want to believe what's happening. But it is too mind-boggling to be real. Do you know what I'm saying?"

"I cannot do any of what you see," Diana says with a laugh. "I might be able to shoot arrows and fight with a sword, but I don't know magic. Well, maybe I do know a bit." She looks out the window. "I'll tell you what. Would you believe me even more if you saw something that I can do in action?"

Bonnie asks, "Like what?"

"Tell you what, Bonnie," Diana says. "Please tell your co-worker we're stepping outside for a moment. Tell her we'll be right back, okay? Then meet us outside." She grabs another French fry off her plate. "And make sure she doesn't clear the table. I still have more fries to demolish."

"Okay," Bonnie says as she stands up and goes to walk behind the counter. "I'll be outside in a second. Don't start without me."

As Diana gets up from her chair, she says, "Okay, you guys. Follow me."

Once Bonnie has joined Diana and her other friends outside, Diana says, "Okay, watch this." She closes her eyes tightly. She begins to mumble things under her breath. The others stare at her like she has lost her mind.

Suddenly, out of nowhere, a stray cat appears from around the corner. It walks right up to Diana just as she opens her eyes. She says, "Hello there, Jingles. How are you?" The cat brushes against her and meows.

Mary laughs. "Maybe it's just a coincidence. It looks pretty cool, but perhaps the cat was coming this way."

Diana chuckles, and then she says, "Oh really? Let me ask you something, Mary. Do cats and birds get along together?" Mary shakes her head.

Bonnie offers, "Birds hate cats and rightly so. My tabby ate my parakeet a few years ago. There was nothing left but feathers. Ugh!"

Diana closes her eyes once more. In a few seconds, five finches appear out of nowhere. Each of the five bird's hovers near one of the girls. Then one after another they land on each of the girl's right shoulder! Naturally, the girls are surprised that the birds landed on their shoulders. However, they are too flabbergasted to move. Anna and Bonnie's faces are expressionless as they stare straight ahead. Edith and Mary look down to the birds on their shoulders. The looks on their faces are ones of "What in the world is happening here?"

Mary abruptly whispers, "Holy mackerel! What you just did was very cool, Diana! I believe you, I honestly do! You are magical!" Just as she says this, a larger bird flies from the trees. It lands in front of Jingles. Jingles lays on the sidewalk and begins to purr loudly. Then the bird nestles in between its paws.

Mary shouts, "Oh, my goodness, a cat and a bird who like each other! Yes, Diana, yes! I honestly do believe you!"

"Thanks, Mary," Diana says, "but that's nothing. Watch this."

She whispers to the bird on her shoulder. She forms a heart with her hands. She nods her head a few times, and then the bird flies away to disappear high into the air.

Anna asks, "What did you say to the bird? Did you tell him to do something cool?" As an afterthought, she says, "You formed a heart with your hands. Were you telling him you love him or something like that?"

Diana says, "You'll see. It's something special I want to give to you as my good friends. I only wish Evelyn were here so that I could show her. But, I'll show her later. While we're waiting, I need to tell you this. The bird that I was talking to is the leader of the five birds. The sixth bird is just a random bird I asked to make friends with Jingles. Because the bird alighted on my shoulder, and not on one of yours, proves he is the leader." She searches the sky. "It'll take him a few moments to get organized. Be patient if you please."

She looks one at a time at each of the birds perched on Edith, Mary, Anna, and Bonnie's shoulders. Each time she looks at one of the birds, she says, "You may join the others." Then the bird flies off into the sky. Naturally, the girls are shocked each time one of the birds reacts to Diana's command.

Diana looks up at the sky. The other girls follow her gaze. As she points, she says, "Okay, watch carefully. He's getting organized. Any second now."

Suddenly, Diana's friends start yelling, jumping up and down and pointing excitedly to the cloudless, deep blue sky. Dozens of birds of varied sizes seemingly fly from all directions. They slowly flock together as a circle in the sky. After a few moments, the birds create a huge heart. The living heart of graceful birds floats back and forth across the sky a few times. All the while, the shape of the heart remains perfectly intact.

Diana suddenly shouts, "Okay, you are finished. Thank you." Then she shouts, "Mortkn, please come to me. I have something to give you, as a token of my appreciation."

Within a few seconds, the leader of the five birds that had landed on Diana's shoulder appears in the sky. He gracefully hovers a few inches from Diana's shoulder. Diana retrieves a small portion of a French fry she had placed in her pocket before she left the café. She offers it to Mortkn. He snatches it from her fingers and flies off. She turns to re-enter the café.

She says, "That heart was my special message to the four of you. To tell you that I love you." She holds the door open for her friends. Then, with a chuckle and a look of satisfaction on her face that seems to say, *See, I told you so*, she eyes her unfinished plate of fries sitting on the table.

"Hurry now. My French fries are getting cold!"

EPILOGUE

Diana is in her room. She is admiring a Sumi project she finished a few moments ago. Sumi is a type of Chinese calligraphy. A good friend presented the calligraphy set to her after they completed a portion of her five-hour photo shoot. She cannot recall her friend's exact words when he presented her with the gift, but it went something like this.

"I hope this gift serves as a token of our lasting friendship. Also, as an expression of my sincere thanks for doing so well during the photo shoot. I also hope this gift serves as a reminder of all the remarkable things of which you are capable, those important things you can and must do in your lifetime.

"Someday I too must depart this earth and join Charles in the ethereal world. But, I promise you this. I shall forever be by your side rooting you on as you achieve remarkable things, but a whisper away and a dream close. Always."

Diana is home alone. Her parents have gone out on the town to take in a movie and to eat dinner. Dan is with some of his friends. Billy is staying overnight with a friend. Charles is also away. He is at the bedside of a young boy who is dying of cancer. The boy is in a hospice somewhere in Germany.

Charles had said before he departed, "You know, Diana, it is strange. The little boy who is dying saw Susan's Instagram profile. He followed her profile even after she died. The little boy with whom I am going to sit as he approaches his final hours had asked his Mom to buy a tee shirt that symbolized Susan's favorite quote. He is wearing the tee shirt as I speak.

"The tee shirt sports a drawing of a large jar of strawberry jelly. The shirt also has words printed on it. They are words that Susan had once said to her friends. 'I know you're jelly I get to see Jesus first but,' and these are the words on the tee shirt, 'if you're gonna be jelly, be strawberry jelly, it's the best!'"

Charles' mention of Susan reminds her of Ariel. Diana did not know Ariel well, but when Ariel passed away, it hurt. It hurt badly. Some of her friends and acquaintances knew Ariel very well. So, Ariel's passing hurt them even more. Ariel had always made a habit of saying, "Live life to your best." Diana and her closest friends intend to do just that.

Diana rubs the invisible scars on her calf. Without thinking, she traces the invisible three-inch vertical scar on her forehead just above her left eye. Now and then, the scars throb. When they do, their pain serves to remind her of her incredible journey in the World Beyond.

She knows she is the only one who can see her scars. So, Charles was correct. The scars and the puncture wounds on the palms of her hands, like her memories of the World Beyond, are imperceptible to everyone but her. To prove to herself that they are, she often moves her hair to the side of her forehead to reveal the scar. She also rubs her calf now and then when she is with her friends. Except for the occasional comment, "Is your calf hurting?" no one seems to notice the scars are there. Evelyn is the only exception. She knows exactly where Diana's scars are. She sometimes traces the scar on Diana's forehead. When she does, she usually says something along the lines of, "Yes, Diana. I can feel it. I guess our being the best of friends allows me to do so."

Diana misses her friends, Uvam, Saccharo, Eros and the other Minima. She also misses I Dunno, terribly so. While she knows that her protector pixie is always by her side in the Real-world, she cannot see or hear her. All the same, she talks to her sweet pixie as if they were having a true conversation. When she speaks aloud to I Dunno, she knows in her heart that her darling protector pixie is smiling.

She also misses Jayvyn. Now and then, during a car ride with her parents, she asks them to stop so she can have a brief conversation with a horse. Sometimes, when she does, people look at her like she has lost her mind. That is because she asks the horse's name and seemingly answers the horse. But, that is okay with her. She is happy, and the horse knows it. Nobody else's opinion counts.

When she is out and about town, either hanging out with her family or friends and when she is playing softball, wild animals stop to stare at her. She never calls out to them in public. If she did, she envisions she would be in the looney bin before you could say, "That girl is crazy!"

The funny thing, when it comes to Diana and animals, is this. She still is allergic to animal dander and feathers in the Real-world. It is strange when you think about it. Here she is, the Empress Artemis-Diana, capable of controlling and talking with wild animals, but she sneezes like crazy whenever animals get too close to her.

Suddenly, the dry paintbrush she is holding in her hand begins to wriggle. She tries to control its movements by grabbing it with her other hand. But, it resists and continues to struggle against her grip. It is like something magical is controlling it! She places her hands on either side of her painting. Then she watches with alarm as something dips the paintbrush into the jar of black ink. The paintbrush moves through the air. A small drop of black ink splashes onto her painting.

She screams, "No, no! You will not ruin my painting!"

She tries to grab the brush, but something forces her hands away. She attempts to grab her painting before the thing can inflict more damage. Once again, something forces her hands away. She speechlessly glares as words begin to appear on her prized painting.

"Greetings, Artemis-Diana. Prepare yourself."

As quickly as the words had appeared, they disappear. Diana grabs the brush from whatever it is that was writing on her paper.

She screams, "You're going to ruin my painting! I've been working on it for days! How dare you!"

The brush is forcefully taken from her hand once more. Whatever it is that is controlling the brush dips the brush into the black ink yet again. Diana frowns as more ominous words penned in calligraphy appear on her painting.

I await you, Artemis-Diana. Then the words miraculously vanish.

At the stroke of midnight on the Fifth. Once again, the words vanish.

Respectfully yours, Bellator! The words vanish yet again.

The Bellator entity has not yet finished taunting Diana. It lifts the jar of black ink from the tabletop, and then it empties the jar of black ink onto her painting, ruining it!

Diana is in a state of bemusement as she stares at her ruined painting. A shiver runs up and down her spine. Her heartbeats quicken, and her shallow breaths haltingly come and go. She wants to run. But, she knows she cannot run far enough from the truth. For she knows the point in time when she must use her weapons as Artemis-Diana has arrived yet again. That realization strikes to the core of her heart like the blue lightning bolt pendant around her neck that is now shining brilliantly. She whispers aloud in an unsteady tone.

"Destiny is calling me, the Favored Child, Artemis-Diana, another time."

CITED WORKS

The following cited works are used in this novel to add realism to the story. Mention of these cited works in no way endorses their products nor does the author have any affiliation with their writers, musicians, producers or business owners.

- In Chapter 2, reference is made to the *Wizard of Oz*. Diana says, "Well, as Dorothy had said in the Wizard of Oz, 'Toto, I have a feeling we're not in Kansas anymore,' I am fairly certain we are not in a place or era of my time." *The Wizard of Oz* was a 1902 Broadway musical adaptation of *The Wonderful Wizard of Oz*, a children's novel written by L. Frank Baum. It was also a 1939 musical film starring Judy Garland.

- In Chapter 3, reference is made to the movie *Dead Man Walking*, a 1995 American crime drama starring Susan Sarandon and Sean Penn. The movie was co-produced and directed by Tim Robbins. The movie was adopted from the non-fiction book by the same name.

- In Chapter 3, reference is made to the thriller novel *The Green Mile*, written by Stephen King in 1996.

- In Chapter 4, Diana recalls lyrics from a song released in 1975 by the hard rock band AC/DC. The lyrics are from AC/DC's Australian album T.N.T. Messer's Bon Scott, Angus Young, and Malcolm Young wrote the song.

- In Chapters 5 and 16, mention is made of Café Coco's. This establishment is a popular Italian café near Centennial Sportsplex, Nashville, Tennessee. The fictional Diana and her friends dine at the café whenever they are in the area.

- In Chapter 8, mention is made of the television sitcom *Mister Ed*. Filmways produced the sitcom. It aired from January 5 to July 2, 1961, and then on CBS from October 1, 1961, to February 6, 1966. The show's title character, a talking horse, originally appeared in short stories by Walter R. Brooks.

- In Chapter 8, Diana sings a few lyrics of the hit song, *Somebody's Hero*. *Somebody's Hero* is a song written by Jamie O'Neal, Shaye Smith and Ed Hill and recorded by Australian country music artist O'Neal. Released in 2005 as the second single from O'Neal's album *Brave*.

- In Chapters 8 and 9, mention is made of the family kitchen, Panda Express. Panda Express is a coast to coast "Family Chinese Kitchen" that serves American Chinese food. Founded in 1983 in Glendale, California. The local Panda Express is one of the fictional Diana's favorite places to eat.

- In Chapter 9, mention is made of the novel *Atlas Shrugged*. It is a novel by Ayn Rand published in 1957. The novel was Rand's longest. She considered it to be her *magnum opus,* her greatest achievement of her fiction writings.

- In Chapter 11, reference is made to Peter Pettigrew. Peter Pettigrew, sometimes referred to as Wormtail, is a fictional character in the Harry Potter fantasy series of novels written by British author J. K Rowling.

- In Chapter 15, the quote, "To err is human, to forgive, divine," is attributable to Alexander Pope. Pope was an 18th-century English poet.

GLOSSARY

Aegolius - (/ē·gō·lē·ės/) The Aegolius is an astonishingly strong otherworldly creature similar in appearance to a barn owl, except it is more than twice the size of the owl. It does not have a true physical form. It is more like a shimmering apparition. The Aegolius has unblinking yellow eyes that are allegedly able to see objects across far-flung distances. Legends claim that if one were to stare into the Aegolius' eyes for more than a glance, one would become petrified.

Agathodaemon - The Agathodaemon, also called the Good Demon, was the god of fortune. It is the opposite of a cacodemon. An agathodaemon is a good spirit or angel."

Anna - Anna is a fictional character.

April - April is Diana's female escort to the World Beyond. Although April plays a secondary role in the novel, she plays a primary role in the Enchanted Gate series of novels as the original queen of the ancient Isle of Spardom beneath the sea.

Aquila - The Aquila is a fictional bird in the World Beyond. It resembles the eagle but is much larger.

Ariel - Ariel is a fictional character mentioned in the text.

Bamao - A plant indigenous to the World Beyond. Leaves of the bamao plant are used as a preservative to wrap foodstuffs. The leaves are edible when boiled.

Banapple - As the name implies, a banapple is a fruity blend of a banana and an apple. The banapple has the shape of a banana. The outer skin, which is edible, is red like an apple. The inner portion, the meat, is yellow like a banana. It has a subtle banana-apple taste.

Beach, Jacqueline - Miss Beach is Diana's school counselor. She is also the official recorder/transcriber during hearings in Miss Davenport's conference room.

Bonnie - Bonnie is a waitress at Café Cocos.

Bob - First name of Mister "Crazy Face" Studeman.

Bob - First name of Mister Cousins.

Cacodemon - The evil spirit or a demon. The opposite of a cacodemon is an agathodaemon, a good spirit or angel.

Caverna Reguli - Full name of basilisk loyal to Mendacium.

Carbatina - Diana's footwear. The carbatina is a one-piece shoe with soles and uppers cut from a single piece of leather. The edges are cut into loops through which a lacing is pulled around the ankles.

Charles - Diana's lifelong ghost, both in the Real-world and the World Beyond.

Christopher - Cousin of Regina Reynolds

Consilii - Minima. She designed a plow harness suitable for a horse.

Coolio - Coolio means the same as awesome.

Conveyor of Lies and Falsehoods - Third, seldom used name for Mendacium.

Cousins - Father of Sarah Cousins. Sarah is a member of the opposing ladies' softball championship team.

Crazy Face - Nickname of Mister Bob Studeman, a cohort of Mister Young, Diana's principal.

Crustulum - Snack made by the Minima and favored by Diana in the World Beyond. The crustulum was a favored food of the Romans as humble nourishment for soldiers. Its ingredients consist of flour, white wine or mead, olive oil, apples, raisins, and nuts. It is shaped like a pancake. For our story, a vinegary, non-alcoholic liquid is used in place of white wine or mead.

Davenport, Miss - School District Superintendent.

Diana (double) - Our protagonist, Diana, is in two places at once - in the World Beyond as Empress Artemis-Diana, Youngster Heroine of the World Beyond. She is also the fictional character Diana Jane Bower in the Real-world.

Dimittetur Illi (/dĭ·vĭ·'tė·tė·rē·lē/) - Miss Hickman's second guardian angel. Miss Hickman's first guardian angel was dismissed because she failed to bring out the best in Miss Hickman.

Diomede - (/dī·à·'mē/) Mythological creature from which Diana is a descendant, the Fifth Unborn Child, Diomede.

Domum - (/dō·müm/) A supposed place of paradise in the World Beyond. Light from Domum radiates over the land during periods of darkness. In this book, Domum is still unexplored.

Downey, Mister - Coach of Diana's softball team.

Dynamite - Diana's nickname on the ladies' softball team.

Elemental attributes - Bursts of air in the tranquility beam designed to increase a person's strong points such as courage, tenacity, and stamina.

Evelyn - Fictional character based on Diana's Real-world best friend, Evelyn.

Edith - Diana's friend in the Real-world.

Eros - Royal Minima son of King Uvam and Queen Saccharo.

Evil Bird - The technical name of Malavem.

Evil Spirit - Not defined in the story. However, its use literally implies the Devil.

Extinctus - Magic word Diana utters to extinguish her magical light.

Favored Child - Diana's title in the World Beyond. Essentially, the Favored Child is the reincarnated, reawakened, all-powerful Goddess Artemis-Diana.

Gloria - First name of Miss Hickman.

He who is Unmerciful - Another name used to identify Mendacium, primarily by his allies.

Hickman, Miss - Miss Gloria Hickman is the school principal's secretary. She bullies and threatens Diana. She also is part of a conspiracy.

Holodi - (/hō·ˈlō·dee/) The currency system in the World Beyond. There are fifty Solodi to a Holodi. Twenty Holodi equals a Potanis, the largest denomination.

I Dunno - (/ˈī·dö·nō/) Diana's protector pixie both in the World Beyond and in the Real-world. A protector pixie is the same as a guardian angel. I Dunno is seen and heard in the World Beyond. In the Real-world, she also protects Diana; however, she is neither seen or heard.

Inania - (/in·à·ˈnē·àh/) - Evil creature loyal to Mendacium. The Inania can become the spitting-image of any other creature. Known as the *Thing* in Latin. The Inania is one of the most dreaded beasts in the World Beyond. In fact, it is the evilest, hideous cacodemon in the Universe.

Industa - A spiritual type of fruit used by the mythological gods that gave them energy before battle.

Insectum - Fictional land that is accessible via the tranquility beam. It is full of insects, including arachnids (and spiders - one of Diana's favorites).

Italian Cream Soda - Diana's beverage of choice at Café Cocos.

Jack - First name of Mister Young.

James - The brother of Diana's ghost, Charles.

Jayvyn - (/ˈjāy·v·ĭn/)Diana's steed in the World Beyond. Jayvyn means the same as "Life Spirit."

Kathy - Girlfriend of Mister Reynolds.

King of Deceit - Another name used to describe Mendacium.

Libum - (/lĭ·ˈbum) - Libum is an ancient food. It was common during the Roman Era.

Life Spirit - Jayvyn's name literally means Life Spirit.

Lux Magicae - (/lux·ˈmāg·ès·tee/) Magical words Diana uses to turn on her magical light.

Malavem - (/ˈmal·ā·vĕm) One of the evilest creatures in the World Beyond. The Malavem is virtually indestructible.

Mary - Diana's friend in the Real-world.

Mendacium - (/men·ˈdà·cee·um/) Our story's villain. Also known as the King of Deceit and He who is Unmerciful.

Minima - (ˈmĭn·ĭ·mà) Subspecies of the Parva Draco. The Minima are friendly creatures.

Missy - Mister Young's oldest daughter and best friend of Sarah Cousins.

Mortkn - Bird that alights on Diana's shoulder near the end of the story. Gathers his friends to form a heart in the sky for Diana's friends.

Opposing diminutions - Bursts of air in the tranquility beam designed to remove negative detractors from a person's body and mind. Examples are indecision, fear, doubt, anxiety, dishonesty, and nervousness.

Parva Draco - (/pàr·ˈvà -ˈdrā·cō/) Evil creatures that can assume the image of any other creature, even those that are not in its presence.

Paulavis - (/paul·ˈā·vĭs/) Name of a bird that befriends Diana in the World Beyond.

Peters, Howard - A student bully in the Real-world.

Prisoner of Innocence - A term Charles uses to describe the ruination of all good in the Universe if Mendacium were to capture Diana.

Protector Pixie - Diana's "guardian angel" I Dunno both in the World Beyond and in the Real-world.

Ray - First name of Mister Reynolds.

Regina (Reg) - Good friend of Diana and the pitcher on the ladies' softball team.

Reynolds, Denise - Deceased wife of Mister Reynolds. Regina's deceased mother.

Reynolds, Ray - Umpire during the ladies' championship softball game. Regina's father.

Reguli - Short name of Mendacium's basilisk, Caverna Reguli.

Ruth - Mister Young's youngest daughter.

Saccharo - Saccharo is the Queen of Minima. King Uvam, her husband, rules the Minima Kingdom. Eros is her son.

Sally Turndle - Star hitter on the opposing softball team during the ladies' softball championship game.

Sana bush - (/sà·'nà/) - A weed in the World Beyond. The Sana berry has remarkable healing qualities.

Sarah Cousins - Member of the opposing team during the ladies' softball championship tournament.

Sine Fine - Name of the spiraling staircase that connects the World Beyond to Domum.

Small Monster - The evil Parva Draco by its other, less common name.

Smith, Miss - School District Union Leader present at Miss Davenport's formal proceeding.

Studeman, Bob - Goes by the name of Crazy Face. Involved in threats to Diana and Regina and a swindling caper with Mister Reynolds and Miss Hickman.

Supreme Lady - Supreme Lady is the Goddess of Ethereal Beings. She oversees all ghosts. She decides what ghosts will do in the After Life.

Susan - Susan is a fictional character mentioned in the text.

The Mechanics of Writing Creative Fiction - Composition authored by Diana. She received an A-plus.

Thing, the - Latin name for Inania. The Inania is faithful to Mendacium. It is the most dreaded beast in the World Beyond. In fact, it is the evilest, hideous cacodemon in the Universe.

Tranquility Beam - Corridor that connects the Real-world with the World Beyond. It zigzags many times. When it does, the traveler is introduced to different realms, such as Insectum and Purgatory.

Uvam - (/ü·'vām/) - King of the Minima Village and its creatures. Husband of Saccharo and father of Eros.

Walters, Miss - Vice Principal at Diana's school.

Whatnots - A type of eatable jerky I Dunno made after watching one of Diana's dreams.

Williams, Miss - Diana and Evelyn's study hall teacher in the Real-world.

Williamson, Miss - District school board member in attendance at Miss Davenport's formal proceeding.

World Beyond - A fictional land where Diana is the Youngster Heroine of the World Beyond, Empress Artemis-Diana.

Yepity yep yep - One of the Real-world Diana's favorite expressions. It literally means "yes." Diana also uses the words in "our" world.

Young, Mister - Diana's school principal.

Vanderbilt, Mister - District school board member in attendance at Miss Davenport's formal proceeding.

Victoria - Cousin of Regina Reynolds.

www.ingramcontent.com/pod-product-compliance
Lightning Source LLC
Chambersburg PA
CBHW060519180626
46817CB00002B/408